*To Mom and Dad,
the alpha and omega of my life*

LISA BLACK

TAKEOVER

HARPER

An Imprint of HarperCollinsPublishers

HARPER

An Imprint of HarperCollins*Publishers*
10 East 53rd Street
New York, New York 10022-5299

Copyright © 2008 by Lisa Black
Excerpt from *Evidence of Murder* copyright © 2009 by Lisa Black
ISBN 978-0-06-154447-7

First Harper paperback printing: July 2009
First William Morrow hardcover printing: September 2008

HarperCollins® and Harper® are registered trademarks of Harper-Collins Publishers.

Printed in the United States of America

Visit Harper paperbacks on the World Wide Web at
www.harpercollins.com

10 9 8 7 6 5 4 3 2 1

CHAPTER 1

THURSDAY, JUNE 25
6:42 A.M.

The sun had barely come up, and already it was too hot. Theresa MacLean felt the first prickles of sweat on the back of her neck as she stared down at the dead man, and wished she had left her lab coat in the car. Humidity kept both the dew and the man's blood from drying, and scattered red spots gleamed against the spring grass. "He hasn't been here long," she told the detective.

The dead man's tie flopped across his chest as he gazed up with sightless eyes, past her to the azure sky. The tiny sidewalk framed his shoulders, and his head rested in the mulch and grass below lush juniper bushes. Two or three heavy blows had caved in his skull; he had tried to defend himself with his bare hands and damaged his fingers in the process. The killer had swung the weapon used with enough force to cut knuckles and dent the man's wedding ring.

"A lady walking to the bus stop saw the shoes sticking out past the bushes." Homicide detective Paul Cleary sketched the scene as he spoke, frowning in concentration over his pad and pencil. The damp morning made his blond hair especially unruly. "He could have been here all night before that. The porch light isn't on, so anyone driving by wouldn't have seen him from the street. It's a quiet neighborhood anyway."

Despite the setting she took a moment just to look at Paul. They would be married in two months and thirteen days. Even her teenage daughter had overcome the instinctive reticence to a stepparent. But Theresa had something to tell him first, and she hadn't yet figured out how.

"You'd think he'd be damper if he'd been out here all night," Paul's partner, veteran detective Frank Patrick, chimed in. He had been in the city all his years and with the police department for the past twenty, but he never tired of complaining about Ohio weather. "This friggin' humidity soaks everything."

Theresa prodded the man's chin with a latex-clad hand; only tiny spatters along one cheek bespoke the damage to the back of his head. A tailored dress shirt held in his expanding girth. A few smears of blood crossed his stomach, probably swiped there by the cut fingers. "He's cold, and his jaw and arms are pretty stiff. His stomach is still soft, though, so I'd guess between four and eight hours." As a forensic scientist with the medical examiner's office, she had learned a lot about rigor mortis, though one of the doctors on the staff would have to give them the official time-of-death frame. She looked up at the two-story Westlake Colonial. "He lives here?"

"Don't know," Frank said. "Whoever bashed his head in also took his wallet. The house is locked up, with no signs of forced entry, and no one answers. We don't know if he belongs here or not."

She frowned. "We've got significant damage to the skull but not a lot of blood spatter, not even a lot of blood soaked into the mulch. It could be lost in the grass or the bushes, washed off by dew, but I would expect to see at least some on this porch railing or the sidewalk."

"You think he was killed inside and dragged out here?"

"Or dumped out of a passing car. He's got some dirt on his shoulder, where the jacket is rumpled." She scraped some particles onto a piece of glassine paper, folding it as a druggist would so none would be lost. "As if someone with dirty hands pulled him from the shoulders."

Paul bent at the waist to examine the porch outside the front door. "I don't see any drag marks, either in blood or in dirt."

"Me neither. But I hate to think the rest of his family is inside, bludgeoned to death. Can't we go in?"

"The search warrant is on its way to the judge right now."

She stood up, stretched a crick out of her back. She loathed having to wait on search warrants. Finding a dead body in front of the place should be sufficient probable cause so far as she was concerned, but in these litigious times . . . "Who does the house belong to? Do we at least know that?"

Frank poked at the dead man's pockets, producing a slight jingle, which proved to be a set of keys. "Mark Ludlow, white male, fifty-four. It could be him. So he pops out of the house on his way to work this morning and someone cracks him in the skull for the money in his wallet—"

"Leaving behind neither the weapon nor the cast-off

blood patterns from swinging it." Theresa looked around at the well-kept houses. "Besides, in this neighborhood? Not common."

"—and then they leave this Lexus in the driveway." He aimed the victim's key fob at the sleek sedan in the drive and pushed a button. The car responded with a loud chirp. "It's him."

"No, it's his car," Theresa corrected. "This could be his girlfriend's house. He stops by for breakfast, and girlfriend's significant other number two doesn't care to serve him coffee."

Paul considered this theory. "And then killer and girlfriend hop over the body and take off, in their car? That's pretty cold."

"Or the killer kidnaps girlfriend," Theresa said.

"Maybe girlfriend *is* the killer," Frank put in. He and Theresa had been bouncing ideas off each other since she could talk; their mothers were sisters.

Theresa moved onto the porch. "Or another victim. I really want to get into this house."

"You and me both," Paul assured her. They turned as a patrol car pulled alongside the curb and stopped. A young man in uniform ducked under the ribbon of crime-scene tape and came up the twenty-foot driveway, sheaf of papers in hand.

"You get your wish, Tess," Frank said before reading the search warrant to the empty house, a process required by law but absurd in practice. The cream-colored siding gave no sign of listening. While he spoke, Theresa crossed the grass to retrieve her small Maglite from the county station wagon and returned to the porch. The sun slanted from the rear of the house, throwing some areas into unexpected dimness.

Paul used the man's keys to open the lock—no sense in breaking the door if it wasn't necessary—and it cemented their theory that the deceased man was Mark Ludlow.

"Wait," Theresa said before the three officers could step over the threshold.

"You were dying to get in here."

"Just hold on a sec." She crowded in beside them and aimed the flashlight at the glossy wooden floor of the foyer. If a trail of blood lay there, she would make the officers go in the back door. But the inside floor appeared as clean as the concrete front porch. "Okay, go ahead."

"Wait here," Paul and Frank told her in unison.

"Count on it." Prowling through rooms that could hold a murderous assailant was so *not* her job, and the whole situation had her nervous enough already. The police did not often call her to fresh crime scenes; usually the murder had occurred days before by the time she got there to spray luminol or collect items for DNA testing. Even if the body remained, the scenes felt empty—whatever destructive collision of personalities had taken place had passed. The aggressors had moved on to damage control, covering up, running. It usually felt as if even the victim had lost interest by that point.

This seemed different. The conflict that produced this death had not been resolved. Bodies were still in motion. It might be preconnubial jitters, but she felt a need to be especially alert, especially observant, especially vigilant.

Frank reappeared at the end of the hallway, where the rising sun flooded the kitchen with light.

"Can I come in now?" she asked.

"Sure. There's no one here. No sign of any murder either."

"Can the patrol officer stay with Mr. Ludlow out here? I don't want some passerby wandering up to our body."

The young man stood guard over the corpse while Theresa photographed the neat suburban home. Two things quickly became clear: There were no indications of a bloody assault, and Mr. Ludlow did not live alone. He had a wife and a very young son, and there was no sign of what had happened to them.

Forty minutes later Theresa knelt on the kitchen floor, her head held at an angle to the surface, as Paul spoke from the doorway.

"This must be her." He held up a framed photo of the deceased man with a young blond woman. A tow-headed toddler sat between them, the boy's cherubic face turned toward his mother.

"Yeah, I saw the picture. If that man died in this house, I have yet to find any evidence of it. There are no signs of cleaning up, no wet spots on the carpeting. There's a mop up against the stationary tub downstairs that's damp but not soaking. She cleans with bleach, which kills DNA, but so do I. This floor has a layer of grit on it, so it's not a freshly cleaned surface. Maybe he *was* attacked outside. I'd just feel better if I had more blood on that sidewalk." One of her knees let out a protesting creak as she got to her feet. "And a weapon would be nice, too. I *did* find this."

He joined her at the sink, peering at three specks of dark red that traveled in a line up the tan ceramic tile behind the counter next to the sink. "It's blood."

"Not much of it."

"Exactly. It could be the only three spots left after a superb cleanup job, or it could be an artifact from last night's steak dinner. I'll take a swab, of course."

"Any scraps in the garbage?"

"No, the bin is clean except for a few paper towels and a tea bag."

After swabbing the blood, she and Paul canvassed the home once more. Toys spotted the living room, along with a *TV Guide* and a half-finished crewel project in colorful yarn. Areas of the master bedroom indicated his and hers; his tastes ran to career-development books and vitamins, hers to paperback romances and matching organizer trays. The baby's room held yet more toys, clean clothes, and a prodigious supply of diapers. If the family had a dark side—a drug or alcohol addiction, abuse, sex parties—all traces of it had been removed.

The third bedroom served as an office. With a twinge of envy, Theresa examined the heavy rolltop desk. "What is this, mahogany?"

"You're asking me?" Paul said. "My taste runs toward Formica."

"Not true—you bought me that walnut bench last month."

"Rachael picked that out."

The idea of her daughter perusing tasteful furniture made her feel proud and old at the same time. The cache of papers in the rolltop came as a welcome distraction. "This seems to be a loan form. Maybe they have money troubles, if they're applying for a loan?"

Paul picked up a stack of business cards and held them toward her. "I don't think so."

She glanced at the cards. The words "Federal Reserve Bank of the United States of America" framed the upper edge. "He's a bank examiner. I see—Ludlow doesn't apply for loans—"

"He approves them."

Frank leaned in the doorway behind them, fingering a cigarette. "That's all I need. The murder of a freakin' employee of the federal government."

Paul explained his partner's mood to Theresa. "The oral boards for the sergeant's position are up this week. Frank might be the boss of the whole Homicide unit by the end of the month."

"And you'll have to break in a new partner."

Frank snorted. "'Gee, good luck, Frank, I'm really rooting for you, seeing as you're my flesh and blood and all.' No, the only thing she cares about is poor Paul having to work with a rookie."

Her older cousin had always been cynical, but now his voice held a bitterness that surprised her. He must be edgier over the promotion than she would have thought possible. "I'm sorry—congratulations, really."

"Forget it."

"I know you'll get it. No one else has more time in Homicide than you do, do they?"

He stared at his feet for so long that she thought he wouldn't answer. "McKissack got there a year and a half before I did. He's a moron, too, but that's neither here nor there in the political world. Anyway, forget it. Find anything else in that desk?"

Paul would not be deflected. "Maybe this is exactly what you need to get the inside track away from McKissack. A nice high-profile fed case—provided we wrap it up before your interview, of course."

"Sure." A smile flickered on Frank's lips, gone before it could settle. "That gives us, let's see, thirty-four hours to find out who killed Mr. Bank Examiner."

Theresa felt a sudden chill of worry. "He works at a bank—"

Paul followed her thoughts. "And now the wife and kid are missing. But that makes no sense. If they were kidnapped to pressure him into robbing his own bank, then why kill him?"

Frank supposed, "Maybe it's got nothing to do with the bank, and she killed him. Then she panicked, fled with the kid."

"That might be preferable," Theresa said. "Because if Theory A is correct, then with the bank executive dead we've got a kidnapper out there who has no reason for keeping Mom and baby around—"

"And every reason to get rid of them," Paul finished.

Theresa's boss, Leo, peered at the dead man on the gurney as if he were something Theresa had picked up at a garage sale on her way to work, using Leo's lunch money for the purchase. "What is *this*?"

"Mark Ludlow. Murdered on his own front stoop." She held a small but brilliant flashlight up to the gashes in the dead man's scalp, prodding gently with her other hand. She didn't want to disrupt the wound pattern or disturb any traces the weapon could have left behind before the pathologist had a chance to examine him, but she might not have another chance before the body was cleaned just prior to the autopsy. The man had died quickly, since his hair was matted but not saturated with blood; his heart had stopped beating early on, stopped pushing the liquid out of the broken capillaries. This told her that he had not bled to death but that the compressions to his skull had halted his brain from directing even involuntary muscle movement, like breathing.

The trace evidence department supervisor took a morose sip of coffee, surrounded by ten other gurneys, each bearing a grim burden. The morning meeting, or "viewing," would shortly commence, as the department supervisors and all the pathologists gathered for a briefing on the day's cases and to decide which doctor would autopsy which victim. "As if we don't have enough to do."

"You say that like it's my fault."

"If I'm not mistaken, you still have three sets of clothing to examine, from yesterday's suicides and that crib death. And we've got the National Transportation Safety Board coming in to see the harnesses from that helicopter crash last week. Not to mention that everyone is going to be late because traffic is backed up now that the freakin' secretary of state is going to grace Cleveland with her presence." But he said all this absently, without any real concern. Their field of work was, by definition, reactive. Without a way to investigate crimes before they occurred, they were always behind. As long as Theresa kept sufficiently current with the caseload so that Leo didn't have to do any of it, all was right in his world.

Now he wrinkled his nose at a heart-attack victim who had lain in her own kitchen for several days before being found, and he opened his mouth to go on.

"Theresa!" Don Delgado, moving with uncharacteristic haste, pushed aside a gurney to approach them in the badly lit hallway. As the occupied gurney was stopped, none too gently, by the tiled wall, the young DNA analyst grasped both her shoulders, and she knew that something was very, very wrong. "Theresa. There's a problem."

Her throat tightened. "Rachael," she rasped out.

"No." His shiny olive skin had paled, which did nothing to reassure her. "Your dead guy from this morning—"

"Him." She jerked her head to the gurney that rested against her hip.

"Yeah. He worked for a bank downtown. Two guys just tried to rob it. Security tried to contain them, and they grabbed a bunch of people in the lobby as hostages. CPD has the place locked down, but at the moment it's a standoff."

Okay, she thought. *Why is that so—*

"It's Paul, Theresa. He's in there with them. He's one of the hostages."

CHAPTER 2

8:14 A.M.

"There's nothing you can do, honey," Frank told her over the phone. "Just don't panic. He'll be okay. No one's dead yet."

Yet? "What happened?" she asked for the third time, her Nextel crammed to her ear. She barely felt the hard folding seat of the old teaching amphitheater underneath her, or Don's arm around her shoulders. Her brain had disconnected from her body, and her body, with animal instinct, knew that survival lay in staying calm and quiet. Hysteria would attract disaster, like lightning to a metal pole.

Her brain, meanwhile, worked to keep up. "What *happened*?"

"We had a takeover about ten minutes ago. Two guys rolled up in front of the bank and went in, armed with some heavy guns. They grabbed some Fed workers before security could do anything, but one guard who's either stupid or crazy ran outside and removed their car. So they stayed put, with the guns and the hostages. Paul had gone to the Fed to talk to the coworkers and the boss about Ludlow. I had roused a neighbor to get the scoop on our little family, so he went on without me. No one is hurt, Tess. You getting me?"

Something smelled bad, she thought. Literally. A pathologist must have opened up the first victim in the autopsy room next door, and for once her stomach rebelled at the odor. "How do you know Paul's there? Maybe he's not there."

"Fed security has cameras in the lobby, and I spoke to the guy who took the car—Paul had to show his ID to get through the metal detector. But he's not hurt, that's what you have to focus on."

"Have you called him? Does he answer his—"

"Tess. He's in plainclothes. If these guys haven't searched him for the gun and badge, then they probably don't know he's a cop, and I don't want to tip them off by ringing his Nextel. *Don't* call him."

She shivered, and Don's arm tightened around her. "Okay, yeah . . . if Ludlow is somehow related to this, then these guys have already murdered today."

"I know."

The upset in her stomach melted into a pain, flowing through her insides like a cancer. The helplessness felt even worse; she failed to see how her expertise in forensic science would help in a bank-robbery case. "I'm coming—"

"The situation is stable at the moment, and they're calling in the negotiator. If everyone stays calm, it might be all right. In the meantime I need you to work, Tess."

"Work?" He might as well have suggested that she paint her nails. How could she possibly work at a time like this?

"The car. I'm having it brought out to you."

She'd crushed the phone to her head so hard that it hurt, and she switched ears. Don's arm slid from her shoulders, but he stayed in the seat beside her. "I'll come there."

"No—"

"You'd have to flatbed it here, to avoid losing any evidence, and how are you going to get a wrecker in there? You probably have the streets full of cop cars, don't you?"

He didn't have an immediate answer, and she knew she would win. "It would be much faster for me to come there. We don't have time to argue about it."

He sighed, surely knowing her argument for the BS it was. "No, I guess we don't. Come on out—at the moment this car is all we've got. I'd like to know if these two are responsible for Ludlow. I'd like to know if they're high, if one is diabetic, if they left their cell phone in the glove compartment, or if the registered owner has been stuffed into the trunk. Look at this car, Tess, and tell me everything you can about these guys."

"I'll be right there."

She took the DNA analyst with her, for both extra help and moral support. They had been through bad times before and understood that the way to keep going when only a heartbeat from disaster was to act as if it were just another day on the job. Don Delgado— younger, the third son of a black mother and a Cuban father, who grew up in the DMZ near East Ninety- third and Quincy—and Theresa had little in common besides attitude, and both could not have cared less.

Now they surveyed the 1994 Mercedes-Benz parked on the grassy mall between the public library and the convention center. She could see the Federal Reserve building, stately and aloof, its pink granite gleaming in the sun. Metal barricades and red NO ACCESS tape closed off East Sixth Street from Rockwell to Superior. The sports coupe had a pearlescent paint job that appeared a pale peach from one angle and a warm caramel from another. "As getaway cars go," Theresa said, "they could have chosen a less conspicuous one."

She barely heard her own words, her mind occupied with Paul's fate. Was he crouched on the floor with his hands on his head? What if his jacket fell open and the badge showed? Would they shoot him? Had they already shot him?

"Maybe that's the idea. Who robs banks in a Mercedes?" Don turned to a uniformed female officer, leaning against her marked unit. "Who is the car registered to?"

She stopped staring at his many physical attributes long enough to admit, "I don't know."

"Find out."

"SRT is probably doing that." She meant the Special Response Team, a catchall phrase for cops who respond to out-of-the-ordinary calls.

"There's no reason you can't do it, too."

Theresa saw the young woman's admiration of the handsome Don turn to a scowl. Perhaps all her friends were around the corner at the standoff or at least on the field trip providing extra security for the secretary of state's visit, and here she was, sweating next to an old German car, taking orders from a hottie with no wedding ring and an all-work, no-play approach.

"Now would be good," Don added, smiling sweetly. "We need that information."

The woman walked out of earshot, with her radio and a notebook. Don continued to click photos of the car, front and back, driver's side, passenger side. "At least the owner isn't in the trunk, right?"

"Yeah, they checked."

"They didn't wait for us?"

"If someone *had* been inside, they'd need medical attention, from the heat if nothing else." In some ways Theresa had been right not to inspect the car at the medical examiner's office. Their only garage had lousy lighting; at least the grassy mall blazed with brilliant sunlight. She would have to stand the heat to have the illumination.

The exterior of the Mercedes had been well maintained, even beyond the fancy after-market paint job, its only flaw being a slight dent in the back bumper. The tires were beginning to bald, however, and the front right showed irregular wear.

"Camber's off," Don said. "The wheel is angled inward just a touch. Probably hit a pothole or something."

"How do you men do that? You can't remember your mother's birthday, but you know the timing sequence on a '68 Mustang."

"The same thing happened to a Riviera I used to have. And I never forget my mother's birthday. Or yours."

Theresa brushed black fingerprint powder over the glossy paint. The tedious work frustrated her, but she knew that the exterior of a vehicle is an ideal surface for prints, and she needed to collect them before any more people, including herself, climbed in and out of the car. The security guard and their young patrolwoman, at the very least, had already been too close to it. She forced herself to work calmly, without missing any of the surface.

"They must have left it running when they went into the bank." She spoke aloud, trying to get her mind around the events of the morning. The pictures would not form. What would Rachael do if he died? How would she react? She didn't seem to *love* Paul, not yet, but he had been well on his way to becoming a second father to her. "The security guy would hardly have the keys to it, so it must have been running when he came out and moved it, which seems really weird to me, but apparently that's the protocol: contain the bad guys and cut off their escape."

"Wouldn't it be safer to let them take the money and run?" Don asked, lifting a piece of tape just enough to slide a card underneath it, lest the weak breeze blow the card away. "Then capture them later when there aren't a bunch of civilians standing around?"

"This is a federal bank." Theresa brushed the powder liberally over the surface, holding her arm out as far as it would go to prevent the fine black grains from settling back on her. "They don't let nobody take nothing."

"A federal bank does things differently?"

Clear finger marks sprang to life; Theresa could only hope they belonged to the criminals. She concentrated, to keep herself from devolving into panic. "It's a Federal Reserve bank. It's like a bank for banks. The Fed lends money to banks, oversees all transactions by check, and controls the physical amount of currency in circulation." She noted her coworker's raised eyebrows. "I chaperoned Rachael's sixth-grade field trip."

"But it's still a bank, right?"

"I guess so. But they'd have been better off going to the Fifth Third across the street."

The young officer returned; her body appeared fit,

but her face flushed red from the heat, and she had used the short trip to her vehicle to snag a bottle of water. She offered her own theory: "Maybe they meant to, and then they got the wrong building. They ain't too bright, and that's a fact."

Enough speculation, Theresa thought. "Who's the car registered to?"

"Robert Moyers. Resides in Brookpark, no record, doesn't answer his phone."

"And hasn't reported it stolen?"

"Hasn't reported squat."

Theresa lifted a palm print with wide, clear tape. "How old is he? Could he be one of the robbers?"

The young woman shrugged again. "Moyers is twenty-seven. But they're wearing hats and sunglasses, so who can tell?"

"Driving your own car to rob a bank is so dumb it should be a charge in itself," Don said. "But then we've already established their level of intelligence. Or lack thereof."

The cop wiped her face again. "All I know is, it's too early in the summer for it to be this hot. It's freakin' *June,* feels like August, and I got to work a special detail at the lake tonight, too. Mosquito heaven."

Theresa stripped off the black-smeared latex gloves and donned a fresh pair, finally ready to move inside the car. She glanced up at the Federal Reserve building, as she had every five seconds since arriving. For a moment she felt more frustration than fear—so close, and yet . . .

Paul could die today. He might be dead already; the walls of that building were thick enough to withstand a nuclear attack, certainly thick enough to muffle a gunshot—

Enough, she told herself. *Focus on what you can do. Focus.*

The interior had been cared for as meticulously as the exterior. The faded leather upholstery had no holes, and the bits of woodlike paneling shone deep and glossy. A steering-wheel cover had been carefully laced up and satellite radio installed. She assumed that Sirius could trace the unit to the owner's account, but that would certainly take days, and Paul didn't have that kind of time. She noted the location of the seat, already positioned so that her five-foot-seven-inch frame could reach the pedals comfortably.

Under the driver's seat, she found a gas receipt from the Lakewood Marathon station, dated the day before, 11:32 A.M. The driver had paid cash. She also found an empty container for candy mints, a wisp of foil packaging, and a toothpick. Great for DNA evidence. Not too informative in the short run.

Under the passenger's seat, she found an empty white number-ten envelope that had been sealed and then ripped open. Oddly, it had no mailing address or return address, only a metered postmark for forty-one cents, dated the previous October.

Both floor mats yielded yellowish grains, which Don lifted with clear packing tape and placed on sheets of clear acetate, labeling each sheet with a Sharpie marker.

The sun ducked behind clouds occasionally, but the humidity persisted. Theresa's handsome coworker disappeared long enough to cart the first set of evidence samples back to the lab, then returned bearing something even more attractive: an ice-cold bottle of water. "You okay out here?"

"Yeah."

"Your face is as red as a beet."

Theresa nearly spit out the water. "Hell, Don, don't say that! My mother always used to tell me that." It had annoyed her at twelve and still annoyed her at thirty-eight.

"Sorry. I took that dirt from the floor mat to Oliver to run in the GC/mass spec." The mass spectrometer, coupled with a gas chromatograph, would separate the substance into its chemical compounds. "I thought I'd have to offer to wash his car, but he heard about . . . about what's happening and took it without argument. I think he likes you."

"Impossible." Theresa lifted the rear floor mat. "Oliver doesn't like anybody."

"I'm not trying to tell you your business, but have you checked the glove compartment?"

"I did. There's an owner's manual and a receipt for an exhaust system from Conrad's in Strongsville, dated four years ago, which our little patrol officer is supposed to be calling about right now. She returned to her air-conditioned squad car the minute you left and emerges only to deliver the occasional bulletin. I also found a travel package of Kleenex and a bottle of Advil. That's it."

"And no sign of the owner?"

"Still isn't answering his phone. They've sent someone to the address." Theresa straightened up and snatched the keys out of the ignition. Aside from the ignition and trunk keys, the ring held a rubberized red profile of some historic-looking figures and a smaller key, apparently meant for a Master padlock. She opened the trunk.

"No body," Don confirmed. "Nothing back here but a jack and a spare and a set of jumper cables. This guy keeps a very neat car."

"Man after my own heart. I hope he's still alive. Maybe out of town or something, blissfully unaware that his vehicle has been used in the commission of a felony, and perhaps a murder to boot." With a flashlight in one hand, she combed through the dark gray carpeting with the other, picking up loose hairs and fibers and dropping them into a petri dish. *This is a waste of time,* Theresa thought. They'd stolen this car to rob a bank—they had no reason to even look in the trunk, much less leave her any clues there. She plucked up a dried twig with two leaves still attached. "You know what this is?"

Don took it from her fingers. "A twig?"

"Thanks."

"Sorry. Magnolia? Birch? You really shouldn't ask me—I flunked botany."

"So did I." And she couldn't see how any of this would help Paul anyway.

The beam of light caught a dark smear on the carpet's surface. She moved the flashlight to study it from different angles. "This could be blood."

"Want a Hemastix?"

"Please."

From the equipment Theresa had piled on a clean paper bag on the pavement, Don slid a paper strip out of a bottle and wet the end of it with a squirt of distilled water. Theresa touched the yellow pad at the end of it to the smear, and it turned dark blue. "Hmmm."

"Blood."

"It could be Ludlow's," Theresa said, more to herself than to Don. "They could have killed him somewhere else and then dumped his body on his own lawn, but I don't think so. He didn't look disheveled enough, and there would be a lot more blood here. It could be from whatever they used to beat Mark Ludlow to death."

Don took up the train of thought. "They stole this car, then went to get Ludlow to tell them how to get into the bank. He didn't cooperate, and they killed him and threw the murder weapon in the trunk, getting blood on the carpet. That's why you didn't find the weapon at the scene."

Theresa sliced out the section of carpet with a sterile, disposable scalpel and dropped the piece into a manila envelope. "But they got rid of it before robbing the bank, because it's not here now, and this jack hasn't moved in five years, from the look of the rust and the spiders' nests. Why take the time to remove evidence from a car that's not yours when you're probably going to dump it immediately after the robbery anyway?"

"They wanted to be careful."

"If they were careful, they'd have had a better plan for getting in and out of that bank." She recapped the scalpel and dropped it into her pocket. With luck, the prints she'd collected would match a set in their database. The blood could be analyzed later; right now they needed any leverage they could get to convince the robbers to give up peacefully. If they had already killed once, either Ludlow or the car's owner, or both, it made them likely to do so again, but if they knew that CPD had a murder charge waiting for them, they would be less likely to let themselves be taken into custody. She slammed the trunk shut. "I'm done here. Can you get on the blood right away, including the swab from Ludlow's house? And have Leo run the prints through AFIS."

"Make the boss man do work?"

"If you have to administer coffee through an IV

drip. Don't let him weasel out of it. Don't let him even hesitate."

Don watched her, worry etching creases into his perfect skin. "Are you coming back with me?" he asked, in a tone that indicated he already knew the answer.

"Nope." Theresa set off toward the sawhorses.

CHAPTER 3

8:30 A.M.

Paul took a moment to appreciate the architecture before facing his death. From his seat on the floor, he read an information plaque: The Federal Reserve Bank of Cleveland was one of only twelve in the country. It was built in 1923 and resembled a Roman basilica; the marble on the lobby's walls had come from Siena, Italy, and the vaulted ceiling was hand-painted in Florentine designs. The lobby seemed appropriately solemn, as the thick walls filtered out all noise from the surrounding city. It should have made one feel insulated and safe, inside with the armed guards and the air-conditioning and more money than he could fathom, all unknown quantities held at bay by the ancient brick. But now the lions had come within the village walls, and it might never be safe again.

The teller cages, with their old-fashioned iron grillwork, sat between the inner and outer walls of the lobby. The inner walls had huge windows, screened with more iron grillwork and each bearing the city seal of one of the twelve Federal Reserves. Unfortunately, the glass in these impressive windows was opaque. The robbers were safe from sniper fire anywhere in the lobby, except for a fifteen-foot-wide band directly in the center. The window over the East Sixth Street entrance was clear glass. Across from that entrance sat the information/security desk, and behind that desk ran an open hallway. Paul could only hope that security forces were massing at the other end of it.

Polished marble tiles on the floor reflected the occupants like a mirror, from the trembling receptionist huddled next to him to the pacing robber with the automatic rifle. A tall, wiry, light-skinned black, he paused directly before Paul.

Right in front of the clear window. *If you're out there,* he thought to the police snipers, *take the shot.* But of course they wouldn't, not while the second robber kept himself tucked farther down the lobby, protected by the opaque windows and invisible from the hallway. That one had blue eyes and blond hair, a faded tattoo on the side of his neck, and a sun-roughened complexion. He also had the husky build of a high-school football star gone slightly to seed, and he kept a black M4 carbine trained on the row of frightened humans.

Both suspects wore dark T-shirts and lightweight Windbreakers, the latter a suspicious garment in the summer heat. The taller one had a navy jacket over jeans, while the stockier blond wore a maroon zip-up with black trim and khaki pants.

The black one removed his sunglasses to look Paul over. "Who're you?"

He had been waiting for this question. "I'm an examiner. I work on the third floor." It seemed a more prudent answer than the truth, and Paul could only hope that if examiners did *not* work on the third floor, this man wouldn't know that. Meanwhile he clenched the corner of his gray blazer between his thighs, to keep it from falling open to reveal his badge. The gun sat far enough back on his right hip to stay hidden, provided he didn't move much.

His fellow hostages stared at him but said nothing. They could not look any more startled than they already did, so their expressions didn't give him away. They didn't know he was a cop—only the security guards knew that—but they had to know he didn't work there. The security guards were at the end of the line, and the man with the gun did not look at them.

"Can you get into that vault?"

Paul didn't have to fake a stammer in his response, since he had no idea what vault the man referred to. There didn't seem to be one within sight. "No—it's not part of my job."

Brown eyes studied him, but only briefly. Then the guy moved away, and the older black man next to Paul let out a relieved breath.

So far, so good. Stay calm and stay alive.

Of course, if they found out he was a cop, staying calm would not save him. Armed robbers didn't like surprises, and they'd already had a number that morning. They must have expected the Fed to be like a neighborhood bank, with the cash at the forefront, physically present for the grabbing. Paul couldn't blame them for their mistake; he also wondered why there'd been no one working at the antique teller windows. Instead the robbers were greeted with a handful of employees and no fewer than four armed guards in fatigues, one with a dog.

Paul had reached the bank at a few minutes past eight, left the car at a meter around the corner, and entered the lobby directly behind an older black man in a green uniform, the man now seated on his right. He had immediately explained himself to the security guard in order to get through the metal detector, then headed for the receptionist's desk. Before he could reach it, the black robber had led his partner into the bank, firing a shot into the ceiling to get everyone's attention, nearly deafening them all. Paul had felt someone's hands on his back even before he could turn toward the noise.

His neck still burned where the gun's barrel had pressed into the flesh. The slightest twitch of a fingertip, depending on what sensitivity the trigger pull had been set to, and a round would rip though his arteries and spine so thoroughly that he'd be dead before he hit the floor. He didn't dare breathe.

Paul had a solid body and good muscle form; he was not, he would have flattered himself, a man easily subdued. But he had not moved—he had only to shift his weight and the guy might feel the gun at Paul's hip. The guards could not fire, not with him in the way, and Paul knew it to be illogical but felt deeply ashamed.

So this is what it's like to be a victim. They're right. It all does happen so fast.

The tall suspect had carried a duffel bag and shouted instructions for filling it with cash, but no one had listened. The fourth security guy, who had been next to the doors, darted outside, a response Paul didn't understand; the slender robber fired at him, leaving a hole and a series of spiderwebs in one of the glass doors and assaulting anew their already-numbed ears.

The other three guards were now kneeling between the solid reception desk and the row of hostages. Two of the guards had their hands on their heads and murderous expressions on their faces. The third, the K-9 officer, had both hands on his dog, as instructed by the blond robber. The blond guy seemed more afraid of the dog than of the guards, and the K-9 guy seemed more concerned about his dog than about the hostages.

Paul turned his head until he could count up the hostages out of the corner of his eye. Besides himself, the guy in the uniform, and the three security guards, he counted two. One man and one woman, each in neat office attire.

The tall one left the front door and faced them, holding the M4 at the ready. He nearly bounced as he walked, and Paul wondered if the manic energy came from adrenaline, drugs, or panic over a plan gone awry. Each source could be bad, all three together disastrous. "Bobby, go through and check both floors."

"What?" The stocky blond didn't care for the idea.

"There could be an army hiding in this place." Paul could see his point. Two rows of teller cages faced each other in the south half of the lobby, and the area between the inner and outer lobby walls in the north half seemed to have been given over to educational displays. Past a sign reading THE LEARNING CENTER, Paul could see a tree stretching through both stories, with dollar bills attached to its branches. Both the educational area and the teller cages had a number of partitions, turning the place into a warren. Now Bobby's partner used his M4 muzzle to gesture at the door in the north wall. "And make sure they can't open that."

"How am I going to do that?"

"Wedge it with something." He spoke without taking

his eyes off the people on the floor. Neither suspect had any particular accent. "And shoot first. Don't bother with questions."

That attitude did not bode well. Nor did using his partner's name in front of the hostages. It sounded as if he didn't expect any witnesses to survive the morning.

Paul pondered what to do. He didn't care to sit there with his hands behind his head while Bobby shot a few secretaries. There were only two of them, against three officers and four civilians. *We could take them.*

And maybe get himself and a few other people killed in the process. That wouldn't do for the department's up-and-comer, the whiz kid whose clearance rate made his boss look not only good but great, the one who was supposed to have all the answers.

Funny, he had not yet thought about how the day would affect his career. Once upon a time, that had been all he thought of. Obsessing over his work had been the only way to stop obsessing over his wife's death. But now he had Theresa.

Could he find an answer to this one, such a smart boy?

He heard muffled thuds as Bobby sped through the Learning Center. He would be passing by the clear outer windows . . . but no sniper's bullet shattered the glass, not with his partner staying out of sight below, right outside the room with the money tree.

Bobby's feet pounded downward into the southwestern section of the lobby.

Behind the grillwork labeled SAVINGS AND LOAN TRANSACTIONS, a woman screamed.

8:57 A.M.

"Where the hell is Cavanaugh?" one of the SRT cops demanded to know. He paced through the aisles of the public library, glancing at the books as if they might be armed.

Frank Patrick shrugged. He had never even met the great Chris Cavanaugh; he certainly had no idea what kept the city's best hostage negotiator from the most spectacular robbery they'd had in ten years. All Patrick knew was, if anything happened to his partner, Theresa would kill him. She'd absolutely kill him.

And he could certainly kiss the Homicide chief's slot good-bye.

The incident commanders had set themselves up on the History and Geography floor of the relatively new Louis Stokes Wing, directly across the street from the Federal Reserve, taking over the staff offices down to replacing the phone and moving the plants off the windowsills, which hadn't pleased the librarians any. The snipers had already dispersed throughout the building, and Patrick hoped their services would not be needed.

He sought out a quiet corner for himself; as a mere detective, he would not be welcome in SRT's insular bosom. At the south end of the floor, he found a cozy nook with painted ceilings and rows of books, though someone had beaten him to it.

Patrick didn't know him. A skinny guy young enough to be his son, he seemed to be the calmest guy in the building. He wore a polo shirt and jeans, but with a vest that read POLICE on the back, and he'd set a telescope next to the floor-to-ceiling window in the east wall, aimed at the entrance to the Federal Reserve. "Who're you?" Patrick asked.

"My name's Jason. I'm Chris Cavanaugh's researcher."

"A *what?*" *Some kind of egghead? That's all we need.*

"Researcher. Hostage rescue works as a team. Chris is the negotiator—"

"I know that," Patrick snapped. "I mean, I know how SRT works. You have a negotiator to talk, a guy to keep track of the details, and a commander to make the decisions."

"And me. I run back and forth looking stuff up and finding out what I can about these guys or what they want. The scribe writes down all the details—that would be Irene Hardstead over there, guiding all the bigwigs into the staff offices so they can figure out who's going to *be* the commander. It's usually the chief," he added, meaning the chief of police, "though this is not a usual situation."

"Why aren't you in there with them?"

Jason unpacked a plastic crate onto one of the cleanly designed reading tables. The nook had been claimed. "We need a quiet area, and a large group of cops are never quiet."

Patrick noted that the walls of the staff office area were silver metal topped with patterned glass, with a two-foot gap above that. "It might not be quiet anyway. What do you mean, *usually* the chief?"

"The police chief isn't here. He's at that luncheon address by the secretary of state. Going to sit right next to the lady. I think those guys across the street could have taken the entire Indians lineup hostage and the chief still ain't going to give that up. We have the assistant chief, Viancourt."

In his heart of hearts, Patrick let out a quiet moan. Through luck, amiability, and a complete lack of any law-enforcement skills whatsoever, Viancourt had been kicked upstairs over and over until he landed on the chief's doorstep, friendly as a puppy and about as effective. But even a puppy can outstay its welcome, and rumor had it that Viancourt would be replaced in the next year if he couldn't learn to do more than interview well. "Crap."

At his side, Jason consoled, "It's an empty point anyway. The FBI has priority."

Great, the Feebs. He'd prefer Viancourt, but no one would be asking his opinion on the chain of command. All hell had broken loose at Superior and East Sixth, and the top brass of three police agencies had closeted themselves in a conference room to hold a pissing contest over jurisdiction. Patrick turned to more proactive matters. "Why haven't we sent a phone in there?"

"We don't need to—there's phones in that lobby. Half the time they call us before we call them, believe it or not. But it's usually best if Chris talks to them first."

"And just where *is* Chris? At a book signing? Or maybe filming another segment on Channel Fifteen?"

"He's on his way," Jason answered smoothly, no doubt used to this kind of jealousy from cops, cops who didn't have Chris Cavanaugh's ability to self-promote. Patrick could only wish it were jealousy. If Cavanaugh could get Paul out of there alive, Patrick would happily volunteer to drive him to the TV station. He bent his head to the telescope eyepiece.

"Hey."

Patrick looked up. A uniformed cop stood next to a section plaque reading GENEALOGY AND HERALDRY.

"Are you Patrick?"

"Yeah."

"Got a lady here who needs to see you. Come on," he prompted over his shoulder, guiding his charge forward. "She says she's—"

"I know her," Patrick assured him. "You find anything in the car, Tess?"

CHAPTER 4

9:04 A.M.

"Remarriage," she had said to Paul only two weeks earlier, "is 'the triumph of hope over experience.'"

"Says who?"

"Dr. Samuel Johnson."

"Then perhaps I should hold on to this check." He had dangled the piece of colored paper over the railing, letting the loose end flutter. The ship beneath their feet rocked gently in the waves. The *Goodtime II* ran charters and lunch cruises, and they were booking it for their wedding reception. They had discussed all its features with the manager and now stood at its bow, letting the crisp, slightly fishy air caress them. The heat wave had not yet hit, and the sun felt good as it bounced off both the water and the glass pyramid of the Rock and Roll Hall of Fame.

Hope over experience. Paul had lost his first wife to acute myeloid leukemia, a disease that attacked with such speed and ferocity that grief arrived before shock had settled in. Theresa had lost her husband to another woman, and then a different other woman, and then several more other women until she'd lost track.

Their experiences had been different, but she believed that their hope remained the same. That this time no lies would be told, mistakes would not be repeated, the fates would give them a break; this time it would work.

She had pulled the check from his fingers. "Let's give the man his money."

Now she could glimpse the blue water only by pressing her cheek to the library window and peeking straight north along the narrow street. The pier sat two city blocks from them, the wedding date two months. Both seemed impossibly far away.

She looked down cautiously, afraid she might see Paul's broken body on the sidewalk, but the buffer zone between the two buildings remained calm. If it weren't for the eerily empty street, the day would appear to be following business as usual.

"We evacuated this half of the library, in case they come out shooting." Her cousin Frank did not ask how she felt, or tell her not to worry, or even look up from the telescope. Like Don, he knew better than to disturb her preternatural self-control. "Ticked off a lot of students and homeless people. And her." He hitched a thumb toward an older woman in a well-cut suit; she hefted a flat-screen monitor onto the reading table as a young man filled the surface with telephone equipment. "The head librarian of the reference wing. She hasn't shushed me once, though."

"What can you see?"

"Not much." He stood back.

Theresa took over the eyepiece, heart pounding. The windows of the two-story Fed lobby were covered with grillwork and reflected the bright street outside. She moved the sharply angled telescope around but saw only a desk here, a chair there. "I don't see anybody."

"They're gathered in the inner lobby. You have to look at the window right over the entrance. That's the only one with clear glass on the inside wall. Otherwise we're just looking at the outer offices, and there's no one there."

She moved the telescope, swinging too far and having to backtrack. "What are we going to be able to do if we can't even see them? They could have killed them all by—"

Past the iron grilles, the outer windows and an inner window, over the metal detector and a revolving door, she saw Paul. At least she thought she did. Next to an older black man was the sleeve of another hostage—a narrow band of charcoal gray, the color of the blazer she had given Paul for his birthday, the one he'd been wearing that morning. Still upright. Still alive.

She watched that sleeve until Frank put a hand on her shoulder. "You okay?"

"A camera," she told him. "We need a camera—"

"Security has cameras in the lobby, remember? We'll have a feed as soon as Jason here connects the monitor." He introduced the young man as Chris Cavanaugh's assistant.

"Don't you usually set up in a van or something?" she demanded of him.

"Usually, but the A/C is on the blink, and we'd get heatstroke if we tried to work out there. And there's not as much equipment as you'd think—all Chris really needs is a phone."

"And where is Chris?"

"He's on his way."

Theresa wiped her forehead, leaving a streak of

makeup on the sleeve of her lab coat. She took it off and pulled her silk blouse away from her wet body to feel the clammy chill of air-conditioning. "Where's everybody else? I expected a mob scene."

"Oh, it is," Frank assured her. "We have fifteen units on the streets, cordoning off the area and redirecting traffic. The Fed security guys guided the employees from the building to the Hampton Inn; they're sending most of them home just to get them out of the way. Snipers are picking their spots now. And the higher-ups are in the staff offices." He jerked his head, indicating the low, constant murmuring that made its way over the headers. "Hashing out who's in charge here."

"Who's in *charge*? Paul's got a gun to his head, and they're divvying up the glory?"

The librarian paused, as if only sympathy restrained her from asking Theresa to keep her voice down. Over her head two stylized Greek gods stared at the group with disapproval.

"Don't worry, Tess. It's better they work it out now so it won't get in the way later."

"So who *is* in charge?"

"Technically, the Fed security force were the first responders, but with Paul in there and the possible Ludlow connection, Cleveland PD is involved. However, since it's both a bank robbery *and* on federal property, the FBI can take over the whole show if they want to, and they want to. So right now the Feebs are nodding solemnly and promising to work together with the utmost cooperation, and not meaning a word of it. Not that I'm bitter or anything."

Theresa had great faith in the FBI—though she was too politic to admit as much to Frank—but found it scant comfort at the moment. The cavalry should be riding to the rescue, not huddled over a table behind stacks of books. "Terrific. And while they're all making nice, are they paying any attention to what's happening across the street? Shouldn't we be calling these guys or something? Finding out what they want? You know, *doing* something?"

Jason had sorted out a phone handset, a tape recorder, a large console studded with knobs and buttons, and enough wires to stretch across the city if placed end to end. "We don't want to do anything right now except let the hostage takers calm down. The first thirty minutes or so of any crisis are the most dangerous."

She crossed her arms, both chilled and impatient. "And besides, Chris isn't here."

Jason answered in a diplomatically even tone, "Yes."

"Won't the FBI use their own hostage negotiator?"

"They'll fly one in, but you never want to disturb rapport once it's been established. So if Chris has already opened negotiations, they'll leave him in place and the FBI negotiator will be the secondary. I just hope it isn't Laura." He rummaged through a plastic bin and came up with an electrical adapter and a book, which he thrust into Theresa's hands. "This is Chris's."

She examined the glossy cover. *Secrets of Hostage Negotiation* by Christopher Cavanaugh. The artwork featured a ninjalike warrior with an automatic rifle, and she wondered if he was supposed to be the good guy or the bad guy. Either way it seemed more scary than comforting. She glanced up at Jason, whose proud smile turned sheepish.

"Officer Patrick told me about your fiancé, and . . . I just thought you might want to see that Chris has a lot of credentials. He knows what he's doing."

"Thank you." She didn't know what else to say and told herself that if Chris Cavanaugh was savvy enough to get published, he would be savvy enough to get Paul out alive. He *would* be.

Jason returned to the electrical cords, and she opened to a page at random. Chapter 11 began, *"The hostage taker will agree to surrender only if he trusts you, trusts you more than his mother or his best friend or even himself. The quickest way to get him to this level of trust is to give him something he didn't think anyone could give him. This will be different for everyone. It can be as small as a compliment, as average as a perfectly baked pizza, or as unique as the cremains of his childhood buddy's pet dog. Do this and you might as well call your wife and tell her to start dinner."*

Humph. No mention of calling your husband and telling *him* to start dinner.

She closed the book and went to set it on the table. The librarian followed its progress the way an Audubon Society member watched even a garden-variety warbler, so Theresa handed it to her. Like teachers, librarians were a profession one wanted to stay on the good side of. "I'm sorry we had to take over your offices."

"That's all right."

Theresa glanced around at the faded book covers and the ornate paint job. "What's heraldry?"

"The study of armorial bearings."

"Like family crests?"

"Yes, and other genealogical records. I'm Peggy Elliott, by the way."

Theresa introduced herself, and they shook hands, forming the instant bond that women do when surrounded by men. Peggy Elliott wore subtle blond high-lights in her shoulder-length hair, no wedding ring, and a sympathetic expression. That was all Theresa took time to observe before hastening back to the telescope, suddenly panicked that she'd been away too long. Something might have happened. The bodies of the hostages might now lie scattered over the tile. Including *Paul's* body.

But the tableau had not visibly changed.

Beside her, via his Nextel, Frank pushed an unseen officer to track down Ludlow's next of kin, to see if they might have a clue as to where Ludlow's wife and child had gone—and to pull his financial information ASAP. He snapped the phone shut and said, "I'd like to know if this guy couldn't make his cable payment. He winds up dead, and an hour later the bank he worked at gets robbed? Tell me that's a coincidence. What's happening?"

"Nothing." One of the hostage takers strolled into view. She could see only the back of his torso. He wore a dark Windbreaker and jeans and carried a very big gun, but his stance conveyed total calm, a commander reviewing the troops. "Why can't we just shoot him?"

"Because there's two hims," Frank told her. "There's only that one window, and they're never both in it at the same time. So supposing we got a clear shot and took out the first guy . . ."

". . . there'd still be his partner left to kill people." And even if they did stand together, they'd be directly in front of their innocent captives. "Can't we gas them? I don't mean tear gas, I mean some kind of nitrous gas that would put everyone to sleep, including the rob-bers."

"The room's too big. There would be no way to disperse it evenly, so some people might pass out before others."

"And one of the robbers might panic and fire." The man in the telescope's sight stopped and turned, glanced up at the library windows as if he felt her scrutiny. She began to pull away from the scope, realized how ridiculous that was, and returned to the eyepiece. The man still stared in her direction.

He had a slender frame, high cheekbones, and light black skin. He wore his hair cropped short and had a small tattoo or birthmark on his neck, slightly behind his left ear. His face seemed as calm as his walk—why? What did he have to feel calm about?

Armed robberies and hostage crises were out of Theresa's area of expertise. She had no idea what had happened, what would happen, or what they wanted to happen. She had no way to orient herself, no way to plan a series of examinations or chemical tests that would give her information or direction. She could only stand and watch.

His partner must have driven the Mercedes; this guy was too tall, so the seat would have been farther back. Unless he had stolen the car and driven it without moving the seat—unlikely, as most men needed to be comfortable while they drove.

There. An interesting piece of deduction that told her absolutely nothing. It certainly didn't tell her why they'd tried to rob a bank without a driver, allowing themselves to be separated from their getaway vehicle. That worried her. It meant they were stupid, and stupidity was dangerous.

She tore herself from the eyepiece and took a moment to run through her usual reaction to any crisis: a mental head count. *Where is my daughter?* Rachael would be in her eleventh-grade trigonometry class right now, with her cell phone turned off; a final exam had been scheduled, and she'd turned down a date the night before to study for it. *My mother?* She was at her job at the corner diner, trying to introduce the clientele to whatever she last saw on the Food Network. It was more a restaurant than a diner, and without a TV, unless the staff had a break room—did they have a break room? Tess couldn't remember. *Paul?* He was in the bank across the street with his hands on his head. All not present, but accounted for.

"Shouldn't we try to communicate with them? Or pretend to, long enough to distract them while the"— she had to make herself say it—"hostages get out through another door?"

Apparently Frank had already sussed out the lobby's structure. "No. The Sixth Street entrance is the only way in or out of the public lobby. On the opposite wall, there's two elevators to the upper floors and a door to the employee lobby. The employee lobby has an exit onto Superior Avenue and the parking garage; however, *inside* the employee lobby is a heavily armed team of Federal Reserve security officers. So our guys have two choices. They can go out the back door into the arms of the Fed security force—"

"Or they can come out the front, into the sights of CPD snipers."

"Exactly. Either way is okay with me."

"Unless they take a hostage with them." Jason spoke up. He seemed to be hunting for an outlet. "Then the situation would get even worse. Here, you'll be able to see for yourself."

Theresa shuddered, suffering from a mental picture

of Paul moving forward, a gun at his spine, serving as a human buffer between the robbers and the snipers. Suddenly, waiting and letting the hostage takers calm down seemed to be a good idea.

She watched Jason set a small box in the window seat between two paintings, one of Clio, the muse of history, and the other depicting a winged figure with a book. A thin wire connected the box to both the monitor and a laptop on the reading table.

"Thanks for the use of your monitor, Ms. Elliott," the young man said. "We have three, but they're all built into our un-air-conditioned van."

"Can you see something?" Theresa moved around the table.

"In a minute." Jason tapped the laptop's keys, and the screen flicked through a number of windows before a black-and-white montage of four pictures popped up. Theresa gasped.

She saw Paul immediately, in the lower left-hand corner. That camera—labeled "West"—faced the center of the east side of the lobby. A gap there led to a hallway and elevator banks behind a marble reception desk. In front of the desk sat seven people. Paul, in his gray blazer, sat second from the end, between a young woman and that older black man. The picture was small but clear, and he was alive. Definitely alive.

"He's all right," Frank said in a low but firm tone, passing her a handkerchief.

She realized that the water on her cheeks did not come from sweat, and she dabbed at it as unobtrusively as she could. She did not take her gaze from the monitor.

With a glance she took in the view from the other three cameras. The east camera faced the entrance from

East Sixth Street with its revolving door flanked by inner and outer sets of glass panel doors. The north camera showed the south half of the lobby, with teller cages facing one another along the east and west inner walls. The south camera showed the educational center on each side of the north half and a single door at the end.

The two men with guns were also visible. One—the taller one—paced in front of the hostages, and the other stayed farther down the south end, shifting his weight from one foot to the other. From there he could not be seen by snipers or hit by an assault force, coming from either the Sixth Street entrance or the employee lobby. But he could stay close enough to shoot the hostages. He wouldn't even need to aim.

"Clear picture," Frank said.

"That's the beauty of working with such an august institution." Jason juggled several cords, then ducked under the desk to retrieve one he'd dropped. His voice grew muffled. "No expense is spared. You should see their security center—they have sensors and monitors up the wazoo in that building."

"Why aren't we over there, then?" Theresa asked. Anything to get closer to Paul.

Frank had jammed his hands into his pockets hard enough for her to count his knuckles. "We couldn't see the street from there. If anything happened to the feed, or if they decided to take out the cameras, or if they left the building—we'd be blind. We're better here."

"We can't see anything except that spot right in front of the door!"

"We can see them if they move into the offices or the Learning Center. Those windows to the street are clear. Plus, CPD is setting up a camera here, six floors down, directly across from the Fed entrance, to fall back on in case they do decide to take out the lobby cameras."

Please don't, she thought. If she could at least see him, it wasn't so bad. Yet she wondered. "Why haven't they?"

"Shot out the lobby cameras? I don't know. They're mounted pretty high. . . . Maybe these guys have enough respect for the marble not to take potshots at it."

"I doubt it."

"Or they're too hopped up to even notice the cameras."

Paul sat cross-legged on the floor, hands behind his head. His arms must be getting tired, and she guessed that he was feeling frustrated. Really frustrated. She watched the slender guy pass in front of him, each step calm and measured. "I don't think so. They didn't have someone to stay with the getaway car and they didn't have a plan for the cameras. These guys really thought they'd be in and out."

Jason plugged in his last wire and stood back to admire his handiwork. "Or they're leaving the cameras in place so that we won't have a reason to install new ones."

"How could we do that?"

"Down air vents, ceiling tiles—well, not that ceiling," Jason amended, in light of the intricately painted and vaulted ceiling. "Around a corner. Letting us see them takes away a big reason for us to approach. Oh, here's Chris."

Chris Cavanaugh entered from between two rows of thick reference books, dressed in a sparkling oxford shirt and expensive slacks. He carried nothing but a boyish look and deep dimples, at odds with the receding hairline. And he smiled, actually smiled, which made Theresa itch to grasp his lapels and shake him. *Where the hell have you been?*

Everyone turned to her.

"Did I say that out loud?" she hissed to Frank.

Cavanaugh's dimples only deepened. "You did indeed." In one sweeping glance, he took in Theresa, the Greek gods on the wall above the books, the windows, the communication center spread across the reading table, and the staff office section with its hum of voices, then settled on the monitor. "They're certainly armed."

The quiet concern in his tone worried her. Knowing that the hostage takers had guns was one thing; seeing the long black automatic rifles held so tightly in their hands was entirely another.

"Any change since you called?" he asked Jason.

"No."

Jason performed quick introductions. Cavanaugh acknowledged each of them with a nod and a smile, though his attention always returned to the monitor; when done, he jerked his head toward the muffled tones and asked his assistant, "Is that the dog and pony show?"

"Yep. They're working out how the FBI is in charge but everyone else's valuable assistance will be greatly treasured."

"Good. Then we'll be up and running before they break for coffee. The stuff looks good. Let's powwow before we make contact. Please sit, everyone. And I got here as soon as I could," he added to Theresa. "I had to shower and change."

She said nothing, well aware that outbursts might get her evicted. At the moment Chris Cavanaugh accepted her presence as a member of law-enforcement personnel. He might not want her around as a distraught family member.

Apparently he took her silence for rebuke and explained, "Negotiations can go on for hours, sometimes days. It's very important that everyone, including me, be comfortable. We eat, we stay hydrated, we take breaks. You'll see how it goes."

This disturbed her even more. What happened to home in time for dinner?

"Sit down," Frank told her, collecting a straight-backed chair for her. "You look hot."

She tried, unsuccessfully, not to glare at him and sat. So did Frank, Jason, and, after a brief hesitation, Ms. Elliott.

Cavanaugh, of course, sat at the head. "How's the perimeter?"

Jason answered him. "SRT has traffic diverted. It doesn't help that Superior is about the busiest street in Cleveland these days, since so many stores closed on Euclid. We've got a lot of whining middle-management types at each roadblock. We've corralled the press in front of the library, where the heat might convince most of them to leave. Phone service going into the Fed lobby has been shut off, except for the reception desk, because we'll use that."

They sounded so matter-of-fact. As difficult as it was for Theresa to believe, this was a rather routine event for everyone except her. They knew what to do, because they followed the same process for each event.

That should have comforted her, but it didn't. This wasn't the same as every other hostage incident. This was Paul.

"Patrick," Cavanaugh said to the detective. "You

worked that domestic at Riverview last month, right? Your partner's in there?"

Frank nodded and summarized the early-morning murder of Mark Ludlow, adding that Paul had been present to interview the man's coworkers when the hostage situation developed.

Cavanaugh said nothing to that, offered no consolation or words of encouragement, but Theresa did not expect him to. Cop machismo would not allow it. When you work with sharks, you don't bleed in the water.

"Snipers are in place?"

Jason said, "We've got five, one on the street and four on different floors here. But there's a problem."

Cavanaugh took in the room once more, the outside light bouncing weirdly off his brown eyes. "The windows don't open."

"Nope."

"Ms. Elliott?"

Theresa had almost forgotten that the woman was there. But then librarians were good at walking softly, and Ms. Elliott seemed versed in camouflage; her tailored suit gave only the slightest hint of what was, to judge from her shapely calves, an outstanding figure. No sense distracting male readers from their tomes. But even the resourceful librarian seemed perplexed. "I'm sorry?"

"Are there any windows in this building that open?"

"No. None."

Theresa hated buildings like that—something to do with mild claustrophobia—but wondered why SRT snipers would show such concern for damaging library windows.

"The books need to be kept at a constant humidity,"

the librarian explained. "Some are quite old. In our Rare and Antique Books section, we have some manuscripts that are two hundred and fifty years old and even in sealed display cases—I'm sorry, I'm digressing."

"That's all right." Cavanaugh spoke warmly, but Theresa could see that Ms. Elliott was made of stern stuff and rather immune to dimples.

"It's also a safety issue, since we're open to the public every day but Sunday and holidays. But—"

Theresa broke in. "What about it? Don't snipers go on the roof, anyway?"

"They're too visible on a roof, silhouetted against the sky. They prefer windows, but then we have to open up every window in the building so that their positions are not obvious. They'll just have to figure something out."

"There are cutouts on the roof," Peggy Elliott said. She spoke reluctantly, with a trace of guilt for suggesting a way to use her building of knowledge for violent purposes. "The roof is ringed with a short wall. It has slots at intervals, for rain and snow drainage."

"Thank you. Jason, SRT has probably already found those, but make sure they know about them anyway." Cavanaugh shook his head. "I don't envy them having to be on a roof in this heat. What's going on over at the Fed?"

"They've shut off the elevators and cleared the employee lobby. They have a team at the other end of the hallway, tucked around the corner." Jason touched the screen, pointing out the area behind the hostages. "They'll keep the two guys from getting into the elevators or reaching the employee lobby, which has entrances to the parking garage and Superior Avenue."

"But they can't approach that way," Cavanaugh

mused. "No cover. Any stairwells or elevators in the public lobby?"

"No."

"So the only thing those two men can do is to go out the same way they came in. Except they've got no getaway car to step outside *for*, because we took it. Did we find anything significant in the car?"

"Registered to a Robert Moyers in Brookpark," Frank told him. "No one answers the phone or the door; the house is locked up tight, with no signs of violence. We've got a guy sitting on it in case he comes home. The car has not been reported stolen. Theresa? You find anything?"

She swallowed. "Not really. Prints are going into AFIS right now. A cash receipt from Lakewood, dated yesterday. An empty Advil bottle. A smudge of blood in the trunk, but we won't have DNA results until, I hope, this is over."

"You're Theresa," Cavanaugh said to her, looking her up and down with such care that she wanted to squirm. "I was just hearing about you the other day."

And he still had that trace of a grin, damn him. "Yeah?"

"I had lunch with Jack. Prosecutor Sabian, I mean. Don't frown like that—he thinks very highly of you. Something about a murderous pediatric nurse and saving his baby's life. Really, stop scowling at me."

"I don't care for being discussed behind my back." *Stop it,* she told herself. *Be smart. He's going to want you to leave; he'd be an idiot if he didn't. Let him think one phone call to the county prosecutor could open any door in the city.* "But yes, Jack and I are . . . old friends."

His gaze grew even more appraising. "Well, I'm

enchanted to make your acquaintance. Why, exactly, are you . . . ?"

Time to wipe the smile off his face, and besides, better he hear it from her than someone else. Men never forgave the withholding of information. "My fiancé's in that lobby, Mr. Cavanaugh."

The grin did indeed disappear, if only for a moment. "I see. Patrick's partner?"

She nodded, not trusting herself to speak. She stared at her hands, refusing to meet his eyes, though she could feel his gaze burning into her temple. Finally he said only, "We'll get him out."

She let a sigh of relief escape between her teeth. He hadn't asked her to leave—yet.

A uniformed cop appeared. "I got someone you're going to want to talk to."

CHAPTER 5

9:25 A.M.

"My name is William Kessler." The man clutched at his tie as he spoke and nearly collapsed into the chair Frank brought for him. *Finally,* Theresa thought, *someone who's as nervous as I am.* "I'm vice president of Supervision and Regulation. The president is in D.C. right now. I had to shuffle cars around in my driveway this morning because my daughter had a late night—anyhow, I got caught in traffic, and that's why I was late to work, and you'd already barricaded the building. Who's in there? Is anyone hurt? No? Thank God. I tried to call the president, but the open-market meeting had already convened." He began to wind down. "I really didn't want to be late today."

"Mr. Kessler—" Cavanaugh began.

"Are they terrorists? Do they have a bomb? What on earth do these men want? Can't you get them out of there? There hasn't been blood spilled inside a Federal Reserve bank since . . . well, ever, so far as I know."

"Has one ever been robbed?"

"Robbed?" Kessler stared at Cavanaugh, then the

rest of them, in dismay, either over their collective ignorance of the Federal Reserve Banking system of America or over his task of summarizing it for them. "You don't *rob* a Federal Reserve bank. The Fed supervises and regulates banks, sets the discount rate—the rate at which we loan money to banks and other financial institutions—and controls the amount of currency in circulation, working with the Mint. We also process all cashed checks for our district, though that's all going electronic now—"

Frank interrupted. "But you're still a bank, right? You have cash in the drawers of those teller windows?"

"Some, yes. Savings-bond transactions are still conducted on the west side of the public lobby. The cages on the east side were left there for show."

"Is the vault in the lobby?" Theresa asked.

The Fed's vice president yanked at his tie once more, distorting the cords in his wrinkled neck. "The money vault is underground. It's also three stories high, and they'd never be able to get into it anyway. . . . This isn't the neighborhood savings and loan—that's what I'm trying to explain."

"You asked about terrorists," Cavanaugh reminded him. "So before I talk to them, has the Fed received any threats lately?"

"Every day. From the people who simply aren't happy with the interest rate to the ones who think the Federal Reserve is a privately owned bank and/or a method for oppressing the American people and/or responsible for JFK's assassination. I'm not kidding. Supposedly we murdered him over Executive Order 11110—"

"Recently," Cavanaugh said. "Have there been any

recent, specific threats? Any that mentioned today's date or referenced the secretary of state's visit?"

Kessler quieted a moment to think. "No. And I insist that PR make me aware of each and every one."

"Okay. If there's a political agenda, they'll mention it as soon as they pick up the phone. Those types are never shy. In the meantime we'll assume they came to rob the place."

"But that's *ridiculous*! We have tighter security than the White House. We have metal detectors, armed guards, and dogs protecting that lobby." The level of Kessler's voice rose with each word. "How could this *happen*?"

"They ran in and put a gun to someone's head," Frank told him. "All the security in the world can't fix that."

"But why?" the man wailed. "Why *us*?"

"Because these guys figured a bank was a bank. And your lobby opens earlier than the other downtown banks'."

Kessler rubbed his eyes with one palm and admitted, as if it pained him to do so, that they opened at eight for savings-bond transactions and school groups.

Frank continued, "Maybe they thought rush hour would slow up our response. They could come in, have the tellers empty their drawers into their bag, and leave. That's how most bank robberies go. That's what would have happened, too, if that security guard hadn't grabbed their car."

Jason cleared his throat. "He acted according to protocol. Containment is the number-one priority with armed attackers."

"Except that if he *hadn't* contained them, they might have just taken the money and left. Instead we have a hostage situation," Frank said. Just as Theresa began to tremble with rage at this error, he added, "But then they might have taken a few people with them, too. You never know."

Cavanaugh theorized, "They go in thinking it's the neighborhood First National, get surprised by the level of security present, and on top of *that* they lose their wheels. They take hostages until they can figure out what to do next."

"Unless they did kill Ludlow," Theresa pointed out. "Then they should know exactly what kind of bank it is."

Kessler started, his lanky body twitching as if she'd applied a shock. "Mark Ludlow? Is he dead? I thought you said no one's been hurt."

Frank outlined the morning's murder investigation for Kessler and Cavanaugh. The vice president had only met the man twice, so he could not positively identify the Polaroid photo of the victim. Frank put in a call to Ludlow's fifth-floor office, where a secretary, waiting to be evacuated by the Fed security force, told him that Mr. Ludlow had not arrived for work. "Unless you've got two Mark Ludlows," he said to Kessler and the rest of the group huddled around the reading table, "I'm guessing he's dead, and I'm guessing he got that way because of something to do with those two guys in the lobby across the street. What did Ludlow do for you? Why would they target him?"

"He's a bank examiner, division of consumer affairs. He monitors banks' operations regarding credit, truth-in-lending laws, interest rates."

"So maybe he found out something about a bank that they wanted to hide," Cavanaugh suggested.

"No," Kessler said immediately. "Ludlow would

have shared any information with the division head. He just got here—Ludlow, I mean. He transferred from the Atlanta bank, not a month ago, so he's still learning our idiosyncratic little ways of doing things. Any officer at the banks we govern would know that killing Ludlow wouldn't hide damaging information, and besides, banks don't do things like that."

Theresa caught a grin before it made it to her lips. She couldn't smile. Paul might end up dead.

Jason worked on a different theory. "They must have tried to make Ludlow tell them how to break into the bank."

Cavanaugh drummed his fingers along the phone receiver, frowning in thought. "But why pick a guy who's only been there a month?"

"There weren't any signs of torture on the body," Theresa said. "The killer hit Ludlow in the head a few times, and that was that."

Frank took out a cigarette but refrained, under Ms. Elliott's wary eye, from lighting up. "Maybe he had enemies in Atlanta and they followed him here. But then why rob the bank? Some sort of afterthought?"

"He told them something before he died," Jason said. "Something worth breaking into a Federal Reserve for."

"What's happening over there today?" Cavanaugh asked Kessler. "What's special?"

The man shrugged. "Nothing. The daily routine: financial analyses, a meeting or two. Banks might come in for some cash transactions, but nothing all that big, except—" He stared at the portrait of Clio, but the muse seemed to make him uneasy and he turned to Apollo and Hyacinthus instead.

"Except?"

"The money shred."

The room's occupants waited for the man to explain about destroying what they all worked so hard to accumulate.

"We handle sending out new currency from the Bureau of Engraving in D.C., and the worn-out bills come to us to be destroyed, shredded. We exchanged old notes for new for the Bank One system yesterday. The old money will be shredded this afternoon—or would have been."

"How much money are we talking?"

"In addition to what we usually have sitting around, probably about seven or eight million dollars."

The room grew even more hushed, no doubt as people tried to picture $8 million. Just sitting around.

"Would Ludlow have overseen this?" Frank asked.

"No. It's got nothing to do with him. He probably couldn't even find that area of the tunnels if he went looking for it. Besides, most of the process is done by robots."

"Robots?" Frank tapped his unlit cigarette on the table. "Like R2-D2?"

"More like forklifts without drivers."

Cavanaugh leaned forward. "And old money wouldn't have sequential numbers, would be nice and innocuous-looking to use. Let's assume that's what these guys are after. What route would they need to take to get to the money?"

"From the lobby? There isn't one. They'd have to take an elevator from the employee lobby, and I thought you said security had that blocked off."

"They have it covered," the negotiator clarified. That, Theresa thought, must be the hallway and elevator bank behind the hostages, past the information desk.

"Then, from the elevator, they'd need a key card to get past the double doors on Sublevel One, and then another to get into the shredding room without setting off the alarm. Not to mention the fact that all these areas have cameras."

"They can't be too concerned about that." Cavanaugh gestured toward the television monitor. "We already have them on camera."

The vice president turned to stare at the sight of his employees crouched on the floor, hands behind their heads. He half stood, then sank back into the hard wooden chair like a deflating balloon. *He's getting it now,* Theresa thought. The futility. The helplessness.

Maybe not. "How are you picking up this video?"

"Streaming Internet link," Jason said.

"This is being broadcast over the *Internet*?" The Fed VP was clearly horrified.

"It's triple-password-protected, and all three will be changed as soon as this is over. Don't worry."

The librarian spoke up again. "We have wireless Internet connections all over this building. Will that interfere?"

"No. It's on the same server, but it's a secure link."

Theresa's head swam. *We have bad guys with guns, and they're discussing the intricacies of modern communication.*

"Don't be afraid, Theresa."

It took her brain a moment to realize that Cavanaugh had spoken to her, and it shocked her gaze away from the TV monitor. "What?"

"I said, don't be afraid." The smirk had left. His dark

eyes appeared somber, and for a moment her soul felt the fleeting touch of comfort. Maybe he really was all that they said he was. Maybe Paul would be fine. "We'll get him out of there. I'm guessing these guys have figured out that they've shut themselves in a box and are already praying for a way to open it. With luck we'll be out of here by lunchtime. There's just one thing, though. I need you to leave."

This must be what it felt like to be sucker-punched. "What?"

"I can't have emotional people in here. I need to concentrate on the hostage takers and on them alone, if I'm going to get Paul out of there." His voice remained calm, hypnotic, and if she didn't take care, she'd find herself agreeing. "I can't have your reactions distracting me."

"I won't react."

"Theresa—"

"No, I mean it," she insisted, unable to stop the babbling undercurrent from her words. "I was married for fifteen years. I learned how not to react, believe me."

"Theresa—"

"I'm sure Jack Sabian would want me to stay."

The weight of his ambitions slowed him, but only for a moment. "I'm the conduit to the guys holding a gun on Paul, Theresa. You don't really want me distracted, do you?"

He had a point. But she kept her gaze steady, the way she did with defense attorneys and Rachael's band director. "You need me. I've been closer to them than you have. I may have inspected their handiwork this morning. I've sat in their car. I know who drove, and that he likes cinnamon Tic Tacs and country music. I need to be here." Theresa turned back to the television monitor, as if this ended the discussion. Hah. She should win all arguments so easily.

From the corner of her eye, she watched him watching her, until a shuffling sound of collective movement erupted from the staff offices in the next section. Apparently the power discussion had been concluded and a decision reached.

To her surprise and intense relief, Cavanaugh said, "All right. But consider yourself on probation. Now let's get this party started." He reached for the handset.

Theresa clapped her palm down on his wrist. "Wait."

CHAPTER 6

9:10 A.M.

Paul's body tensed, waiting for the shot. Nothing. Just the woman's scream, cut off. Then Bobby's voice, raised and peremptory. Then footsteps over the polished marble tiles.

He turned his head to see two more hostages join them. Three—one of the two women carried a small boy. He had huge eyes and clung to his mother, and Paul recognized him from a photo seen just that morning, in a dead man's house.

"They were hiding under a desk," Bobby reported to his partner.

The tall robber barely glanced at them. "On the floor. Anyone else?"

"Negative."

"Take care of that door."

Bobby headed toward the north wall of the lobby. The tall robber kept his gun aimed at the three security guards and the dog. The two women sank into a sitting position, aligned in a row with the other hostages. The little boy didn't make a sound, simply clutched a small stuffed animal to his face. His mother dropped her oversize handbag beside her to put both arms around him, all without taking her eyes from the robber—or perhaps his gun.

So this was what was left of the Ludlow family. The woman almost certainly didn't know that her husband was dead and must have come here looking for him. She hadn't been home since early in the morning, at a minimum, or else how could she miss a corpse on her front step? Where had she been?

And now the hostages included a baby. This had gone from bad to worse.

Bobby returned. "I used a shelf to wedge that door. I don't know how long it will hold. They'd be nuts to come in there anyway—we'd see them long before they'd reach us."

"I don't want them even tempted. You'd better hang out in this half of the lobby and keep these people between you and that door and that hallway, in case they decide to come in all commando-like."

Bobby zipped quickly past the vulnerable center section. "What about the elevators?"

"They probably turned them off. But if you hear a 'ding,' dive for cover and come up shooting."

"Now what?"

"Get the tie-wraps."

Bobby laid aside the automatic rifle to dig in his duffel bag. Dust motes danced in the sunbeam above him as it slanted down from the high windows.

"You, in the pink," the tall robber said to the woman next to Paul. "Stand up."

The young woman trembled.

Should I stop this? Paul wondered. Bobby had the gun back in his hand.

"Come on, get up. I'm not going to hurt you, I just

need to borrow you for a minute. Now turn around.
I'm going to put my hand on your shoulder, like this.
That's all you have to do. Now you three." He nodded
at the three security guards, who knelt in a line between the rest of the hostages and the two new women.
"Now that Bobby has relieved you of your weapons,
he's going to cuff you to the teller cages there. Don't
get nervous. No one's going to get hurt as long as you
do what I say."

The three young men gazed at him, and Paul could
see them working out various methods of attack in
their minds. They had been trained for exactly this—
which was no doubt why this guy had to neutralize
them.

"But if you try to rush me, this girl—What's your
name, sugar?"

It came out in a whisper. "Missy."

"That's a pretty name. Missy here is going to stay
between me and you three. And if you get in a scuffle
with my partner, the next sound you will hear is Missy's
guts spattering all over these other folks. On the other
hand, if you come along real nice, Bobby won't make
the cuffs too tight. We'll take some money, and then
we'll leave, and everyone, even Missy, gets to keep their
guts. Do we understand each other?"

Silence.

"I asked if we understand each other."

The three nodded, one at a time, ever so slightly.

"Okay. You with the dog. Take him with you and
tie-wrap the leash to the cage. Make it secure. If he gets
loose, I will be able to shoot him before he ever makes
it to me."

Paul watched as Bobby and each guard moved slowly,
carefully, down the iron grillwork wall to the south end

of the lobby. The metal bars made a handy thing to tie people to and appeared as solidly constructed as the rest of the building. From there the guards faced the savings-bond teller cages and the opaque windows hiding East Sixth Street from view. Missy, her brown eyes seething with both fear and anger, didn't seem to breathe at all. Paul thought of the gun at his hip. What should he do with it?

It occurred to him that he had to live. He had a wedding to attend. Theresa would not forgive him if he missed it.

He shifted slightly, as if his legs were getting stiff—which they were. The tall robber's eyes flicked to him, watched for a moment. It could have been a trick of the light on the sunglasses, but Paul didn't think so. The man's finger only had to twitch against the trigger of that M4 carbine he held and Missy would be cut in half before Paul could blink.

His gun would stay in its holster for now.

Odd as it seemed, what he longed to do more than anything was call Patrick and tell him the dead man's widow and child were here. It seemed relevant to the investigation.

And what about the Nextel? If it went off, it could startle the two men. But if he tried to turn it off, he would attract attention, and he did not want attention from these guys. If they had gotten anything more than a speeding ticket in their lifetime, they would know a cop when they saw one. Ex-cons always could. Besides, he couldn't bear to deaden his only connection to the outside.

Bobby finished tie-wrapping the security guys to the grillwork, arms up, facing out. It looked uncomfortable, not to mention embarrassing, and Paul felt for them. It was now all up to him, as the last loose law-enforcement person in the room. Training mantras came back to him: Watch for an opening. Wait until they're both distracted, then fire quickly. Take out whoever's closest to the hostages first. Don't risk a civilian.

He assumed that either the police or the Fed security force, probably both together, were planning a response. The door at the north end had been closed off, according to Bobby. That left the hallway behind them and the street entrance. The ceiling was out—too high, and no handy acoustic tiles to hide behind, only ornate artwork and gilt edges.

"Nineteen twenty-three," the black guy in the uniform whispered when he noticed Paul's gaze. "They're the original paintings."

"Beautiful," Paul told him, though he would rather have had ugly white tile that SRT guys could creep through.

"Yeah." The man sighed. "You should see the executive offices. One has a Picasso and a collection of Murano glass."

The tall robber watched them over Missy's shoulder but said nothing. Still, Paul piped down. No sense pressing his luck.

When the dog's leash had been secured to the grating, Bobby returned to the southwest corner of the lobby, where sniper fire through either the Superior or East Sixth windows would require an impossibly sharp angle. "Okay, Lucas."

Another name. Either these guys weren't very good at this or they didn't intend to leave witnesses.

Lucas ordered the rest of them to slide down toward the two women, and Paul inched across the floor.

It felt good to let his arms down and even better when Lucas did not tell them to put them up again. Clamping his left arm to his side kept the blazer from opening and exposing his firearm.

He came to rest against a rounded reception desk of solid marble, standing alone before the employee lobby with the elevator bank. The three security guards were tied at least forty feet from Paul, making communication difficult, if not impossible. If Paul turned his head to their direction, he also faced Bobby, in his safe zone in front of the savings-bond teller cages.

"Sorry, Missy," Lucas said to the quivering hostage. "I'm going to need you to stand in front of me for just another minute. You, the gentleman in the green." He stared at the black man next to Paul, the one who knew how old the ceiling paintings were. "Where's the money?"

The man swallowed hard but answered in a steady voice. "In the tellers' drawers. The rest of this floor is an educational area now, classrooms and displays."

Lucas cocked one eyebrow. "You think I'm doing all this to empty a few drawers?"

That didn't clarify matters. "There's cash in various areas all over this building. Is there some amount in particular that you mean?"

"I mean the really big pile of it."

"Well—"

The phone rang.

"Missy," Lucas said, "I'm going to need you to answer that, please."

CHAPTER 7

9:40 A.M.

Theresa squinted at the screen, dimly aware that she still pinned Cavanaugh's warm arm to the table. "Does that woman have a *child* with her?"

Everyone else looked, leaning toward the small television screen as if a magnetic force pulled them.

She could make out the woman's light-colored hair and the outlines of the small person in her arms, but beyond that the image shaded into pixelated blobs of gray tones. "Frank, you don't think—"

"Why the heck would she have a kid in there?" Jason asked of no one in particular.

"Do you have day care on the premises?" Cavanaugh said to Kessler.

"No."

Theresa let go of Cavanaugh's arm and patted Frank's in agitation. "Our dead guy from this morning— could that be his wife and child in the lobby?"

Now Frank squinted, and Cavanaugh regarded the screen with new interest. "What makes you say that?"

"They match the description. We saw their photos this morning, and it could be them."

Frank said, "You think she went there looking for her husband?"

"It would make sense. Of course, it doesn't explain why she didn't notice him on the front stoop."

"No," Kessler contradicted, and the heads at the table swiveled back to him. "She works there. It was part of the deal to get Ludlow to come here from Atlanta."

Cavanaugh nodded at the screen. "Is that her?"

"I've never met her."

"Jason, do we know who's in that lobby?"

"Not them. Security made up a list earlier, from the cameras. But they only list one woman and now we have . . . three. Where did they come from?"

"Probably hid under their desks at the first gunshot. Who are the identified hostages?"

Jason read off the names and vital statistics of the three security guards and the three hostages, not including Paul or the three recent additions. The five employees ranged in age from twenty-four to seventy-one. Most were married with children. *This is more than Paul*, Theresa thought. *This is a larger tragedy than mine.*

None had a criminal history or so much as a reprimand in their personnel files. None of them worked in high-security areas.

Frank said, "No one stands out as an obvious inside man. But Ludlow's murdered, and Mrs. Ludlow happens to be in the lobby when it's taken over. I have a hard time believing that's coincidence."

The hum of voices from the staff offices next door continued to disperse. A young woman approached the group, carrying a notepad and a chair, which she placed slightly behind Cavanaugh, on his right. Without turning, he said, "This is Irene, our scribe. It's time to start."

Before, Theresa assumed, the FBI had told him to wait for the unwanted Laura. Cavanaugh needed to be the first to the hill, or telephone, in this case, possession being nine-tenths of the law. Now he dialed in a phone number from Jason's notebook, using their impressive array of telephone equipment. Three phones, as well as a digital recorder and a speaker, flowed from a central hub.

It's all about words, Theresa thought. No microscopes, no chemicals, no databases. Just words.

A woman's voice answered with a quavering "Hello."

"This is the police department calling. Can I speak to one of the men with the guns, please?"

Without discussion a man's voice took over. Theresa figured out that his side of the conversation came over the speakerphone, so that everyone in the room could hear it. But on their side, Cavanaugh spoke into his receiver so that the hostage takers couldn't pick up other conversations going on around the room.

"This is Sergeant Chris Cavanaugh of the Cleveland Police Department."

"I don't much care who you are," the guy said, with what sounded like utter repose. "I need to know if you're in charge."

"I'm the negotiator. I'm here because we have a situation going on, and I want to help you find a way through it so that no one gets hurt. That's our most important goal, that no one gets hurt. Not you, not the bank employees, not the cops. Does that sound reasonable to you?"

" 'A situation.' That's an interesting way to put it."

"As I said, my name is Chris. What can I call you?"

"It's so nice to be talking with you today, Chris. My name is Lucas. I'm going to want some things, and I'll need a yes or no from you. Can you do that, or should I be talking to someone else? I don't intend to repeat myself."

"I'm not trying to argue with you here, but all the conversation is going to go through me. That's the way we do it. How's everybody doing in there? Anyone hurt?"

"Let me tell you how *I* do it, Chris." The man's derision came over the speaker loud and clear, but with a slight wobble. He probably wasn't as tough as he liked to sound, but Theresa knew enough about the psychology of criminals to know that that would not be a help. Any insecurities would only make him more desperate. "I talk to the guy in charge."

"How are the people in there? Is anyone hurt?"

"They're going to be if I don't talk to the guy in charge."

Theresa let her breath release from aching lungs. Sixty seconds in, and already they could not meet a demand, couldn't produce the person in charge, and all because Chris Cavanaugh had acted prematurely in order to keep the limelight directly on himself.

And he could, because those from the corridors of power were not here but at a fancy luncheon. Theresa turned to Frank and whispered, "Is the secretary of state's motorcade coming through this area? Could this be some sort of ploy—"

He shook his head, which needed a haircut. "Their route from the airport to the convention center goes down Ontario. They won't come within two blocks of this place."

Cavanaugh let out a theatrical sigh. "I'm going to tell you the truth, Lucas, and I want you to consider that statement carefully—all day long here, whatever else happens, I'm going to tell you the truth, because I've found that that's the only way these situations work out to everyone's satisfaction, including mine. You with me so far?"

"Uh-huh." The hostage taker did not sound convinced.

"Then here's the truth: There are three police agencies here, the Federal Reserve security force, the Cleveland city cops, and the FBI, and right now they're fighting over—I mean discussing—who's going to get to be the boss. As soon as I know, I'll put them on the phone. But no matter who it is, today is going to be all about you and me."

"I'm sure you're a great guy, Chris, but why should I waste my time with you? You put the lucky winner on the phone, and I'll put my gun in the ear of one of these people here, and we can work this out fast."

His words brought scenes of carnage to Theresa's mind, so that she got up and returned to the telescope. Paul had moved as the line condensed in front of the reception desk, but he still breathed. His hands were in his lap, and he stared straight ahead. *Look up, honey. I'm here.*

Footsteps padded over the low carpeting. Two young men, too well dressed to be anything but FBI, entered the reading area and stopped short to observe Chris Cavanaugh and his conversation with the hostage taker. Their eyes glowed with excitement; they were clearly tickled to death to be in the thick of it. After a flash of anger, Theresa confessed to herself that she would feel exactly the same way if all the players were strangers to her, if she weren't in love with one of the hostages, if the man who had jolted her emotions from their self-imposed hibernation didn't sit across the street with a gun to his head.

The young men hurried back the way they'd come, no doubt to let their higher-ups know that CPD had started without them.

"There's reasons for this," Cavanaugh was explaining. "I can't concentrate on you and make decisions at the same time. Also, we might talk for a while, and there's always the chance I could start to like you, and then any decisions I made would be biased."

"Oh," the voice drawled, "I don't think there's going to be much chance of that, Chris. As soon as I kill one of these hostages, I bet you'll cross me right off your Christmas-card list without a second thought."

It worried her that the man called Lucas referred to them as "hostages" instead of "people." Killers often tried to dehumanize their victims, to make their murders seem more reasonable. It would be up to the negotiator to make Lucas see his captives as human beings, with jobs and families and dreams worth living for.

Cavanaugh must have had the same thought. "Speaking of which, could you tell me who-all you have in there with you? We know the receptionist is there, Missy, and the three security guys, Greg, Antoine, and—"

Lucas interrupted. "Four million. In hundreds. And while you're coordinating that, let me tell you something about the lobby of the Federal Reserve Bank of Cleveland. It's big. It's pretty, really—paintings on the ceiling and all that shit. But big. We will always be closer to our hostages than you are, and we can kill them before you get to us. You throw tear gas in here or try to smoke us out, we can kill them before you get to us. You got that down?"

"I understand. Four million is a lot of money, Lucas. But you know what? It's doable. We can do that. It's going to take some time, though—certainly more than an hour."

"We're in a building full of money, Chris. There's a lot more than four million in cash in this place, and we all know it. So it shouldn't take more than ten minutes, really. I'm only giving you an hour so that you can get the car here from wherever you took it. Either drive it or put it on a flatbed, by the way. Do *not* use a tow dolly. You got that?"

"Lucas, I don't know much about the Federal Reserve building, but—"

"You got it down about the car? Just have someone drive it here. No towing."

"No towing, got it. But about the money. That place is like Fort Knox. You need to cooperate with us in order to go get your money, because there's a lot of security measures in place to pass through—"

"Don't be stupid, Chris."

Cavanaugh stopped.

"I'm not going to go and get anything. There are robots downstairs that move cash around, and we have elevators. Have it brought to me. One hour. Or someone dies. And don't screw up and use a tow dolly."

CHAPTER 8

9:46 A.M.

The click of his hang-up filled the room, and then everyone began to talk at once.

"He didn't mention his partner," Theresa observed.

Frank lit a cigarette, and Theresa resisted the urge to snatch it from his fingers and take a few puffs. "Have the money come to him," Frank said. "These guys aren't as dumb as I thought they were."

"And they know something about the Federal Reserve. Please don't smoke in here, Detective," Cavanaugh added, nearly in unison with the librarian, Ms. Elliott.

Theresa watched while Frank stared at the smoke curling up as if wondering how it got there, dropped the cigarette into his water bottle, and gave the librarian a sheepish smile. She also wondered why the librarian had been allowed to remain, but then they might need further assistance from the building, and after all they *were* occupying her workspace. Besides, she wouldn't become emotional. *Her* fiancé wasn't one of the hostages.

Cavanaugh addressed the Fed executive. "Mr. Kessler."

"Yes?" It seemed to require physical effort for the man to tear his gaze from the television monitor.

"How long would it take to bring up the money from the vault?"

"Actually, he's right," Kessler admitted, his voice steeped in misery. "We could do it in about ten minutes. The *paperwork* would take two days, but I assume he means for us to skip that step."

"I think that's a reasonable assumption. Can a robot really deliver the cash?"

"Not to the lobby. They won't fit on a passenger elevator. They're designed to use the freight elevators at the back of the building, and they don't go to the lobby."

"I wonder if he knows that," Cavanaugh said.

"But I suppose it could install the pallet in the passenger elevator and send it to the ground floor. I'm not really sure—it's never happened."

Theresa spoke. "He knows about the robots but not that there's eight million piled downstairs to be shredded instead of four. It's possible these two guys *don't* have anything to do with Mark Ludlow's murder."

"That's true." Cavanaugh wiped the phone receiver down with a disposable alcohol swab as he talked. "Or maybe they couldn't carry eight million. Wouldn't that take up a football field or so?"

"In ones," Kessler said. He spoke firmly and calmly once on a familiar subject. "If they took only the hundreds, four million dollars in hundreds would weigh about eighty pounds and fill six hundred forty-three cubic inches, or four good-size briefcases. Between the two of them, they could carry it out. Or they could make more than one trip."

"They'd have to let go of the hostages." Frank

fingered his water bottle as if he regretted using it as an ashtray. "They couldn't keep a gun on them and carry all that at the same time."

Theresa found it hard to take her eyes off the TV screen. "That looks like a duffel bag on the floor. They could fill that up, sling it across their backs, and still be hands-free. Or they could make the hostages help them carry it."

Cavanaugh murmured, "That's another good point. We keep forgetting they have a ready supply of labor in there with them."

Theresa thought of something else. "What if Ludlow was their inside man? That's why there's no signs of coercion on his body—he gave them the information freely. Then they decided to cut him out."

"Leaving them short one getaway driver. But Ludlow's only been here a month. Not much time to hook up with a team."

"He'd be an unlikely suspect for that very reason, and a month's long enough to get the layout."

Kessler stirred. "Mark Ludlow came with an excellent recommendation and has—had—worked for the Federal Reserve for a long time. At least ten years, I think."

"I'm sure he did," Cavanaugh soothed. "Why did he want to move here from sunny Atlanta?"

"I don't know. The weather, maybe. It can get miserable there in the summertime."

"Do me a favor—most of the employees should have been evacuated to the Hampton Inn. Would you call whoever recruited Ludlow and the Human Resources person who coordinated his hire and get them over here? Maybe they'll know how Ludlow came to transfer here, and why, and something about his wife."

"Certainly."

A new voice sounded. "What's going on here?"

Theresa turned from the window. The bigwigs had arrived.

At the head stood a towering man with gray hair and a matching mustache. Despite appearing a little too paunchy and florid to be an FBI agent, he introduced himself as the special agent in charge of the Cleveland office, and the two young men Theresa had seen earlier flanked him like a pair of groomsmen. "My name's Torello. You're Cavanaugh?"

"That would be me. I just spoke with the hostage taker named Lucas. He wants four million and his car back. In an hour."

"He called you?"

"We're on a first-name basis already," Cavanaugh said, which of course didn't answer the question.

In the three steps it took Torello to reach the reading table, Theresa could see his mind churning as he analyzed Cavanaugh's actions, motives, and results, accepted same, and moved on. This did not surprise her—one didn't make it to the top FBI slot in a large city without possessing both sense and self-control. "Laura Reisling will get here from D.C. in an hour and a half. She can be secondary."

Cavanaugh spoke with every appearance of sincerity. "It will be great to see her again."

SAIC Torello did not sit but kept the psychological advantage of looming over the upstarts at the table while the rest of his party filtered in. Theresa recognized Viancourt, the assistant chief of police, who took a seat next to a graying man in fatigues. This man's name tag read MULVANEY.

She remained by the wall, close enough to the

window to grab a peek through the telescope but not close enough to be warned away from the opening should the robbers emerge shooting. She tried to make herself invisible and glanced over at the librarian, Ms. Elliott, who had retreated into the rows of texts in order to do the same. Or perhaps they'd simply been pushed back by a mushroom cloud of testosterone.

The diplomatic Jason opened the discussion with a refreshingly nonjurisdictional question. "What about the secretary of state's visit? I know we're several blocks away, but what if this is some sort of diversion? We get every cop in the city over here, it might put holes in the security at the convention center."

Assistant Chief Viancourt shook his head. "No, the plan for the secretary of state will stay intact. There's Secret Service coming in, too, to fill out the ranks."

"Still, the timing is suspicious," Cavanaugh pointed out. "Any available cops not working the luncheon will be working that Rock and Roll Hall of Fame induction concert tonight, so if this thing goes on, our resources are going to get stretched pretty thin. Maybe one or both should be canceled, or at least change the venue for the State luncheon."

"Are you nuts?" Viancourt began to flush at the very idea. "*Cancel?* Cleveland needs this exposure, needs to show the rest of the country that we're still a major city. Our star began to fade shortly after the paint dried on Jacobs Field, and by now it's in an all-out spiral. Canceling is not an option. Besides," he added, "it's too late now. The secretary's going to land any minute, and—"

"Okay," Torello broke in smoothly. "We'll keep our security detail informed of what's happening here, and they can make their own decisions. Surely these two don't have any sort of direct assault planned, since they couldn't affect the convention center from a block and a half away unless they set off a nuclear bomb. Let's talk about his demands. You, sir—you're the Fed president?"

"Vice president," Kessler told him. "The president is in Washington at a Federal Open Market Committee meeting. The presidents of all twelve Reserve banks are there, plus the board of governors," he added morosely. "They only meet eight times a year, and it had to be today. I don't—"

Cavanaugh interrupted. "Are you willing to give them four million dollars?"

"It's not mine!" Kessler protested at first, then hedged: "Can you guarantee we'll get it back?"

Receiving no response from Cavanaugh, he appealed to Torello, who said, "No."

Mulvaney, the man in fatigues, announced without heat, "We don't deal with terrorists."

"No, we don't deal with terrorists," Cavanaugh clarified. "But we'll *negotiate* with anyone. At least I will. We want them to take the money and leave the hostages. It's only money. It's not worth lives."

Maybe I could like Chris Cavanaugh, Theresa thought, *even if it's his own reputation he's really trying to protect.*

"And if they will, then our situation goes from being a complicated standoff to the relatively simple pursuit of an armed felon. The problem is," he went on, "that the money is usually the stalling point. I can put people off for hours over the difficulties in raising a large amount of cash. But in this case the money is right there and he knows it. Mr. Kessler, you said those robots aren't designed to use the lobby elevators?"

"Correct."

"Okay, we'll use that. Meanwhile the car. Where is it?"

"We sent it to the medical examiner's office," Theresa told him, wincing as nearly every man in the room turned to wonder who the hell she was.

"That gives me something to work with. His insistence on a flatbed will help, too. I can delay about finding one."

"Tell him they're all broken," Viancourt suggested.

"He won't believe that. Besides, I can't lie to him. Stretch the truth, maybe—after all, the robots *aren't* designed for the lobby, and we *don't* have a flatbed standing by."

"He's a scumbag," Mulvaney said. "Lie through your teeth."

Cavanaugh inched his console farther out onto the table, expanding his personal work area and lessening everyone else's. Theresa wondered if that was one of the tricks they taught you in negotiator school. "That won't work, and it gets people killed. The two hardest things about this are, first, figuring out what it is they'll give themselves up to get. Usually *they* don't even know, and that's what makes it tough. Second is resisting the urge to promise them anything, including the moon. Unless they're mentally disabled, they'll see through it in a second, and then people can get hurt. Theresa, what's special about this car?"

Again he caught her off guard, which annoyed her. "What?"

"Usually they ask for *a* car. But he wants *his* car. You examined it—what's so special?"

"Nothing. It's a Benz with a nice paint job and a clean interior."

"Maybe that's all the reason there is," Frank said. "It's hard to find a decent used car these days."

Cavanaugh persisted. "Has it been modified in any way? Police scanner installed? High-performance engine?"

"I didn't look under the hood." She didn't add that she wouldn't know a high-performance engine from a four-cylinder econobox.

"Go look. And take someone from the bomb squad with you—they might have explosives strapped to the frame as some sort of Plan B. We can't snow him about the money, so we're going to have to work with the car. Jason, go with her, and take a remote. Get me—us—some answers. We've got forty-five minutes."

CHAPTER 9

10:09 A.M.

Theresa had even bought a dress. A wedding dress. A floor-length white dress with lace and a few modest sequins. Hope, this time, would triumph over experience. That was what she hadn't told Paul about, what she felt a little silly about confessing. Now, not telling him seemed a vote of no confidence, a betrayal. Never mind that if he didn't make it out of there, the damn dress would cease to matter anyway.

She waited behind the M.E.'s office, in a sliver of shadow along the brick wall, eyeing the Mercedes, which now sat in the middle of the parking lot as three outfitted bomb squad members worked on it. Two examined the undercarriage with small mirrors on retractable handles, and a third attached a wire to a latch embedded in the front grille.

Be careful, her grandfather had always instructed her. *Don't ride your bike in the street. Don't talk to strangers. Don't drive too fast.*

She had always listened. But surely there had to be a time when caution produced diminishing returns. "Do they understand that we're in a hurry?"

Beside her, Jason sketched the coupe's outline on one page of his notebook. "They understand they don't want to get blown up."

She swallowed her frustration. The poor guys must be close to passing out, working with all that protective gear in this humidity. And an explosion would cause a great deal of damage to her coworkers' automobiles, not to mention what it would do to herself and Jason. *Be smart and think,* she told herself. This car was all they had. If Cavanaugh had sent her to it just to get rid of her, he wouldn't have spared Jason. "What's that on your belt, that remote that Cavanaugh told you to bring?"

"It's a one-way radio. It connects with our phone equipment, so I can listen to both sides of the conversation. I can't talk to them on it, but it will keep me up with current events if they call Chris again."

"Is he always so . . ." Words failed her. Abrupt? Peremptory? Unsympathetic?

"Chris? He's pretty matter-of-fact, but he has to be. Aren't you matter-of-fact around dead bodies?"

"They're already dead before they get here," she said, aware that this did not answer the question. "There's nothing I can do about that."

"Chris has to stay calm because no one else will. There isn't time to second-guess. This has been a reasonable job so far. Sometimes the bad guy just shouts threats for an hour or two, nonstop, and Chris has to stay with him for every second. These guys, I'm beginning to think, are professional criminals. They rob banks for a living."

Despite the sweat trickling down her spine, a chill swept her skin. "So they're more likely to use violence."

"Less likely," Jason assured her. "They have a more

reasonable assessment of what will and will not happen, and they're able to judge accordingly. They know that should they go to jail—and by the time they come out of the bank, they'll have accepted that they're going to jail—their sentence will be much less if they haven't hurt anyone. Other hostage situations—like political terrorism or psychotics or domestics, which are the *worst,* let me tell you—are much more dangerous."

She suspected that unlike his boss, Jason had a few minutes to try to make her feel better, and that he had slanted his statistics for her sake. But she appreciated it.

"You might want to duck," one of the bomb squad guys told them, shouting to be heard from behind his Plexiglas face shield. "Or go inside."

She crouched in the shelter of a Grand Marquis. It belonged to a pathologist of whom she was not particularly fond, and she hoped any flying debris would shatter its rear windshield instead of herself or Jason. But if they blew up the Mercedes, what would Lucas do? If they didn't . . . "Do you have a tracking device to install on this?"

"They have that downtown and can pop it on just before we give it back. It only takes a second. We'll also add a remote switch, so that even if they take off in it, we'll be able to kill the engine at any time."

The bomb squad yanked the wire, which pulled the latch under the front grille and released the hood. Nothing happened. They slowly opened the engine area and continued their exam. After another ten minutes, they started stripping off gear. "It's clean."

Theresa pushed herself up from the bumper of the Grand Marquis just as Don appeared on the loading dock.

"What are you doing out here, *chica*?" the DNA analyst inquired. "Trying to get yourself blown up?"

"Risking heatstroke."

"You're doing okay?" The young man came closer, studying Theresa's face, ready to provide comfort if it was wanted or put it aside if it wasn't.

"Aside from the heatstroke." She could not take time for sympathy. If she started to cry, she wouldn't stop.

Don nodded. "You've brought company?"

She introduced Jason.

Don told them, "Come on in for a minute. I'll tell you what I've got so far."

Reluctantly Theresa abandoned the car a second time and followed her coworker. Jason went with them, pausing to stare at the array of cotton-draped gurneys in the dock area. "Don't you refrigerate these things?"

"These people," Theresa snapped. "People. Yes, of course we do. These folks are either on their way in or on their way out. I need to stop at autopsy. You can wait in the parking lot if you want to."

Jason remained in step with Don and her. "No. I've seen dead bodies before. More than I care to think about."

"I hope that's not a reflection on Cavanaugh's negotiating abilities." She was being a total bitch, and she knew it—but felt powerless to stop. Being back in her own world loosened some inhibitions, and stress freed the rest.

"Nope. Gulf War."

She let out a breath, moved past the door with letters spelling AUTOPSY on its frosted glass. "Sorry. I'm glad you're not going to faint on me, though. I want to ask Dr. Johnson here about her victim. Okay if we take a detour, Don?"

"Always a pleasure to visit the good doctor." He followed them through the door.

Mark Ludlow's autopsy had just been completed. The diener, or autopsy assistant, had placed the victim's partially dissected organs inside a red biohazard bag and then into the torso's cavity. He'd sewn the flesh back into place, over the bag, with heavy black thread and not particularly neat stitches.

Christine Johnson stood near the head. The exposed skull lay in fragments, which she was piecing together on the stainless-steel table like a macabre jigsaw puzzle. She peered at Theresa with that all-seeing doctor gaze that can tell when you're not sleeping well or haven't touched a vegetable in a month. "How are you holding up?"

"Okay. Paul's all right, so far."

Christine, tall, black, and caring, stripped off a glove to reach out and put a hand on Theresa's shoulder. Theresa remained rooted to the ground. As with Don, if Christine hugged her, she might collapse in her sympathy and hunker there for the rest of this crisis. "What can you tell me about this guy?"

Christine summarized, "The late Mr. Ludlow had deposits of cholesterol in some veins and a precancerous lump in his left testicle that might have become a bad scene in another few years. Otherwise he was perfectly healthy until someone hit him over the head with something heavy, three times."

"Can you tell me what it was?"

"A piece of thin pipe, maybe. But one impression has more of a defined, oval shape to it, so there might be two different weapons, or two surfaces on the same weapon." The doctor frowned. She didn't often encounter a weapon she couldn't immediately identify. Her interest in the instruments of death bordered on the unhealthy, or so Theresa occasionally pointed out.

"Metal?"

"I can't be sure, but I haven't found any wood splinters." With blue-latex-gloved fingers, Christine turned the right wrist outward to display the victim's palm. "He held up his hands to defend himself and got two fingers broken, but he also had some skin scraped off. Whatever they used, I'm betting it isn't smooth."

"I think I should wait in the hall," Jason said. "If you don't mind."

Christine glanced at him. "Who's this cutie?"

"His name's Jason, he works with the negotiator."

"So you met Chris Cavanaugh? What's he like? Does he look as good in person as on TV?"

"No."

"I don't believe you," the doctor said. "Jason, tell him I read his book."

"Christine—"

"Okay, okay. That's all I have, anyway. I wish it were more."

Theresa continued to stare at the remains of Mark Ludlow, noting the reddish areas where the blood had pooled after death and then coagulated. "The lividity is all on his back, consistent with the way we found him."

"Yep."

"Don't blows to the back of the head force someone down on their face? You'd think the last blow would be on the ground."

As in any full autopsy, the scalp had been cut at the top of the head and flipped forward to reveal the skull. Christine moved it back into place. "When someone's down and having their head pounded into the pavement, it usually leaves injuries to the face. He has none, which makes me think this attack was quick and brutal, with massive force applied to the skull. He died before he had time to fall."

Jason sidled toward the door. "I'm going to—"

"Come with me." Don led him out.

"What about time of death?" Theresa persisted.

"From the rigor I'd say four to eight hours before he arrived here. So any time between midnight and four A.M.? Of course, if he died inside and they had the air-conditioning on, the time of death could be last evening. If he stayed outside the whole time, with this heat, he could have died only an hour before you found him. I can't be sure."

Theresa thanked her and rejoined Don and Jason. Under the receptionist's watchful eye, they continued through the lobby and punched the button for the elevator. The woman had come with the building and meant to stay there until the walls fell down.

The doors slid shut, and Jason asked if there was a men's room handy.

The third floor housed the trace evidence and toxicology departments, decorated in the same worn 1950s linoleum and shabby paint as the rest of the building. At least the air-conditioning had been having a good day, and the temperature hovered around sixty-five. Theresa felt clammy in her sweat-soaked clothing but didn't complain. If anyone tried to adjust the thermostat, it would turn off, and tomorrow they would all swelter. A happy medium could not be found.

"Oliver had something to tell you," Don said as they stepped off the elevator. "You want to see him first?"

"Yeah."

Jason lunged for the door labeled MEN.

Theresa knocked for admittance to the toxicology department and made her way past a row of plastic bottles—gastric contents, something she avoided whenever possible. She found Oliver, the overweight, ponytailed toxicologist, in his usual lair at the rear of the building, protected by a fortress of compressed air tanks and scarred countertops.

"I suppose you want to know about your dirt. Seems an appropriate summary of my professional life: I work with dirt."

"Dirt is important," Theresa told him. "It's what the earth is made of. Can you tell me something about the stuff from the floor mat?"

"Aluminum and silicon, mostly. Clay. Clay with a little rust in it. That tell you anything?"

"Not really. Any industrial applications?"

He snorted with enough force to ruffle the papers on his desk. "About a million, from bricks to paper to toothpaste. But the grains are coarse and the sample is anything but pure, so my extremely well-educated guess would still be dirt."

She sighed. "Okay. Thanks."

"You find anything more useful, bring it back."

"Volunteering for work, Oliver? You're going to ruin your reputation."

"Good point."

"What about the stuff from the victim's suit jacket?"

"Again, dirt. I can't get enough of the stuff today." He patted the dusty beige box that housed the mass spectrometer, possibly the only physical entity in the universe to receive his affection. "It's running as we speak. I'll page you if it's interesting."

"Call me even if it isn't, okay?"

Oliver nodded and turned back to his desk without another word, and she went to find Don and the coffeepot. En route she rang Frank for an update, which he could not provide. The robbers were pacing in front of the hostages, but their body language did not seem particularly agitated.

"Actually," he said, "they seem to be the coolest guys in downtown Cleveland today."

"I know you're trying to make me feel better, but that doesn't make any sense. We assumed at first that they thought they were robbing a regular bank and could grab the cash and run. But if they know there are stacks of it in the basement, then they know exactly where they are."

"Lucas never mentioned the basement. He just knows there's a lot of money somewhere, and that's hardly a tough deduction once you're in the building."

"If they thought they were hitting the local savings and loan, then they're not the deducing type. I think they know exactly where they are," Theresa said. "Did you notice that Lucas's demand is exactly half the amount to be shredded?"

"But then why not all? Besides, if they knew it was the Fed, they'd have expected the tight security. They'd have had a better plan."

"Yeah, but all they had to do was get close enough to grab a clerk and put a gun to her head. No security force in the world can do much once that has happened."

"Hell of a chance," Frank grumbled.

"It worked." She wondered why they were even debating it. It didn't matter whether the suspects meant to hit the Fed, a regular bank, or the corner 7-Eleven. All that mattered now was getting them to come out without killing anyone—except she still couldn't shake the nagging feeling that all was not as it seemed.

"I don't know," Frank was saying. "These guys aren't even smart enough to bring a driver."

"If they did get the setup from Ludlow, they knew that the money wouldn't take long to come up the elevator. Is it risky? Sure. But it could have worked. If they hadn't lost the car, they could have been in and out in ten minutes. I sure wish they had been."

"Hang in there, baby."

Hopelessness flooded her, trying to seep into her bones, and she snapped the Nextel shut. Her cousin's calling her anything other than her name could not be a good sign. All might be calm for the moment, but they had a long way to go.

10:23 A.M.

Theresa grabbed a coffee, for once not for the caffeine but for the heat. She'd gone from sweltering to shivering in a flat ten minutes, the silk blouse having cooled to a wet shroud.

Don sat in front of a computer terminal, explaining the images to Jason. "Of the prints we got from the car, seven fingers and the palm match Robert Moyers. Ten other prints don't match anyone in our database."

"There's ten other people on this car?"

"No, it could be ten fingers from one person or, more likely, ten fingers from two or three other people. There's no way to tell for sure."

"That doesn't help much," Theresa admitted. "Moyers owns the Benz—Wait a minute. Why is he in the database?"

"Armed robbery."

"So that could be him in there." Theresa sipped, letting the scalding liquid aggravate an already fluttering stomach. She had begun to think these crooks were smart, but who would use their own car for a burglary?

"Is there still no one at his house? Do we have a work address or anything?"

"CPD just called Jason about that. The address is old—the woman living there bought it last spring. Doesn't know anything else about him, not even what he looks like. CPD checked her out, and she's, like, Snow White: a fashion designer, two kids. Not the type to be an armed robber's moll."

"So where's he been since last spring? He sure hasn't been living in that Benz, unless he's a neat freak of the highest order. It's *clean.*"

"You keep saying that," Jason said.

"We see a lot of cars," Theresa explained. "Most are filthy. Some have their own supply of cockroaches."

Jason made a face. "I see. This is the Ohio state database that these prints turned up in?"

"You betcha. And before you ask, we can't search the country unless we send it to the FBI and wait four or five weeks."

"Wonderful."

"It's not like TV," Don explained gently. "Moving right along. I superglued the Advil bottle, the Tic Tac container, the Kleenex package, and even that little piece of foil but didn't get any fingerprints of value. The fumes only brought up a smudge here or there. I used mag powder on the owner's manual and the envelope and the receipt, since the pulverized metal is better on porous surfaces. And tell Paul," he added to Theresa, "I hope he appreciates it, because I hate that black powder crap."

"Duly noted."

"I got nothing with the mag powder either. CPD called Conrad's about the receipt, but it had been paid with cash by Robert Moyers, with the same address, the one he sold to the fashion designer. No one at Conrad's remembers anything about one sale four years ago. And no one at Sirius will tell me anything about the satellite radio account either, so the cops are running that down."

"Have you called about the meter on that envelope?"

"The what?"

"Where is it?"

Don moved to a counter and picked up the number ten envelope, now sooty from the mag powder used to process it. "It's blank. Nothing but the forty-two-cent imprint."

Theresa peered through the plastic at the inked red markings. "Postage meters are closely regulated. You have to lease them from a dealer authorized by the United States Postal Service. This is a Pitney Bowes; if we call them with this serial number, they should be able to give us the name of the company that metered this envelope."

Jason listened attentively. "That easy, huh?"

"Not really—they'll want faxes on letterhead and a few other forms of identification before they'll release the information. I'll take the envelope back with me and get some police VIP to call."

Don thrust a printed form and a pen at Theresa. Chain-of-custody procedures had to be maintained, even under extenuating circumstances, up to and including Armageddon. "Sign here and it's all yours. Now, follow me."

She led them into one of the back rooms, pausing at the door.

"That looks—" Theresa stopped.

Don nodded. "Yep."

"Like *Leo*. At a microscope."

"Yep."

"It's like he's *working*."

"You betcha."

"I can hear you, you know." Her boss spoke without moving his lean face from the ocular lenses of an old polarized light microscope. "I can also hear the percentage of your cost-of-living increase dropping like a sow's litter."

Theresa approached with caution, as if a heavy tread could shatter the tableau. "What are you doing?"

"Pollen."

"What?"

"Remember pollen? The powdery stuff that busy little bees carry from one plant to another, making most of our food supply possible? Identifying them with polarized light was a big deal in the fifties and sixties, tracking dastardly criminals back to the apple tree behind the crime scene." He replaced a pair of glasses on his nose, long fingers flicking with excess energy. "It's a dying art, sadly. No one does it anymore."

"Yeah, like hair comparisons," Theresa commiserated. "We have a reference collection for pollen?"

"In the basement. Way back in the corner, behind the piece of fence from that torso in the park and the skull-under-glass thing from those satanic wannabes. I've probably breathed in enough dust to give me pleurisy." Indeed, the one-by-three-inch glass slides scattered around on the countertop appeared dusty, and the mounting media had yellowed. The corners on their hard vinyl case had abraded into powder.

"So what is it?"

"Pine."

Her shoulders slumped. "That's all?"

"Nothing exotic, sorry. It's kind of odd to see so much of it, though."

He skittered his chair back a few feet as Theresa bent her head to the eyepiece, viewing the pink-stained grains. They seemed to have three sections, a central orb with two kidney-shaped appendages. "Why is the amount odd?"

"It rains regularly here, even in summer. That knocks most of the pollen out of the air."

"So they might be from some other area?"

"But I thought your guy lived here."

"His car does. Or did. Where would we expect to find a lot of pine pollen?"

Leo began to fit the glass reference slides back into their kit. "I remembered how to use a polarizing microscope, Theresa. That doesn't make me a botanist. But I'll see if someone at the Museum of Natural History can help us."

Leo, volunteering to make a phone call, hunt up a specialist? Tears pricked the backs of her eyelids. *Don't start,* she warned herself. *Don't.*

Jason's remote radio chirped at the same time as Don's Nextel.

Jason put it to his ear, then held it out so they could hear it. "Chris just called them. The receptionist answered."

She heard Cavanaugh's voice, full and deep even on the radio's tiny speaker. "Can I speak to Lucas?"

Don took his call out of the room.

"Chris." Lucas's voice sounded much less real than Cavanaugh's and had an echo to it. The robber had them on speakerphone, so that the hostages could hear every word of the process meant to free them. Theresa wondered if that made Paul feel better or worse. "You're early."

"I needed to give you the heads-up. First, though, is everyone in there still doing okay?"

"They're getting tired and thirsty and will probably have to go to the bathroom soon, Chris, so it would be best if we could take our show on the road. What are you telling me? The chief won't part with four million dollars that's not even his?"

"No, they're still talking about the money. It's the car. They took it to the medical examiner's office and—"

"What did they do to it?"

"Nothing. It's fine. It's just that the flatbed isn't there to pick it up yet, so I know it isn't going to be back here to you by the one-hour deadline. There's no way. And I didn't want to wait until the last minute to tell you. Things usually go smoother with that policy—I don't surprise you, you don't surprise me, okay? Can we agree on that at least?"

"Too late, Chris. I'm already surprised that you'd risk losing a few of these people because the entire police department is at the Winn-Dixie drinking coffee instead of getting a tow-truck driver off his ass. Makes me think there's some other problem with the car."

"There's nothing wrong with the car."

"You didn't cut up the interior, did you? Bobby will be really mad if you did. I mean *really*."

A pause.

"Robert Moyers." Don spoke from the doorway. "CPD just ran him down. He sold the house because he had to serve eight months for a parole violation from the armed-robbery charge. He got out on Friday."

"Is that Bobby Moyers with you?" they heard Chris ask.

"The one and only!" a distant voice shouted. The other robber. "What'd you do to my car?"

"The car's fine." Lucas sounded fainter for a moment, as if his head had turned away from the phone. "Chris says so."

"I don't believe them," the faraway voice continued.

"Now, Bobby, if Chris says the car is okay, it's okay. We're happy about that, Chris, and we'll give you another ten minutes to get it on a flatbed. And don't talk to me about traffic jams, because everyone in town is over at the convention center, so there *isn't* any traffic. Talk to me about something else—like why I don't see any money coming up the elevator. What *have* you been doing for the past forty minutes, Chris?"

"We've been working on the money, too. The problem is, the robots never place money in the passenger elevators, only the freight elevators. To get them to move money to a new place, the Fed engineers have to write a whole new program."

"You're telling me the tech geeks can't handle that?"

"They've begun to work on it. When you"— Cavanaugh paused here, no doubt trying to think of a less offensive word than "invaded"—"took over the lobby, we evacuated the building. Nearly three hundred people work in that building, Lucas, and they couldn't all hang out at the Hampton Inn. We sent them home. Everyone's getting a paid day off because of you, so you're a fairly popular man among the staff right now."

Theresa snorted.

Jason told her gently, "I know he's laying it on a little thick, but if you can get them feeling good about themselves, for any reason, they'll look at the hostages that much more generously."

"So you don't have any programmers?" Lucas pressed.

"Oh, yeah, we got hold of two. One has arrived, I've been told, and the other is stuck in the convention-center traffic."

Lucas said nothing. Theresa asked Jason, "Is he lying?"

"Chris? No. He meant what he said about not lying to them."

"I'd lie to them." Leo sat with one ear cocked toward the radio, as if listening with all his might.

"He can't. As bizarre as it sounds, the whole thing works on trust. If he says the pop machine doesn't carry Diet Coke and they know it does, it's all over. If they can't trust him, we'll never get them to give up."

The radio sprang to life with Lucas's voice. "Here's a thought: Why don't the programmers just pick up the damn money and throw it into the elevator themselves? Bypass the robots."

"Only the robots enter those rooms. It's designed that way."

"Are we standing on procedure now?"

"The rooms are made to keep people out. If any body of matter other than a robot enters, the alarm system trips and all hell breaks loose."

"I don't mind if the alarm rings. My ears are tough."

"It also closes the doors and locks them for twelve hours. It's a fail-safe thing. I'm sorry, but there's nothing anyone can do about this. We are all at the mercy of modern technology, my friend."

Then Lucas said, "I am not your friend," so that the

words coursed through Theresa like a river of ice. *We're not going to make it through this. Paul is going to die.*

Then Lucas added, "More than that, Chris, I'm beginning to doubt your commitment to this endeavor."

"Don't doubt me yet, Lucas. I might have a solution. There's a shipment of cash scheduled to arrive this morning. It's only three million, but at least we mere human beings can touch it without triggering a mechanical lockdown."

"You trying to haggle with me, Chris? This is priceless. Someone over there decided that these people aren't worth four million, only three? Or that you only want three-quarters of them back, is that it? Then I might as well kill the last quarter of the group, if I'm not going to get paid for them anyway."

"Come on," Theresa said to Jason. "Let's get that car down there so at least that will be in place."

"But the tow—"

"We don't need a tow. I'll just drive the damn thing."

"But—"

She stopped as Cavanaugh spoke, dying to move but afraid to miss a word.

"It's not the money, Lucas. You can empty every last cent out of that building as long as you don't hurt anybody. *We don't care.* If you want four million instead of three, I'm sure we can scrape together the last million for you—that's not a problem. The problem is, the three million on the truck isn't going to arrive until two. It's on 80, just passing State College."

Another pause. "Clever. Very clever. Hang on a sec, Chris. I just need to talk this over with Bobby."

Jason scratched his chin with the radio antenna, staring at nothing. "That's not good."

"Why? What's wrong?"

"Sorry. Didn't mean to startle you—it's just that we had Bobby pegged as a follower, not an equal. Negotiations are more complicated when you have more than one person on the other side, because you have to get a consensus. When you go to buy a car, the salesman wants you to come in by yourself, but he'll have the floor manager and the finance guy on his side. It means he has an excuse to slow down, whereas you don't. What we need," he went on as the radio remained silent, "is for the hostage taker to make decisions. If these two have to discuss everything first, it will drag on that much longer. That's why sometimes a lone gunman is easier than a takeover."

She stared at him.

"A single robber instead of a group of two or more," he clarified.

"He sounds so calm," Don said.

"They usually do. That's something I've never been able to figure out either. Even the psychotic ones are often calm. They're focused, I guess."

"Let's go—" Theresa began to say, but then she stopped once more, arrested by voices from the small device in Jason's hand.

"Bobby doesn't want to wait until two o'clock," Lucas said. "He's not the patient type."

Cavanaugh didn't miss a beat. "Then I don't know what to do, Lucas. Those money rooms can't be bypassed."

"Tell you what, Chris. You just get that car here and let me worry about the money. I have an idea."

"Good, let's talk about that. What's your idea?"

"Never mind, just get the car here. Oh, and one more thing—we won't be leaving alone. In case you get any ideas about installing a remote kill switch in the engine or a GPS tracker, you should know that we've made some friends here and we'll take at least two of them along for company. I thought you ought to know that. It might figure into your thinking."

Click.

"Lucas?" Cavanaugh asked, without result. He sounded worried to Theresa, but perhaps this was a projection of her own terror.

"Come on," she said to Jason. "We're going."

She turned and led the way out of the lab without looking back. They took the stairs.

"What's on your mind, Theresa?" Jason's voice sounded almost as smooth as his boss's, and that only irritated her.

"He isn't going to hold out much longer. I don't know why he wants the stupid car, and I don't care. All I know is that I can at least get that into place in case he decides to start shooting. He's melting down, this Lucas."

"All due respect, Mrs. MacLean," Jason told her as he followed her down two flights, "but you've never been through a negotiation in your life, right? Perhaps you're not the best person to predict what's going to happen."

She reached the bottom, held the door as he caught up. "All due respect, Jason, but you can't stop me."

CHAPTER 11

10:55 A.M.

"The car's here," Theresa announced as soon as she reached the reading table. Cavanaugh sat in front of the phone system, with the scribe, Irene, at his side and another woman next to Irene. Both Frank and the head librarian had left; Kessler sat drinking coffee as if it were an act of penance. Jason took a seat on the other side of Cavanaugh. Assistant Chief Viancourt browsed the library shelves with polite interest, the way one might do at the in-laws' house. "It's down on Superior, in front of the Hampton Inn," she added.

Cavanaugh looked at her with a gaze so sharp she wondered what he saw. A red face and a crumpled blouse, a voice tight enough to tune a violin—not a professional scientist but a woman on the edge? She forced herself to take a deep breath, slow to a stop, drape one hand over the back of a chair as if she had nothing better to do than drop by the library on this sunny morning.

He said only, "Can they see it from the lobby?"

"Not unless they go through the employee lobby and the security team to the Superior entrance."

"Good." He turned back to the woman in front of him, middle-aged, black, wearing a navy suit and sensible shoes. "Go on, Mrs. Hessman."

Theresa sidled over to the nattily dressed assistant chief of police, now perusing the spine of *The British Museum Catalogue of Seals*. She introduced herself to the man, who cooed with admiration over how "cool" her job must be before she could go on. He did not seem to know about her relationship with Paul, and she did not see the need to inform him. "I can use your clout on something." She handed him the blank, powder-processed envelope from the robbers' car and explained about the postage-meter number. "They won't be able to give it to me, not immediately. I'd have to fax them all sorts of letters and forms. But someone in your position . . ."

Theresa had never been much of a manipulator, and she couldn't believe how easy it was. The man's chest expanded, and he nodded with great solemnity. He even patted her hand and told her he'd have it taken care of in no time before striding forcefully from the room. She watched him leave. The poor guy just wanted something to do.

Now if she could convince Cavanaugh to give Lucas his car back, her day might end well after all.

Theresa leaned against the metal shelving, listening to Cavanaugh question the woman, trying to stay still and quiet and patently under control. She wished Frank were there. She worked with cops every day but was not one of them, and she liked having Frank and Paul to buffer the unfamiliar faces.

"You handled getting Mark Ludlow on board?" the hostage negotiator asked.

"Yes. A number of our bank examiners were hired

at the same time, so they all retired at the same time, and we didn't have enough qualified replacements locally. It's hard to find an experienced Fed examiner who wants to move, much less move to Cleveland, I'm sorry to say."

She chuckled, and Cavanaugh nodded. A survey of large cities with good self-esteem would not have Cleveland in the top ten. Or fifty.

"So you convinced him to leave Atlanta?"

"No, he responded to the online posting. He wanted to come here."

"Why?"

She paused, fingers stroking the gold cross around her neck. "I think he said Atlanta had gotten too crowded. It *is* a huge city. But he still drove a hard bargain—he got a promotion and a job for his wife out of it."

"What does his wife do?"

"She's a secretary in the savings bond unit."

"She doesn't work with her husband?"

"Oh, no. Family members can't be in a supervisory relationship with other family members. She can type and had done some clerical work before the baby was born, so we fitted her in with the support staff."

"Did you meet her?"

"Yes—Jessica, her name is. Sweet girl."

"How did she feel about the move, about her new job?"

Again the human resources manager fingered her pendant. "I don't really know. I only met her twice, once for the testing and interview process and once to sign all the paperwork. She seemed excited about the job but expressed some . . . misgivings, I guess you could say, about moving to the new city. I suppose that's normal. She's young and probably away from her family for the first time. I was a new bride of nineteen when I left Biloxi. It's hard."

"True," Cavanaugh said, so briskly that Theresa winced. He didn't understand. Didn't he have a family, some sort of foundation he'd be reluctant to leave? "Did she seem angry about it?"

"No, not at all. Just nervous. She also, I think, would have preferred to stay home with her little boy instead of working. She said something about 'at least until he started kindergarten.' I could understand that, too. The first years are so important."

"So her son is in a new house, a new city, and then has to start day care, too," Cavanaugh said, showing more sensitivity than he had a moment before. "That probably worried her."

"It was a lot of changes at once. Scary but exciting. She really is a sweet girl—an artist, too, likes to paint, and I told her about our art museum. I remember she joked that her son is taking after her and draws constantly, sometimes on the walls." She chuckled again at the memory. "I think that's all I can tell you. Why are you so interested in Jessica?"

"We believe she's one of the hostages." Cavanaugh pointed at the flat-screen, its images flickering silently on the tabletop. "Can you tell us if that's her, on the left?"

The blood drained from the woman's face to see her coworkers crouched on the marble floor, guns pointed at their bodies. "Oh, my Lord."

"No one is hurt, and I'm sure we can get them out safely. But does that look like Jessica Ludlow?"

She squinted. "Yes, I'm sure. She has the *baby* with her?"

"Yes."

"Why?"

"We're wondering that ourselves. Thank you for your help, Mrs. Hessman—"

Theresa interrupted. "What time does she start work?"

"Seven-thirty," the woman answered without hesitation.

Cavanaugh took a swig from his water bottle, allowing Theresa to continue her questioning.

"What time does Mark Ludlow start work?" she asked.

"Eight, usually. But a senior examiner . . . well . . ."

"Doesn't punch a time clock."

"Exactly," Mrs. Hessman told her. "Some are more flexible, come in at eight-thirty or nine and stay later, but only a few. They're all accountants, so they tend to be a bit regimented."

"Do you know what day-care arrangements she had for their son?"

"No, I sure don't."

Theresa mulled this over while Cavanaugh thanked the woman again. "This officer will see you out."

The room fell silent, except for the hum of distant cars and the terse, quiet exchanges from the staff offices. Then Theresa said, "Maybe they drive separately to work because she starts earlier. It still seems funny, considering the price of gas these days."

"Come here," Cavanaugh said to her. He pushed an empty chair out from the desk, next to him. "Sit down. Need a bottle of water?"

"No—yeah, actually. That would be good."

Irene pulled an Aquafina from a small cooler and passed it down.

Cavanaugh handed it to her. "Or she drives separately because she drops the baby at day care. Are there still officers at the scene? We'll have them ask the neighbors while they canvass."

Theresa soaked her hand with the bottle's frigid condensation and rubbed it on the back of her neck, hot again from the six-flight jog. "They're probably done."

"Jason, get Homicide. Have someone come over here with everything they found out about Ludlow. If they didn't find the day care, send someone back to the neighborhood."

Theresa sipped, watching the TV screen. "This woman's got a gun pointed at her little boy, and she doesn't even know that her husband is dead."

"I haven't lost a child on one of my jobs yet, and I don't intend to start today."

"You haven't lost anybody yet." Jason stood as he dialed, adding to Theresa, "Chris has a perfect record. Two hundred and sixteen hostage situations ended without bloodshed."

"Not totally—there's been some blood lost. But not fatally."

That should make me feel better, Theresa thought, *but it doesn't. He talks about loss of life as if it's a running bet on a basketball team.* As Jason walked off with his cell phone, she asked Cavanaugh, "How did you get into this line of work? How do you talk them into giving up when they have to know they're going to go to jail?"

"Mostly it's about listening. You have to be a good listener. I'll bet you would be good at it."

"Not me." She shuddered. "I don't want live people depending on me."

Cavanaugh laughed. "Dead ones are okay?"

"Precisely. I could fail to solve their case, to get justice for them, but I can't make them any *more* dead." She finished the water. "That probably sounds wimpy, but I don't care."

"It sounds sensible."

"You, on the other hand—do you ever have to decide who lives and who dies?"

"Not in this case," he said, neatly sideswiping the question. "The hostages are all together, and that simplifies matters. In domestics, particularly, you can have them scattered around in different rooms, so that at any given moment some are safe, some are not. We adjust our thinking accordingly."

If it came down to Paul, who had chosen to be in the line of fire by virtue of his profession, and a civilian, he would adjust his thinking accordingly. She needed to stay with Cavanaugh, to be sure that did not happen.

She let out what had been weighing on her mind for the past hour. "Can't we give them their damn car and let them move on?"

"Not in light of his parting statements. They take any person with them out of that bank, that person's dead. Otherwise I'd be happy to let them have the car and all the money they want, and I don't even care if they get away. That's someone else's problem. But I can't give them a hostage." He glanced at her face. "Don't look like that. It's not hopeless. I'm going to try to trade the car for leaving all the hostages behind."

"They'll never go for that. They have to know that once they poke their heads out that door without a hostage in front of their face, they're dead."

"That's why it makes more sense to give themselves up. You have to let them reason through the scenarios themselves. Eventually they'll get a grip on what is and is not a realistic option." He glanced at her face again. "I just said it isn't hopeless. I didn't say it'll be *easy*."

Kessler stood to throw out his coffee cup. "But why kill Mark Ludlow? And if they've already killed once, doesn't that make them more likely to . . . um . . ."

"We're not completely sure they had anything to do with Ludlow," Cavanaugh said. "We're not even reasonably sure. But if they did, they don't know that his body has been found or that we suspect he's connected to this robbery. They want to have the option to walk away from this without anyone getting hurt, because they're certain to get a lighter sentence that way. If we let them know that we're waiting to hang a murder charge on them—"

"They have nothing to lose," Theresa finished.

"Exactly. We need to keep them believing that it's in their best interest to avoid hurting anyone." Cavanaugh moved one hand to pick up the phone, then hesitated, long fingers stroking the receiver. "Tell me about your fiancé, Theresa."

Would this man ever stop startling her? "Paul?"

Well, duh. How many other fiancés did she have? She took another deep breath. "He's been a cop for seventeen years. He's currently a detective in Homicide. He's a good cop."

Cavanaugh waited as she tossed her empty bottle into the wastebasket. "I'm sure he's a great cop, Theresa, but I'm not writing a brochure for the department. Tell me what he's *like*."

Not a word came to mind, and she stared at him in confusion. Glass slides and databases were her bailiwick, not psychology. "I don't know what you want."

"It's an open-ended question, I know. This is why I ask: He's a cop in their midst, but he's in plainclothes and he's not tied up with the security guards, so our two guys in there clearly do not know that he's a police officer. That means they haven't searched him, haven't found his gun, so now he's ten feet away from these guys and he's armed. What is he going to do?"

She glanced at the TV screen again; she had trouble looking away from it for more than a few seconds. Not much had changed in her absence. Paul still sat second from the end of the row of hostages, fidgeting now and then but obviously unhurt. "All he'll care about is protecting those people. Frank says he's a Boy Scout."

"What do you think?"

It took her a while to answer. "I think he cares about doing the right thing. That's why I want to marry him. My ex-husband never cared about the right thing. Paul is more like—"

"Your father?"

She gave a tiny jump, glared at him, and then looked away. She would never admit that; it made her sound like a neurotic little girl. No matter how true it might be.

Cavanaugh, mercifully, moved on. "Where did he propose to you?"

"*What?*"

"I'm just trying to gather information here, Theresa. Where did he propose?"

She smiled, unable to help it. "In an alley. In the rain. We had just cleared a triple homicide at a bowling alley, with about fifteen shots fired over three rooms—"

Cavanaugh's dimples were showing, but his eyes seemed deadly serious. "So he's kind of impulsive? You hadn't expected a proposal?"

Her mouth formed a no, but that would be a lie. She had expected a proposal from their first kiss. "It wasn't a complete surprise, but yes, a diamond popping out of nowhere sort of threw me."

"Ah, he had the ring already. So he's not *that* impulsive."

"No, no. He'd had dinner reservations at Pier W, champagne on ice, the whole scenario, but then the pagers went off." Apparently impulsivity was not a desired trait during hostage negotiations, which made sense. But what about the hostage *takers'* impulses? "What did Lucas mean about having an idea to get the money?"

"I wish I knew. I called back, but he made Missy answer. She said Lucas does not wish to speak to me at this time, and neither does Bobby."

She nibbled a fingernail, a habit she thought she'd broken in high school. "It would help if we could communicate with Paul. Can't we text-message the Nextel?"

"It would beep. I already asked his partner that. We can't risk drawing their attention to him."

"No," she agreed fervently. "We can't. Where *is* Frank—Officer Patrick?"

"Trying to find someone in this city who knows Bobby Moyers. Supposedly he's got a brother who works for Continental Airlines, and Patrick went to run him down."

Jason returned, finishing a sandwich. "They have food in the conference area, you know."

"Good," Cavanaugh said. "Can you grab me something on rye?"

Jason tossed a cellophane-wrapped square at him. "I anticipate your every need, boss."

"Glad to hear it. Now tell me who Lucas is."

"I just got off the phone with Corrections. There are no known associates under that name in Moyers's file for the original armed-robbery charge. No cellmates by that name at Mansfield. He only served eight months for that, due to a combination of prison overcrowding, good behavior, and a shaky ID on the 'armed' part of the armed robbery." The young man paused to swig Cherry Coke. "Theresa? You want a sandwich?"

Even the idea of food made her want to retch. "No thanks. I'm fine."

"Then he got picked up for violating probation."

"What'd he do?" Cavanaugh asked, breathing a puff of rye-scented breath in Theresa's direction.

"Bought some cocaine from a gangbanger in the Flats. He used up all his luck on the first charge and had none left for the violation. He not only got six months, he wound up in a test group for prison reform. The theory goes thus: Prison isn't rehabilitating anyone because they wind up in prison with the same old people operating in the same old gangs and then get out and commit crimes with the same old people in the same old gangs. Send the cons far away where they don't know anyone and they're forced to function on their own, so when they get out, they're better able to resist falling back into their old habits."

"That almost makes sense."

"As with all great social experiments, only time will tell."

"And that's where he met Lucas."

Jason shrugged. "Either that or Lucas isn't his name at all."

"Where is this far-off reformatory?"

Theresa rubbed the back of her neck again, trying to keep the stiffness there from spreading to her brain. "I bet I know."

"Hey." Kessler, the bank executive, stared at the TV screen. "I think something is happening."

CHAPTER 12

Paul watched the tall robber pace in front of them, moving slowly down the line. At least he kept the M4 carbine pointed at the floor. He stopped again, near Paul.

"You."

The robber spoke to the black man next to him, in the green uniform. Paul felt a wave of relief and hated himself for it.

"What do you do here?"

The older man gave his name as Thompkins and said he worked in Support Services. "I vacuum and empty wastebaskets. I'm a janitor, I guess."

"Mmm." Lucas nodded. He still wore his hat; its emblem featured a red eagle. "I suppose I should identify with you, one lower-class workingman/oppressed minority to another. But that's not what I'm thinking, Mr. Thompkins. I'm thinking that you may be the most valuable man in this building, because janitors go everywhere. They have to, to empty all those garbage cans. They have access to places they lock vice presidents out of, you know what I mean?"

"I'm thinking there's nothing so 'working' about what you're doing." The old man's gaze stayed as straight as his back. "Nothing at all."

Everyone else tensed, Paul included. His legs trembled from the hours of inactivity. If he had to take them down, could he get to his feet fast enough? Should he even try? What about Theresa?

The line of Lucas's jaw wavered as he clenched his teeth, then relaxed. "That's a good point. I've given up on honest work, I admit that. But it's going to be worth it. With great risks come great rewards. How long you been here?"

"Twenty-five years."

"My, my. That's impressive. You know this building pretty well, then? Don't hesitate, Mr. Thompkins, if it means you're thinking about lying to me. That wouldn't be a good idea."

A single bead of sweat slid down the janitor's left temple. "I know it pretty well."

"Good. Did you hear what that negotiator told me on the phone? About the robots?"

"Yes."

"Is that true?"

"Yes."

"No one can just walk into the storage rooms downstairs and pick up the money?"

"No." His answer came promptly, with assurance. Paul believed him. Perhaps Lucas did, too, since he switched his attention to the next hostage and asked for his name.

The kid's pale skin stood out in sharp contrast to his black hair. "Brad."

"What do you do here, Brad?"

"I'm in the public-relations department."

"The Federal Reserve needs PR?"

"Sure." The young man gave a sickly grin. "Everybody hates the government."

Lucas rewarded the joke with a sardonic twist of his lips, so that his target's shoulders seemed to relax an inch or two, only to tense again at the next question. "What exactly do you do for the PR department, Brad?"

The young man mumbled.

"What?"

"I'm a tour guide."

Now Lucas's grin looked genuine, and Paul watched the points on Brad's collar quiver as he trembled.

"So you must know this building pretty well, huh? Maybe even better than the janitor."

"No." Brad's air of nonchalance wouldn't have fooled a three-year-old. "I take them to our museum and then the vault—the old vault. It's empty now. A historical conversation piece."

"No money or robots?"

"No. The old vault was part of the original 1923 construction—anyway, I'm never in the work areas. We can't have hordes of middle-schoolers disrupting the staff."

"Still, you know the layout. What else is in this building? And, just as with Mr. Thompkins here, lying to me would not be a good idea." Lucas stroked the M4 to make his point.

The young man swallowed hard. "There's offices, for the analysts and the examiners. There's the security team. There's the bank officers' rooms on the ninth floor. We have a little vending area—"

"Bank officers. Do they have vaults up there?"

Brad snorted, envy overcoming fear, if only for a

moment. "Hardly. More like Oriental rugs and Ming vases."

"Really?"

His head bobbed in his desperation to please. "The vice president for general counsel even has an original Picasso."

"Uh-huh. Where does this hallway go, this one behind y'all here?"

"The employee lobby—it opens onto Superior. There's also the elevator to the parking garage and the one to the loading dock, where that shipment is coming in at two."

Lucas came closer to the boy. "You're all pushing me toward this two o'clock shipment, aren't you? Why is that?"

"I'm not pushing anything."

"You just want to go home, is that what you're saying?"

"Yes." Fear etched crow's-feet into his face as Brad screwed his eyes shut, trying to blot out the image of the M4's barrel, a yard from his nose. "Yes."

Paul kept gazing at Lucas, trying to remember every detail, just in case the guy got away. In case Paul *lived* to see him get away.

"If it makes you feel better, Brad, I may change my mind about that shipment. Hell, at this point what's another few hours?" Without warning he walked away from Brad, disappearing behind the reception desk to return with a box of Kleenex.

"Here." He handed it to the receptionist, seated next to Paul, who hadn't stopped crying since the first shot rang out. "Clean yourself up. Missy, isn't it?"

"Thank you," she breathed.

"That's okay. You hang in there, because I need someone to answer the phones."

She wiped her eyes, which did not stop filling up. "Please let me go. You have to let me go."

Lucas had begun to walk away, but her speaking up seemed to surprise him. "Why is that?"

"My little girl. She's three years old, and she needs her mommy. She's so precious—"

The sobs that accompanied this appeal would have softened the heart of Genghis Khan, but Lucas showed no signs of sympathy or even interest. Instead he moved over to the woman who had brought her baby along, one of the two women who'd been hiding behind the teller cages. Mark Ludlow's wife, now his widow, though Paul figured she did not know of her recent change in status. "What's his name?"

The woman's eyes were huge and sea blue under untidy lengths of dishwater-blond hair. She clutched the child to her, his head resting against her shoulder. He seemed to be dozing, the skin around his nose slightly reddened, but he kept his grip on a tiny stuffed dog wearing a Browns football helmet. Mother and son appeared well fed and neatly attired. "His name is Ethan."

"That's nice. You name him after his daddy?"

"N-n-no. I just liked it."

"Uh-huh. So why ain't Ethan in school—What's your name?"

The woman next to her spoke up, tossing auburn curls from her eyes. "She's Jessica. Can't you let them go? He's just a little boy."

Lucas considered her. "It's not polite to jump the line. And I'm sure Jessie here can speak for herself."

"He's only two," Jessica Ludlow said with a delicate southern accent, so softly Paul could barely hear her. "I found a nice day-care lady, but he wasn't feeling well this morning, and she wouldn't take him."

"So you brought him to work?"

"I didn't know what else to do. I was just going to tell my boss that I'd have to take the day off." Her lips crinkled, and she gulped in a breath. "Then I was going to leave."

"Take it easy. Follow your son's example and just chill out," Lucas told her before moving on. "You, Talking Tina. What do you do here?"

"My name's Cherise." About thirty years of age, the slender woman eyed Lucas with more anger than fear. Paul felt that this could not be wise.

"Thanks for sharing, but I don't recall asking your name. I asked what it is you do here."

Bobby had been pacing along the teller cages like a hyena before feeding time, but now he stopped, perhaps sensing something in his partner's voice. *They're too far apart,* Paul thought—*I can't hit them both, not before one gets me.*

"I'm a savings-bond teller."

"What are those?"

"Savings bonds? They're a promissory note guaranteed by the government. They're also tax-exempt, so they're a secure way to save. The bonds are bought and cashed in at those windows." She ducked her head to indicate the teller cages behind him, on the East Sixth side of the lobby. "The ones you tied these guys to are empty, just there for show."

"So there's cash money in those cages? How much?"

"I wouldn't know."

The M4 carbine came up slowly, as if this were

only a random movement and not connected to the sudden tension in his frame. "I'm beginning to not like you, Cherise. I'm beginning to doubt your concern for your coworkers. Jessie, you might want to block your baby's ears."

The young mother gasped.

"So how much, Cherise?"

"Three to five hundred thousand."

"Hmm." Lucas lowered the submachine gun, reached into his oversize duffel, and pulled out a red nylon backpack. He tossed it to her. "Fill this up."

Cherise didn't move. "What?"

"You work in those teller cages, right? You must know where the money is."

"Well, yeah—but I only have keys to my drawers, the ones assigned to me. I'll have about—"

Before she could complete her mental calculations, Lucas reached into the duffel bag again and pulled out an eight-inch-long Craftsman screwdriver. "That's all right. I have this. It might screw up the locks a little, but then again, I don't really care."

She still did not move.

"Do you want to sit in this lobby until two this afternoon?"

She stood up slowly, never taking her eyes off the barrel of his gun.

"Good job, Cherise. We're going to walk a wide path around these friends of yours from security and their puppy. Don't forget I have twenty-nine rounds of .223 shells pointed at your back, and all it would take is one twitch of my finger to let them all fly into you. Keep an eye on the rest of them, Bobby." He had to shout over the K-9 unit's dog, barking at their passage.

"I've got 'em," his partner said, raising his own

carbine to his shoulder. He sighted down the barrel in Paul's direction, and Paul felt the ooze of sweat along his spine grow to a trickle. Lucas's words made him think the robber had military training. A civilian would probably call the rounds ".22s."

Lucas and his captive dipped past Bobby and disappeared, only to reappear behind the antique grillwork of the first teller window.

The conversation, if it could be so called, between Lucas and the querulous Cherise bounced off the eighty-six-year-old marble walls and curved along the elaborate ceiling frescoes. Paul could make out most of it, once the dog piped down, as they moved in and out of sight behind the wall.

"How much is that?"

"Thirty-eight thousand, four hundred."

"Okay. Next drawer. Fit the screwdriver into the lock."

"It won't move."

"Pry it. Get the tip into the crack there and twist."

"Tell you what." Paul heard Cherise's words as clearly as if she stood next to him, though he could not see either of them. "Why don't you try it? I'll hold your gun."

"She's always like that," Thompkins muttered, and shook his head.

"Quiet," Bobby told him, including the rest of the row in his glance. "And stop fidgeting."

From the stress in his voice, it seemed that some of Lucas's cool had evaporated. "Do it!"

Cherise said a few words Paul couldn't make out. Then *"No!"*

The gunshots echoed through the lobby. The sound seemed to gather strength with every rebound off the polished tile until the waves deafened him. Missy screamed, Jessica Ludlow held her son's head to her chest, and Thompkins came partially to his feet. Paul's hand moved toward his gun. But he froze when Bobby and his M4 carbine materialized three feet in front of them.

He's in the center! Paul screamed silently to the unseen police snipers who *had* to be stationed in the windows of the library across the street. One of them must be able to get a bead—*Shoot! Shoot! Shoot!*

But now Lucas could not be seen, not by the snipers and not by Paul.

"Did he shoot her?" the janitor asked. Missy sobbed. The security guys were all shouting, mostly obscenities, but Paul heard one say, "I can't see."

Brad moaned, "We have to get out of here. He'll kill us all, one by one."

"Are there offices behind the teller cages?" Paul asked Thompkins. "Other rooms back in there?"

"Three. Mine and—"

"I said *shut up*!" Bobby shouted at them as he backed up to the teller windows. "Lucas, you okay?"

"I'm fine. Be there in a sec."

"If he killed that girl, then you're both in very serious trouble," Paul said to Bobby.

"Gee, like we weren't before? You wanna act as my lawyer? Get me a deal?"

"You haven't hurt anyone—yet. You should get out now, quit while you're ahead." Paul fought to keep his voice steady, reasonable, watching every minute for an opening. If Bobby would turn away, even for a second, Paul could fire, close the fifteen-foot gap between them before Lucas emerged, grab Bobby's gun, and—

Bobby not only pointed the rifle at him, he raised it

to his eye as if taking special aim. "You should shut up and quit while *you're* ahead. I'll hang with Lucas and kill all of you—"

Missy gasped.

"—but I ain't never going to trust no cops. My whole family is dead because of them."

Lucas reappeared behind him, with the backpack but without any sign of Cherise. "What's going on?"

"This guy thinks I should give myself up."

"Well"—Lucas dropped the now-stuffed backpack onto the floor—"a man's entitled to his opinion. We have four hundred and eighty thousand and some-odd dollars, Bobby. I don't think that's enough."

"Me neither."

"Did you kill that girl?" the janitor asked again.

Lucas said, "Let's just say we won't be seeing Miss Cherise again soon. But right now we need to put our heads together. Where else in this building can we find some money?"

CHAPTER 13

11:36 A.M.

"Something just happened," Theresa said. "Every person there just jumped a foot."

"I wish we had *sound*," Cavanaugh said.

Jason picked up the phone. "They have sound at the monitor station. I'll ask."

Theresa caught her breath as she saw Paul's hand move to his side, going for his gun. It was an ingrained response, she knew. He wouldn't even have time to think about it, wouldn't even have time to stop himself, but Bobby Moyers would have time to pull the trigger on that submachine gun before Paul could get his Glock up and pointed.

She watched Bobby approach Paul. But the robber merely shouted something, and Paul's hand stopped midmotion. He did not pull out his gun. "What the *hell* is going on?" she demanded.

"That young woman didn't come back," Cavanaugh pointed out.

"Shots fired," Jason said. "It sounds like he killed that girl."

Don't move, Paul. Don't do a thing.

Cavanaugh let loose a string of expletives. "Can security see behind the teller cages?" he asked Jason.

"Just the counter area at each window. There's no camera coverage in the offices behind the cages. She went back there with Lucas, and only Lucas came out."

"Can't we see through the windows? The ones in the outer walls are clear."

Jason knelt on the window seat, phone in one hand and a pair of binoculars in the other. Where did he get those? Theresa wondered, resisting the urge to rip them out of his hands. She moved to the telescope instead.

"I don't see anyone," the young man reported. "There's cabinets stacked against a few of the windows. They must be behind those."

"So she could be alive."

"The other hostages are asking if she's dead," Jason went on. "He's not denying it. They can't make out much else."

"Why not?"

Jason dropped the phone onto the table. "Fed security snaked a mike down an air vent. It's over on the east wall, so most of the talk is unintelligible. You can only make out what someone's saying when they shout."

"Crap. Who was that girl? Kessler?"

"I don't know," the bank executive told them. Theresa watched Paul through the telescope. Did he know she was there? Sense it, maybe?

"Is she an employee?"

"Oh, she *works* there. She looked familiar to me, but I don't know her name."

"Call your security team. They should have names to go with all the faces now."

"I asked them an hour ago," Jason told him. "They

were too busy trying to keep the FBI agents out of their desk chairs."

Kessler reached for the phone, then hesitated.

"What?" Cavanaugh demanded.

"I felt this sudden desire to ask if I could just go home." The man's face had become ashen over the course of the morning, approaching the shade of his shirt. "Cowardly, I know. I'm just not used to this."

"You're not supposed to be, sir." Cavanaugh spoke more gently. "It's not your job, it's mine, and I should have thought to get a list of the hostages an hour ago. Maybe everyone on it would still be alive."

Theresa couldn't help but wonder if the bitterness in his voice had more to do with a woman's untimely death or his perfect no-bloodshed record. "Now that he's started killing people, he might keep on going."

He did not thank her for stating the obvious. "If we're right about Ludlow, he had already started. It may be time to let him know we suspect him of Ludlow's death, to let him get used to the idea he's not going to be walking away from this, even if we can't confirm the woman's murder." Cavanaugh's hand strayed toward the phone, then stopped. "Wait a minute. When we were talking about Bobby having been sent out of state, you said you bet you knew where. I'll bite. Where?"

"Atlanta."

Bobby Moyers had a brother. Eric Moyers worked as a baggage handler for Continental Airlines. He described his job as slinging golf clubs and countless wheeled suitcases onto a moving belt for people who could afford to go to much nicer places on vacation than he could. He had the same sandy hair and stocky build, a head cold, and he didn't want to talk about his brother.

"What's he done now?" he asked Patrick as they both had a cigarette on the tarmac outside Concourse C. An Embraer jet began to push back from the elevated walkway.

The heat levitated from the asphalt in visible waves, but Patrick wanted a smoke badly enough to risk passing out. "He's robbing a bank and has taken a bunch of people hostage."

"What?"

Patrick repeated himself, shouting this time.

"Can't say I'm surprised," Eric Moyers said, once the jet left for the runway.

"Why not? Has he said anything about it?"

"He hasn't said anything to me in over a year. I didn't even know he'd been released from jail, or that he came back to Cleveland. No, I mean I'm not surprised about it because Bobby has been going from bad to worse his whole life, and I can't see any reason why he'd stop now. It killed our mother, you know, seeing her baby go to jail."

"I'm sorry for your loss," Patrick said automatically as he mashed his butt beneath one shoe. "Is there anyplace we can talk? With air-conditioning? And maybe less noise?"

As he followed the young man through a heavy door into the building, Patrick wondered, for at least the tenth time that day, how this case would affect his chances of becoming the head of the Homicide unit. He had passed the sergeant's exam with flying colors, but then he'd been doing that for years. There had always been guys with more seniority and a better grasp of ass kissing to move ahead of him. This time, though, he had a shot. McKissack, though not truly a moron, had only slightly more schmoozing ability and nothing like Patrick's case-clearance rate. This time he had a chance.

He had never thought of himself as an ambitious man. But then, most humans didn't think of themselves as carnivores until they spied a perfectly grilled filet mignon.

And for the tenth time, it bothered him that he could even think about such a thing at such a time. Though he told himself that the bad guys would give up and Paul would emerge with a wisecrack and a rumbling stomach, Patrick had been a cop too long not to know that it could all go very badly wrong at any moment. They hadn't killed the security guards, true, but the guards were expected and clearly labeled by their uniforms. If they discovered Paul's profession, it would startle them, and that was the worst thing anyone could do.

He hadn't worked with Paul even a full year yet, and they probably wouldn't even socialize if they didn't have to work together—the kid was too damn virtuous. He'd have the chief's slot in an instant if he asked for it. The department's golden boy. And why his cousin didn't want more of a . . . well, a *man's* man . . . it was beyond him.

Maybe it wasn't. Theresa just wanted the opposite of her asshole ex-husband, that was all. And Paul was a good cop. Frank would work like hell to get him out of there in one piece.

But *still*.

At the back of the luggage sorting room, the employees had a corner that doubled as a lounge, with some beat-up armchairs and a pop machine. It was out of everything except Mountain Dew, which Patrick loathed but drank anyway.

The air-conditioning worked. Well.

"Everyone keeps asking me how I catch a cold when it's ninety-five freakin' degrees outside," Eric Moyers groused. "This is how. The tarmac is like a blast furnace, and then in here it's a refrigerator. In, out, in, out. Then you have people flying in with germs from everywhere in the world. I'm sick all the time, working here."

Patrick nodded, feigning sympathy but watching the moving belts instead. He decided to invest in a sturdier set of luggage and one of those locks that only TSA could open. "Bobby is the youngest?"

"Yeah. I'm thirty, he's twenty-seven."

"How many kids are there?"

"Just the two of us, and Mom. I guess it's the old 'growing up without a father' thing. Our dad split just after Bobby was born. We had my mother's brother and his wife around for a while, up the street from us for . . . I don't know, at least ten years. Then the steel mill cut back. My uncle went to Gary to work, and Bobby didn't have anyone to follow around. I was working by then, just trying to keep the rent paid." Eric Moyers stared at the floor, hands hanging loose between his knees. "First he started coming home from school early. Then he started getting *sent* home from school early. Then he started getting sent home from school in a police car."

"How did your mother react?"

"She did her best. She tried understanding, she tried

tough love. At first he stole from our neighbors, friends, people who knew our situation and wouldn't press charges, at least not heavy ones. But Bobby never had the sense to stay where he was safe. Let me describe my brother to you, Officer. He's never had a job. Ever. Not flipping burgers or delivering the damn paper. The only thing he's ever done is steal, and he can't even do that right. I'd understand if he were dumb, but he reads books, he's a whiz at math. He'd just rather die than work for a living."

No surprises so far. Frank said the cop's prayer to himself: Please, God, let me find out something useful. "So he went to jail."

"He robbed a check-cashing place on Lorain, him and this guy he knew from his high school gym class. Unfortunately, the clerk was the kid they both used to toss into the locker-room trash can, and he sent the cops their way. Bobby got one break—the surveillance tape sucked so bad that you couldn't tell if he had a gun or a bag in his hand. He got a decent sentence."

"Where's the other guy now?" Could this be Lucas? "Tried to cozy up to a gang of skinheads, thinkin' they'd protect him inside. They killed him within a week."

Patrick looked around for a place to dump his empty pop can. The only wastebasket in sight was filled to the brim. "That's Bobby's only conviction?"

"That's the only felony. He's got all sorts of juvie stuff."

"Then he went back for the parole violation."

"My mother's hair went gray during his stint at the Mansfield prison. When he got out, it was the whole 'I've learned my lesson' song and dance that we'd heard a thousand times and that Mom still believed. But when he started bringing drugs home, to the place his mother slept, the place I was paying the rent on, it was time for more tough love. I called the cops, gave him another chance to learn his lesson. Which obviously didn't take any better than the first time."

"That's why I'm here." Patrick balanced the can in the unsteady pyramid of trash.

"They empty that twice a day," Eric Moyers told him. "We just dehydrate so fast in this heat."

"Mr. Moyers. Your brother is in a very dangerous situation right now. I think we're going to need your help to save his life."

Eric Moyers pitched his can at the wastebasket, collapsing its contents into a noisy jumble. "Why on earth would I want to do that?"

CHAPTER 14

11:43 A.M.

"You think Bobby and Lucas are from Atlanta, Georgia?" Cavanaugh asked. "Why?"

Theresa spoke rapidly, without taking her eyes from the TV. Paul sat terribly still, left arm clamped to his side, hiding his firearm. "The key chain for the car is a red, rubberized relief of men's faces. I think it's from Stone Mountain State Park outside Atlanta, where Jackson, Lee, and Davis are carved into a cliff. The dirt I found in the floor mats is clay with iron oxide. Rust, that's what the toxicologist told me."

"Georgia's red dirt," Cavanaugh said.

"Exactly. Don thinks the twig in the trunk is from a magnolia. They grow here, but they're especially abundant in Georgia."

"Jason? Is that right?"

"Yep. Bobby just served eight months on felony parole violation at the federal prison in Atlanta."

"Give the girl a cigar. What about his cellmate?"

"Thirty-one-year-old black male from Raleigh, name of Dunston Taylor."

Theresa saw her own disappointment mirrored in Cavanaugh's face.

"Not Lucas, not even as a middle name, but he did get released the week before Bobby," Jason went on. "They're searching the database now for *any* Lucas who would be out now."

"What about guards?" Theresa asked.

"They're searching the employee list, too."

"So how do two run-of-the-mill scumbags in prison hook up with a bank examiner from the Federal Reserve?" Cavanaugh asked.

Jason didn't have an answer, and Theresa didn't care. "Can't we figure that out later? Right now they just shot and killed one of the hostages. What are we going to do before they shoot the rest?"

Cavanaugh perched himself, catlike, in front of the phone. "I'm going to ask Lucas who he shot and why. And then we'll talk about his feelings."

Theresa returned to the telescope. The line of hostages remained one short, but otherwise nothing had changed.

Ms. Elliott, the head librarian, materialized at her elbow. "How are you holding up?"

"Fine," Theresa said.

Ms. Elliott waited.

"I keep breathing in and out. Beyond that, I don't know." Theresa sank against the wide windowsill, leaning one thigh against it; even the marble had turned hot in the overhead sun. She breathed in the scent of book dust. "My grandfather used to work here."

Peggy Elliott questioned her kindly, as if Theresa were a particularly bashful student asking to use a periodical. "At the Federal Reserve?"

"No, here at the library." She spoke without turning

from the glass, but she could see the other woman's solid form, safely tucked against the wall between the windows, watching her. "Of course that would have been . . . what, 1930? He was a page. Do they still have those? Pages?"

"Sure. We call them clerks now."

"What do they do?"

"Shelve books, help readers find what they're looking for."

"He always read a lot." Theresa gazed across the street, at the building for once, instead of its windows. These stone structures had been here for a long time, but so much had changed. What had it been like in 1930, when a fourteen-year-old boy could go downtown to work by himself and no one worried, before terrorists blew up planes and automatic rifles had been invented? The study of crime told her that the world had always been a dangerous place, but at least it used to require more effort.

Ms. Elliott hadn't moved. "We have a staff lounge. Would you like to come and sit down for a while?"

The woman's gentle tone frightened Theresa. She must look like she was about to collapse. She straightened her back, brushed what curls the humidity had left her out of her eyes, and said, "No, thank you, I need to stay here," in as firm a voice as she could muster.

Cavanaugh then ruined the effect by asking her to stay away from the windows, in the same tone one would use to a child. It infuriated her, mostly because she knew he was right. She and Peggy Elliott moved back into the reading nook, and Theresa sat across from the hostage negotiator as he got Lucas on the phone.

"What happened to that young woman?" Cavanaugh

asked. He might as well have been discussing copier toner or the need to order more coffee.

"Which young woman would that be, Chris?" If recent events had rattled Lucas, he did a masterful job of hiding it. His voice flowed from the speaker like melted butter.

Cavanaugh looked at Kessler, still on his own phone with the Fed security unit.

"Cherise," the vice president said. "Shur-EESE. It's her name."

Cavanaugh repeated it and asked Lucas again what had happened to her.

"What makes you think anything has?"

"As I said before, Lucas, this has to work on trust. Everything we've talked about so far, I've told you the truth. But it has to be a two-way street."

A voice sounded in the background, over the speaker.

"Lucas, what was that?"

"That was Bobby. He don't trust cops much, as I think I told you."

"Why not?"

"You got a few hours, Chris?"

"Yes."

"Well, I don't."

Cavanaugh went on. "I have to be able to believe that you're going to tell me the truth, if we're going to be able to work out a comfortable solution here, Lucas. You and Cherise went back into the cages and only you came out, so I have to ask you. Where is Cherise? Is she all right?"

"Are you watching me, Chris? You have hidden cameras in here?"

"I'm beginning to think you're jerking me around, Lucas."

The pace of the conversation wore on Theresa. "Why does he say his name with almost every single sentence?" she whispered to Jason. "More humanizing?"

"Yeah. Getting him to think of the hostages as human beings instead of objects sometimes means getting him to think of himself as a human being—capable of choice and compassion. It also might make him feel special, that Chris is focusing just on him."

"But he uses Cavanaugh's name all the time, too."

"Yeah. That's kind of odd."

Cavanaugh continued, "There's a camera in every corner of that lobby, Lucas, in plain sight. You know they're there, so you know bloody well we're watching you. Why wouldn't we be? So why are you wasting time talking about the cameras instead of telling me what happened to Cherise?"

"I would have taken the cameras out," Lucas said. "But they're at least twenty feet off the ground, and I'm not that good a shot."

Ha, Theresa thought. *Like I believe that.*

"What happened to Cherise?"

"Cherise," Lucas stated, "was not cooperating. You know how important cooperation is in an exercise like this. If anyone knows, Chris, you do."

"I don't like this guy," Jason muttered, in what should have been an almost inane comment; instead it chilled Theresa down to her veins. "Calm is one thing, but he's actually cool. He's so cool he's flat-out cold."

"So Cherise—"

"Cherise is dead," Lucas said. "See what I mean about cooperating?"

Cavanaugh paused. "Why did you kill her, Lucas?" He seemed to be fighting to keep his voice calm, but Theresa couldn't be sure if that was part of the act. He had to make Lucas aware of how serious the situation had become, but he couldn't yell at the robber and possibly antagonize him further. This way it sounded as though he was fighting his inner feelings to stay fair and evenhanded, to continue to assist Lucas through this crisis. She began to see why the police department held him in such high regard. But had he met his match?

"Why did you have to shoot her?" Cavanaugh was saying. "Why couldn't we have worked things out? I said I'd get you the money and I'd get you the car. Why did you give up on that plan, Lucas? Now that innocent girl has lost her life, and for nothing."

"You're breaking my heart. I love the 'innocent girl' part. You never even *met* the bitch, so how would you know how innocent she was?"

"Had *you* met her? Before today?"

Everyone in the room fell silent, waiting for this answer.

"We had an acquaintance of about, all told, ten minutes. With some people that's enough."

"This changes things, Lucas. You see that, don't you? My boss is going to be a lot less inclined to deal with you if he thinks you're going to shoot people no matter what, for no reason."

"Tell him to imagine how many I'll shoot when I *do* have a reason."

"I don't understand you, Lucas. You stay so calm through this whole thing, you take over the lobby without spilling a drop, and then, without motive, you shoot a woman."

"You don't need to understand me, Chris. I understand you."

"Then understand this: Before we go any further, I need your word that you won't hurt anyone without giving me a chance to work with you on it first. No more surprises. If you are considering hurting someone, tell me about it first, and we can work it out. Can I have your word on that?"

"No."

"They usually go for that," Jason said.

Theresa had thought her stomach couldn't sink any lower, and now she discovered she'd been wrong. She also wished Frank or Don were there with her. Or Paul. Especially Paul.

"No one out here is going to give you what you want if they think you're going to shoot people anyway. You're not giving us any incentive to work with you, is what I'm saying."

"I understand that perfectly, Chris. So here's your incentive: I want that car parked and running, with the keys in it, outside the door in twenty minutes, or I shoot another hostage. How about that for incentive? I bet that will work."

"You can have the car, Lucas. You just can't take a hostage away in it, that's all."

"And how are we supposed to get to the car without your snipers taking us out? You worked that one out, Chris?"

"If you leave that bank, just the two of you, no one is going to shoot you. I can one hundred percent assure you of that."

"We can get in the car and drive away? And how far are we going to get?"

"That, I can't answer. I can only handle what's happening on this block of East Sixth."

"Not good enough," Lucas told him, and hung up.

Cavanaugh thought for a moment, then redialed.

"Now what?" Theresa asked Jason.

"He'll keep talking to him. As cool as Lucas plays it, he's got to be uptight or he wouldn't have shot that woman. He needs a deal, he needs a way out, but he's going to play hard to get so that he can look like a hero to Bobby and himself. Chris will just keep talking and talking until he wears him down."

"My ex-husband used to do that. Especially when he wanted to buy something expensive."

Jason laughed, startling her. She hadn't meant it to be funny.

Frank appeared next to a matching set of *Vital Records of Concord, Massachusetts* and beckoned to Jason and Theresa. They followed him out of earshot to the glass-walled map room at the north corner of the building. Ms. Elliott or one of her staff had set up a second television next to a glossy blue globe; Assistant Chief Viancourt watched Channel 15's coverage of the secretary of state luncheon. He sat on an antiqued wooden bench with two other men in suits, like overgrown boys in a class they hadn't wanted to take.

"I've got the brother here." Frank kept his voice low. "Bobby's brother."

"Here?" Jason asked. "You brought him *here*?"

"He's the closest thing we've got to insight into these two guys. He doesn't know Lucas, never heard of him. But he knows his brother. Can't stand him either, but that's not my problem."

"Yes it is," the young man insisted. "If he hates Bobby, the feeling's probably mutual."

"He can still talk to him," Theresa said. "If Lucas will even put him on the phone."

Jason shook his head so hard his tie shifted. "No, you don't get it. This isn't TV, where the criminal melts into tears when his sainted mother tells him to come out. These guys are losers who blame everything that's gone bad in their lives on other people, and most often the people closest to them. He isn't going to feel sentimental about his family members. He'll probably hold them responsible for every problem he has."

"Especially this one," Frank said. "Eric turned him in. Said he did it to save the aforementioned sainted mother. Her baby's wild ways wore out her heart."

"What about her? Would she—" Theresa began.

"She's dead. He really *did* wear out her heart."

"Then why did you bring Eric Moyers here?" Jason asked again.

"Well, gee, I had nothing else to do, and he needed a ride home from work. And because my partner's in there with an M4 carbine in his face, and this guy is the only life-form we have that can tell us anything about the guy *holding* the M4 carbine besides his age and ID number. Maybe that's why."

"Okay, okay. Did he tell you anything else about Bobby that might help us?"

"Just that's he's a lousy thief. I'm guessing Lucas is not only the mouthpiece here, he's the brains."

"No surprise there. Okay, we'll tell Chris what you've learned from the brother, but not that he's on the premises."

"Wait, you're not telling your own *boss* all the facts?"

Jason mopped his forehead with one sleeve cuff. "It's for his own sake. We don't know how Bobby will react to even the mention of his brother, and what Chris doesn't know, he can't slip and reveal."

Theresa tried to imagine Leo's take on this operating procedure. *You keep things from me, MacLean, and you'll spend a week in the deep freeze putting blood samples from 1994 in numerical order. Then I'll fire you.*

"Hey." Channel 15's reporting turned to how Cleveland had finally won the Rock and Roll Hall of Fame's induction ceremonies from New York City and Assistant Chief of Police Viancourt now tore himself away, clutching Theresa's plastic evidence bag and a sheet of paper. "I've got that postage-meter information."

"That was fast," Theresa said.

The assistant chief beamed under her genuine praise; if he'd been born with a tail, he'd have been wagging it. "It was nothing. Hi—Patrick, isn't it? You're up for the chief of Homicide, aren't you?"

"Yes, sir."

Theresa goggled. She'd never heard Frank call anyone "sir" before.

"Best of luck to you. I'm glad you're in on this—we need to keep a cop approach going here. Cavanaugh's good, but these specialized units can get too wrapped up in themselves."

Theresa could see a sort of struggle pass over her cousin's face, as if the desire to be honest—at the moment Cavanaugh seemed their only hope—warred with his desire to be the head of the Homicide unit. Jason said nothing. She intervened. "Could Pitney Bowes trace the postage meter?"

Viancourt's expression clouded. She could swear he had forgotten what they were talking about, finding the politics of the police department a far more fascinating topic. Then it cleared. "Yeah. They have over five hundred meters leased within city limits, did you know that? Just about any large office concern has one. Anyway, this machine is at a storage facility in Decatur, Georgia. Gray's Store-All, on Forrest Avenue."

Frank had his radio in hand. "I'll get the Georgia cops to send someone out there now."

"I thought of that. A unit's on their way," the assistant chief told him with a touch of reproach. Frank's stock had just lost a few points on the Dow.

Theresa butted in again, even batting an eyelash or two at Viancourt. "Bobby probably had his car in storage while he served his time. But I don't understand how the car got to Decatur from here—they'd hardly let him drive himself to prison, would they?"

"Not in this case. It was an interprison transfer, so he'd have gone by bus."

"Then maybe the storage facility can tell us who brought it there or who paid the bill." She thanked the assistant chief profusely. He wandered back to the hypnotic waves of broadcast news as she turned to Frank. "Where's his brother? I'd like to talk to him."

"So would I," Jason said.

Eric Moyers's disposition had not improved greatly since he'd left his workplace. He had gone from one inhospitable climate with a partially stocked pop machine to another. He sat at an abandoned microfilm-viewing station, drinking Sprite without enthusiasm.

Theresa planted her body in front of him and introduced herself. The guy looked exhausted and breathed with a raspy wheeze, but he gamely fielded questions from her and Jason without argument. Theresa had the feeling he'd answer questions from Peggy Elliott, should she care to ask any. An air of hopeless resignation bracketed every word.

"Does Bobby have a white Mercedes?"

"Not white," the baggage handler corrected her bitterly. "Pearl."

"And he put it in storage while he served this last sentence in Atlanta?"

"I wouldn't have any idea where he put it."

"Could he have paid to store it for six months?"

"Sure. Bobby always had money—stolen money, of course, but he'd have it." He snorted. "He put his car in storage? That's probably the only time my brother thought ahead in his life."

Jason asked, "Did he live in Brookpark before he went to jail? The car is registered to a house there."

"We all lived there. That's where Bobby and I grew up. But he was gone and Mom had died—no point me living there all by myself. I sold it months ago."

Jason's phone rang, and he answered it, walking a few steps away and pulling out his notepad before he even flipped the receiver open.

Theresa tried another tack with Eric Moyers. "Is Bobby good with mechanics? Did he work on the car, know how to modify it?"

"Bobby couldn't change a tire if his life depended on it. If he had any work done, he got someone else to do it. What are you guys doing about this anyway? Can't I sit somewhere so I can see what's going on?"

"Unfortunately, we can't all fit in the command center," she told him, thinking, *Damn, I'm learning to deflect people as smoothly as Chris Cavanaugh.* "Does Bobby have a friend named Lucas?"

"I told this guy here I don't know any of Bobby's

friends. He always had plenty of them, I'll admit that. Everyone liked Bobby, especially kids and dumb animals. But I don't know his friends—I didn't want to know them then, I don't want to know them now."

"Has he called you since he got out?"

"He might have tried, but I doubt it. I changed my address and phone, left no forwarding. We only had my aunt and uncle in common, and they died in a car accident. Truth is, lady," Eric Moyers summed up, "I didn't even know he *was* out."

CHAPTER 15

12:05 P.M.

Paul had stretched his legs out straight, Theresa noted, probably to release some of the pressure on his butt. He wasn't used to sitting so much. He still wouldn't look up at the camera, instead following Lucas's pacing movements.

I'm failing miserably at this investigating gig, honey. I haven't discovered one useful fact, and we still have no idea how to get you out of there.

Kessler had disappeared. The scribe, Irene, wrote steadily now that Cavanaugh had Lucas back on the phone. He asked the bank robber, "Where are you from, by the way?"

"I could say the depths of hell, but I hate to be overdramatic."

"Bobby is a Cleveland boy, born and raised, we know that—"

"Really. What else do you know?"

"—but where are you from, Lucas? Where did you two get to be friends?"

"I fail to see how that's relevant, Chris."

"Did you meet when Bobby served time in Atlanta?"

A pause. Theresa could see him on the monitor, talking on the phone from the information desk. It had a cord and limited his movement to pacing in front of the hostages, the curly wire stretched over their heads. Any minute now he would tug the body of the phone down onto one of them. "I don't see that car pulling up outside. And don't give me any more lines about a tow-truck driver."

"That's just it, Lucas. The last time you mentioned the tow-truck driver, you also mentioned Winn-Dixie, which is a chain of grocery stores, right?"

"So?"

"So there aren't any in Cleveland. There aren't any in Ohio. They're a southern chain."

"That's just fascinating, Chris. I guess your cops will have to get their coffee somewhere else, then, which is a pity, because they make pretty good stuff. I still don't see that car. Who do you want me to shoot next?"

"I just want to know where you're from, Lucas."

"Is there a reason you're wasting my time with this? Please tell me there's a reason."

Cavanaugh sighed. Didn't he ever get tired of these games? Theresa wondered. She could see herself yelling at people: *Just spit it out already!*

Cavanaugh didn't yell. "Bear with me here, Lucas."

Lucas's sigh could be heard clearly over the speaker. "Okay. Since you ask all polite like, and since I'm obviously supposed to be impressed with your keen grocery-store reasoning here, I'll just tell you if it will make you feel better: Bobby and I served time together in Atlanta. That's where we met."

"Again, telling us stuff," Frank muttered. "Does this guy even want to get away? Or is he just that stupid?"

"He's not stupid," Theresa said, back at the telescope.

Cavanaugh opened his mouth, then stopped. Then he said, "Thank you, Lucas. Give me a second, okay?"

He tapped a button on the phone console and turned to the rest of the sweltering group. "It sounds like he has us on speakerphone. If Bobby can hear what we're saying, so can the hostages."

Maybe we could get a message to Paul, Theresa thought. But what would they say? Run for it? Don't run for it?

"I can't ask him about Ludlow. Ludlow's wife is sitting there with a gun to her baby's head and then hears that her husband has been murdered? She'll freak out."

"She'll be uncooperative." Theresa shuddered. Lucas hadn't stopped at an unarmed woman; there was no reason to think he would stop at killing a child.

"Just as well," Jason said. "I still think he'll become more desperate if he knows we know about Ludlow's murder."

Cavanaugh rubbed his eyes.

"I spoke with Atlanta again," Jason went on. "Bobby did not have any visitors during his incarceration. He gave exactly one name for his visitors' list, his mother's, and they erased that after she died."

Theresa said, "His brother didn't even know Bobby had been released."

Cavanaugh stared at her, and too late she realized they hadn't told him about Eric Moyers's being in the building. But he didn't ask how she knew that, and

Jason went on, "They had nine Lucases incarcerated at the same time as Bobby—four in his cell block—who've been released in the past six months."

He paused, his eyes going to the blinking red light indicating that their Lucas was on hold. But Cavanaugh said, "Details."

Jason rattled off four names, then added, "One white, thirty-two, Arkansas resident, second conviction for selling marijuana within five hundred yards of a school. The other three are black. The first is twenty-one, did four years for assault after nearly killing a guy in a bar fight. No other record. The second is forty, two and a half years for credit-card fraud, first offense. Third is thirty-one, did five years for putting his ex-girlfriend's boyfriend in intensive care. No other record."

"Military backgrounds?"

"The white guy got kicked out of the National Guard. The last black guy got kicked out of the regular army for medical reasons."

"What kinds of reasons?"

"They didn't know. His record just said honorable discharge, medical deferment."

"None classified as mixed-race," Cavanaugh mused.

Frank said, "We can't eliminate by that. He'd be entered as whatever the arresting officer considered him, which depends a lot on the arresting officer."

The light on the phone went out. Lucas had hung up. Cavanaugh glanced at it but did not seem concerned.

Please don't make that man angry, Theresa thought.

"What's that last one's name again?"

Jason checked his notes, but the scribe read first, from hers: "Lucas Winston Parrish."

"Why him?" Cavanaugh asked.

"We figured this guy's age at twenty-five or thirty, right? He and the white guy would fit, but the drug dealer doesn't have a record of violence, and he does. Besides, the bottle of Advil in the car might have been his. Maybe his medical condition involves headaches or some other kind of chronic pain."

"It's slim."

"Everything we have is slim." She could not keep the bitterness from her voice.

"Good point. Okay, Jason, call whoever you have to call to get Parrish's military history. I'll try to keep him occupied talking about Cherise."

Theresa's Nextel rang. The caller ID read OLIVER TOX. She moved to the window seat facing Superior and cupped the tiny phone with her hand, to keep from disturbing the negotiations.

"Here's the thing," he said without preamble. "The dirt from your victim's shoulder?"

"Yeah?"

"Vaseline. With cyclotrimethylene trinitramine."

The vast library felt airless all of a sudden. "Shit."

"Yep. Whatever the hell you've gotten yourself into down there, don't bring it back here."

She snapped her phone shut. Apollo and Hyacinthus rested stiffly in their painting overhead, aware that Hyacinthus would die from a misdirected discus. His life-blood would drain out at the feet of someone who loved him.

Who the hell decided to put *that* on the library wall?

She went back to the reading table, where the conversation between hostage taker and hostage negotiator continued. "I'll pick one from the middle of the row this time," Lucas was saying, "if I don't see that car outside the door in five minutes."

"What's your hurry? I thought you wanted more money," Cavanaugh pointed out.

"I did. But I've decided I can live with what I've got. I'm tired of this place, and I need a drink. I want my car, and I want to get out of here."

The scribe, Irene, made a note, which Theresa read over the girl's shoulder. *"Drinks?"*

"This guy goes back and forth," Frank groused.

Cavanaugh said into the phone, "I thought it was Bobby's car."

"You're nitpicking, Chris. Does that mean you're out of ideas?"

"I'll be happy to give you the car, Lucas. But you can't take any of those innocent people away in it."

"There you go with the 'innocent' bit again." The robber paused, perhaps to think. "Tell you what. The hostages will walk to the car with us but won't get in. That will protect us from the snipers, at least until we drive away. Then they'll riddle us with bullets, like Bonnie and Clyde or something, but it will just be us criminals."

"That doesn't sound like a good plan for you two."

"Hardly your problem, is it?"

"It is. I don't want you to die any more than I want one of the bank employees to die. If we can come to some agreement, some conditions under which you'd turn yourselves in, then we could be sure to avoid the whole 'riddled with bullets' thing."

Bobby said something in the background.

"The bullets sound better than trusting you cops, that's what Bobby thinks."

"What do you think?"

"Trying to create a difference of opinion over here? It's not going to work. We're a team, me and Bobby."

"Then decide as a team. Under what conditions would you consider letting those people go and turning yourselves in?"

Lucas did not hesitate. "The team answers: None. We are driving away from here under our own power, no matter what. So let's get back to the central point, because I think we've digressed. I want the car outside, keys in, engine running, in ten minutes."

"Can't do it. Not like this."

"The middle of the line this time. I'm thinking Brad. I don't really like Brad. He looks like the kind of pencil-necked little geek who cashes postdated checks a day early just to watch them bounce."

"I don't cash checks!" they heard the young man's distant protest. "I'm just a tour guide!"

Appropriating Jason's binoculars, Theresa could see the left half of Brad and his crisp white shirt. He held his hands up to his shoulders, palms out, and even without high resolution she could see the look of horror on his face as the barrel of Lucas's gun came to rest a few inches from his nose.

Paul sat no more than five feet away. He would not let Lucas shoot another hostage. Theresa knew that. He would die, and they would not be married. This did not surprise her. She could be a good mother, a good daughter, a good employee, and be happy in those roles. But romance would never be hers; like Apollo and Hyacinthus, they had been doomed from the start.

"I think Brad," Lucas said again. "Or maybe Missy."

Next to her, Frank whispered, "If they head for the door, Theresa, get away from this window. Immediately."

"I know."

"Besides, I'll need room to aim."

Cavanaugh kept talking. "And then what, Lucas? You're already on the hook for whatever you did to Cherise. You want to make this situation even worse? Or do you want to quit while you're ahead?"

"Shooting Cherise put me ahead? You must not have liked her any more than I did."

Theresa opened her mouth to tell Frank about Oliver's call but broke off with a frown when Cavanaugh said, "You told me she struggled with you. Did she grab the gun, make it go off?"

"He's giving him an out," Frank said, "not blaming the victim. He's trying to guide Lucas into thinking he can weasel out of the murder charge with self-defense. He needs Lucas to think he can get out of jail again someday, which of course he can't."

"I understand that. My back aches, that's all."

"Want to sit down?"

"No. I want to curl up in a ball and die."

He put his arm around her, but only for a moment. It was too bloody hot in the sunny window for that. "Your mom won't see this on TV, will she?"

"She's at the restaurant. What about your mom?" The sisters had perfected the science of instant communication.

"She doesn't watch anything but the Weather Channel."

"You've just wasted five minutes, Chris," Lucas said.

"You're afraid to come out because you're afraid of the police snipers. But don't you think they'll be even more trigger-happy if you shoot that young man?"

"Or Missy."

"Or Missy."

They could hear the girl wail, "But my baby—"

"That's good reasoning, Chris. You have four minutes remaining."

"What's the hurry, Lucas? You've been in there for over four hours now. What's another twenty minutes or so to work this out?"

"I think we're done here, Chris. It's been a pleasure talking with you. Have the car outside in four minutes."

Click.

"I don't get this." Frank lit a cigarette in his agitation. "He said he wanted more money. Now he's leaving without it. What's up with that?"

Cavanaugh rubbed his face, an agitated tic Theresa hadn't seen before. "I don't know. And don't smoke in here."

"Give him the car," Theresa said.

"We can't."

"It will keep him from shooting that kid."

"He'll take the kid with him to shoot later. And maybe Mrs. Ludlow and her little boy. They'll get in that car with him and Bobby and they'll drive away and we won't be able to stop them without harming the innocents, so they'll *get* away, and then those people's lives won't be worth a pack of gum."

"We'll follow them. They can't drive forever. And at least most of the hostages will be safe."

His chair turned on a swivel, and he spun around to look at her. His face held neither encouragement nor condemnation. "And what if Paul is one of the hostages he wants to take with him, Theresa? How would that affect your decision?"

He was right, and she hated him for it. But her growing desperation made her willing to be inconsistent. "We have to do something."

"We delay. That's how this works. We keep him busy with details and small decisions. We send in food, cold cuts, and bread so that the hostages will have to put a sandwich together for them, which creates more bonding than a ready-made sub would. And we keep talking."

"Until what?"

"Until his sense of self-preservation overrules his ambition." Cavanaugh's hand went to the phone.

Lucas picked up on the tenth ring. "I don't see our car, Chris."

"It's on its way. But I can't turn it over to you until I can be sure no one else is going to get hurt."

"Oh, someone's going to get hurt," Lucas said. "And it's going to be Brad. Sixty seconds."

Theresa gave up on the telescope's narrow view and watched the monitor. Lucas pointed his gun at the young bank employee, who covered his eyes with one trembling hand. His mouth moved, but his voice did not reach the speakerphone.

"We can't work this way, Lucas."

"You can't. I can."

"Are you on speakerphone, Lucas?"

"Why, yes, Chris. I kind of need my hands free at the moment."

"Can you pick up? I need to talk to just you."

Theresa saw Lucas hesitate, glance at the phone, consider his options. Perhaps curiosity won out.

Into the receiver he said, "Trying to cut Bobby out?"

"No, no. I don't care if Bobby's in on this conversation, but I don't want the hostages to be able to hear us."

Theresa watched as Lucas turned, glanced at Bobby, then picked up the receiver. He stood at the side of the information desk, slightly behind the hostages but not totally exposed to the employee lobby.

"Please just listen to me for a minute, and don't say anything. There's a woman there who's going to be very upset if she hears what we're going to discuss, and I don't want anyone in there getting bent out of shape. You with me?"

"I haven't shut the timer down, Chris, so you may want to get to the point."

Water trickled down the back of Cavanaugh's neck.

"He's sweating," Theresa whispered to Frank.

"He's calling an armed killer's attention to a young woman and a baby. It's a hell of a risk. I'd be sweating, too."

"I suppose that's why he just said 'a woman,' no specifics. She's one of two, if Lucas doesn't know what she looks like."

"He hasn't given any indication of it so far."

On the phone Cavanaugh spoke quietly but clearly. "Do you want to tell us why you killed Mark Ludlow, Lucas?"

Lucas said nothing. But on the screen Theresa saw him turn away from the reception desk, phone receiver still to his ear, and gaze in the direction of his partner. He said nothing, and the video did not give sufficient clarity to show if they exchanged some sort of signal. Then Lucas said, "Never heard of him."

"He was a bank examiner for the Fed, previously worked in Atlanta. We found him murdered this morning."

"Never heard of him."

"There's an off chance he's telling the truth," Frank whispered to her. "It would explain why he's not paying any attention to Mrs. Ludlow. You'd think if he knew Mark Ludlow enough to try to extort inside information about the Fed, he'd know about his wife and kid."

"And we still can't be sure Cherise is even dead. What if she was in this with him? What if *she* was the inside connection, not Ludlow?"

"Then why is Ludlow dead?"

"Maybe he found out, or maybe he had access to something she didn't."

Cavanaugh, meanwhile, continued, "You have to understand our point of view, Lucas. We found a man dead this morning, and now Cherise has been killed. To let you take people out of that bank . . . well, how can we have confidence that you wouldn't hurt them?"

"You're going at this all wrong, Chris." Lucas set down the receiver and punched a button to turn the speakerphone back on. Unencumbered by the cord, he moved back to the young man in the tie, Brad. "I want you to have confidence that I *will* hurt them. And time's up."

He had left the phone line open. He wanted them to hear this.

The M4 carbine came up.

As Theresa watched, Paul stayed on the floor but brought his sidearm out and upward in one fluid motion.

"Stop." His voice sounded light-years away, but still she heard the strength of it, the clarity of purpose. "Police."

Two shots, in quick succession.

Paul fell back, both hands to his right leg. He dropped the gun, and the janitor kicked it across the tile, shoving it away from himself as if it were a live grenade.

Someone screamed, "He's hit!" When Theresa's throat tingled from the effort, she realized who it had been.

"Anyone else?" Cavanaugh scanned the monitor, his face flushed as if with heat and fear. "I heard two shots."

"No one else acts hurt." Frank squinted at the scene. "Not Lucas. Bobby—No, there's Bobby, he just darted out to pick up Paul's gun."

"He's *hit*." Theresa didn't know what to say, and she didn't have enough breath in her lungs to say it anyway.

Frank tried to guide her to a chair. "Just in the leg, Tess. He'll be okay."

"*Just* in the leg?"

Cavanaugh punched the phone's numbered buttons with savage force, nodding at Frank. "Get her out of here."

She voiced some unintelligible protest.

"I can't have screaming in here, Theresa. They have that second monitor in the map room. You can watch from there. Hello, Lucas?"

"Well . . ." the robber drawled. "That was interesting."

"What the hell is going on?"

"Where I come from, we call that a snake in the grass. Guy was a cop, and I didn't know it. Serves me right for not searching everybody at the beginning, but I *am* a little shorthanded. And you know what? I still don't see my car."

"Shooting a cop is not a way to demonstrate good faith."

"Point A." The gunshots had rattled him; he seemed to be fighting to keep his voice low and insolent, but higher tones kept slipping out. "I didn't know he was a cop because he neglected to mention it at the start of this exercise, which really wasn't demonstrating any good faith on his part, don't you think? Point B: What makes you think I'm interested in showing good faith? I don't care if you have faith in me. All I want is my car!"

Theresa watched the monitor, her vision of the world narrowed to one nineteen-inch black-and-white screen. Paul had his back up against the reception desk; he had not moved his hands from his wound. The older black man next to him removed Paul's suit jacket and began to wrap it around the injured leg, revealing the now-empty holster. "Trade him the car for Paul."

Cavanaugh held the phone against his shoulder. "Get the special agent in here and her out."

Jason trotted off to the conference room. He left Theresa to Frank.

She tried to modulate her tones, with extremely limited success. "He's wounded in the thigh. If the bullet hit or even nicked an artery, he could bleed out in five minutes. Give Lucas anything he wants to get Paul out of there, or he's going to die."

"I understand that, Theresa. But there's eight other people in that lobby I have to think of." He pushed the "talk" button on the console. "Lucas, we need to get that wounded man out of there."

"That would be good. He's bleeding all over the freakin' tile. Really ruins the look of it."

Theresa let out a tiny sound, a whimper. Cavanaugh shot Frank a murderous glare.

"Honey," the detective said to her, "I think he's right. We should—"

"Tell you what." Lucas's voice continued, grating

on the air like a sandblaster. "You give me our car, and we can leave. You can whisk EMS in here to fix this guy up, and everybody's happy. Especially me."

"Will you leave all the other hostages there, so just you and Bobby drive away?"

"There you go, thinking I'm stupid. No! All five—not the security guards—will come out to the car with us, as a wall between Bobby and me and your snipers. Once we're in our car, they can rush off to your waiting arms."

"How can I be sure you won't take one of them with you? I'd be putting that person's life at risk. I can't make that deal, Lucas, not under those conditions. You have to leave the hostages in the bank."

"Then this guy's going to die, sooner or later. Probably sooner. He ain't looking so good."

"You have to give him his car, or Paul's going to bleed to death," Theresa said. She thought she said it slowly and clearly, but it came out jumbled and very loud.

"Get her out of here," Cavanaugh ordered her cousin.

"Give him the car!"

He stood up so fast he knocked his chair over backward. "I can't sacrifice a few bank employees just so your wedding will proceed as planned! It doesn't work like that!"

On the monitor a dark stain began to show through the suit coat around Paul's thigh, inexorably growing in size, spreading though the layers of fabric as the blood seeped from his body.

She moved closer to Cavanaugh. She was only going to touch his shoulder, that's all, just to remind him that they were real people and not theories on which to practice his "perfect record" techniques. She didn't intend to grasp his lapels or push against his chest with both hands. "Give him—"

"Patrick, get her out of here, or whatever happens next will be on you."

Frank didn't hesitate. "Just save his life," he told Cavanaugh as he dragged Theresa from the room.

CHAPTER 16

12:21 P.M.

The street had not cooled any in the past hour. The sun hung directly overhead. Her white lab coat did its best to reflect the rays, but it did not allow any air through to her skin, and sweat soaked both her blouse and her pants.

She would not remove the lab coat, though. Even with her reddened eyes and a hurried pace, a lab coat meant she belonged there, a trained professional, an impartial observer. Besides, the keys to the Mercedes were in the pocket.

The officers lining Superior Avenue, obviously bored and hot, did not see anything amiss in her passage. They let her go past them without comment, past the yellow crime-scene tape, up to the sawhorses blocking the East Ninth intersection. They let her walk right up to Bobby Moyers's 1994 Mercedes-Benz. Why not? She'd already been in and out of it twice that morning.

They didn't even question her when she opened the door and sat in the driver's seat.

Cavanaugh was right, she thought as the engine turned over. There were eight other people in there, including a little boy, and if Lucas got his vehicle back, some of those eight would disappear into it. Driving this car around the corner was akin to signing their death warrants.

Be careful, her grandfather always said.

She was not trained in hostage negotiation. She was jumping into a process in the middle, startling two men with guns who had no idea who she was and had never seen her before in their lives.

But she had spent enough time around blood to know how much was too much. And Paul was losing too much. He would not last until Lucas gave up. Cavanaugh had said it himself—situations like these could go on for days.

Think things through, her grandfather had said. *Keep a savings account. Don't quit a job until you have another one.*

She put the car into gear. Two uniformed officers, wedged into a sliver of shade next to the Hampton Inn, looked at her oddly but did not move toward her.

The bank employees also did not know who she was, had never seen her before. But they might come to curse her name in their last few moments of life.

But her grandfather had also said, *Make your decision. Then don't worry about it anymore.*

Hope over experience.

She put her foot on the gas and drove around the corner. Now she heard shouting behind her, the officers telling her to get out of the road. She pulled up in front of the East Sixth entrance between a fire hydrant and a sewer grate.

Now she slipped off the lab coat, left it in the car. Every surface of her body needed to be visible. Keys in hand, she got out and moved to the sidewalk. There she stopped with her arms up, keys dangling from her right index finger. "Lucas!"

It seemed like forever—she hoped that man was keeping good pressure on the wound—until the broken glass door opened. She saw Lucas flip the doorstop down before retreating back into the lobby, which appeared dark beyond the brilliant light outside. The ten feet between them felt like the Grand Canyon, but she could hear him clearly. "Who the hell are you?"

"I'm the woman with your car. Send out the wounded officer, and I'll give you the keys."

A confused pause. "Are you crazy?"

"Yes. Send out the wounded officer. If he can't walk, send someone with him. Then I'll give you your keys."

"Did Cavanaugh send you?"

The sun felt as if it were singeing her hair, and the waves of heat from the pavement made her queasy. She could smell the sausage cooking in a lunch cart down the street and heard a sharp metallic ping, as if a sniper had accidentally dropped a penny, or a bullet, several stories to the sidewalk below. "No. I just want the officer to get help before he dies. You should want that, too."

"Why don't I just shoot you and take the keys?"

"Because I'm standing next to a sewer grate. It has nice wide gaps between the slats. You shoot me, I drop the keys, and you're stuck here."

"What if Bobby has an extra set on him?"

"Then I'm screwed." She had a fifty-fifty chance, right? Sweat rolled downward, tickling her sides.

Another pause. "I thought Cavanaugh said—"

"Cavanaugh's screwed, too. I just want that wounded officer out of there." When he didn't answer, she pressed. "Look up and down the street, Lucas. There's an army out here. No matter what else happens today, what do you think they're going to do to you if a cop dies?"

"Who *are* you?"

"I'm a forensic scientist with the medical examiner's office."

"What are you doing here?"

"I'm engaged to marry that cop." The truth, Cavanaugh had said. That's the only way it can work.

"Really."

Having to hold her arms up ached. She needed more push-ups in her routine.

"Theresa!" Frank called from somewhere behind her. She did not turn. The poor guy could forget about the Homicide chief's position if he couldn't handle one hysterical relative—another corpse littered in the wake of her decision.

"So I let him go," Lucas said, "and you'll walk in here with the keys?"

"I'll throw them to you."

"I don't think so, sugar. I'm going to be down one hostage, and a cop makes a good one. You're close enough. He goes out, you come in. *With* my keys."

Her personal phone rang. She didn't want to answer it. It was probably Cavanaugh, and she didn't want to think about the names he'd call her.

But it gave out the first few notes of "Devil in Disguise" before she could turn it off. "My phone is ringing," she said to Lucas. "I have to answer it."

He only laughed.

She took that for permission and slowly pulled the phone from its clip.

"Mom?" her daughter said. "The math final wasn't so bad after all. The first question had this triangle—"

"Rachael, I can't talk right now."

The briefest of pauses, a hiccup of time. "What's the matter?"

"I'm glad your test went okay, but I have to go. I'll call you back as soon as I can, okay?"

"*What's the matter?*"

"Nothing's wrong. You should probably go to your dad's after school. You know he likes to see you."

"Something's really wrong, isn't it? You always think you sound so calm, and you don't, you never do! What is it? Is it Grandma?"

"No, no. I just have a situation at work."

"Don't give me that shit!"

"Language," Theresa said automatically, but didn't blame her. Her daughter had just walked into her own personal Twilight Zone, and they both knew it. Theresa didn't take her sight off of Lucas, hovering beyond the door. "I have to go. But I love you, Rachael. No matter what, I love you more than anything."

The last thing she heard before flipping the phone shut was her daughter screaming. "*Mom—*"

Theresa pushed the "power" button.

She had just terrorized her daughter and might render her motherless before the day was out, and all to save her boyfriend. Looked like the Mother of the Year award would slip through her fingers once more.

To her surprise, Lucas asked, "Are you okay?"

Make your decision.

Then stick to it.

"Keys," she reminded him, making them jangle for emphasis.

"You stay right where you are. You don't move, you don't drop those keys for nothing, right?"

"Yes."

"Then you got a deal. Don't move."

She saw the shadowy figure retreat, listened to the bottom tones of a conversation. She heard Lucas say, "I don't care!" but everything else was unintelligible.

Let him still be able to walk, she thought.

Where was Rachael? She had to be in school, probably in lunch period. Was she screaming at the phone now, demanding that her mother answer her? She'd probably call her grandmother next. Who was sixty-four. With a bad mitral valve.

I may have just destroyed every member of my family.

Paul appeared in the doorway, with the black man in the uniform who had been sitting next to him. Theresa could see why. Paul's face looked ghost white in the brilliant sun, and he leaned his weight on the other man until they both staggered. The blood-soaked suit coat around his thigh had begun to slip from his hand. They emerged from the door. Usual city noise went on in the surrounding blocks, but this stretch of East Sixth had become as silent as the grave.

Two hostages for one. *That's something,* she thought. *Cavanaugh should be pleased with that.*

Her sweat turned to ice. Paul's face reflected his bewilderment as his conscious mind receded. He didn't seem to recognize her at first, but then he stretched out a hand. "Theresa—"

"Step down," the man told Paul. They had reached the curb.

"Keep walking, baby." She extended her left arm, and their fingertips met in a touch so light she might have imagined it. Her throat closed up. "Just keep walking."

The older man tugged at his burden, and they continued their shambling gait across the burning street.

She listened to their footsteps, and with each one her heart urged him to take one more.

"Now you come in here," Lucas ordered her from inside the bank. "*With* my keys."

"I'm going to turn my head to see that he makes it. That's all—I won't move anything else."

"I can just shoot you, you know."

"Then I drop the keys." She turned her head, straining her neck, expecting to feel a bullet rip through her heart with every breath. Frank and two other officers emerged from the library building to help the two men, and her spirit lifted a millimeter to hear a siren on the next block. Someone had thought ahead to call an ambulance; maybe Cavanaugh, or Frank.

Her cousin caught her eye over Paul's shoulder. Shock there, and anger.

"Okay, he's gone. Now get in here."

Part One has ended. Time for Part Two.

The light reflected off the glass doors, blinding her, or perhaps the heat had made her faint. *If I run, I won't make it. If I go in, there's no reason to assume he'll kill me. He has plenty of other people to shoot first, and I brought him his car.*

Make your decision. Then stick to it.

Slowly, hands still up, she moved toward the door.

Her traitorous body longed for the marble lobby—anything to escape the sun. With its blinding rays blocked from her eyes, she saw him. His skin, the color of caramel, had become shiny with beads of sweat just under the ball cap. He had slender lips and a wiry frame. "You wanted in here awful bad."

"No," she corrected him. "I wanted him out of here awful bad."

He appraised her with light brown eyes. "Hope he was worth it."

So do I, she found herself thinking. Would Rachael think so? Would her mother?

Up four or five marble steps, she saw the lobby, saw the terrified people cowering in front of the information desk. Saw the pool of red liquid that Paul had left, in a large puddle and then a heavy trail to the door, his living tissue, his lifeblood. The thought of stepping in it . . . She jumped away with a shudder.

"Give me the keys," Lucas snapped. "And don't pass out on me neither."

She held them out for him to snatch.

He eyed her trousers, the clinging silk blouse. "I'm guessing you're not hiding anything in there."

"I'm not a cop. I don't carry a gun." The other hostages watched, wide-eyed, except for Brad, who did not look up from Paul's blood.

"What are you, then?"

"I'm a forensic scientist."

The lines on his face wrinkled as he broke into a laugh. "A freakin' scientist. Okay, ma'am, welcome to the club. The hostage club."

The automatic rifle dipped toward the floor. Her hands began to sink as well.

"However."

She froze, hands splayed at hip level.

"I obviously screwed up with that guy you just sent out of here, and I'm not big on making the same mistake twice. No excuse for it, my mother used to say. So I'm going to have to pat you down. Be assured I'll do so with regret as well as the utmost respect."

She blinked at him.

"That means stand still. Very still, because Bobby over there has you covered. Got it?"

She nodded. Bobby peeked from around the corner, gun at the ready.

He came closer. She could smell aftershave mixed with sweat, as well as a sour, oily smell, perhaps gun lubricant. It felt odd to have a strange man's hand passing over her body, but he went lightly and quickly and didn't linger. He took her cell phone and stuffed it into his back pocket.

"Okay. That's cool. I was lying a little bit, though—I don't regret it. Now have a seat with the rest of the group over here, and we'll proceed."

She headed for Mrs. Ludlow and the little boy. She could not force herself to take Paul's place, to sit by his blood while it dried to black.

The phone on the reception desk rang.

"That's probably that negotiator dude. Can't get rid of him." Lucas snatched up the receiver. "Thanks for calling, Chris, but I really don't need you anymore. I've got my car, I've got my posse, and we're going to be leaving now." He listened. "She's fine. . . . Why? . . . . Yeah, but why? . . . I'm putting you on speaker."

He turned. "Are you Theresa?"

She had stopped her motion toward the desk, afraid to move while he'd been distracted by the call, afraid to startle him. "Yes."

"He wants you to get on the phone."

She knew what he would say. "No. I don't want to talk to him."

"I don't really care what you want, ma'am. Get over here."

She began to shake, coming down from the adrenaline rush. Hadn't she been through enough today? "No. He'll yell at me."

"You're lucky I need a laugh, ma'am, because you're sure giving me one. But that's it. Get over here."

She moved to him, breathing in gasps. The body of the telephone, a black and silver model, perched on the raised ledge of the reception desk. The "in use" light glowed red. Cavanaugh's voice sounded tinny and much too far away. "Theresa?"

"I'm sorry, Chris." Her hurried breaths dissolved into sobbing. "I'm sorry."

"Theresa, it's all right," he soothed, and sounded as if he meant it. But then, feigning empathy was his stock-in-trade. "We'll get through this okay."

"I'm sorry."

"Calm down. It's all right."

"I'm sorry. Tell Oliver I'm sorry."

"Just calm down, okay? I will get you out of there."

"Shouldn't make promises you don't know you can keep," Lucas observed.

Theresa choked out, "Is Paul all right?"

"He's in the ambulance now. They're—"

Lucas interrupted. "Okay, you spoke. Now the lady is going to sit down and you're going to hang up, Chris, because, like I said, I don't need you no more." He gave Theresa a small shove. She walked with leaden feet to join another woman who had lost her other half.

Perhaps Paul would live.

Perhaps she would not.

Was it worth it? Would Rachael agree? Would the girl ever forgive her mother for taking the risk, even if she lived? Even if Paul lived?

Ultimately it didn't matter. She couldn't stand by and do nothing while he died. She could not.

It was too late now anyway.

Stick to it.

Across the street Cavanaugh ripped off his headset and turned to Patrick. "Who the hell's Oliver?"

CHAPTER 17

12:35 P.M.

"Listen up, people." Lucas addressed them as a group while Bobby hovered nearby, out of sniper range.

Theresa took in her surroundings; the room she'd been watching in black and white had suddenly blossomed into reality, like Dorothy's Technicolor Oz. The polished granite and the soaring, painted ceilings were quite beautiful. Pity to turn it into a mausoleum, a place for the dead.

"It's twelve-thirty," Lucas said. "I don't want to hang around here waiting for that afternoon shipment, do you?"

He didn't get a response but didn't seem to expect one.

"So let's forget that, and let's forget the computerized vaults downstairs and their uncooperative robots. Where else is there money in this building? Anyone? Brad—jeez, relax, Brad, I'm not going to shoot you. I've got my car, so you're safe. Where is the money?"

"If I tell you, will you let me go?"

Lucas studied him. "You getting cute on me, Brad?

You think because Theresa and I made a deal that the table is suddenly open?"

The young man swallowed hard. "Yes. I'll tell you if you let me walk out of here."

"That doesn't sound like a bad deal. I'd still have six of your coworkers, right?"

Brad nodded, his head bobbing quickly; his fellow hostages were on their own.

Next to him Missy clenched her fists as if restraining herself from slugging him. "Thanks a lot."

"Don't blame Brad because he's less than altruistic. Some people are. Okay, tell me where the money is. When I have it in my bag, you can leave."

The man opened his mouth, shut it again. He frowned in thought.

"You don't really know, do you, Brad? You figured I'd take your word for it and shove you out the door. There'd be no one around but your fellow hostages by the time I found out you lied."

"No, really, I just need to think a minute. I'm usually guiding little kids around. . . ."

"You work on it, Brad."

"But I'm only twenty-four!"

"And that's relevant to me . . . why, exactly?"

"I can't *die*."

"I thought that once, too, Brad. Anyone else? And before you ask, no, I won't let you walk out. But once I have enough cash, I'll leave, and then you can all go."

No response. Theresa's breath had finally steadied, and the white spots had disappeared from her vision. Next to her, Jessica Ludlow fidgeted, her son shifting in her lap.

"Missy? I'll bet you can tell me. Receptionists know everything. They're almost as good as janitors."

"I don't."

"The way I figure it, if I can pick up another million dollars, I'll just go on my merry way. Or I can hang out here and continue to shoot people. Which do you think is a better idea?"

"I thought you wanted to leave," Theresa said. "You said you didn't want any more money."

Lucas barely glanced at her. "I only said that to get my car in place before the next stage of wealth accumulation commences, because that sort of activity makes cops antsy. Missy?"

"If I knew where a million dollars was, you think I'd be working as a receptionist?"

"Yes, I do. Because you're an honest girl, Missy. And also because you'd never get it out of here without one of these." Lucas gestured with the automatic rifle, its barrel drawing a loop in the air. "Neither condition restricts me."

He stood in front of them, in scuffed Timberland hiking boots, a crisp black T-shirt under the nylon Windbreaker. His jeans seemed crisply new as well, but they had already been stained. Dark droplets made a vertical line on his right leg, difficult to see against the dark fabric. Their tiny tails pointed toward his head, indicating that the liquid had been cast off by a soaked object traveling upward. He had been doing something messy before entering the bank.

"I'm always down here," Missy said. "That's it. I don't have the run of the building."

"We'll go logically. What's on the second floor?"

"Research."

"And the third?"

"Check Services. Verifying and correcting."

"No cash?"

"That's the beauty of checks," Missy pointed out. "All electronic."

"Where are the security guards?"

"Sixth. No cash there either."

They stared at each other.

"What's in the security offices?"

"Desks. File cabinets. Lots of food."

"Food?"

"For the dogs. Monitors. A meeting room."

"Monitors showing what?"

"The building."

"What parts of it?"

"All of it. There's cameras on every floor."

"This lobby?"

Why did he ask? As Cavanaugh had pointed out, the cameras were clearly visible.

"Sure, this lobby. The vaults. The loading dock. Third floor. The—"

"What's on the third floor?"

Missy hesitated. She had erred somehow, and the knowledge showed clearly on his face. "Bank Loans."

"What's that?"

"How would I know?"

"I'm willing to bet you could run the department if you had a fancy degree after your name. I'm willing to bet you know all about it. So don't make me shoot Brad after all, okay? What's in the bank-loan department?"

The girl sighed. "If banks are having a shortfall, or some other temporary crisis, they come in here and get a loan to tide them over. They get a certain interest rate and—anyway, most of it is done by electronic transfers."

"But some isn't?"

"Some cash," Missy admitted, less reluctant now

that the subject had been broached, "is kept on hand in case of an old-fashioned run, where customers come in and want to withdraw all their funds. Never used to happen before 9/11. Now, with terrorism scares and worries about another blackout—"

"Thank you for the financial analysis, Missy. Where is this money kept?"

"Don't know," the receptionist told him, with a trace of smugness. "I'm always down here, like I said."

"How much cash?"

"I wouldn't know that either."

Lucas watched the young woman, his stare on a slow simmer. "Well. We need to get that money."

Missy shook her head.

"You got a problem with that, sugar?" Lucas asked.

"No, but you might. There's still security in the rest of the building. You won't make it."

"Of course not. It'd be suicide even to try. That's why I'm going to send someone else."

His eye fell on Theresa, producing a mixture of feelings. She'd be more than happy to wander around the Fed, more than happy to be anywhere except in this lobby. She could probably find a phone to check on Paul's condition and call Rachael.

Lucas said, "Jessie."

All eyes swiveled to the young mother, so that Theresa could openly study the recently widowed woman. Jessica Ludlow had luminous blue eyes and washed-out blond hair that hung, without much form, past her shoulders. Her body type fell between average and chubby, and her hunched-over posture did not help. Like Theresa, she wore a silk blouse, and it clung to her perspiring sides.

The little boy clutched to her chest had the same

hair, though with a few darker blond streaks. He dozed now, his eyelids lifting momentarily, then closing again. His mouth and nose had reddened, and his breath came out in small wheezes, ruffling a wrinkle in his mother's sleeve. Her arms tightened around him.

"You're going to go to three and find the bank-loan cash."

"Me?" She squeaked the word. "I work down here. I print certificates and send out interest statements, that's all."

"You don't have to join the staff on three, just bring the cash back here."

"How?"

"Excuse me?"

She pressed the child closer to herself. Theresa wondered how the kid could breathe. "How? I don't even know where it is. If it's locked up, how do I get it out?"

"You'll figure something out."

She seemed surprised at the idea. "I will not!"

"Now, Jessie." Lucas being soothing sounded even more terrifying than Lucas being threatening. "You're not cooperating. Do you remember what happened to the last person who didn't cooperate?"

Jessica Ludlow bent her head over her child's and closed her eyes.

"I'll go," Theresa said.

Lucas regarded her coolly. "I don't recall asking for volunteers."

"How much can she do with a baby in tow? I can do it."

"You don't even work here."

"I've only been here a month," Jessica pointed out, much to her captor's displeasure.

His scowl deepened when Brad raised his hand as if in class. "No, I'll go. I can get it—I have the combination."

"You? You're a tour guide. Why would you have access to bank-loan money?"

The man hesitated for only a moment. "I used to date a girl who worked for the auditor. She knew everything about every department here. I can get you as much as you want."

Theresa didn't believe him, and she tended to believe everybody. Lucas didn't either. "This is not up for discussion. I'll even explain my reasoning, to make it perfectly clear. You"—the barrel of the automatic rifle tipped toward Brad—"have no reason to come back to this lobby and every reason not to. Same goes for you, Theresa—you got your man out of here. If you get out of this room, you can go hold his hand in a hospital somewhere and not give a thought to all these people I'm going to shoot because you didn't come back. Why not? You don't know them."

"I wouldn't do th—"

"I'm not casting aspersions on your character, now, just assembling the facts from my point of view. Jessie, on the other hand, has that maternal-instinct thing going. She's going to go and get the cash, but her baby will stay here."

She gasped, cupping the boy's head against her shoulder.

"That makes her the only person in this room I *know* will come back. Isn't that right? Even if you're scared. Even if the cops tell you not to. Even if you have to smash down the bank-loan department chief's door with a desk chair. You'll do that, and you'll come back here, won't you?"

She nodded, with horror in her eyes.

Lucas winked at Theresa. "Motherhood. Never underestimate it. You can hold the kid while she goes on this scavenger hunt. Hand the kid to Theresa, Jessie. She'll take care of him."

The young woman couldn't make herself relinquish her child, not until Lucas aimed the automatic rifle at her head. Then she shifted the small, warm body to Theresa with the solemnity of a death knell and an expression to match. Her hand lingered on his back until Lucas told her to stand up.

Theresa accepted the boy almost as reluctantly as his mother had given him up. The situation was about to deteriorate even more.

She watched as Lucas picked up the red backpack off the floor and dumped its contents into the oversize duffel at Bobby's feet. He brought the bag, a simple red nylon sack with a Spider-Man logo, over to them; his passage set off another volley of barking from the K-9 unit's dog, so that he had to raise his voice to instruct Jessica Ludlow, "Take this. Fill it up. Do not let the cops add any dye packs, GPS devices, et cetera. As soon as you get back, I'm going to unload this pack into another bag, so anything planted in here will be found. Every item I find in this bag that isn't money is one bullet that goes into your boy there."

The young woman paled.

"You've got twenty minutes. Every five minutes after twenty minutes, I put a bullet in your boy. You don't come back at all, then neither does he. Got it?"

"But how . . . ?"

"I'm sure security is running all over this building. They can help you. They'll want to use you to get to me, but I've got a gun pointed at your little boy's head and they don't, so who wins here? Hmm?"

Jessica didn't take long to think about that one. "You do."

"Right." He handed her the empty backpack. Then, with a hand on her shoulder, he turned her around and gave her a slight shove toward the elevators in the employee lobby. She did not take her eyes from her son until she disappeared around the marble information desk.

The boy twitched violently in his sleep, as if rocking in the wake of her departure. Theresa rubbed his back and wished the dog would pipe down. She didn't relish the thought of having to explain to a two-year-old that his mother had gone on a bank robber's errand. She had no faith that the security force would allow Jessica's maternal instinct to overcome her self-preservation. They certainly would not have allowed Theresa to trade herself for Paul. If they could have stopped her, they would have.

The baby stirred. *They always know,* Theresa thought, *a parent from a nonparent. I don't smell like her, I don't pat his back like she does. My shoulder is bonier.* A host of subconscious clues were telling him that he'd been abandoned to a stranger, and they would prod his conscious into investigating. And she doubted that Lucas would have much patience with a crying child. She rubbed his back again. *Please sleep.*

"You," Lucas said to her again. "Scientist lady. What are they doing at the command center?"

"Watching you."

"Through the windows?"

She nodded.

"And the cameras here?" Lucas gestured at the walls, where the lobby cameras nestled in the corners.

She nodded again.

That didn't satisfy him. "Answer me when I ask you a question."

She pointed at the small boy's back. "He'll wake up. My voice isn't familiar."

"I don't care much about baby's naptime, Theresa. I can handle cryin' kids. What do they know about us, me and Bobby? Ah, you're hesitating. That's not a good idea, Theresa. It makes me nervous. It makes me think you're lying to me."

Again she gestured at the small boy in her arms, keeping her voice as quiet as possible. "I don't want to wake him. They know that Bobby's last name is Moyers and that he just got out of jail in Atlanta."

Bobby moved closer, listening.

Lucas had been standing still, but somehow he became even more so, a change minute enough that it could have been a trick of the light. It prompted her to explain, "They traced the car. It's registered to him."

"Uh-huh. And what do they know about me?"

"Nothing." The child stirred in her arms.

Did he relax just slightly? "Nothing at all?"

"Not a thing. About that car—they didn't want me to take it. I sort of stole it."

Now Lucas actually grinned. "A car-stealing scientist lady. I'm *so* glad you decided to join us, Theresa."

"My point is, they don't want you to have it. You might want to leave sooner rather than later, in case they move it away again."

He threw a glance over his shoulder, but said, "I'm not too worried about that. Bobby and I can shoot one or two of you before any cop could even make it to the car."

"Unless they use an armored vehicle," she persisted—perhaps unwisely, but she so desperately wanted them to *leave. Now,* so she could get to the hospital and see Paul before she was fired and possibly jailed for interfering with a police operation. "They could just push the car out of the way without exposing anyone to your fire."

"Damn," Bobby said. "That would screw up the transmission for sure."

"Relax," Lucas told him. "We see anyone or anything come near the car, we shoot one of these fine people here. That will get them to back off. No one's going to do anything to your pearl."

"They probably already have," his partner grumbled. "You can't trust them."

The little boy gave one more convulsive shudder, lifted his head from Theresa's shoulder, looked directly into her eyes, and screamed.

12:36 P.M.

"I don't know any Oliver," Patrick said. The idea of Theresa's trying to pass them a clue made him nervous. He wondered what the hell she was doing—first she walked into the lion's den to save Paul Cleary, his partner, whom *he* should have been saving, and then she starts playing Nancy Drew? If she got out of this alive, he would kill her.

The FBI special agent in charge had been and gone, shaking his head in disbelief at Theresa's actions. Assistant Chief of Police Viancourt had wandered back in and taken a seat at the small desk, his gaze ping-ponging between Patrick and the hostage negotiator.

"She must have said that for a reason," Cavanaugh insisted. "Who might know what she meant? Jason, get us through to that ambulance. Maybe the wounded cop knows."

"Or the lab," Patrick said. "Her boss, Leo, or Don might know."

In five minutes Jason reported that Paul had lapsed into unconsciousness and the medics didn't think he would be coming around soon. In fact, the medics didn't sound too enthusiastic about his overall condition, Jason added to Patrick, using a gentle tone that only grated on the older cop's nerves.

All Patrick needed to know was that Paul was still alive. Though he wondered why. . . . Why hadn't Lucas taken a second shot, finished him off? Sure, Paul had been incapacitated and was no longer a threat, but still, most guys kept shooting once they began. Maybe Lucas thought of Theresa's idea even before she did. Bargaining over Paul had certainly gotten him what he wanted.

Or maybe the guy just wasn't a killer. But then, what had happened to Cherise?

Cavanaugh, meanwhile, had Don on the speakerphone. "*¿Qué hace allí?*" the DNA analyst snapped. "*¿Cómo pudo usted dejar Theresa ir—*"

"*La sacaremos,*" Cavanaugh said. "*No se preocupe.*"

"You had *better* get her out safely! How could you let her go in there in the first place?"

Patrick leaned over the desk to interject, "Don, who's Oliver?"

The young man paused, probably in surprise. "There's a guy named Oliver in Toxicology."

Cavanaugh explained what Theresa had said to him. "We're assuming that's some kind of clue. What is her relationship with Oliver? Are they friends?"

"Nobody's friends with Oliver—he's too big a pain in the ass. But Theresa can get more out of him than anyone else. She gave him some stuff from that dead guy this morning. That's probably what she meant. You want me to transfer you?"

"No, stay with me a minute. Jason will get Oliver on another line. What can you tell me about Theresa? Have you ever seen her under pressure?"

"*Pressure?* We work for Leo."

Apparently Don also had them on speakerphone, because they heard the boss's voice in the background. "Hey!"

"This job is nothing *but* pressure. Theresa handles it. The bodies just keep coming in, attorneys get in her face, she just gets colder and quieter."

"Is she likely to take action?"

Patrick wondered why the hell Cavanaugh wasn't asking *him*. He had known Theresa since the day she was born—but then Cavanaugh didn't know that. He spoke up. "No."

"No," Leo said.

Don sounded defensive. "She's very tough."

"But not assertive," Patrick said.

"I don't know," Leo put in. "She certainly gets up-pity enough with me."

"So she's more likely to cooperate, to try and keep things calm," Cavanaugh said.

"Unless they're going to hurt someone," Don insisted. "Then she'll rip the guy's heart out."

"I guess we've just seen evidence of that. Thank you. I'm going to hang up now. Jason's got Oliver on the other line."

"*Espero que usted sea tan bueno como dicen,*" Don warned. I hope you're as good as they say you are.

"I'm better," Cavanaugh told him, and hit a button on the phone. "Is this Oliver?"

"Who wants to know?"

Patrick leaned over the microphone. "Oliver, this is Patrick from Homicide. Did you talk to Theresa today?"

"Yeah."

"What about?"

"*Now* what's going on?"

"*What did she say?*"

Patrick didn't care for the appraising look Cavanaugh gave him, perhaps considering if Patrick would need to be evicted from the command center as well.

"I told her the dirt from the floor mat of that car was oxidized soil. Red clay, if you will." After another moment he added, "I assume from your silence that means about as much to you as it did to me."

"Like from the southern states," Patrick said. "Georgia."

"Sure, could be."

"Anything else?" Cavanaugh asked.

"Yeah. About forty-five minutes ago, I called her back with the smear that was on your dead guy's shoulder this morning. She collected it from . . . let me see—"

"His suit coat," Patrick supplied.

"Yeah. And I told her it was cyclotrimethylene trinitramine." Not even the hollow sound of the speakerphone could disguise the disdain in his voice. "Now I assume from your silence that you have no idea what I just said."

"Is that C-4?" Cavanaugh asked.

"RDX, actually, but you've got the general idea."

"Plastic explosives?" Patrick sat down. "Can this get any worse?"

Oliver pointed out with unseemly haste, "Things can always get *worse*."

"Where would they get RDX?" Patrick mused. "Maybe Lucas was in the military. Bobby sure wasn't."

Oliver spoke again. "Considering the liberal use of Vaseline as a plasticizer, they probably made it themselves. All you really need is bleach and potassium chloride."

"What are they going to do with that?" Patrick wondered. "And where is it? It's not in the car."

Cavanaugh stared at the monitor. "They could have it strapped to themselves, but I can't see it. The jackets hang open, and there doesn't seem to be anything on or under the T-shirts."

"It's hard to tell," Jason offered, "with dark colors against dark colors on a black-and-white monitor."

"That leaves the duffel bags. Oliver, how stable is this stuff?"

"It all depends on the skill of your amateur terrorist, how thoroughly he filtered the crystals out, et cetera. If it hasn't gone off yet, that's your best indication." The toxicologist paused for a split second, then added, "It's . . . um, not near Theresa, is it?"

"It's about ten feet away," Patrick told him. "I assume from *your* silence that this situation is less than ideal."

"I couldn't have said it better myself, Detective."

Patrick eyed the monitor. "I'm going over there."

The air hung still, without even a fishy breeze from the lake to lift the sand-colored strands of hair from Patrick's forehead. He took the long way around, down East Third and up Rockwell to the rear of the Federal Reserve building. Beyond the sawhorses blocking the roads, Clevelanders were going about their daily business, working, eating lunch, ducking out of the heat and back into the air-conditioning before their ties wrinkled and their makeup ran. He passed the corner where Pat Joyce's Tavern used to sit and found himself wishing for his younger years, when whether or not to write out a parking ticket would be the toughest decision he had to make the whole day.

Unless he wanted to walk all the way around the Hampton Inn to the Superior entrance, Patrick needed to enter the building via a plunging vehicle ramp overseen by a guard turret encased in glass, which Patrick assumed to be bulletproof—and air-conditioned, or the poor guy in it would have passed out by now.

His badge got him inside without getting shot. One of the many Fed security SRT responders, sweating in his assault gear, escorted Patrick up to Mulvaney's office on the sixth floor. The chief of the Fed security force wasn't happy.

"What the hell did she do that for? Driving that car up to the door! One of my guys got shot at in order to take their wheels away, and she gives it *back* to them?"

"Trying to save a cop's life."

"And did she?" Mulvaney's head bobbed from side to side as he studied his mosaic of surveillance videos. "Did he live?"

"Don't know yet."

"There she is, that other girl." Jessica Ludlow appeared on one of the monitors. She had just stepped out of the elevator onto the third floor. "Let's go."

He didn't seem to care, or even notice, if Patrick tagged along.

They caught up with her in the hallway—the young mother no doubt further terrorized to have a group of large, heavily armed men descend upon her, but that could not be helped. Mulvaney identified himself.

"You have to let me go back," she said. Her entire body shook, the jumbled blond hairs quivering like plucked harp strings. "If I don't go back, he'll kill my son."

Without thinking, Patrick reached out to pat her shoulder, and she jumped away like a startled rabbit. "Don't worry, Mrs. Ludlow. We're doing everything we can."

"You know who I am? Is my husband here? Where's my husband?"

Patrick kept his expression neutral. The woman seemed close enough to collapse; learning of her husband's murder would finish her off. "We've evacuated the building."

"All the employees are next door or sent home," Mulvaney added.

"I have to go back," she repeated. "You can't stop me from going back to the lobby. He'll kill Ethan—"

Mulvaney stepped forward, which only made her retreat farther until she bumped into the glass door labeled BANK LOANS. "We understand, Mrs. Ludlow. We're not going to stop you from delivering the money if your child's life is at stake. I hate to let you go back there, but we don't appear to have any choice."

She breathed in a huge sigh of relief; it seemed to fill her entire body with air. After she let it out, she spoke a good deal more calmly. "He wants me to pack this bag with money, like a million dollars or something."

Mulvaney extended a hand for the backpack, but she held it to her chest. "No, he wants this exact bag back. He's going to make me or one of the other hostages unpack it and repack all the stuff, so we can't put any dye packs or locators in with the money. If there is, he'll kill my son." Her moment of relief, of trust that the cavalry could ride in and save her, had passed. The pitch of her voice rose with each word, and she seemed more afraid of them than of the robbers in the lobby.

"Okay," Mulvaney soothed.

"You have to help me get the money."

"It's okay," the security chief told her. "That, we can do. Come this way."

"I've never even been on this floor." She followed him, flanked by Patrick and four security guards. "When I got in the elevator, I went to the eighth floor because I pushed the wrong button. But then I used the restroom. I had to. I thought I was going to pee my pants." She sniffed. "I *had* to. But if I'm not back in twenty minutes—"

"It's okay, Mrs. Ludlow. You have eleven minutes left, and this won't take that long."

Patrick longed to ask her . . . what? How Theresa was doing? He could watch that himself on the monitors, and Jessica Ludlow had barely met Theresa; the young woman wouldn't have any insight as to her mental state. Ditto the robbers, but he had to try. "We've been watching on the lobby cameras, Mrs. Ludlow, but is there anything you can tell us about those two men? Anything they might have said to each other?"

"No." She answered Patrick without taking her eyes off the security chief as she followed him through the glass door, nearly tripping in her haste. "They don't talk much. He says more to us than the other guy."

"Anything stand out about them? A tattoo? A smell?"

"No. I can't think of anything, I'm sorry. All I can think about is Ethan and that big gun."

Mulvaney led her and her escorts past a grouping of desks to a set of double doors too narrow to lead to a room. The metal latch system in the middle of the two doors had a thin gap for a magnetic card, and a numbered keypad. Mulvaney punched in six numbers in quick succession.

Despite his agitation Patrick found himself curious about the Fed's building security. It seemed pretty thorough. Lucas must know something about it, at least enough to know better than to try to get around it. "You have the code?"

"The director of this department whispered it over his cell phone about five minutes ago," Mulvaney said as he gave the latch a twist. The heavy metal doors opened to reveal a set of drawers, each with its own lock. "As soon as this crisis ends, he'll come in and program a new code, known only to himself and the board. You know how it goes. They don't let us cops near the money, only the guns."

Jessica Ludlow stared in dismay. Set into the wall were twelve drawers, three across, four down. Each seemed as wide as paper money was long. Each had a smaller version of the card swipe/numeric keypad latch on its face. "Is that where the money is? How are we going to get in there?"

"Ten minutes." One of the security guards, who held a stopwatch, announced to Mulvaney.

"That was the second thing the director whispered in my ear," Mulvaney said in answer to Jessica Ludlow. "I think he found it personally painful." He opened three drawers with what seemed to be the same numeric code, sliding each one out and setting it on the carpeted floor. Each had been filled to the top with one-hundred-dollar bills, held in bundles with paper bands.

Jessica Ludlow sank to her knees and opened her backpack. One of the security guards tried to pull it away gently. "I'll fill it for you."

She wouldn't let the nylon bag out of her hand. "No! It has to be me. . . . It's my son's life. Please."

"Of course," the young man placated. "But it will go faster if I help you."

She held the bag open as the young man dropped in the bundles. "There can't be any dye packs, you know, or whatever other security things you might have."

"Don't worry, Mrs. Ludlow," Mulvaney assured her. "We don't put anything like that in these drawers. We've always assumed a robber would never get this far."

His tone did not convince Patrick, who caught his eye. Mulvaney seemed to nod, and the Homicide detective said nothing. He was in another agency's house now and would have to trust their judgment in an area of crime that he, Patrick, seldom dealt with. But any surprise Lucas received might prompt him to kill another hostage. He'd shot Paul; choosing Theresa, who had traded herself for Paul, might have an appealing symmetry to the sick son of a bitch. "We wouldn't do anything to startle the robbers," Patrick said, speaking to Jessica Ludlow's bent head but looking at Mulvaney.

"We won't," the security chief confirmed.

"That's all I can fit." The blond woman struggled with the bag's zipper. "How much is it? I lost count."

The guard who had helped her said, "Eight hundred forty thousand."

"Seven minutes," the other one reported.

The young woman hefted the backpack with a grimace. Patrick thought for a moment that he could smell her fear, a sharp, sweaty odor. "That might not be enough," she worried. "I'm sure he said a million."

"It's all you can fit in that bag," Mulvaney pointed out.

Jessica slung one strap over her shoulder and weaved through the cubicles, making for the elevator like a student late for class. The men had to trot to keep up with her.

The elevator doors stood open; this apparently confused her, because she stopped and did not go in.

"We shut it off," Mulvaney explained, reaching in and flicking a red switch before holding the doors for her. "So you wouldn't have to wait for it."

Then she moved inside quickly and stood at the front, as if trying to bar them from entering. "You can't come with me. He said I had better come back alone."

"I know," the security chief said. "And I'm sorry. We'd rather do anything in the world than have to send you back there, Mrs. Ludlow. You're a brave woman."

She pushed the "L" button. "He has my baby."

The doors began to slide shut. Patrick's stomach seemed to shrink; it went against a cop's grain to let an unarmed civilian walk into a criminal's power, it battled with every instinct he had. But he could not see a solution.

With five inches to go, her palm slammed against the moving door. She spoke to Patrick, as if answering one of his earlier questions. "One thing. It was after they shot that guy in the blazer, the one that new lady asked them to let go. Lucas said to the other guy,

'If the cops come in after us, we have to kill them all.'
But he nodded his head at us as he said it. He didn't
mean you cops, he meant he'd have to kill *us*. The hostages."

The doors slid shut.

Before he left, Patrick asked the Fed security chief
about the money packs. "There's really nothing in
there?"

"Nothing this scumbag is going to figure out."

"If he does, who do you think he's going to pick for
his next example? He's already shot one cop—why
not one of yours? Or our scientist?"

Mulvaney held the door to the stairwell for him,
possibly implying that Patrick shouldn't let it hit him
in the butt on the way out. "It's not in the money. You
have to keep this to yourself, and I mean it—the employees here don't even know about it, for obvious
reasons. There's a metallic tracer in the bands, but all
it will do is show up at the metal detector by the doors.
I wasn't lying—a robber, under normal circumstances,
would never make it to that vault, so there aren't any
standard security devices there. The bands are meant
to catch thieves who work here and decide to cut out
early one day and head to Aruba. Last time that happened was 1963."

"So Lucas won't notice—"

"He might hear a beep when they go out the doors,
but since the guy's carrying a damn M4 carbine, I don't
think it's going to worry him much. Unfortunately, it's
not going to help us at all either."

"Mmm." Patrick checked Theresa's status on the security unit's monitors but grew frustrated with the

lousy audio quality. At least in the library he could hear the phone conversations. He hurried back up Rockwell, hoping nothing had happened to Theresa in his absence. Not that he could do a bloody thing about it anyway.

CHAPTER 19

1 2:4 6 P.M.

Six stories down, Theresa remained occupied with the squirming child on her lap.

Two-year-old Ethan pushed at her, trying to get away from this stranger, and hit her with the stuffed Cleveland Browns dog. She gave him a bit of space but wouldn't let go. His screams pierced her eardrums.

"Told you so," she said to Lucas.

"Don't hassle me, ma'am. You should be able to handle kids—you've got your own."

He must have overheard her conversation with Rachael. "Just one, and it's been a long time since she was two."

Lucas glanced at his watch. "Hang in there. His mama's only got seven minutes left. And how'd you know he was two?"

Her lungs seemed to seize up, and she covered herself by getting a firmer grip on the writhing boy and turning him to face outward. "He's pretty solid for his size. And he's definitely got all his teeth, since he just bit me with them."

Lucas watched her with a cool, shark-eyed stare, but said only, "Don't bite, Ethan. It's a nasty habit."

The boy quieted, distracted by the sweeping room and the mysterious man in front of him. He straddled Theresa's thigh, with one of her arms firmly around his waist. "Bo," he said, suddenly and clearly, shaking the stuffed animal. "Bo."

"That don't concern me," Lucas answered, his eyes on Theresa still. "What concerns me is your mama has five minutes and twenty seconds left."

"I still don't see how you expect a young girl to find and then break into a small vault, or whatever the heck is up there," Theresa said.

"You'd be amazed what people can do when they have the proper incentive."

"You've got some money, you have your car. You could leave now and come out way ahead." Theresa wished she could have read Cavanaugh's book before getting herself into this. Whatever she said might agitate him, spur him on. On the other hand, she couldn't sit idly by while he shot a two-year-old.

"You think so, do you?"

"I'm probably going to get fired for giving you that car, if not thrown in jail. I'd hate to have it be for nothing."

"Yeah, what about that?" He crouched in front of her, putting them at the same eye level, submachine gun across his knees. The sudden advance startled her. "You did that because you love that cop?"

"You're not watching the street. They might come for your car."

"The marble behind you, Theresa, is as smooth as a mirror. I can see any movement outside. Cops are many things, but invisible is not one of them. Now, did you come here because you're in love with that cop?"

Love. Something she had almost convinced herself didn't exist until one night when Paul suddenly put his arms around her, outside a ring of crime-scene tape in the Metroparks after everyone else had left. He hadn't asked her to dinner or a movie or out for drinks, knowing that her defense system would rise if forewarned. He simply stepped inside the castle walls before she had time to lower the gate.

She swallowed. "Yes."

"Crazy, the things people do for love."

She couldn't speak around the lump in her throat.

"Bo," the child insisted.

"Is that what you're robbing this place for?" Theresa asked him. "Love?"

"You trying to analyze me, Theresa? Figure me out? Or just distract me from the fact that Ethan's mom has twenty-seven seconds remaining?"

"I'd like to know why my fiancé is bleeding to death and why my daughter may have to grow into adulthood without a mother."

He edged closer to her, so close she could see the red veins standing out against the whites of his eyes, could smell the last traces of a breath mint on his tongue. "I'd really like to tell you, but I'm afraid you wouldn't understand."

"I might understand a lot more than you think."

He didn't actually roll his eyes, but he came close.

She went on. "I understand that someone didn't take very good care of you when you were a little boy."

The red-rimmed eyes narrowed, and his body

receded from her ever so slightly. "You saying I wasn't raised right?"

"I'm saying someone burned the inside of your left wrist with a cigarette, at least four times that I can see. I had a young man about your age in last month. The abuse had occurred when he was five, but his wounds were less distinct than yours. So you were, what? Ten? Twelve?"

He stood as quickly as if he had discovered a scorpion at his toes, checked his watch, and said, "Mama's time is up."

"You're not going to shoot this little boy."

"And who's going to stop me, Theresa? You?"

"What will it gain you, except a quick trip to a lethal injection?"

"That's assuming I get caught."

"You know you're going to be caught eventually. You're not stupid."

They certainly didn't seem to be bonding—in fact, she seemed to annoy him more with every word. Yet he kept talking to her. Why?

"I'm not going to get caught." He did not say this as if he believed it, however. The tone of his voice sounded neither boastful nor wistful; it sounded resigned, as if he knew he would do exactly that.

"Let's say you do. If you leave here without hurting anyone, the cops will pursue you, yes. But if you hurt a child, they will chase you to the very ends of the earth."

Bobby shifted in the background, but Lucas did not turn. "You seem to forget I've already killed someone."

She didn't want to mention Mark Ludlow again; it might make things worse. But he had freely discussed the bank teller. "You mean Cherise? What happened to her anyway?"

Without raising his voice he asked, "You think I didn't shoot her? You think maybe I'm faking all this?"

"No." But her voice lacked certainty.

"Anybody else here think I'm faking this?"

The other hostages, who had been present to hear the gunshot and Cherise's voice, abruptly cut off, shook their heads. Missy even cast Theresa a murderous look.

What am I doing? What she'd said to Cavanaugh was true. Forensic work burdened her with only a limited amount of personal responsibility. Sure, she cared about solving an innocent victim's murder, but if she could not, she didn't take it personally. Sometimes the evidence just wasn't there. But now she had to be proactive, and other people could die as a result. The idea made her heart pound even more than Lucas's threats.

"Set the boy down," Lucas said to Theresa, referring to Ethan. "Just leave him there."

"He'll run away."

"Missy, you hang on to the kid. I need to show Theresa something. Just hold the back of his shirt so he don't run around."

Missy moved to the other side of Brad and slid the boy from Theresa's lap, gently easing him into her own. Ethan seemed sufficiently interested in Lucas's movements and did not protest.

"Get up."

Theresa stood, her knees reluctant to move but not half as reluctant as her mind. Why had she antagonized him? Why hadn't she kept her mouth shut?

On the other hand, Lucas seemed to have forgotten Jessica Ludlow's tardiness.

The phone began to ring.

He ignored it. "Come here."

She complied. It didn't seem that she had another option. But Lucas merely grabbed her right elbow with his left hand, leaving his gun ready in his right. He prodded the muzzle of it into her rib cage, and she flinched.

"We're going to take a stroll. Just walk with me, nice and easy, and I won't have to pull this trigger, understand?"

"Yes."

He gripped her elbow tightly enough to stop the circulation, and they made a careful excursion past the other hostages. The pool of Paul's blood had developed a yellow halo as the serum separated out from the red blood cells. She looked at the security guards with a wincing glance; their barely contained fury hurt her eyes. The dog growled. The phone kept ringing.

The teller cages continued in the marble and gilt tradition of the rest of the lobby. Behind the fancy ironwork grates sat counters filled with the accoutrements of work: tape dispensers, staplers, rubber stamps of all sizes and shapes, framed photos of adorable children. The third drawer down at each station had been pried open, the locks mangled, except for one. Cherise's work area, complete with a nameplate and a photo of herself and a boyfriend with a beach in the background. The entire drawer, undamaged, lay on the floor.

Theresa took this in as they passed. Lucas did not pause but continued past the tellers' cages, around to the narrow, walled-off section behind them. Theresa could already smell it. The burnt gunpowder and the tinny odor of blood.

On a worn section of carpet, directly below a stack

of computer printouts and a half-empty coffeepot, the young woman had bled out onto the springy carpet. This, then, was the missing Cherise.

1:00 P.M.

Patrick had never felt more helpless. Returning to the library's video monitor only to find Theresa missing from the hostage's lineup had been déjà vu in the worst way. Cherise had gone off in the same direction and hadn't come back. Paul had been shot before their eyes, or before the cold black-and-white eyes of the video monitor. Now Theresa, and he couldn't do a damn thing to stop it. He should have stayed over there. No, he should have stayed here, made Cavanaugh distract Lucas. "Why didn't you do something?"

"I called. He ignored the phone. But she's all right. We're catching snatches of her voice."

"Maybe it's time to use the snipers. Or the assault time. Or the 101st Airborne."

"The snipers are ready," Cavanaugh said. "They've had a hundred opportunities to pick off Lucas, but Bobby stays out of range. He could shoot a few hostages or set off their RDX, wherever they've got it. For amateurs they've been pretty careful so far."

"Do we know they're amateurs?" Assistant Chief Viancourt asked.

"We don't know much of anything at the moment."

Jason hung up his cell phone. He had spent enough time on it to leave a red slash across his face. "Lucas Winston Parrish was injured five years ago in an explosion during a training mission in Germany. He was stationed at the base there. He still carries a few pieces of shrapnel against his ribs."

Patrick sighed. "Theresa called it."

"Maybe," Cavanaugh said. "What else?"

"He told the military that both his parents were dead, and the prison said he had one visitor during the five years he spent at Atlanta—his sister. She lives in North Carolina and isn't answering her phone."

Cavanaugh massaged beads of sweat into his face. "What did he do in the military?"

"Armory clerk."

"So he knows guns. And at least the basics of explosives."

"I'd like to know where he got those two." Patrick nodded at the monitor. "That's a lot of firepower for a bum just out of jail."

Cavanaugh asked Jason, "Did Atlanta say he and Bobby were friends?"

"No one there knows. Of the regular guards on their cell block, one is off on a fishing trip and the other one is in the hospital."

"Prison riot?"

"Heart attack."

"And Bobby had no visitors."

"There's one more thing. Parrish had one other person on his visitor's list—a Jack Cornell in Tennessee. The guy never visited, but he had him listed. There was a Jack Cornell in his unit in the army."

"That's his gun connection, I'll bet," Patrick said. "Lucas came here from Atlanta by way of Tennessee."

Cavanaugh opened the cooler next to Irene and pulled out a dripping bottle of water for Jason. "Here, you deserve it. Get us Cornell on the phone. We definitely need to talk to him."

"*Talk* to him." Patrick perched on the window seat and lit a cigarette. "We need him picked up by the Tennessee cops. He's the best suspect for providing not only the guns but the plastic explosive as well."

Cavanaugh swiped at the sweat on his temples with one hand. "If they show up at his door, they could be walking into a literal powder keg. On top of which, he might wind up too preoccupied with his own problems to talk to us about ours. We've got two dead people here and a bunch of hostages, and he's not going to be willing to own up to his part in that. Jason, you silver-tongued devil, get the right cops in Tennessee on the line and tell them everything we've got. They'll have to handle it as they see fit. They might even know the guy."

Patrick took one more deep puff before tamping the butt on the bottom of his shoe. "I'd send someone to the sister as well. At least she's got more incentive to help, if she wants her brother to live through the day."

CHAPTER 20

12:55 P.M.

Theresa gazed at the dead girl. Auburn curls crowned Cherise's face, in which a slash of red lips and sightless blue eyes stood out against the paled skin. A screwdriver lay a few inches from her right hand. She had been wearing a shiny cream blouse and dove gray slacks; the slacks were spattered with a fine mist of red dots, but the center of the blouse disappeared into a gaping, bloody hole. He must have fired more than once; Theresa did not know how delicate the trigger on such a weapon would be, how easy it would be to blow away a target's entire rib cage before the index finger could loosen. It looked pretty damn easy.

"You killed her," Theresa breathed, the words sounding ridiculous even to her own ears.

"I said so, didn't I?"

"I had hoped—Why the hell did you *kill* her?"

"She didn't cooperate."

Theresa eyed the Craftsman. Did he make Cherise use the screwdriver to pry open the cash boxes, and she pulled it on him? Did he shoot her in a bizarre parody of self-defense?

But what were they doing behind the cages? Tiny dots of high-velocity blood spatter and one neat bullet hole speckled the cabinet doors to the left of the body, so she had been shot right where she lay. "What were you doing back here?"

"What?"

"What did you come back here for? The cash is in the cages, so why come back here?"

"I thought there might be more."

"That's why she had the screwdriver in her hand? Because you thought there might be more boxes for her to pry open?" *Not* self-defense, then.

"What are you doing, Theresa? Investigating?"

I look at scenes like this every day, she wanted to tell him, *and this one isn't adding up.* Besides, every moment she kept him occupied gave Jessica Ludlow another moment to return. "I want to know why you killed her. What happened?"

"I walked her up to the teller cages and told her to pry open the cash drawers." He began to guide Theresa out, talking as they walked. "Everything was cool. But when I wanted to check out the areas back here, she turns around and starts to argue. She says this area is just for paperwork, which is okay with me, but she waves this screwdriver under my nose. At that point I felt it both necessary and prudent to shoot her. She also served as a good lesson for the rest of you." His words, so mocking, did not match his voice.

"You might have gotten out of this without murdering. Now there's no going back."

He squeezed her elbow again in a vein-crushing grip as they exited the teller area. "What makes you think I *want* to go back? What do you think is the whole point of this?"

"Good question." She turned to the security guards this time, taking in their faces, the way their bodies tensed at her passage, as if frustrated that they could not help her. The dog let out one sharp whine. "What *is* the point of all this?"

"The point is that I'm more than willing to kill to get what I want." He announced this not only to her but to her fellow hostages as they returned to the reception desk. "Isn't that right, Theresa?"

They turned to her with pleading looks, wanting her to disagree. She could not. Despite the reluctance in his voice, if not his words, Lucas *had* killed without apparent hesitation or remorse. "He killed her. Cherise is dead."

Missy cried out. Brad and the security guards gasped, a single, unanimous drawing-in of breath.

Lucas released her arm, leaving a tingly sensation as the blood flowed back. "Sit back down, Theresa. Missy, let go of the kid. His mama's overdue."

"You can't shoot this baby," the receptionist intoned, just as Theresa had a scant ten minutes before.

"I'd set him aside if I were you. The bullets will go right through him into your lap."

"You ain't going to shoot this little boy."

"Theresa," Lucas said. "Take the kid from Missy."

She had been scanning the street outside—was that a movement, or a wave of heat distorting the air?—and blurted out without thinking, "Why me?"

"Because Missy wants to be a hero, an inspiration to receptionists everywhere. You, on the other hand, will do anything to get back to your man and your daughter."

"Not hold up a baby boy as a target for you."

"You sure?"

Was she? Didn't she owe it to her own child to stay alive, no matter the cost? Then what the hell was she doing here? Why hadn't she let Paul go, to be sure she could keep being a mother to Rachael?

But could she sacrifice someone else's child?

Make your decision, her grandfather had said. *Stick to it.*

"No," she told him. "I won't."

He lifted the automatic pistol, aiming downward at both the young boy and the receptionist. "Suit yourself."

"It isn't smart," Theresa warned.

"Who said I was smart?"

"You did," she insisted desperately. His finger closed on the trigger.

The phone rang.

The elevator bell dinged. Theresa heard a frenzied rush of footsteps.

Jessica Ludlow threw herself into the lobby, toting a visibly stuffed red backpack. "Stop! Don't kill him!"

Lucas ignored the phone and pointed his automatic rifle at the floor. "Well, well. Ethan's mommy has returned."

The young woman threw the backpack at Lucas's feet, went to her knees, and pulled her child back from Missy. He clutched his stuffed Browns mascot, crying.

Lucas snatched up the bag with one hand. "Take a look at this, Bobby. The little lady came through."

"I filled it up." Jessica's breath came in gasps. "The bank-loan department had cash in drawers. Hundred-dollar bills."

"Just lying around?" Lucas said. He crouched on the floor next to the large black duffel and opened the red backpack as if it were a present plucked from under a

Christmas tree. Theresa had just seen his handiwork in Cherise, but she felt positive, in her heart of hearts, that Lucas felt relieved to spare Ethan. Most people had a soft spot for children, she thought. It didn't make him any less dangerous.

The phone continued to ring.

"No," Jessica Ludlow explained. Stress made her voice bounce off the walls. "The cops met me. You said that was okay as long as I came back."

"I did. Relax, Jessie." He had emptied half the backpack when he asked, "Did they fill this bag?" He began to remove the bundles of money and place them in the oversize end pocket of one of the black duffels. He stacked them carefully, perhaps to fully utilize the space.

"No, I did. I told them not to add any dye packs or anything." She cradled Ethan's head under her chin. He let out a shout now and then, but, it seemed, more as communication than as notes of distress.

Lucas's movements slowed. "How much is here?"

"I'm . . . I'm not sure."

"Of course you are." His momentary elation faded before Theresa's eyes, and his voice turned cold and accusing. "They would have told you, because they'd expect me to ask."

Jessica Ludlow trembled. "Eight hundred forty thousand. I know you said a million, but—"

"That isn't good enough."

"I filled the bag."

"Not enough."

Jessica wrapped her arms around her baby and sank back against the marble information desk. Lucas continued to transfer the money in quick, deliberate movements.

"You have over a million," Theresa said, "with what you got from the teller cages."

He glanced at her, and somehow the fury in his eyes frightened her more than his gun. "I didn't ask you."

After he emptied the bag, he zipped the end compartment closed and folded the now-empty red backpack into a side pocket. Then he stood and whirled in a quick 360, surveying his partner as he spun. "Keep an eye on your car, Bobby. That two o'clock shipment is getting closer. We might as well wait for it."

"Come on!" Bobby didn't care for the idea. "Let's just get out of here!"

"We need more money."

"Send her back upstairs, then!"

"It worked once because the cops had no time to plan. It's not going to work a second time. Besides, we'll have all the money we can carry pulling up to the curb outside in less than an hour. Then we can go."

Next to Theresa, Jessica sighed, either in disappointment at Lucas's decision or in relief at her son's narrow escape. The phone still rang.

Between Bobby's scowl and his rough skin, he could have been a villain in a comic book. "I think it's a mistake."

"We're not done here. Do you think we're done here?"

Bobby didn't answer.

Lucas turned back to the hostages. "Missy, would you please answer that damn phone?"

CHAPTER 21

Lucas got back on the line with Cavanaugh. The pool of Paul's blood had coagulated, though the humidity from the open door kept it from drying very fast. Theresa rubbed the back of her neck and wondered if Paul had needed a transfusion. . . . Silly thought—of *course* he would need a transfusion, probably several. She wished Lucas hadn't taken her cell phone, even if she couldn't risk using it. Cell phones had become the security blankets of the twenty-first century.

Ethan took a swipe at her with his stuffed dog, as if he didn't want her to get any ideas about holding him again. He wanted his mother, and that was that.

Theresa tried not to think about Rachael's reaction, should she die.

Hell, what if she *survived*? The thought filled her with fresh terror. Rachael was not stupid. Once the shock wore off, her mind would reconstruct the events and come to this conclusion: Her mother had made a choice between her daughter's best interests and those of a boyfriend, and the boyfriend had come first. There were few crimes less forgivable than a lack of maternal instinct, and Rachael had inherited her mother's process of anger: slow, cold, and implacable.

Suddenly, dying did not seem the most frightening option.

The little boy continued to watch her, warily. Jessica Ludlow's breath had not yet slowed to normal.

Theresa leaned toward her. "Cute Browns dog."

The young woman glanced down at the stuffed animal her baby held. "He loves it."

"I remember when Burger King gave those away—it was years ago now. My daughter collected the whole set."

"I think our new neighbor gave it to him."

Dogs, Theresa thought. The dog with the security guard was trained to sniff explosives, not drugs. It barked up a storm every time Lucas passed by. She'd assumed that the dog had also been trained to recognize a bad guy when it saw one, but what if he scented plastic explosives in Lucas's aura?

She had been close to the man twice, once when he frisked her, once when he pressed an automatic pistol into her side before escorting her to see Cherise's body. She had brushed up against his chest, his sides, and felt nothing under the clothing but muscle. Even with the dark colors and the loose jacket, she could not see any suspicious bulges. And the explosives were not in the car. They could be in the duffel bag on the floor in front of her. Or they could have been installed somewhere in the offices behind the teller cages, and that was why he'd killed Cherise. He needed her to open something—what? a vault? a computer server?—so that he could set the explosives, but he couldn't leave her alive to tell the other hostages, who might panic.

But why not just detonate the explosives, if that was his plan? What he was waiting for?

And why would a target worth blowing up be found in a minimum-security area on the ground floor?

She watched Lucas converse with Cavanaugh. He had to have a plan. She shouldn't let his super-cool persona convince her that he had more brains than he really had—perhaps his only talent lay in acting—but everything she felt about him gave the impression that he did have a plan. He'd also have a backup plan, and a backup to the backup.

Maybe there was nothing of financial value in the cubicles. Maybe there was only a part of the foundation, a structural support, without which at least a few floors would collapse. She knew that four or five pounds of RDX would turn a good-size truck to pieces of rubble. He could have carried twenty pounds back there in his trip with Cherise, and no one would know. But why set the charges out of sight? There were no cameras back there, and he had killed the only witness.

Perhaps the real hostage here was the Federal Reserve building, a historic landmark built in 1923. Or was it the backup plan? Is that why Lucas had not blown it?

Perhaps he needed the RDX for his escape. A large explosion would make a great diversion. All eyes and rescue personnel would head for the destruction, while Lucas and Bobby and a hostage or two made for the Mercedes.

It could be a booby trap, so that after all the excitement had ended and the workers poured back into the building, an explosion would take some out. But deaths under those circumstances would not help him, and they would produce a relatively low body count if he meant it as some sort of protest. Whatever else he was up to here, politics did not seem to be part of it.

She needed to talk to Cavanaugh.

"Thanks for holding him." Jessica Ludlow startled her out of her reverie. "He's getting hungry, is the problem." Bobby watched them but did not tell them to shut up. Jessica Ludlow had been through an extremely stressful morning and, like most people would, needed to vent. "He's fussy now, but he's going to be ten times worse in another half hour. I have his snacks in my bag, but I don't know what that monster will do if I try to get them."

Theresa tried to soothe the worried mother. "I don't think he wants to hurt a child."

"I think he wants to hurt all of us." Jessica frowned. "Why don't these guys just *leave*?"

"I keep asking myself the same thing."

"My husband must be frantic."

Theresa's chest tightened up for a moment. She had no idea what to say. Jessica's husband lay on a gurney at the M.E.'s office, but Cavanaugh had been right. She could hardly tell Jessica that now. "I'm sure the authorities will let him know you're okay."

"But Ethan—" The young woman ran out of words, no doubt imagining her husband imagining his child's demise.

Theresa patted her shoulder. Ethan knocked at Theresa's hand with the Browns dog, pointed at his mother's floral-print handbag, and said, "Baba."

"Bottle," Jessica translated. "I told you he was hungry. We don't do bottles anymore, remember, baby? You're a big boy now."

Maybe we can use that, Theresa thought. Cavanaugh said to keep the hostage takers occupied with details to wear them down. Bringing in food would do it. She felt amazed that no one yet had asked to use the bathroom, though Cherise's fate might have put them off asking for anything.

"Theresa," Lucas called her, as if on cue. "Come here."

1:07 P.M.

"What's he doing with Theresa?" Patrick demanded to know, stalking the monitor. "What did you say to him?"

"I asked if he'd reconsider the two o'clock shipment, since it's only fifty minutes away now. That's all."

Over the speaker they heard Lucas's voice, slightly muted as he turned away from the receiver to speak to Theresa, but still clear. "Chris wants me to take the two o'clock shipment and go. This is acceptable to me, provided a SWAT team doesn't come along with it, provided all the people here cooperate in moving the money for me—got that, team?—and provided no one and nothing comes near that Mercedes parked outside. That's the deal we're working on, Theresa, to bring you up to speed. The problem is, like Bobby, I don't trust cops, and I don't trust the great Chris Cavanaugh. I think maybe he thinks I won't strike back when double-crossed. So I just need you to clarify what happens to people who don't cooperate, like Cherise, because obviously they have no camera feeds in the cubicles behind the teller cages. Understand?"

Silence, but on the monitor, Patrick could see her head move in a small nod.

"So, Theresa, what happens to people who don't cooperate?" He held out the phone.

A slight brushing sound, then Theresa's voice. "Cherise is dead. He shot her."

"Damn," Cavanaugh muttered.

"Hardly a surprise," Patrick said.

Theresa asked, "Is Paul all right?"

Patrick dropped his cigarette into Jason's empty water bottle. He hadn't even called to check. Cavanaugh caught his eye, and Patrick shrugged. Cavanaugh pushed the "talk" button on the phone.

"He's at the hospital, Theresa. That's all I can tell you," he added before changing the subject. "Did you see Cherise?"

"I did. She's very, very dead, believe me. It was an explosive sight."

A second of quiet and then a whistling sound. The receiver made a clanging noise, as if it had been dropped.

Patrick stared at the monitor in disbelief. "He hit her!"

"What?" Cavanaugh stood, moving closer to the screen, though he could see perfectly well from his chair. Lucas had ripped the phone from Theresa's hand before punching her in the face with his right fist. It had to have been hard; it knocked her completely off her feet, so that now she sprawled across Missy and Brad.

"*Shit!*" Patrick screamed.

Lucas picked up the receiver, dangling by its cord against the outer wall of the reception desk. "Excuse me a minute, Chris. Theresa and I need to have a chat."

He hung up.

Theresa had curled and rolled to all fours, trying to raise herself. With the M4 carbine in his left hand, Lucas grabbed her hair at the nape of her neck and pulled her up, marching her away before she could get her feet underneath her.

"Take the shot!" Patrick shouted, looking to the assistant chief for some backup, but the man merely stared at the TV screen with a dumbfounded expression. "He's going to shoot her just like he shot Cherise!"

Cavanaugh stared at the monitor. "Don't panic."

"Why the hell *not*? Where is the SWAT team? Where's Mulvaney?"

"He's not heading for the teller cages," Cavanaugh pointed out. Indeed, Lucas headed away from the cages, toward the east wall of the lobby.

"There are classrooms there," Patrick said. "He's trying to get her off camera."

"Why? If he wants to force us into a concession by killing someone, why do it out of our sight?"

"That's how he killed Cherise. Maybe he can't work with an audience. Take the shot. We have to take the shot." In another few steps, they would leave the center of the lobby, the small area where the snipers could see through the clear glass.

Cavanaugh hit another button on his telephone console. "Harry, you there?"

"Roger."

"Target A is taking a hostage away from the others, moving northeast. Anyone got a clear sight?"

"In sight, but chance of deflection too high. Target B not in range also."

"What's he talking about?" Patrick demanded, though he knew. A sniper could hit Lucas from across the street without a problem, but shooting through a window was another proposition altogether. The glass would alter the path of the bullet, perhaps a little, perhaps a lot. The glass in the antique Fed building might be particularly thick, and the two people were a good distance from it, so that any deflection would be amplified by the time the bullet reached them. The odds of its striking Theresa instead of Lucas were much too high.

They continued to move, two silent, dark figures on the screen.

"Oh, God." Patrick heard his own voice and hated the sound, almost like a whimper. "He wouldn't rape her, would he?"

Cavanaugh snatched up the phone, hit a button. "I'll get him back to the phone. It's all we can do."

"That's not all. SWAT has to go in." He turned to the assistant chief of police. "Viancourt. Send in the assault team."

"I can't. FBI's in charge of this operation."

"You're here, and they're not. You can act before they can stop you." What Patrick heard himself suggesting was insane, he knew. It did not even slow him down.

Viancourt gave the detective his full attention. "Sucking up to me won't get you the Homicide chief's slot."

Shock silenced him, the idea that he would use Theresa's imminent murder to get in good with the assistant chief. Patrick put one hand on the man's shoulder to make his point. Unfortunately, he wrinkled the lapel of the expensive suit by bunching it in his fist and gave the guy a little shake while he persisted in requesting the assault team. Again, déjà vu—he now played the same scene with the chief that Theresa had played with Cavanaugh, and it would have the same effect. He'd be shut out of the operation.

The assistant chief knocked his hand away with more force and speed than Patrick would have anticipated. "Get your hands off me, Detective, and control yourself."

Cavanaugh's call went through. On-screen they saw the hostages glance toward the ringing phone, but Lucas did not pause until he reached the other side of the room. Then he spun Theresa around and slammed her up against the marble wall, holding her there with one hand at her throat.

Patrick swallowed hard. He would never be able to explain this to his aunt. "He's about to kill a hostage. We have to act."

Cavanaugh answered him. "They go in shooting, we'll have an instant bloodbath. You told me yourself that Jessica Ludlow said exactly that. We can't do it, Patrick. Not even for Theresa."

"We're just supposed to stand here and let him kill her?"

"He didn't kill Paul."

"But he killed Cherise, with a lot less provocation. Who knows what this guy will do?"

Patrick's hands hurt, and he glanced at them. Bright red semicircles appeared where his fingernails bit into the flesh of the palms.

She was in sight, and still alive. But for how much longer?

"He's underneath the air-conditioning duct," Cavanaugh observed.

How *could* the man be so damn cool? Patrick wondered, then saw the point. "Do we have a microphone in that one?"

Cavanaugh disconnected his phone call to the receptionist's desk and dialed Mulvaney's HQ instead.

Within seconds they could hear Lucas's low tones and Theresa's choked replies.

"What was that all about?" the robber demanded.

Theresa gasped for air. "What?"

"Cute choice of words."

"You wanted me to tell them about Cherise."

"What do you know about 'explosive,' Theresa?"

A pause. "I can't breathe."

Patrick couldn't breathe either, standing in front of the TV screen.

"She's stalling," Cavanaugh told him.

"How do you know?"

"She's debating with herself. Should she tell him we know about the explosives? Will it make him more likely to give himself up, or less?"

They saw Lucas pull her slightly forward, in order to slam her head once again. Instead she knocked at his arm with her elbow, trying to twist away, and kicked him in the groin. The M4 carbine clattered to the ground.

This time it really was a whimper. "Oh, God. Tess."

She was going to die.

CHAPTER 22

1:10 P.M.

The kick to his groin worked. Lucas doubled over. Unfortunately, he bent right into her and kept going, throwing her to the hard floor and knocking every molecule of air from her lungs. As soon as she sucked a few back, she pushed him off. The automatic rifle lay on the other side of him.

Take him out, Theresa told herself. *Then you can shoot Bobby.*

She reached over him, and he punched her in the rib cage. It hurt, but not as badly as it would have if he'd hit the stomach. She struck back, but she had about one-third his weight and muscle. She sank her knee into his groin once more, but he pressed his thighs together, deflecting most of the blow.

She reached again for the gun.

He bucked and rolled, and suddenly she felt the cool stone floor against her back and a sharp pain at the base of her skull. He sat on top of her, suffocating her, hands and legs pinning her down in a tidy spread-eagle.

What was that about taking somebody out again?

"You really shouldn't hit me, Theresa."

"Can't breathe."

His weight shifted upward as his face came down to hers. She felt his hot breath against her ear. "You know, if I didn't have so much on my mind right now, I might enjoy the position I find myself in. How about you, Theresa? You enjoying this?"

Her fingers stretched toward the gun and found nothing but smooth marble. "Get off me."

"Not until you explain your choice of words to Cavanaugh just now."

She was out of air and out of ideas. "They know about the explosives."

His mood got unsexy in a hurry. He sat up, with the unfortunate result of again settling his weight on her slight body. "What?"

"Can't breathe."

"What explosives?"

"My ribs are going to break."

He lifted himself off her, just enough to let her lungs expand. "What explosives?"

"The stuff you have. The homemade RDX. We know you brought it in here and set it where you killed Cherise."

His face loomed over hers. "What else?"

"That's it. We don't know why."

"I don't like conflicting with you, Theresa. Of anyone here, you ought to understand what I'm doing."

She wouldn't be sidetracked. "What's back there worth blowing up?"

"You'll have to ask Bobby. He's the one with the detonator." He stood, yanking her to her feet by the front of her shirt. She felt the stitching come loose beneath the arms.

It felt better to be standing under her own power. At least it did until he swung her against the wall again, the barrel of the gun under her chin. This time he had his finger on the trigger. She tried not to breathe, but her lungs ached for it, to keep up with the demands of her pounding heart.

"My balls are going to hurt for a week now. I help you out by releasing your boyfriend, Theresa, and this is how you repay me."

He hadn't killed her for asking once, so she tried again. "What's back there worth blowing up?"

"I told you to ask Bobby. But consider this: When the government has killed your whole family, there's no part of it *not* worth blowing up."

"What do you mean?" she gasped. "What happened to his family?"

"He's got nobody left, that's what I mean. But I do, and here's where you come in. As soon as that three million arrives, it's going to be moved into my car. And you, Theresa, will be at the head of the assembly line, with me on your back like a remora. The snipers try to take me out, they're going to hit you instead."

With that, he escorted her to the reception desk, not gently, but at least he clutched the back of her shirt instead of her hair. She collapsed next to Jessica Ludlow and wiped her sweating face on her sleeves. She could only hope that one of SRT's microphones had been dropped behind that particular air-conditioning grate.

The phone was still ringing.

Patrick collapsed onto one of the upholstered chairs. The clock read 1:12, and yet he felt as if he'd pulled an all-nighter.

No, what I did was pull the rug out from under my career. The assistant chief went by, giving him a cold stare and a wide berth. Patrick had made the guy look ineffectual in a crisis, and that would not bring any recommendations his way.

But Theresa still lived. He could breathe again, maybe quell the tremors in his legs.

"Detective Patrick?"

Peggy Elliott stood next to him, still as fresh and neat and she'd been hours earlier. She'd removed the suit jacket to reveal a tailored white blouse with a gold Summer Reading Club pin on the breast pocket. "Are you all right?"

"Oh, sure. Fine."

She waited for more without comment, then gave up. "There's a phone call for you."

He followed her to a communication system set up on a reading table in the map room, where other staff could make calls without disturbing the negotiator. Kessler spoke to someone, apparently his wife, telling her not to worry. Jason trotted toward them, listening to his cell phone while devouring another sandwich. Once upon a time, Patrick could eat all day and all night like that. Once upon a time, he'd had that kind of enthusiasm for his job as well.

The librarian handed him a receiver. "It's the hospital."

A doctor at the Metro General trauma center introduced himself and asked Patrick if he was Paul's partner.

"Yes. Thank you for calling me, Doctor. How is he?"

"We tried a plastic graft. It took thirty units of blood, but it's in place."

"Is he awake?"

"Off and on. Not much."

"Can we ask him a few questions, do you think?" Who knew what the two guys might have discussed in front of Paul, when they took him for another bank employee? They might have mentioned their exit strategy, assuming they had one.

"I'm not calling to tell you to come and interview him," the doctor said with a tougher edge to his voice. "I'm saying if you want to speak to him again, you might want to come here now."

It wasn't as if the possibility hadn't occurred to Patrick. He had been to the full-dress funerals of too many cops killed in the line of duty for that. But he hadn't really believed it. "He's going to die?"

The doctor didn't pause. "He'd be dead already if the nick hadn't been at the lower end of the femoral and someone hadn't gotten that belt around his thigh immediately. He *could* recover, but I'm not fully confident of it, and that's why I'm calling. The police department said you are listed as emergency notification. You and a woman named MacLean, but she's unavailable."

Not fully confident. Patrick had heard versions of that, too. It meant the doctor didn't think Paul would live through the end of the day.

His eyes drifted to the windows, through which the Federal Reserve building gleamed in the afternoon sun. "You say he's conscious?"

"Off and on," the doctor repeated. "I can't make any promises about that either."

Patrick sighed. "I'm sorry, I can't come right now. We're in the middle of something here. I'll send another officer out in case he wakes up. But I have to stay here."

"Okay," the doctor said, and hung up. He had done what he could and undoubtedly had other patients and phone calls to see to.

Patrick called another detective, Sanchez, and asked her to go to Metro. She was sensitive but smart, and Paul had always gotten along with her. She would know what questions to ask if he woke up, know when to call Patrick and when not to. But he, Patrick, couldn't spend the afternoon sitting next to an unconscious man on the off chance that he *might* come to and he *might* be able to tell them something of Lucas and Bobby.

"How are things going?" Ms. Elliott asked him gently.

"Not good."

"I had guessed as much. I wish I could help."

Patrick gestured at the books around them. The tomes held centuries of accumulated knowledge and yet couldn't tell him how to defeat one man with a gun. "Not unless you know a formula for invisibility. Or how to neutralize RDX."

"The plastic explosive?"

He probably shouldn't have mentioned that, but Peggy Elliott had been in and out all day and nothing confidential had found its way to Channel 15. Still, he didn't clarify. "Or how to deflect bullets. Lots and lots of bullets."

"No." She shook her head. "Sorry."

He needed to get back to the monitor, to Theresa's grainy black-and-white image. He could do nothing for Paul, but he still might be able to do something for her.

He stood up and reached for the glass door when Jason said, "Detective, wait."

The young man held a cell phone to his ear, and a cop had just handed him a receiver from a table unit.

"This is the PD in Tennessee, and I'm already on with Lucas's sister. Can you talk to them?"

Patrick nearly leaped over the row of flat-drawer filing cabinets to grab the phone and identify himself.

"Slow down." The voice on the other end did not conjure up images of honky-tonks and moonshine stills. The syllables were as neatly pronounced and accentless as any TV anchorperson's, the pace measured and calm. "Who is this again?"

Patrick repeated himself while enunciating and using a sleeve to mop the sweat from his forehead. He leaned on the cabinets and closed his eyes, the better to concentrate on the man's voice.

"This is Captain Johnson from the Hudson County sheriff's office in Tennessee. I went out and talked to Jack Cornell, just like you asked."

"We appreciate that," Patrick said with fervor. He pulled out his notepad and opened it, discovering that he'd mislaid his pen. He lost a precious second or two patting his pockets before Ms. Elliott handed him hers. "We have a real bad situation up here. One person dead and one cop almost dead, with eight hostages still inside."

"Yeah, that's what that first guy told me. It wasn't any trouble anyway. We know Jack real well, and he lives near town."

Patrick didn't like the sound of this. Cornell probably *was* someone's brother-in-law, and they wouldn't give him up no matter how many northerners got shot.

But the police captain went on. "Jack isn't a bad guy. He's a little loopy since he got out of the army, but hell, he was a little loopy before that. He's never hurt anybody, and he sure could if he wanted to, with that arsenal he's got."

"He's got firearms in his possession?"

"It's his business. It's all legal. He's a licensed dealer, and his paperwork is in order. I should know—he and I go over it regularly. Anyway, what you want to know is, he *did* get a visit from those two boys you've got up there, and he's more'n happy to tell us all about it. He doesn't want any trouble that would threaten his livelihood, see?"

"When did they get there? When did they leave? Did they say—"

"Hold on, I can do better than that," the captain said, his voice spilling into the stuffy, sunny map room like a cool spring breeze. "I'll let him tell you. He's sitting right here."

"Thank you, Captain. Thank you."

"I'll get back on the phone when he's done. Here y'go, Jack."

A pause, and the sound of a receiver being handled. "Hello?"

Patrick introduced himself for what seemed like the millionth time that day. He spoke too fast again, but Jack Cornell didn't seem to care. "Yeah, the cops here told me that Lucas is in some sort of trouble. He didn't tell me nothing about it, and I didn't ask. And what you're saying doesn't sound like Lucas anyway. Could be that nut Bobby, but not Lucas."

Patrick forced himself to slow down. Their first real break in the case, and he had to make it count. "Let's start from the beginning. When did they show up at your place?"

"Day before yesterday—yeah, Tuesday. Out of the blue."

"They had just gotten out of prison?"

"Yep."

"What were they driving?"

"A white Mercedes." The man laughed. "I just about bust a gut. A damn Mercedes with pearly paint. That was Bobby's doing, I think."

"You knew Lucas from the army?"

"Yeah, that's what I'm telling you. Him 'n' me were in the same unit over in Germany. We worked at the armory. That's where I learned so much about guns—course, I already knew a lot about guns—so I started this business when I came back. Lucas went and robbed a place, I guess, so he wound up in jail down in Georgia, but I'm telling you, that's not like him. He's a real nice guy. Sensitive, even. He was sweet on this girl who worked at a bar in town, and every day he had leave he'd show up on her shift with a couple of roses. That's the kind of guy Lucas is."

"Did he tell you where he was heading?"

"Cleveland, yeah. I guess Bobby lives there."

"What did they plan to do here?"

"Hook up with some of Bobby's old gang, I guess. They didn't have any real big plans, I didn't think. They sure as hell didn't say nothing about robbing no bank, let me tell you. Bobby was going to look up some old friends, and Lucas said he had to find him a girl. That's Lucas. He always has a girl."

"That's it?"

"That's it."

"Did Bobby mention any friends by name?"

"Nope, not that I recall. He might have, but I wasn't paying much attention."

"Did he say anything about storing his car in Atlanta while he did his time? Mention who drove it there for him, maybe?"

"No."

"You didn't drive it there for him, did you?"

"Sir, I never met this Bobby until the day before yesterday."

"How were they fixed for cash?"

"No one comes out of prison a rich man. But I guess Lucas had saved a few pennies in some work program at the prison, and Bobby had stashed some in his car before he put it in storage. They didn't ask me for any, so they must not have been hurting too bad."

"You say Lucas isn't a violent type. What about Bobby?"

"I don't know nothin' about Bobby, even though I spent most of Tuesday talking to him. Lucas was kind of quiet. I guess after being in jail for a while, he didn't have much to say. That Bobby, though, he couldn't stop talking."

"About what?" Patrick swallowed, needing something wet in his throat. He thought longingly of the cooler down by Cavanaugh and decided that all phones that still had cords should have been thrown out years ago.

"His car. It needs new carpet—he said that about a million times. His friends, how it was going to be just like old times. You know how that goes, you can't ever go home again because you just ain't the same person, you know what I mean? But I didn't say anything. I felt the same way after I got out of the army, so free I could bounce off the walls. Oh, and his family."

"What did he say about his family?"

"That they're all dead and he's the last of his line. Like in that book about the Mohicans, you know? He seemed to think this was important in the grand scheme of things, that there weren't nobody left but him. I'm not making fun of him, mind, though he did get on my nerves a bit. But family's important, so I could see why he felt bad about it."

"What happened to his family?"

"Cops."

"Cops?"

"That's what he said, cops killed them. No, actually he said 'the damn justice system of the United States of America' killed them, that's what he said." Cornell's voice faded for a moment as he said to someone there with him, "Shut the door, will you? It's freezing in here."

"You're cold?" Patrick couldn't remember what cold felt like.

"June in the mountains. Anyway, I told Bobby to find a nice girl and have some sons, and then the whole bloodline thing won't bother him so much. He just laughed."

"What about Lucas? Did he mention his family?"

"He's only got a sister. He said he called her and she didn't answer, but she's in the service, too, so she might have been transferred. They never seemed to be too tight anyway."

"Did either one of them mention the Federal Reserve Bank?"

"Nothing about no bank, no." He seemed firm on that, but then he had seemed firm on everything so far.

"Did they pay you for the guns? Or were they a gift?"

Silence. Then, "Guns?"

"Two M4 carbines?"

More silence before he said, "They stole them."

"They stole the guns from you?"

"They were part of my private collection, like, not for sale. When I woke up yesterday morning, Lucas and Bobby were gone, and so were the guns."

"They never asked you for them."

"Nope."

Patrick didn't believe him. Apparently the Tennessee police captain didn't either, because Cornell's voice continued, muted, as if he had turned away from the receiver. "I didn't tell you, Johnson, because I didn't want to get the guy in trouble. He's my friend. We took enemy fire together."

Patrick heard the Tennessee cop asking: "In *Germany*?"

"Well, sort of."

"But the guy stole from you. What sort of a friend is that?"

"I don't believe he did." Jack repeated this into the receiver for Patrick's benefit. "I think it was that Bobby. He and I got on okay, don't get me wrong, but I don't know him. I don't know what he'd do or not do."

"Cornell," Patrick put in.

"Hmm?"

"Any other guns—missing? Besides the two M4 carbines?"

No hesitation this time. "Nope."

"What about the RDX?"

Another pause, but when he spoke, he had none of the prior sheepish tones. "Say what, now?"

"The plastic explosives. Did Lucas or Bobby get those from you, too?"

"I don't have no plastic explosives, I don't know nothing about no plastic explosives, and I don't want to know about no plastic explosives. That shit's wicked. Some of it exploded at our base in Germany.

Lucas took some shrapnel, and another guy got his hand blown off. They say it's so safe, but not if the guy with the detonator don't know what he's doing."

"You don't know where Lucas would get some?"

"Lucas wouldn't fool around with that stuff either. He'd wanted to go Special Forces, underwater demolition, until that injury. And he knew the guy that lost his left hand, too. Combat engineer."

Patrick straightened his spine, stretching the vertebrae. Cornell sounded positive again, truthful. "Where is he now? This combat engineer?"

"He's not in the army, I can tell you that. They shipped him out on permanent disability."

"Where does he live?"

"Hell, I don't know. Michigan? Montana? I heard he went to work for a civilian contractor—demolition work—and got blown up his second week. You can't tell me it wasn't on purpose. It broke his heart to leave the army. He was weird that way."

"He's dead? You sure?"

"I heard that from someone. I forget who, though."

"What was his name?"

"I don't think I ever knew that. He was just the guy who got his hand blown off, you know what I mean?"

"Did Lucas know anyone else who worked with explosives?"

"Not that I know of. But it's a big army."

"Yeah." Patrick could not think of anything else to ask. No doubt a million questions would occur to him as soon as he hung up, but he couldn't help that. He thanked Cornell, asked to speak to the police captain again, and thanked him as well.

"I believe him," Captain Johnson said. "For the most part. I think he's fudging a bit on the two guns—he might have given those to Lucas, for old times' sake—but whatever you asked about plastic explosives, he told you the truth. I've known Cornell a long time. He don't lie too often and he's transparent as hell when he does."

"Thanks for the help. We appreciate it."

"Good luck up there, Detective."

"Thanks." Frank Patrick sighed. "We're going to need it."

CHAPTER 23

1:25 P.M.

Theresa sat with her knees to her chin, hugging her damaged ribs, and watched her captor. His actions had been quick and brisk before, but now he moved with a sense of real urgency. She wondered if he'd been stalling all this time, waiting for the two o'clock shipment while convincing everyone else that he neither knew nor cared about it. Why?

He conversed with his partner, both of them tucked out of the snipers' line of fire, in front of the teller cages on the southwest side of the lobby. They seemed to be arguing.

Bobby had the detonator, Lucas had said. Bobby wanted to blow up the building. Maybe that was all Bobby wanted, because he certainly didn't seem interested in the large amount of cash due to arrive at 2:00 P.M. He wanted to leave, and he wanted to leave *now*.

Lucas murmured for a few minutes. Bobby interrupted, and Theresa heard him say, "—not the way it was supposed to go. My opinion counts, too—" before they lowered their voices once more.

Did the explosives have a timer? Perhaps Lucas planned to cut things too close for Bobby's comfort?

"Are you okay?" Jessica Ludlow whispered to her.

"I guess."

"I can't believe he really killed Cherise."

"Who was she?" Theresa asked. "What did she do here?"

Jessica shifted her little boy, now gnawing on a Pop-Tart; apparently his mother had found a way to extract his snacks and his cough medicine from her oversize purse. A juice box with a tiny white straw sat on the floor between them. Theresa felt like asking if she had a spare. "Cherise was a savings-bond teller. She was really nice, sort of took me under her wing when I first came here."

"You worked together?"

"In the same department. I'm a secretary, not a teller, but Cherise and me would eat lunch together every day. I didn't know anyone else here, and I'd talk her ear off. I talk a lot."

"Did your husband join you?"

Jessica stroked her child's hair, the skin on her fingers roughened and peeling slightly—she probably needed to go easier on the bleach while scrubbing her floors. "He usually worked through lunch. Or he had to go out with other bank examiners or executives in order to get acquainted with them. He was so busy, trying to learn everyone's names and titles and, you know, sort of get on their good side right away."

"I see." Perhaps Mark Ludlow had been conscientiously trying to get a handle on his new job. Perhaps he had been a snob. "Had Cherise worked here long?"

"Yeah, about ten years."

"Eleven," Brad added. He sat with his back against

the cool marble. All three conversed without moving their gaze from the two robbers, watching for any sign of agitation. But Lucas and Bobby did not seem to care if they spoke among themselves. Perhaps they had larger concerns.

Bobby's voice rose enough for them to hear: "Brian said—" Theresa wondered who that might be.

"Had Cherise always worked in Savings Bonds?" She intended the question for Brad, but Jessica answered.

"No, before that she was an administrative assistant to the vice president for public relations. She worked up in the fancy offices on the ninth floor."

"How'd she get to be a teller?" Brad asked, his voice tinged with curiosity despite the circumstances. "Quite a switch from an admin assistant."

"She was too outspoken, I guess. She wouldn't call a mule a horse even for a sack of gold."

"She sounds like a handful." Theresa felt angry all over again that such a vital woman had been snuffed out so carelessly.

"Top dogs don't care for that," Brad groused. "You should see how they live up there—Karastan rugs, bone china coffee sets."

"Our tax dollars at work, huh?"

"It belongs to the building," Jessica clarified. "This is a historic landmark."

"Of course." Theresa had no interest in debating the ethics of executive perks. She cared only that the sound of their soft voices had made Ethan's eyes close, and he dozed against his mother. She also wanted to know why Cherise had died, but no detail so far could explain that.

"Landmark, my ass," Brad went on. "The first vice

president's Picasso and his original Monet sketch and the Egyptian cartouche are all in storage on eight because he had to have new carpeting. The stuff being replaced was only a year and a half old."

"There's a firm line between the townies and the po' folk here," Jessica agreed.

"The vice pres for research isn't as showy," Brad admitted.

Jessica sniffed. "But his taste runs more to Thomas Kinkade."

Theresa interrupted the watercooler talk. "Did Cherise resent that? Moving to Savings Bonds?"

"No, she liked it. She said it was real work, where she could see a result instead of a pile of useless memos designed to stroke her boss's ego. Cherise was sort of a Communist."

"Did she have any worries on her mind lately? Here at work, or in her personal life?"

"No. Her last boyfriend broke up with her just before I came, but she figured that was just as well. . . . Why?" Jessica turned from the robbers long enough to stare at Theresa. "You think she *knew* about this?"

"No, I don't. . . . I'm just trying to figure out why she's dead, her in particular."

"Knowing Cherise," Jessica said, sighing, "she probably refused to give him the money."

"And it wasn't even hers." Brad shifted his legs, rubbing one knee.

"That's what Lucas said," Theresa told them. "But I don't believe him, not the way he told it to me."

Jessica brushed some dark flakes off her pants onto the marble tile. Ethan woke up enough to play with them, pushing the specks around to create a pattern. "What do you mean?"

"When he described robbing the teller cages, he spoke in the past tense. That's consistent with describing an event from memory. But when he spoke about shooting her, he switched to present tense and said, 'She waves the screwdriver' around and 'She starts to argue.' That's more consistent with a fabrication."

Jessica patted her little boy's back, furrows between her eyebrows. "Always?"

"Almost always. Especially when there's a change in tense for only part of a story. The part that stands out is most likely untrue."

"Wow."

"It's called forensic linguistics, analyzing the probable truth of people's statements from the words they use."

"But if you think he's lying, does that mean someone else killed her?"

"No one else could have. I think he's lying about *why*."

They broke off as Lucas returned. Bobby stayed in the back, as usual.

"This is how it's going to work, people. Listen up." With his brisk manner, he could have been one of the SRT commanders. "Theresa's going to wait at the door. The Fed cops will form a line outside to pass you the money, which you're going to hand off to Brad and him to Missy and my roomy duffel bag. I will have Jessie and Ethan between me and them. If they try to come in, Bobby and I can shoot a bunch of you first. If they throw in tear gas, knockout gas, a smoke bomb, or put same in the bundles of cash, Bobby and I can shoot all of you before we're incapacitated. If they try to pull one or two out, Bobby and I can shoot the rest of you. Do you understand that?"

No one nodded or spoke, but he did not press them.

"And though I know you all deserve a tip for your hard work today, no skimming. Don't let a few bundles get pocketed before they make it to the end of the line. And you, Theresa."

She felt as if a spotlight had picked her out in a dark room, blinding her with a sudden glare.

"You're going to be my front man. My sights will be on you the whole time. If you go through that door and keep going, I'll kill half the people in this room, starting with the security guards. I figure I can count on you, since you stood up for little Ethan there. Am I right?"

She nodded her head to confirm it. He had spared Paul, so perhaps he did not prefer to kill, but she had no doubt that Lucas would do so whenever he thought it prudent. The sight of Cherise's body had taught her that.

The phone rang, piercing the stillness of the warm air. "That must be your buddy Chris."

CHAPTER 24

Across the street Patrick told Chris Cavanaugh everything he'd learned from Jack Cornell. The hostage
negotiator listened. He did not mention Patrick's earlier agitation or express any relief at Patrick's current
calm. He did ask about Paul.

"The doctor seems to think he's going to die."

Cavanaugh said, "You don't have to stay here, you
know. You can leave someone here in your place if
you'd rather be at the hospital."

Diplomatic as hell, Patrick thought. Cavanaugh
knew he didn't have to be there at all—Patrick was a
flippin' Homicide detective, not an SRT member, and
surely the negotiator could work better without his
emotions taking up space in the room. Yet he didn't say
that, nor even imply it.

Still, Patrick felt grateful. "No. Selfish, maybe, but I
couldn't stand sitting there next to a guy who's out
cold, without any idea what's going on here. You talked
to Parrish's sister?"

"Yeah. She's not in North Carolina anymore. She
went army, too, and is stationed out in New Mexico.

She hasn't seen her brother in five years; they write each other at Christmas, that's about it. No surprises in the family history. Mom was a schoolteacher, Dad knocked her and the kids around regularly and then took off on Lucas's fourteenth birthday."

"Great guy. And this was in Atlanta?"

"Outside Columbia, South Carolina." Cavanaugh's pager made a buzzing sound.

Patrick waited while Cavanaugh took his phone call. After Cavanaugh's quick discussion of foreign rights and hardback editions, Patrick asked him, "What's his plan for getting away? He *must* have a plan."

"Oh, yeah. Every vibe from this guy says he has a plan. Unfortunately, he's really good at keeping it to himself. I need another phone conversation before this shipment exchange happens. If he'll talk about his ideas for a getaway, I can make him see how unrealistic they are."

"Look, something else keeps sticking out. Bobby seems to believe that his brother is dead."

"He could mean dead to *him*. Didn't the brother turn him in?"

"Yeah, but I don't know if Bobby knows that." Patrick patted his shirt pocket but didn't bother to remove the pack of cigarettes from it. "I can ask the brother."

"It's interesting. It could be the only psychological advantage we can get. Neither of them has anyone else we could use for leverage, no close family, no job, no political agenda. And it might be a way to drive a wedge between Bobby and Lucas if we need to."

"Bobby will put family over friends."

"Exactly. If they're going to take the money and run, fine. But if they're going to take some hostages with them—and they'd be insane not to—then we have to stop them before they reach the curb." He watched the monitor, where Lucas slowly herded his captives toward the front of the lobby. "They're getting ready to receive the money shipment. Maybe now I can get Bobby on the phone."

"He's never let us talk to Bobby before," Patrick observed.

"We've never asked to, and Bobby has expressed his opinion throughout. He's no flunky."

"In that case there's something else you should know." Patrick scanned the area for Jason and didn't see him. "I know we're not supposed to tell you everything, but if you do happen to get Bobby on the phone and he really does believe that his brother is dead . . ."

"What is it, Detective?"

"His brother—Eric—is here. He was getting off work at the airport, and I thought he might come in handy."

Cavanaugh absorbed this. "We usually try not to do that. I know in old movies they always bring the beloved mother or long-suffering wife in to talk the guy down, but in real life that backfires more often than not. Hostage takers tend to blame everyone else for their troubles, and the people closest to them most of all."

"I know that."

"However, when Lucas hit Theresa, he said that Bobby wants to use the RDX on the building because he blames the government for losing his family. If you're right and he really does believe that his brother is dead, discovering that he's not could change everything."

"We've got nothing else," Patrick reminded him. "Lucas doesn't seem to *have* an Achilles' heel. At least Bobby has this family hang-up. We could use it to distract him at an opportune moment, if nothing else."

"I'll keep it in mind. Otherwise we'll have to continue doing what we always do." Cavanaugh picked up the receiver and punched a few buttons. "We pick our way through the minefield wearing a blindfold, using nothing but a toothpick and some chewing gum."

They watched the TV screen. Lucas apparently did not want to give up his surveillance of the street and called to Bobby, who approached the phone. The stocky blond adjusted the position of the M4 carbine, finally tucking the butt onto his hip so that he could keep his finger on the trigger while leaving his left hand free.

They waited, letting the phone ring. Patrick felt as if they were trying to tempt a smallmouth bass by jiggling the hook.

"Hello?" Bobby said at last.

Cavanaugh introduced himself again, then asked, "This is Bobby Moyers, right?" as if he didn't know.

Bobby ignored the question. "Is the money here?"

"Not yet."

"Well, where is—"

"The truck is tied up in the traffic around the convention center. You know, that luncheon for the secretary of state. It will just be a few more minutes. If you stay on the line, I can keep you up to date."

"Uh-huh."

"I wanted to ask you something anyway—you said you don't trust cops. I need to ask why, because if we're all going to go home today without having shed any more blood, we need to establish a little trust between you and me, at least in some areas. You see what I mean?"

"Trust really isn't an option here, *Chris*."

"Why not?"

"You killed my family. I mean the Cleveland Police Department killed my family."

"No one told me about this." His voice dripped with sincerity and concern. Not for the first time, Patrick wondered how he did it. He *had* to feel like crawling through the wires and choking the life out of the scumbag. "How did it happen?"

Bobby didn't waste time with sarcastic preambles as Lucas would have. "First of all, my dad had to skip town when I was a kid because you guys were going to arrest him for robbing a jewelry store, which he didn't do. It was some other guy who lived on the same street and kinda resembled my father. So he had to leave town and never come back."

"I suppose that's what Mommy told him," Patrick muttered. Cavanaugh glared at him, and he shut up.

"Then you guys could barely get your charges to stick the first time, so you sent me as far away for as long as you could on a probation violation." He made buying drugs sound akin to jaywalking, and in his mind it probably was. "My mother had a heart attack after a month. You put my mother in her grave over a damn *probation violation*."

Bobby sounded agitated, and on the monitor they could see him pacing back and forth in front of the reception desk. They did not want a hostage taker agitated. Cavanaugh's voice seemed to walk a precipice, sympathetic without falling over the edge into a valley of schmaltz. "That must have been very hard on you."

"I couldn't even go to her funeral."

"What about your brother?"

A pause. "My brother turned me in. He was the one who called you guys."

Cavanaugh waited. On the screen Bobby had

stopped pacing, and now he leaned on the desk, hanging his head as if worn out. Jason returned and took a seat but did not speak.

"I hated him when they sent me to Atlanta."

"Do you still hate him?"

"How could I? He was right. I was destroying our mother—her hair went gray during my first term. She worried about me day and night. I would have killed her eventually if you guys hadn't beaten me to it. He was right."

"So now you think he did the right thing?"

"He tried to protect Mom. I can't blame him for that. But I never got a chance to tell him, because you bastards killed him, too."

Cavanaugh exchanged a frown with Patrick. "What do you mean by that?"

"What do you think I mean? He got picked up on a DUI charge, and two guys in the holding cell with him beat him to death. The guards threw him in with the biggest psychos they could find and then looked the other way."

"When did this happen?"

"A few weeks after you sent me to Atlanta."

"Your brother was arrested for DUI?"

"My brother never drove drunk in his life—the jail cops wanted to get back at me, and I'd been sent out of reach. So they took the only person I had left."

Patrick retreated between the stacks and pulled out his Nextel. He had already called Records for a criminal history on Eric Moyers—clean—but wanted to double-check. He listened to Cavanaugh and Bobby's conversation while he waited.

"How did you find out about this?"

"A buddy of mine, the guy who drove my car down to Atlanta and put it into storage for me—he told me."

"What's your friend's name?"

"I'm not going to tell you! You'd go and harass him, too. Forget it, he's got nothing to do with this. What?" He spoke this last word away from the receiver, but loudly, apparently shouting to Lucas. The response sounded like a distant murmur to Patrick. "Lucas wants to know if the truck is here yet."

Cavanaugh looked at Jason, who nodded a yes.

"It will pull up any minute now—that's why you need to stay on the line with me. You obviously feel very bad about your mother and brother."

"I'm alone now. How would you feel if I came into your house tonight and took out everyone but you?"

"At the moment I'm very confused, though, because as far as I know, your brother is not dead."

"Yeah, sure. Did you wave your hands over his grave and bring him back to life?"

"Have you been to his grave?"

"No-o-o."

"Is there any chance your friend was mistaken?"

"You're just playing with my head. You think I don't know that? I should believe you over a friend? You'd tell me the sky was orange if it made me toss down my guns and let your sniper take me out."

"What if I could let you talk to your brother? That would show you that I'm not lying, right, that I can be trusted?"

"What are you going to do, hold one of those séance things?"

"Your brother is not dead, Bobby."

"Sure."

"I know this for a fact. One of our officers interviewed him this morning. He works for Continental Airlines, right?"

A pause. Bobby started pacing again, within the length of the phone cord, back and forth, back and forth. He had room, since Lucas had moved their hostages away from the desk.

Patrick retook his seat. "Records has nothing on Eric Moyers. No arrest for DUI. Neither does Lakewood. They're checking the other suburbs as well."

"Bobby? Your brother was never arrested for DUI. I don't know why your friend told you that. He must have gotten Eric confused with someone else."

"He knew who my *brother* was."

"Well, so do we, and he's very much alive and well. More than that, he's here with us, in the library across the street from you. If I get him on the phone, then you'll have to admit that I told the truth, right? That if I say I can get something to happen, then I can. Right?"

It didn't take a Ph.D. to see where Cavanaugh was heading. He needed Bobby and Lucas to believe that they could come out, give up, and not be killed or even mistreated. And they wouldn't do that unless they trusted him.

"Sure," Bobby said at last. "Go ahead, get him on the phone."

"Okay. It will take a few minutes. He's downstairs."

"Is that truck here yet?"

"I don't see it." Of course he didn't, unless he could see through stone walls.

"Then we got time."

He covered the mouthpiece and whispered to Patrick, "Go get him."

Patrick returned in four minutes with Eric Moyers in tow. The man seemed considerably less enthusiastic about the idea than his brother had. "What am I supposed to say to him?"

"Just tell him you're not dead," Cavanaugh said. "Otherwise just keep it neutral and calm. Don't be judgmental or tell him he's screwed up."

"Even though he has."

"But we're trying to make him calm and sentimental here, right? Don't get drawn into an argument. I'll be right here listening to every word, but we're not going to be on speakerphone, in case you and I need to consult. Are you ready?"

Moyers couldn't have looked gloomier if he had been in line for the guillotine. "I suppose."

"Bobby? I have your brother here."

"Sure you do."

Cavanaugh plugged a second receiver into his console and handed it to Eric Moyers. He put it to his ear, carefully, as if he might need to pull it away again in a hurry. "Bobby?"

"Is this supposed to be Eric?"

"It *is* Eric, Bobby. I don't know why you think I'm dead, but I'm not." No answer. He looked at Cavanaugh, who made a rolling motion with one finger—*keep it going.* "I see you're in a jam over there. I want to help you out of it."

"I'll just bet you do."

Eric Moyers glanced at Cavanaugh again. The hostage negotiator said, "Talk about something only you would know."

"Bobby, listen to me a minute," Eric tried. "For Mom's sake."

"Don't say a word about my mother! You cops will

stoop to anything to blast me out of here! I don't know who you are, pal, but you're not my brother Eric, so get off the phone and put Cavanaugh back on so I can tell him to go to hell."

"Bobby, it's *me*."

"You don't sound anything like Eric."

Calm and nonjudgmental had been thrown out. "I have a cold, you idiot!"

"Call back when the truck is here," Bobby said. A clicking sound came from the phone's speaker.

"Did he hang up?" Eric Moyers asked. "I can't say I'm surprised. Listening never was a specialty of Bobby's."

Cavanaugh rolled his head from side to side, stretching neck muscles. "It was worth a try. Maybe he'll think about it. In the meantime I can't stall them about the money anymore, and there's no reason to try. There is the possibility that he's telling the truth, that they'll just take it and go."

"Go where?" Moyers asked.

"That's the hard part."

Somewhere behind the books, Patrick heard the voice of a very young woman: "—don't care. I don't give a *crap* whether they like it or not. That's my *mother*—"

He hadn't thought that the situation could get much worse. He'd been wrong.

Cavanaugh started to turn toward the noise and caught the look on Patrick's face. "What's the matter?"

Patrick pinched the bridge of his nose between forefinger and thumb. "If you thought Theresa was a handful," he told Cavanaugh, "you're not going to believe her daughter."

CHAPTER 25

2:10 P.M.

"Okay," Lucas said, surveying his motley brigade. "Are we clear on this?"

Theresa stood in front of the open door, feeling the cruel heat and the even crueler glimpse of freedom. Flowing in as a wave of hot air that pricked her pores into sweating before her skin even felt the warmth, it beckoned to her, a slice of paradise more irresistible than a glittering canyon or a Caribbean beach. The street stood empty, her path unencumbered except by an armored truck and a group of armored men.

The blinding sun reflected from slowly moving automobiles along St. Clair, two streets over; the secretary of state's luncheon had finally ended. Metal barriers along Rockwell kept back the curiosity seekers, people who had left their offices for lunch and wanted to see what would happen. People who were free to come and go. Free.

She could make it if she ran. The guards wouldn't stop her.

I have to live, Theresa thought. *Rachael might forgive me for this risk if I live. If I die, never.*

But did that mean she should dart through the door in front of her if she saw an opening, leaving the other hostages to their own fates? Lucas would almost certainly start shooting, start a firefight with seven innocent people in the way.

Or should she stay calm, stay in place, pass him his money and hope he'd take it and run?

Out at the reception desk, the phone rang. Lucas merely nodded at Bobby, and by craning her neck she could see the other robber cross the floor to pick it up. Lucas, against the northwest wall, must have been out of the line of sight of the clear windows, or he would never allow Bobby to walk into it.

Bobby held a lengthy conversation, then put the receiver down with what sounded like enough force to break it. A minute later it rang again, but this time Bobby kept the chat brief and didn't slam down the phone. He told Lucas that the cops were ready to start moving the money. Everyone in the lobby sighed.

"Missy, you have to unwrap all the money packs before putting it in the bags. No dye packs, no GPS, no booby traps. I'll be watching you."

Brad, behind Theresa, groaned. "Is this day ever going to end?"

"Sooner or later," she told him. "Though the circumstances of 'sooner' might not make it the best choice."

"Shut up," Lucas told them. He had Jessica and Ethan Ludlow in front of him, against the wall on the other side of the door. He used them as human shields to protect him from invading security guards, but also, he explained aloud, because Jessica could not both hold her son and pass packages of money to and fro, and he didn't want the little boy running around loose.

The phone rang again.

"Answer it," Lucas called to his partner.

"I don't want to. It's some nut who says he's my brother, like I'm going to believe that. Those cops must think I'm a total wack job."

"I told you they'd try anything. But you're right, stay where you are."

Should she tell Bobby that she'd spoken with his brother earlier?

"Okay, Theresa." Lucas gestured at her with the tip of the automatic rifle, which she really wished he wouldn't do. "Step up to the opening. After that, your feet do not move, not even an inch, right?"

And there she stood. In front of her, there were at least ten aggressive, heavily armed men. Behind her, there were two aggressive, heavily armed men.

Theresa found herself face-to-face with a stocky guy of about thirty, with brown skin and an SRT uniform that had been crisply starched when he put it on that morning. It had since wilted in the heat, leaving circles of wetness under both arms.

"Hi. I'm Sergeant Filmore, CPD. Everything's going to be all right."

Part of her found that very sweet. Part of her thought that Sergeant Filmore might not be the best judge of future events.

"Mrs. MacLean?" he went on. They must have told the young sergeant her name. "You with me?"

"Yeah."

"Everyone okay in there?"

"So far," she told him. "How's Paul?"

He blinked. "Who's Paul?"

"Less chatting, Theresa," Lucas called from behind Jessica Ludlow. "I want to see some money start changing hands."

Sergeant Filmore turned, and most of the other guards did as well. Theresa followed their gaze to the open doors of the armored truck. A neat pile of plastic-wrapped squares occupied a space about five feet by five feet.

"Is that it?" she asked.

"That's it. Let's *go*," the sergeant called, and the guard closest to the pile plucked the top package from its perch. He handed it down the line until Sergeant Filmore put it in her hands. She could see the green-printed pieces of paper through the thin wrap. It weighed about twenty pounds. She handed it to Brad, who trotted up the few steps to the main lobby floor to toss it at Missy and the duffel bag. Then Theresa accepted another from the sergeant.

She could only think of it as surreal, to pass down packets of money as if they were sandbags and the hostages were concerned citizens awaiting a flood.

But if the tenuous calm were breached and all the armed men in this city block began shooting, the room *would* be flooded—with the blood of people. The image sickened her. Better to concentrate on her actions, grab the package, hold it firmly. She couldn't let it drop, didn't know what might set Lucas off.

The phone rang.

"Don't answer it!" Lucas shouted to, she assumed, Bobby.

"But—"

"He's trying to distract us. Stay where you are."

Lucas seemed to think Cavanaugh had an assault planned but needed to lure Bobby into the open. Would they try it with Jessica and her son standing in front of Lucas, his gun in her back? Theresa hoped not. Cavanaugh seemed too proud of his no-fatalities record.

"We're going to get you out of there," the sergeant said to her, very quietly. "Just keep everyone calm. Did you see the explosives?"

"No."

"But you think they're behind the teller cages." He spoke when he turned to accept another package from the man behind him, so Lucas could not see his lips move. If Brad heard them, he gave no sign.

"I'm guessing." She kept her head down, as if focusing on the money, and chin pointed slightly away from Lucas and Jessica.

"Do they have anything strapped to them? Chest? Waist?"

"No. Not that I see."

"Bobby keep his hand in his pocket a lot?"

She tried to think over the past hour. Lucas always held their attention; she glanced at Bobby only when he did something to warrant it. "I don't know. I don't think so."

"Any other ordnance besides the guns? Any grenades? Any idea what's in those bags?"

"Don't know." *Hell, Theresa,* a voice in her head asked, *exactly what have you been doing? You're supposed to be on our side, you know.* The lives of seven other people at stake, and she'd spent the past hour admiring the architecture. "Investigate Cherise. He's lying about why he killed her."

"What do you mean?"

"We're not chatting, are we, Theresa?" Lucas called, making any pores that weren't producing sweat suddenly shove it out in waves.

She paused to wipe her forehead. "This stuff's heavy."

It didn't answer his question, but he did not ask

another. She could feel his eyes on her, hotter than the summer air and just as suffocating.

"What do you mean?" the sergeant repeated. She could barely hear him, so Lucas couldn't—she hoped.

But she had once taken Rachael to a museum in Cincinnati where you could stand at one corner of a busy, cavernous room and whisper and someone standing elsewhere could hear every word. She hoped the lobby had not been similarly constructed.

"Mom!"

Theresa almost dropped the package of money in her sweating hands. Had her brain snapped? She could have sworn that was Rachael's voice and not just the memory of that day in the museum. But it did not sound like a whisper this time.

"Mom!"

Past all the guards and the money and the expanse of hot asphalt, across Rockwell where the sawhorses held back the Cleveland office workers watching the show, her daughter waved her arms. "Mom!"

Theresa froze.

Rachael stood with her stomach pressed against a metal barrier with CAUTION! stenciled on its side. She wore the same clothes she'd worn to school that morning, pencil-thin jeans and a black V-neck T-shirt that Theresa felt was too tight for a buxom seventeen-year-old. Rachael's boyfriend, Craig, who must have been pressed into service to drive her downtown, flanked her. On her other side, Frank had a hand on each of her shoulders, almost certainly to keep her from leaping the barricade and rushing to her mother's rescue. That would be Rachael.

"Who's that?" the police sergeant asked.

Theresa's shock instantly ceded to fury. What was in Frank's mind, to let Rachael get this close? If bullets started to fly, who knew how far they could go, not to mention allowing her a ringside seat to her mother's potential murder? Wasn't this traumatic enough—did she have to be an eyewitness as well? Had he lost his mind? She was seventeen bloody years old! He should have locked her in the back of a police car if he had to, just *get her out of there.*

And she would throttle Craig, if she lived through the day.

But the two men hadn't told her to sacrifice herself for her fiancé. They did not create this situation.

If I run, I could make it. The cops wouldn't stop me. I'd be halfway up the street before Lucas could react, and he couldn't hit me. He might shoot everyone else, but not me.

And he might not shoot anyone. He'd have seven hostages left, it's not like he couldn't spare one. Unless everyone else tried to run out, too. Then he'd shoot. He'd have to.

"Mom!"

If she ran, she could make it.

"Lucas." She spoke calmly and clearly. "My daughter is out there. I'm going to wave to her, just wave my hand. I won't move."

"She's out where?"

"Behind the barriers."

"Really." His head poked out from behind Jessica Ludlow's, just an inch. "Invite her in."

She snarled an obscenity at him, startling in its ferocity.

Perhaps it startled him as well, or merely amused.

"Okay, okay. Relax, Theresa, I was just kidding. Your feet don't move. Go ahead and wave—once. Then get back to my money."

She gazed at her daughter, so far away that her face was not clear, just the shape and the hair and the voice. Was she crying? Was she angry? Which would be worse?

If she ran, she could make it.

Theresa waved, two swipes of her right arm. Rachael saw it; she stopped her frantic movements, and as her body stilled, it seemed to deflate. *It's hitting her now,* Theresa thought. She came there, she saw her mother, and now she was figuring out that that was all she could do. That was all anyone could do. Theresa was stuck, and no one could help her.

Unless she ran.

"Don't take one step forward, Theresa," she heard Lucas say. "If you do, I'll kill half the people in this room. I'll still have the other half."

Then you'd give the authorities no choice but to take you out, no matter the cost, she thought, but she knew it didn't make any difference. Her decision had been made, and she felt almost grateful to him for helping her make it.

She kept moving packages but could not take her eyes off her daughter.

Craig put his arm around Rachael's waist, and Theresa wished he wouldn't. The girl might pass out in the heat. But Rachael must have calmed some, since Frank had removed his hands from the girl's shoulders. *Maybe it did her good to see me,* Theresa thought. *Maybe then the whole thing won't seem so bad.* If she survived.

The sergeant interrupted her thoughts. "Any of the hostages seem to be working with them?"

She thought of Jessica Ludlow. Where had she been last night, if not at home to notice her husband's dead body on the sidewalk? Or had he been killed early that morning, after she left? Theresa hadn't seen the least sign of familiarity with the robbers, and the young woman could not have faked her terror on Ethan's behalf. "No."

"Either of them seem to have any medical problems?"

The cops wanted to know anything that might cause the situation to become unstable—a heart attack, asthma attack, psychotic behavior. "No."

Suddenly his questions worried her. They could have gotten this information from Paul, surely better versed than she was in observing criminals for behavior and armaments. If they had not, that meant Paul was unconscious. Or dead.

"How is Paul?" she asked again. "The cop that got shot in here."

He hesitated. She switched her gaze back to him from Rachael, and knew she should have done it sooner, because now he was molding his face into that blank, "I know nothing" calm that meant he didn't want to tell her. She had done it herself when family members intercepted her outside a crime scene, wanting to know if the body underneath the overturned vehicle was their husband or son or brother.

She stopped, holding a heavy bundle of money. "Is he dead?"

"I don't know, ma'am."

"Is he *dead*?"

"I don't know." Now he spoke clearly, since Lucas must have heard her question. "Really, I've been upstairs all morning. I don't know anything."

"Keep going, Theresa," Lucas said. "We're almost full up."

She didn't believe the sergeant, but she wanted to, so she didn't ask again. She couldn't tell Jessica Ludlow that her husband was dead, because she might freak out, get hysterical, upset the fragile calm until Lucas and Bobby killed her to shut her up or panicked and began firing at everyone. And now this man wouldn't tell her that Paul was dead, for exactly the same reason.

"Anything else you've observed?" the sergeant asked.

"Lucas was abused as a child." She hadn't intended to say that; she didn't see how it could help them, and if Cavanaugh brought it up, Lucas would know she had passed information to the sergeant. But childhood trauma had some real relevance to her at the moment. How would Rachael deal with this? Eventually fear would turn to resentment, an anger at her parent for bringing her that close to grief.

She looked back at where her daughter stood sweltering and hoped Rachael would not become motherless in the next few minutes. "Tell my daughter—"

"What?"

Should she tell Rachael to go to the hospital, to stay with Paul, assuming he still lived? Was it fair to leave the burden of a death watch to a seventeen-year-old who hadn't quite sorted out how she even felt about her future stepfather?

But Theresa didn't want him to be alone.

"Get moving, Theresa." Lucas spoke with more urgency than before.

"Tell her I love her," Theresa said, and passed the package in her hands to Brad.

The sergeant said, "If they start shooting, get everyone under the reception desk if you can. It's marble, it will protect you."

"Okay."

"Otherwise just stay down."

"Mmm."

"This is the last one."

Theresa held it but looked at the crowd behind the sawhorses. This might be the last time she ever saw her daughter. It might be the last time Rachael saw her.

"Tell her I love her," she repeated.

"Will do," the sergeant promised, and began to back away from the door.

"Wait!" Brad shouted. "You're *leaving* us here?"

She understood him. To be this close to help, to rescue . . . There were limits to one's discipline, even in the cause of self-preservation.

"What did you think?" Lucas asked. "They'd ride in on white horses? Shut up and turn around. If a cop enters this room, all of you die. Is that what you want?"

Brad groaned again, a low, grating sound.

"Don't worry," the sergeant told all of them. He continued to walk backward, and the expression on his face told her that it pained him as much as it did them.

"Get us out of here!" Missy screamed at him.

The other officers withdrew as well. Leaving them.

"Move back, folks," Lucas ordered. "Don't make me shoot Jessica. Brad, help Missy unwrap those packages. Separate the one-hundred-dollar bills. That's all we'll be taking."

Theresa made her feet shuffle backward as she watched her daughter until the thick wall of the Federal Reserve building blotted out the rest of the universe. Her world once again shrank to a room of cold stone and strangers.

Missy muttered, "But I've got a baby."

"I'd like a chance to have a kid," Brad said, sinking to the floor.

"My little girl is used to me being there."

"So?" Brad demanded. "You deserve to live more than me?"

Theresa, unasked, began to unwrap the plastic from the money bundles as well. She spilled the bills, held in stacks by paper bands, onto the floor. "You're wasting your breath, I'm afraid."

Missy struggled with the wrappings. It would have been much easier with some sort of knife. "At least your daughter got to see you."

Theresa's self-control slipped. "As a captive! With a gun to my head! You want to talk about *trauma*?"

"Shut *up*." Brad dropped the loosened bundles of hundred-dollar bills into one of the two duffel bags. "Will you guys drop it with the kids business? He doesn't care! No one else cares! Why do all you people with children think that you're more important than everyone else just because you have *kids*?"

"It means something," Missy insisted.

"Only to you!" Perhaps fear had turned to anger; Brad ripped open another plastic-wrapped pack. "Anybody can have a baby. You don't get a medal for it."

Lucas followed this exchange with the ghost of a grin. "Is this a sore spot, Brad?"

He's a student of human nature, Theresa thought. Or perhaps of child rearing, given the history written in scarred flesh along his arms.

"They take days off and assume you can cover for them. Their vacation week gets approved because it's Junior's Little League tryouts or something. They act like I don't have a real life because it doesn't revolve around some little rug rat."

Lucas had reached the end of his attention span. "People—"

Missy ripped the paper band off a packet of money with enough force to send a few stray bills wafting to the floor. "No, because you're a self-indulgent party boy who—"

"People!"

They fell silent.

"Let me reintroduce some reality here. None of you are getting out of here until Bobby and I have this money safely stowed in our car. I don't care who has kids and who doesn't. It may be a noble undertaking, but it does not confer any special immunity in life. I also don't give a crap if you're caring for an elderly parent, or your dog has diabetes and needs its medication, or if you've won the lottery and intend to donate it all to charitable organizations. *I don't care.* Are we clear on this?"

The phone rang.

"Nobody move," Lucas said. "Bobby, don't answer that. Missy, you got that one zipped up?"

She had filled it to bulging. A small stack of leftover bundles rested on the floor. "Yes."

"Good. Jessica, go sit down where you were before. Missy and Brad, slide the bag in front of the reception desk. It's going to be heavy, but you're both so ticked off you can probably pull it without too much trouble. Then everyone sits down. Theresa, you, too."

Lucas followed behind Theresa, close enough that the barrel of the gun prodded her spine with every few steps. The phone continued to ring. Lucas had the money and the car, with nothing to stop him from taking off with a few hostages in tow. Except Chris Cavanaugh, assuming he really could talk anybody into anything.

"I think you should answer that phone," Theresa said to him.

Lucas ignored her suggestion. "You could have run for it, Theresa. You could have been out that door before I shot you. Why didn't you go?"

"How many people would you have killed if I had?"

"Half of them." The answer came so quickly, so lightly, that it chilled her blood. "Just like I said. But so what? You love your daughter. Aren't you willing to sacrifice others for her well-being?"

The question made her heart pound, more so than the gun at her back. *Should* she have been willing? Why did Lucas ask? Trying to sort out what happened during his childhood, what the adults in his life should have done versus what they did? Or did he simply enjoy poking an open wound?

Should she have run, put Rachael above these other people, these strangers?

"Love has to be balanced," she said as they reached the reception desk, "with being a human being. You can't truly do one without being the other."

His face grew still again, hard, almost disappointed. "I disagree, Theresa. Real love is *un*balanced, and you have to be willing to sacrifice everything and everyone for it."

For the second time, she asked, "Is that what you're doing this for? Love?"

"Sit down, Theresa."

She sat.

CHAPTER 26

2:35 P.M.

"What did you do with the daughter?" Cavanaugh asked.

Patrick, Cavanaugh, and Jason sat at the librarian's desk. Assistant Chief Viancourt perched on a folding chair, one ankle over the opposite knee. He seemed to have forgotten his irritation at Patrick—he'd never been the sort to hold a grudge—but he also seemed to have lost interest in the whole ordeal.

Patrick could not remember when he'd last felt this tired. He didn't have the energy to light a cigarette, and his clothes, even his pants, clung to his sweat-soaked body. Yet the last active cell in his body rose up at Cavanaugh's tone. "Rachael. Her name is Rachael."

"Rachael, then. Where is she?"

"She's watching the monitor in the map room."

The hostage negotiator studied him. "If this goes bad—"

"She might witness her mother's slaughter, yes, I know that. But what else could I do? Stick her in a closet and tell her to be quiet like a good girl? If it was my mother, I'd sure as hell want to see what was going on."

"It will give her nightmares for the rest of her life. Why don't you send her to the hospital to stay with the fiancé? Paul," he added hastily, seeing the look on Patrick's face. "He was almost her stepfather."

Is going to be, Patrick thought, but he felt superstitious about insisting, felt afraid to acknowledge Cavanaugh's use of the past tense when it came to Paul Cleary. "I thought of that. She didn't ask much about him before, but I'll have to tell her what kind of shape he's in. I won't make her go—I keep picturing Tess bleeding to death on the floor of the Federal Reserve building. Having to be here if that happens, yes, would traumatize Rachael for life. But knowing she might have had a chance to say good-bye if I hadn't sent her off to Metro . . . well, she'd hate me forever."

"So are you basing this decision on her feelings or yours?"

Patrick damned the man. That was probably what made him a good negotiator, the ability to cut through words to the crux of the matter. "That's just it—it's going to have to be her decision."

Cavanaugh shrugged. "Whatever. Just keep her out of here." He dialed the phone again. "He still isn't answering. This is not good."

It felt better to discuss anything besides himself or Theresa. "What's his plan?"

"That's just it, I don't know. After the entrance, the exit is the most dangerous time, and it's best to have every detail worked out. You think they were trigger-happy before. . . . They should be even more worried about it than I am. I don't get it. Did we hear from the storage facility that had Bobby's car?"

"Whoever left it there gave his name as Bobby Moyers. Surveillance tapes have since been recorded over, and the employee who assigned the unit got fired three months ago. Decatur PD is trying to track him down on the off chance he can give us a description." He dialed again.

"Where's the secretary of state now?" Patrick asked suddenly. "The luncheon should be over."

"Yeah, it's over," Viancourt answered from the couch, a bitter edge to his words. He had probably hoped to attend at least part of it. "They're bundling the secretary into a bulletproof limo as we speak. So I guess this had nothing to do with that after all. I'm glad I didn't even suggest to the chief that we cancel it," he added pointedly. He had been right and they wrong.

Patrick checked his Nextel, hoping the hospital would call him if Paul's condition changed. "Maybe he was waiting for the traffic to clear."

Cavanaugh asked what he meant.

"We've gotten the feeling all day that Lucas was stalling. First he refused to wait for this shipment, and then he changed his mind, even after going through the whole rigmarole of sending the Ludlow woman to rob the bank-loan department. Maybe he wanted to wait until the secretary departed, taking a lot of traffic and a lot of cops with her."

Cavanaugh nodded. "It could be. It works in our favor as well—if we have to pursue, which I pray we don't, at least we won't be running into the motorcade or convention-center traffic. Of course, if he heads east from here, it wouldn't have made any difference anyway. I need to know what he's planning. If he waits any longer, we're going to run into that Hall of Fame concert traffic." He dialed the phone again, punching the numbered plastic buttons with violence.

"What about Cherise?" Patrick said. "Did you check out what Theresa told that SRT guy?"

Cavanaugh gestured at Jason, who answered. "I spoke with her parents—as much as I could; they were hysterical—and her brother, and three other Fed tellers. She's had no recent changes in her behavior or her habits. She's been dating the same guy for a year and a half, a production assistant at WMMS. They break up off and on, but he's been away with a church mission trip for the past ten days, rebuilding homes in New Orleans. Her finances have stayed steady. She deposits her salary and pays her bills. No big purchases. If there's some dark secret in her life, she's hidden it well."

Cavanaugh kept dialing, so Patrick lowered his voice and spoke to Jason. "Lucas, then. Did we ask his sister what Theresa told the sergeant about abuse?"

"I tried her, but the line was busy. Apparently there are still people in this country who don't have call-waiting. Or a DSL line."

"Mind if I try?"

"Be my guest." Jason stood up. "I've got to have a bathroom break anyway, or it's going to get messy in here. Here's the number."

Patrick moved out to the center of the building, by the elevators, where the early-afternoon sun slanted through the wall of windows facing the courtyard and the Eastman Reading Garden. Miraculously, Lucas Parrish's sister answered on the first ring. As soon as he identified himself, she said, "I'm not interested in helping you kill my brother, and besides, I have to be at my post in ten minutes."

"Ma'am, he's surrounded by approximately thirty-five cops and security guards. I don't want anyone to shoot him, because once one bullet flies, you know more will follow, and there's a lot more people down there besides your brother. So I'm as desperate to keep him alive as you are, understand?"

Slowly she agreed.

"Do you have any idea why your brother is doing this?"

"Why he's robbing a bank? Because he's a dreamer without a real job, that's why."

"He doesn't want to work for a living?"

From the tone of her voice, she took no offense at the question. "He's not lazy—he's impatient. He wants grand adventures, tons of money, a beautiful woman who will love him forever and ever. He aims too high, I guess you could say."

"I've been told Lucas suffered some abuse as a child. Can you tell me how that happened?" He tried to sound knowledgeable, when in truth he had no idea how Lucas's friggin' childhood could help them in this situation. But Theresa had taken some risk to pass along this information, and he would act on it.

"You mean the burns?"

"Uh . . . yeah."

"My mother's husband. Our father, I guess, though I've never really been too sure about that."

"He left when you two were kids?"

"Yeah." She waited, no doubt wondering what the hell Patrick was getting at. He wondered, too.

Patrick began to pace, then entered the stairwell to move down one floor. "Is that when Lucas began to get in trouble?"

"No. He didn't go in for petty stuff—he's never

aimed low. I got in more trouble than he did. He liked
school, worked part-time here and there. He read a
lot. I guess that's how he got so dreamy—he read books
and drew pictures to get through the days at our house.
I went out and played football with the boys, climbed
fences, anything to be with other people. We all cope
in our own ways."

Patrick couldn't stand in one place. He escaped the
sunlight and slipped between the cool stacks, up to
the glass-walled map room. Rachael had her back to
him, glued to the monitor, watching the small group
of pixels representing her mother.

Patrick asked, "Did he show any violence to other
people? Act out against what his father would do?"

"Again, that was me. *I* fought. *I* got expelled for
throwing another girl into the high-school trophy case.
Lucas was more philosophical, like our mother. I guess
that's why him and me aren't close."

Through the glass he could see Rachael's boyfriend,
Craig, offer her a bottle of water, wet with condensation. She took it, and Patrick felt oddly comforted. At
least the kid hadn't gone completely comatose. "What
do you mean?"

"Mom put up with our dad. She said she loved him,
and you had to be willing to do anything for love. I
never quite got where loving the kids she brought into
the world figured into the equation, but apparently
that's normal. The nonabusive parent—some kids side
with them, while others, like me, resent them even more
than the abusive one. A shrink told me that once. Question is, why am I telling you?"

"Because your brother murdered one, maybe two,
people this morning for no apparent reason."

"One thing I know about my brother," the woman

said. "He's got a reason. It just won't make sense to anybody but him. And I've got thirty seconds to get to my duty station."

"Thank you, Ms. Parrish."

"Good luck."

He steeled himself to enter the map room. He had held Rachael in his arms three days after her birth, true, but on the other hand he had no children and went to some effort to avoid dealing with anyone under twenty-five. Now he moved toward Theresa's daughter as one might approach an injured tiger. The analogy fit almost too well—Rachael was desperate, unpredictable, and definitely wounded.

He pulled up a chair, sitting in front of her so she could see him and the monitor at the same time. The boyfriend—a pretty even-keeled kid, to Patrick's great relief—noticed him first, then Rachael. She regarded him warily, wondering if he now functioned in the capacity of cop or loving uncle.

"I don't have any news. The situation is still just as you see it on the TV here—your mom is fine."

"What are you guys going to do?"

"We're going to negotiate until they give themselves up peacefully. That's how these things usually end, especially bank robberies. But I wanted to tell you that the hospital called, about Paul."

"How is he?"

She looked like her mother, he noticed for the first time. Her eyes, brown instead of Theresa's crystal blue, had always thrown him off, but now he could see it in the shape of her lips and the line of her jaw. And like her mother, she hid her vulnerability well, refusing to even hint at its possibility.

But Rachael was only seventeen, and about to face

a decision he wouldn't want on his shoulders at fifty. "He's in pretty bad shape."

She seemed surprised, but then teenagers still believed in immortality. And she hadn't seen the blood. "Is he going to die?"

"They don't know. But I have to tell you it's a possibility."

She did not respond, simply absorbed. Just as her mother would have done.

"I'm sorry to have to tell you this, Rachael, when I know you're so worried about your mother. I wish it could be avoided." Seventeen or not, Rachael was a human being and deserved the truth. Paul had been about to become her stepfather. "I'll let you know as soon as I get any further news."

"Mom would want me to go and stay with him."

Patrick wrote down the names of the hospital and of Paul's doctor but said nothing. Theresa would probably prefer him to get Rachael away from the scene, both for psychological reasons and to be out of harm's way in the event of explosions or gunfire, but he couldn't bring himself to influence the girl. Deciding things for other people did not come as easily to him as it did to, say, Chris Cavanaugh.

He left her there to think about it, sighing with guilty relief as he left the room—on little cat feet, the way one leaves a funeral parlor.

Moving back upstairs, he turned his mind to Lucas Parrish and tried to fit the information Lucas's sister had provided into some useful framework. He couldn't. The conversation had served only to convince him that Parrish had a loftier goal in mind than getting a teller to stuff some cash in a bag.

On the other hand, the sister had listed "wealth" among his aspirations. Perhaps Lucas Parrish was exactly what he appeared to be, a kid blessed with enough smarts to have a dream but not enough to bring it to life. Maybe it really was just the money.

CHAPTER 27

"Detective?"

Peggy Elliott skipped up a few steps to catch him. She carried a textbook that must have weighed seven pounds, easy. "I've been reading up on RDX."

He paused on the landing. "That was quick."

"I'm a reference librarian. It's what I do."

His partner had an appointment with death penciled in, Theresa sat out of reach with a gun to her head, and yet Patrick found himself wondering if Ms. Elliott had a significant other, and if not, how she might react to an offer of coffee or lunch. . . .

Later. "Thanks. Please don't tell anyone else—I'd get in trouble for discussing an investigation in progress. What did you find?"

"Nothing, unfortunately. There is no way to neutralize it—chemically, I mean. You could always throw it in the lake or blast it into space. Or just pull out the detonator."

"The lake, huh?"

She nodded. "Then run like hell."

Patrick returned to the negotiator's area like a moth

to the flame, afraid to look at the television monitor but unable not to. He retook his seat just as Lucas Parrish finally answered the phone at the information desk across the street and said, "Hello, Chris."

"Thanks for picking up, Lucas. I was getting worried about you."

"That's so sweet, Chris. Remind me to drop you a card on your next birthday."

"I'm glad you have your money, but now we need to work out where you're going to go from here."

"I have an aunt in Chicago. I figure she'll let me sleep on her couch for a few weeks. After that, I'll head for Las Vegas. Ever seen the Grand Canyon, Chris?"

"I'm mostly concerned with Cleveland right now. You know there's a whole lot of cops with guns on this block who are pretty worried that you're going to hurt some of those hostages. You have to know they're willing to take you out to make sure that doesn't happen."

"I wouldn't respect them if they weren't, Chris."

"We're going to have to work together to come up with a good exit strategy, one where no one gets hurt."

"Exit strategy. I like that. It sounds all corporate-like."

Again Patrick felt a desperate need to travel through the wires and strangle the little shit.

"Why don't you tell me what you have in mind?"

"I could tell you, Chris, but then I'd have to kill you."

Cavanaugh wiped moisture from his nose, then pinched the bridge. Patrick wouldn't say he seemed worried, exactly, but he did not speak with the confidence he had earlier that morning. It scared him. Cavanaugh had been through this process hundreds of times more than Patrick had, and something about this situation was atypical. But then, hell, from Paul to Theresa to Rachael, nothing about the day had been typical.

"I'll go first," Cavanaugh offered. "If you put down the weapons and come out, you have my word that you will not be harmed in any way."

"You can go first, last, and always, Chris. It doesn't matter, because this is not a negotiation. We'll leave when we want to leave, and if your cops try to stop us, we'll kill a few hostages. End of story."

"If you hurt people, I can't guarantee your safety."

"We've already hurt people, in case you haven't been paying attention. So I'm guessing our safety has become irrelevant. At least I can still pick the way I go."

Patrick found himself chewing on a knuckle. Lucas had gotten it, finally—he had no way out. He could collect the money, he could keep the cops at bay by threatening the hostages, he could trade barbs with the famous negotiator—he could do everything but leave. He had two choices: He could give up, or he could go out in a blaze of glory or some other suitably dramatic ending.

Dreamy, his sister had said. Romantic.

Patrick had no doubt which choice Lucas would take.

"That's not true." Cavanaugh continued to work on it. "We can still salvage the situation. No one else has to die today. We can work this out as long as we trust each other."

"See, that's just it. As I believe Bobby and I have made clear, we are not going to trust cops, ever, ever, ever. You're not going to negotiate us around that, Chris, do you understand? You fail. Period."

Cavanaugh's voice grew hard. The word "fail" had

LISA BLACK

a rejuvenating effect on him. "I don't get this, Lucas. You told me who you were, you told me what you wanted, you sent Jessica upstairs, and we let her come back. We worked together on the money shipment. Now we get to the most critical part of the day and you won't tell me what you want?"

"I don't believe you care what I want."

"If you try to leave with hostages, they'll kill you. You'll be giving them no choice. I know you're intelligent enough to see that."

"I'm intelligent enough to know that your goals and my goals have never coincided. Y'all gave me the money figuring you'd get it back after we die, and we'll die if we put these guns down. I know it. Bobby knows it. So stop wasting your breath and my time."

He hung up.

Cavanaugh dropped the receiver into place with a clatter. "I just don't get this guy." He sounded almost plaintive for a moment.

"What's he going to do?" Patrick asked, feeling worse than Cavanaugh sounded. "Keeping hostages with him is the only way to get to that car. He has no choice."

"I know that. What makes it worse is that Theresa is an obvious choice for him. He thinks we'll place more value on her life than on a stranger's."

Jason returned from the direction of the command center. "Laura's plane finally landed. She'll be here in ten."

"Fifteen," Cavanaugh said, dialing the phone. "She exaggerates. I need to stall them, to let SRT figure out how to get a hook on that car. And we've only got one card to play. . . . Lucas? May I speak to Bobby, please? There's a loose end I'd like to tie up."

Eric Moyers, Patrick thought.

"Is this about his brother again?"

"I want to show you I can be trusted, that I have told you the truth every minute of this day, and that if I tell you you won't be harmed, you won't be. I can prove I didn't lie about Bobby's brother. Will you at least give me the chance to do that?"

"No."

"What about Bobby? It's *his* brother, the last of his family. Shouldn't he be the one to make this decision?"

The phone gave a snapping sound, which led to a low hum. Lucas had switched to speakerphone; they heard his retreating voice as he changed places with his partner. "He wants to talk to you about your brother. I don't know, just talk to him. I want to check out the street anyway."

Patrick said, "I thought you never—"

Cavanaugh covered the receiver while he answered him. "Use the family? This is different. I don't expect the sight of his next of kin to fill Bobby with remorse. But I do expect it to convince him that he has based all his actions today on erroneous assumptions. If one crumbles, they all may, including his assumption that getting away scot-free is a possibility."

Patrick dropped it. "If Lucas doesn't want to talk to us, why does he keep picking up the phone?"

"Because deep down he wants me to find a solution for him, to find a way to make this come out all right. He's a little boy who started out to steal an apple and instead set fire to the orchard, and now he's scared. Most of these guys are like that."

Patrick wasn't so sure. Lucas seemed like the least frightened guy on East Sixth, and Cavanaugh needed a reason to keep the reins from the imminent Laura.

She would only be secondary anyway—but maybe that was still too much for Cavanaugh. It didn't matter, really. They had to do something. Maybe this would drive a wedge between the two robbers.

The monitor showed Bobby's approach. In the background Theresa seemed to be conversing with Jessica Ludlow. *Be careful,* Patrick silently warned her. She should stop trying to investigate and keep her head down.

The other half of the criminal team spoke into the phone. "What?"

"Family seems to be the most important thing to you," Cavanaugh told him. "Is connecting with the last member of your family more important than robbing a bank?"

"I don't get you."

"I'm saying if I can produce your brother, not just on the phone but let you *see* him, would you put down your weapon and end this day peacefully?"

"If you can bring the dead back to life, Cavanaugh, I'll do anything you say."

"I'm serious, Bobby. This is a real deal we're making here. I can only hold up my end if I can trust you to hold up yours."

"There's just one problem," Bobby said. "I know you're lying."

"I'll bring him down, and we'll stand in the doorway, across the street at the library building."

Bobby's derisive snort exploded over the wires. "I sure hope this guy you've got *looks* more like my brother than he sounds, or you'll have to stand in the next county to convince me."

Cavanaugh paused, his finger off the "talk" button.

"You're not going to have us walk Eric Moyers across the street?" Jason whispered. "That's against the rules."

"We're not going to hand him over, just let his brother see him. We can break Bobby, and we have to. . . . Okay, Bobby, we can make this work. I can let you converse with your brother if that will satisfy you that I'm telling the truth. But what are you going to do for me?"

They heard—and saw, on the monitor—Bobby turn from the phone and explain the situation to Lucas.

Lucas sounded more strained than ever. "Give *up*? Are you nuts?"

"If it's not him, we can waste 'em. But if it is—if he's really still alive—then I don't want to die, man."

"*What?*"

They heard a clunk as Bobby dropped the phone. He moved across the tile and joined Lucas for what appeared to be a heated talk. They both stood at the corner to the entranceway.

"Snipers!" Cavanaugh barked into his radio. "Green light!" Meaning they were far enough from the hostages—take the shot.

"Negative. Out of range." One or both were sufficiently hidden by the teller cages.

"Damn."

The two conversed with a number of hand gestures but only an audible word here or there.

Cavanaugh next contacted Mulvaney. "Can we turn up the volume on those mikes? We really need to hear what they're saying."

"If we could," the captain's voice drawled over the radio, "don't you think we would have hours ago?"

"True, sorry." Cavanaugh set the radio down.

"They're keeping their voices low. They don't want the hostages to hear."

"What's the plan?" Jason asked. He seemed truly worried, which didn't make Patrick feel any better.

"They're going to make a run for it. At least debating this issue will delay them a bit. It also seems to be breaking down the partnership—best-case scenario, they get in a fight and shoot each other." Cavanaugh tilted his head back, drained another bottle of water. "Second best, I can make this deal with Bobby and they give up. No one else gets hurt."

Patrick tried to loosen his tie, only to realize he had removed it hours before. "Lucas didn't come this far just to make Bobby feel all warm and fuzzy inside."

"But it gives him an out. He's got to know by now that he isn't going to drive the Mercedes into the sunset with a trunkful of cash. Giving up for the sake of his buddy is a much different animal than giving up to save his skin."

"Altruism has drama," Patrick agreed, though he couldn't shake the feeling that Cavanaugh might be drawing the conclusions he preferred.

"It all depends on what's going on in Lucas Parrish's mind," Cavanaugh said, as if he'd read Patrick's.

Jason still worried. "How are you going to get Eric Moyers to go along with this? He went to great pains to avoid even a phone call from his brother, much less a visit."

"He won't like having those people's blood on his hands either." Cavanaugh straightened his collar, tucked his shirttails more tightly into the slightly wrinkled khakis. "You've talked to him more than we have, Patrick, what do you think?"

"Hmm?" He'd been watching the monitor, where

Bobby and Lucas continued to converse with intensity but not, so far, apparent anger. "He isn't a bad guy. He'd want to do the right thing, and he's not afraid of his brother, more contemptuous of him. But he also strikes me as having a well-developed sense of self-preservation. Look, they're done talking."

Cavanaugh leaned over the communication set just as Bobby, on the monitor, swept up the phone receiver. The robber's first words came as something of a surprise.

"Tell me again what you have in mind," he asked.

Patrick noticed the slight breath of relief Cavanaugh let out before going back into the dance.

"If I produce your brother—so that you can see him and talk to him, long enough and close enough to satisfy you that he *is* your brother, Eric Moyers, then you and Lucas put down your guns and come out. You will not be harmed by the officers."

"That sounds like weasel words. Who *will* we be harmed by, then?"

"No one. No harm will come to you from anyone, as long as you put down your weapons and come out, leaving those people safe. We're not interested in shooting you, Bobby, or hurting you or Lucas. We just want to get those bank employees back to their families and all these police officers back to *their* families."

Patrick thought he laid the family emphasis on a bit thickly, but it kept Bobby talking.

"One condition," he said. "We don't serve any time. Lucas and me, we've already seen the inside of prison for longer than we ever cared to."

Jason shifted in his chair and muttered to himself. "This part is always sticky."

"That's not really up to me, Bobby, but I'm not going to lie to you and tell you that you can both walk off free after this has ended. You know that's not how it works. But if you give up peacefully, without hurting anyone else, it will count in your favor with the courts."

"Meaning we'll go to jail and you'll throw away the key."

This could lead to several more hours of negotiation. Hostage takers never wanted to go to jail, but all knew that they would. Just like escaping with the money—the trick was to keep them talking until they accepted the reality of the situation. It had to be so tempting to lie to them, Patrick thought, to tell them anything they'd like to hear just to end this. But unless they were completely insane, they'd know you were lying, and further discussions would be pointless.

However, that they were even considering jail time represented a huge concession. The brother card might actually work.

"I don't know what kind of sentence the judge will require, Bobby. As I said, that's not up to me. But I know what kind of sentence you'll get if anyone else dies today, and you won't like it better." Cavanaugh spoke almost gently. He did not wish to threaten, his voice said. Merely inform.

They waited while Bobby went back to Lucas for another conference.

"I still can't believe Lucas would do this," Jason grumbled.

"I wouldn't have either," Patrick said, "but his sister said that Lucas learned loyalty from his mother—she'd put up with anything to keep her husband, her loved ones. Maybe he'll act out that lesson. Or maybe it's like you said," he added to Cavanaugh, "an out, a way for him to give up and still save face."

Jason did not seem reassured. "But Lucas has been the leader all this time. He's called all the shots."

"Or he's just the spokesman," Cavanaugh pointed out. "Like me."

"He insisted on staying to get the money shipment. Bobby didn't want to."

Patrick's head swam with the what-ifs and maybes. He got into other people's heads all day long, trying to understand what skeletons they didn't want the cops to dig up—how they broke into the apartment, why they murdered their wife. But never for so many hours at one stretch. Besides, none of their speculation seemed to help; they still wound up simply watching what the robbers did and then reacting as best they could.

"Okay." Bobby's voice startled them all. "We can deal on this. But we have some conditions."

"Let's talk about them."

"I'm putting Lucas back on. He's better at this."

The two robbers changed places, careful as always not to be in sniper range at the same time.

"I don't believe you, Chris," he said without preamble. "I think you're lying—"

"I'm not."

"—but I know how important family is to Bobby. That's all he ever talked about in therapy, so believe me, I know."

Patrick glanced at Jason and raised his eyebrows. Irene made a note. The prison in Atlanta would have records of which programs the inmates attended. Perhaps this solved the mystery of where Bobby and Lucas had met—a group-therapy session, each revealing his secret dreams and goals.

Lucas, meanwhile, continued. "I'm willing to go along with this. You bring Bobby's brother over here—and by you, I mean *you,* Chris, no one else—and he will lay down his arms and leave with you."

"What about you?"

"I stay here. I'm happy for Bobby if this is the choice he wants, but I'm not giving up my freedom for it."

"What about all those bank employees?"

"They stay with me."

Patrick had not expected this, but it made sense. Lucas could respect his friend's wishes without giving himself up. He'd still have the hostages and the money.

"That might work," Cavanaugh said, though Jason frowned and shook his head. "However, I've been assuring your safety all this time—are you going to assure mine?"

"Why would I shoot you, Chris? Provided you're telling us the truth and this really *is* Bobby's brother."

"He is. But this is a highly unusual undertaking. We don't normally make piecemeal deals like this—"

"You'd be down one robber without any bloodshed. How is that bad for you?"

He was correct, of course—so correct that it made Patrick nervous. The man needed to get a large amount of money out of a city block filled with trigger-happy cops, and he seemed *too* cooperative about it.

Cavanaugh proceeded with caution. "I think this plan can work, and I'm willing to escort Eric Moyers across the street to talk to Bobby. But I'm concerned about the rest of the bank employees. That's a lot of people for you to handle by yourself."

"That almost sounds like a challenge, Chris. I'm

not worried about it. I can always tie them up, like the guards."

Jason continued to shake his head. "The guards are tied to the teller cages, the same place we think Lucas set the explosives. That's got to be his exit strategy—he fills the cages with hostages and then walks out with the detonator. We let him go or they get blown up."

Cavanaugh argued, "That would last for about sixty seconds before our team got in there and freed them all."

"With the roads cleared he could be on I-90 in sixty seconds."

The negotiator nodded, then pressed the "talk" button on the console. "I mean this would be a good time to cut some of them loose. As a show of good faith."

"I won't shoot you when you show up. That should be good enough faith for you."

They haggled a while longer but finally settled on a plan. Cavanaugh and Eric Moyers would walk across the street and converse with Bobby Moyers outside the East Sixth Street entrance. If satisfied, Bobby would leave with them, along with four hostages of Lucas's choosing. They had ten minutes.

CHAPTER 28

3:14 P.M.

Theresa watched these negotiations closely while listening with half an ear to Jessica Ludlow. Like a child in class, the young woman took advantage of the lull in their captors' attention. "At least I found a decent day-care situation for Ethan. Our neighbor recommended her, and she's really good, feeds them lunch and everything, but she's real firm on not taking any sick kids, so when he looked sniffly today, she said he couldn't stay."

Lucas and Bobby conferred over Cavanaugh's offer. She expected Lucas to refuse it, but he had deferred to Bobby's wishes. This didn't make sense to her. Lucas had been so strong-minded all day. . . . Had he lost his nerve with the end in sight, figured out that it would not, could not, end well for him? Or had he been deferring to Bobby all along?

"I wasn't real big on working at all. I'd rather be home with him. I had a part-time job in Atlanta, and that was perfect—an hour or two three times a week, enough to get me out of the house and bring in a little extra money, but not enough for Ethan to really miss me."

Bobby returned to the phone, then handed it over to Lucas. Now Theresa could hear every word, but they still did not make sense. Why would Lucas agree to this? Pulling off an escape with the two of them would have been extremely difficult; by himself, impossible.

Unless he had never intended to escape.

"But Mark insisted. He insisted on a lot of things. He assumed because I was born in Georgia that I was some sort of barefoot high school dropout." She measured out a spoonful of cherry-flavored cough syrup for Ethan to take and rubbed his back. "It's okay, honey. We'll see Daddy again soon. Do you want another fruit roll?"

"I can't believe this. He's going to come here!" Theresa exclaimed softly.

"Who?" Jessica Ludlow asked.

"The hostage negotiator. He's going to walk Bobby's brother over here. I can't believe that."

"Why not?"

"They're not supposed to get involved—the negotiators, I mean. They always stay on the phone. He's not supposed to put anyone at risk, even himself, and *definitely* not a civilian like Bobby's brother." According to his book's table of contents, Cavanaugh had devoted an entire chapter to the topic of acceptable risk. Had he become desperate for a solution? Or did he know something she didn't, such as when the explosives were due to go off—and that the answer was *soon*.

The younger woman pulled her child closer, letting him smear her sleeve with his thin sheet of strawberry gel. "Is something bad going to happen?"

Theresa tried to sound more positive for the girl's sake. "No, it will work. Cavanaugh must believe it can

save us or he wouldn't do it." The man had his record
to think about.

"They're going to give up?" Jessica asked.

"Only Bobby. Lucas isn't the type to give up." But
he was the type to cut his losses. Perhaps he realized
that he couldn't fight Bobby and the cops both and so
gave in to his partner's wishes. "I wonder what they'll
do about the car."

"What about it?"

"It's Bobby's car, and he made a pretty big deal
about it. But Lucas will need it to escape." She also
wondered what they would do about the explosives.

"What did you say, Theresa?" Lucas's voice cut
through the air like a deadly missile. "I don't like being
discussed behind my back."

"You said you'd release four people when Bobby
leaves. Let Jessica and the baby be among them."

"What about me?" Missy asked. "I have a baby,
too."

Lucas stood in front of Theresa, giving her the considering look she had learned to recognize. "Interesting,
Theresa. You don't ask for yourself, only for someone
else. Very altruistic."

Brad said, "What is this, women and children first?
What kind of last-millennium shit is that?"

Lucas pivoted so that the barrel of the automatic rifle pointed at Brad. "You're not much of a gentleman,
are you, Brad?"

"Why does a kid have more of a right to life than
an adult? Or some bitch more than me?"

How *do* you decide who lives and who dies? Had
Cavanaugh decided? Had his answer prompted this
new strategy?

"Let me go." Brad would not give up, and, Theresa admitted to herself, why should he? "Just. Let. Me. Go."

Lucas raised his hand. "How many people think I should ship Brad out of here if only so we won't have to listen to him whine anymore?"

No one moved. The other people in the lobby had been through too much that day to joke about anything.

"Then listen up. You're all staying. I'm going to get rid of the three goons tied to the teller cages over there, bless their little hearts." He gestured toward the three security guards. "They're going to suffocate if they can't lower their arms soon anyway. And Theresa."

She started. "Why me?"

"I have my reasons. You can thank me later." He reached down and, with a grip like a screw clamp, pulled her to her feet in one motion. "But I need your help on something first."

Brad continued to protest. "Come *on!*"

"Stop whining, Brad. And don't nobody think that you can use this as a diversion. You move out of line, you get shot."

Theresa couldn't guess Lucas's reasoning. He seemed to want to remove all law-enforcement personnel from the room. Did he think they—three trussed-up security guards and a science nerd—could overpower him, once left without Bobby?

He took the precaution of tie-wrapping her hands behind her back. Though this changed very little about the situation—she still could not run without getting shot—it made her feel more vulnerable than she would have believed possible. He also slung the automatic rifle over a shoulder and pulled one of the guards' handguns from the duffel bag; the pistol pressed easily into her spine. Then he walked her over to the small glass door, still propped open, and positioned them at an angle so that both the wall and her body blocked him from gunfire. He could see out, over her shoulder. A slight turn of his head and he could keep track of the hostages. Then Bobby skittered to the opposite side of the door, mirroring them.

No one appeared in the street outside, only wavering mirages of heat, shimmering up from the asphalt.

Cavanaugh's book prohibited bringing family members to the scene. Would they have a cop playing Eric's role? If so, he would never fool the man's own brother—unless Cavanaugh only intended to get close enough to get a good shot at Bobby. The robber had kept himself out of the snipers' scopes all day, and this ploy would draw him into the open, with Lucas nearby, and only her body blocking him from a kill shot. She began to tremble.

"What's the matter, Theresa?"

"I'm scared."

"Why?"

"I'm afraid they're going to shoot at you and hit me."

His left arm slipped around her waist, and his hips and thighs pressed against her rear end. Her bound hands were caught between them, the plastic straps biting into her flesh. He rested his chin on her shoulder, lips next to her ear. "That's why we're going to stick together, so close that they won't even try. You don't mind, do you? I mean, about me being so close. I don't expect you to be too happy about facing the snipers."

Bobby rested his back against the cool marble wall. "You shouldn't be huggin' up some other girl."

They sounded relaxed for two guys about to take on three different police agencies, but she could feel the tension ripple through every muscle in Lucas's body.

"This isn't huggin'. This is self-preservation."

"Call it what you like, brother. I ain't the one you're going to be explaining it to."

From the corner of her eye, she watched the row of hostages, but no one moved. They had nowhere to go anyway—any movement toward the employee lobby would be noisy and immediately obvious, and there was no other way out. Besides, Lucas switched his gaze between them and the street every half a second. She could feel each swipe as his chin brushed her hair.

Bobby held his automatic rifle pointed down, the folding barrel resting against his chest. Tiny glints of deep red speckled the butt. She kept her voice very low. "Is that what you beat Mark Ludlow to death with?"

Lucas's arm tightened.

Bobby scowled. "I don't know what you're talking about, lady."

"He had two types of injuries—a long, rounded indentation, probably from the barrel when you swung the rifle like a bat, and an oval shape just like the flat end of that rifle stock."

"What are you doing, Theresa?" Lucas asked her, his breath warming her ear.

"I still don't understand why. Did he tell you about the money shipment? Give you the layout of the building? Obviously he didn't provide you with any special access, or you wouldn't have spent the whole day stuck in the lobby. What did he have that you wanted?"

The very ends of Bobby's mouth turned up, though his eyes remained cool. "That's a good question, lady. I wish I had a good answer."

She pondered that opaque response for a split second, getting nowhere. "Or did you screw up and kill him before he could tell you what you needed to know? I saw his body—he didn't suffer any physical question-and-answer session. Is that why you seem to have been making it up as you went along?"

"That's where you're wrong. This day has gone exactly according to plan."

That did not sound good.

How could Bobby have planned for his brother to be alive? Only if he knew all along that his brother wasn't really dead—but why the charade? If he wanted to see his brother, there was nothing to stop him from showing up on his doorstep. Eric Moyers had said he'd changed his address and phone, but surely some old friend or relative could have clued Bobby in.

Unless Eric Moyers was part of this plot and his appearance part of what the cops had wondered about all day—the robbers' exit strategy. Though one of the cardinal rules of hostage situations was *never* to bring family members to the scene, these two might not know that. It happened on TV all the time.

Either way, it seemed clear to her that Bobby Moyers had expected Cavanaugh to produce Eric and that Bobby had no intention of giving up afterward.

Cavanaugh was about to walk into a trap and bring a possibly innocent civilian along with him. A civilian—or a reinforcement?

She couldn't warn Cavanaugh. She didn't even know if she was right.

Sunlight slanted off one of the glass doors across the street as it opened. A young man in fatigues, rifle in hand, stepped out and held the door open. Cavanaugh and Eric Moyers filed out.

Cavanaugh wore the same shirt and pants she'd seen him in earlier, but a bulletproof vest covered his chest. They had put one on Eric Moyers, too. They must have been sweating in those, for all the good it would do. Even Theresa could squeeze off a head shot at this range.

"Here they come," Lucas said.

Bobby said nothing. He seemed suspiciously unsurprised at his brother's existence.

Theresa let her gaze roam the street without turning her head. Did a sniper have her in his sights? Trying to leave the doorway would get her a bullet through the spine, and cops and robbers alike would assume she had tried to escape, instead of tried to warn them away from the subterfuge about to take place. She looked up at the sixth floor. Surely Frank stood at the telescope, though she saw only a row of dark holes. The sun had shifted to the west.

Despite the heat, Eric Moyers's skin shone a pasty white. He had to be terrified. Agreeing to walk across the street and talk to his brother probably didn't sound so bad until he stepped out in front of all the guns, glanced at the barricades demarcating the safe areas from the unsafe ones, and noticed that while the hum of the city went on around them, East Sixth remained deathly silent.

I hope you're watching, Frank. She slowly shook her head in a one-inch arc.

"Hold still," Lucas hissed.

Cavanaugh and Eric Moyers stepped off the curb and into the waves of heat rising from the pavement. Bobby pushed on the metal frame of the door closest to him.

Behind them Ethan let out a laugh, his high-pitched giggle bouncing off the walls.

Cavanaugh and Moyers reached the middle of the street. The negotiator spoke. "Bobby, we're here. Come on out."

I have to warn them. I'll have to scream, and quickly. But if I take a deep breath, Lucas will know.

If she could even get a deep breath, he held her so tightly. She began to suck in air, slowly, steadily.

Bobby pushed the door completely open.

Now. "Don't—"

Lucas's hand covered her mouth, pulling her head back against his shoulder. *Damn, he was fast!*

She wriggled, more to keep him from slicing the insides of her lips against her teeth than to reattempt her plan. She needed only a split second to shout a warning, but the more she twisted, the tighter he held her.

On the other side of the glass, Cavanaugh waited with Eric Moyers in the street while Bobby crossed the sidewalk. Both men watched him; Cavanaugh gave no indication of noticing her struggle just inside the door.

"That's close enough, Cavanaugh," Bobby said to him. "Hands up, and turn around in a circle. I want to see that you're not armed."

She watched Cavanaugh turn slowly, fingers splayed above his head. Defenseless, unless he had a handgun underneath the bulletproof vest.

Bobby stood about eight feet from them, blatantly armed to the teeth. "Okay. You can put your hands down, but don't come any closer."

Eric Moyers spoke. "Hi, Bobby."

From behind him she watched Bobby cock his head. "It don't sound like you, bro."

"I *told* you I have a cold."

"What are you doing alive?"

"Why would I be dead? Who told you that anyway?"

Bobby's shoulders slumped. The hand holding the gun fell to his side. He began to say that it didn't matter, but then his voice trailed off and he put his other hand to his eyes.

Cavanaugh took the moment to glance her way, but she couldn't even shake her head in Lucas's vise-like grip. Perhaps he saw the panic in her eyes, because he opened his mouth to speak, possibly to tell Lucas to let her go, before realizing the futility of it. Talking to Lucas all day had proved futile. Cavanaugh could not help her, and she could not warn him.

"I'm sorry," Bobby said. "I'm sorry, Eric. I'm sorry about Mom and all the pain I caused her. I'm sorry you had to spend most of your life looking out for me." The level of his voice continued to move up and down, so that the two men in the street moved a few steps closer to hear him.

No! Theresa tried to shout. *Go back!*

"What was that?" Lucas whispered in her ear. "I didn't quite catch it."

Between the heat and the tension, she wouldn't have believed it was possible for Eric Moyers to look any more uncomfortable, but he managed. "Listen, Bobby . . . we all make mistakes."

"But I made more than my share. I never thought about anyone else. At the prison we had to paint a picture of our family, and I did the whole thing in red. The therapist said that's because blood and pain is all I see when I think about us."

Eric Moyers took another step toward his brother. "Mom never stopped loving you."

Bobby's voice turned harsh, and the hand on the automatic rifle tightened. "I know that. You think I don't know that?"

Cavanaugh spoke up. "It's really hot out here in the sun, Bobby. Do you think we could talk about this inside the library? Are you ready to put the gun down and go?"

Theresa shifted her weight to her right. She kicked at Lucas. He ground the barrel of the handgun into her kidney. "I *will* shoot you, Theresa. Please don't make me."

Bobby shook his head. "I can't believe you're really alive."

"It's me, Bobby. Come on, let's go." Eric Moyers took another step toward his brother, but Cavanaugh moved up and put one hand on his arm.

"Wait here, Eric. Where are the bank employees, Bobby? The ones that are coming with us?"

"They overheard our plan," Bobby told him. "It led to quite a squabble in there. It's amazing what people will do or say to save themselves."

"They only want to live, Bobby, to go on with their lives. We all do. You have dreams you want to realize, don't you? Here is where we can start. Bring out the bank employees."

The pressure of the gun in Theresa's back eased. The drama outside commanded Lucas's attention.

"Come on, Bobby," Eric Moyers urged.

"I know I gave Mom gray hair."

"We can talk about this later," his brother told him.

"No, I need to say it now. I know my troubles wore on her, but she could have handled that. My going to jail, she could have handled that. But when you talked her into cutting me off, not calling, not writing, not coming to visit me—she couldn't handle that."

"Let's go, Bobby."

Theresa fought to separate her jaws, leaving a gap just wide enough for one of Lucas's fingers to slide in. She bit, catching part of her lower lip in the crush and tasting blood. Instinct made his grip loosen.

"Run!" she screamed.

Lucas muffled her again and pulled back. Eric Moyers turned to her voice in confusion. Cavanaugh somehow understood and grabbed Eric's arm, moving backward toward the library building. Bobby left his automatic rifle at his side but pulled a handgun from the back of his waistband, underneath his loose Windbreaker. He used this to shoot his brother in the face. Then, retreating, he shot Chris Cavanaugh.

CHAPTER 29

3:26 P.M.

At least three snipers hit Bobby Moyers. The force of each blow pushed him back across the sidewalk, where the last shot hit his skull. A splash of red exploded over the glass of the open door, and a faint mist sprayed Theresa's face. He fell at her feet, half in and half out of the entrance to the Federal Reserve building.

Theresa screamed something—what, she never knew, since Lucas muffled her sound to just a panicked whimper. His body tightened, but he did not move. He said nothing. *He doesn't seem surprised.*

Eric Moyers lay motionless on the hot pavement. Cavanaugh's hand twitched, and she wept to see it. No hope remained for Bobby; the lower part of the back of his skull had been shredded.

He must have hit Cavanaugh in the vest, because the man now sat up and checked Eric Moyers's condition.

Let Eric be alive, she prayed. *He was trying to save us, and enough people have died today.*

But Cavanaugh did not shout for an ambulance, or

even radio for one. From his demeanor she knew that Eric Moyers had passed beyond help.

Lucas maneuvered her into the doorway. Rays of light struck her, heating her clothing until it burned the skin. "Cavanaugh!" he shouted.

The negotiator looked up, squinting in the sunlight, and slowly got to his feet.

"Come in here," Lucas commanded. "Join us."

I'll bet he didn't cover this *situation in his book.*

"I really need to stay out here, Lucas. I need to be able to make the arrangements you need, to get our efforts organized. I can't get anything done from in there."

"Let me clarify." Lucas took the gun out from behind Theresa and pressed it to her right temple, skulking behind her so completely that her hair muffled his voice. "Come in here or I'll blow her brains all over this nice marble."

Theresa stood as still as if she'd been carved from that same marble. Snipers would be trying to get Lucas in their sights, waiting for him to move from her shadow just enough to squeeze off the shot. But he stayed so close. His body plastered hers from ankle to neck; she could not pull away or even sink down.

They could do it. They were trained for this. *Just don't move.*

"Why?" Cavanaugh demanded. "What do you want me for?"

"Because your boys are getting desperate, and they'll never launch an assault with their leader in cuffs on the lobby floor."

"I'm not their leader. I'm only part of th—"

Lucas removed his hand from her mouth, placed it on her throat. She could feel a smear of blood, heavier than sweat, along her jaw. An expression crossed Cavanaugh's face, something dangerously close to compassion.

"Don't!" She didn't need to shout; he stood only ten or so feet away. Lucas's hand squeezed her larynx, but only for show. If he wanted to silence her, he could. "Don't do it."

Why weren't they taking the shot?

Worry etched lines into Cavanaugh's face as he looked at her. "Theresa—"

"Don't let your hero persona think for you, Cavanaugh! It's a trick." She wasn't a damsel in distress—she was *bait*.

"Come in here or she dies. I've got seven other people, Cavanaugh."

Take the shot! "He's lying! He won't do it."

"What on earth makes you say that?" Lucas asked her. To Cavanaugh he raised his voice. "Do you really want to take that chance?"

The hostage negotiator echoed Theresa's sentiments. "Enough people have died here today, Lucas."

"You can say that again."

The snipers were not going to risk a shot unless she wriggled away. They would need only a couple of inches and a split second.

"I'm going to count to three, Cavanaugh. One."

"If you shoot her, what then? I'll be back inside the library building before you can pull out another hostage."

"Person, Chris, person. The term 'hostage' is so dehumanizing. Two."

She had forgotten all of her martial arts training except for the side kick—devastating to the knee. But she would have to be very, very fast.

"All right," Cavanaugh said. "I'm coming in."

She kicked. Lucas exhaled with an expression lost in the fabric of her shirt as his legs buckled, pulling her backward. His gun went off. She might have been shot, but she couldn't feel anything past the pain in her ears.

Falling backward only protected Lucas, putting more of his body against the wall and leaving her still between him and the snipers. Her plan had not worked.

From their tangle of arms and legs she saw Cavanaugh emerge from the sunlight and reach for her, saying her name. At least his lips moved; she couldn't hear what he said.

He pulled her off Lucas, who rolled once and then jerked up the automatic. The barrel pointed up at her with an unwavering grip. Neither Theresa nor the snipers had disabled him.

There was only him now, and two of them, and Cavanaugh had a bulletproof vest. It dug into her side as he held her up. She turned to the hostages. "Run! Get out of here!"

They didn't need to be told twice. Brad scrambled to his feet.

Lucas fired another shot, painful even to her already numbed ears. A chunk of marble leaped out of the floor, five feet to the left of the little boy, Ethan. Everyone froze.

Lucas darted against the wall on the other side of the doors, safe from the snipers and with a clear shot of everyone in the room. She and Cavanaugh were not close enough to attack. The advantage of the situation had righted itself in his favor.

"Step back," he told them. "Go over to the desk, by the others."

Cavanaugh shoved her slightly behind him, out of either chivalry or convenience—she couldn't do much with her hands still tied behind her back. "It's over, Lucas."

"It's nowhere near over," he said. "Chris."

CHAPTER 30

3:39 P.M.

The plastic tie-wrap around her wrists must have stretched during the tumble, because she could now, painfully, slide one hand free of the other. She stayed pressed to Cavanaugh, their bodies so close she could smell his sweat; her hands swiped the back of his vest, searching for the hard outlines of a concealed weapon. If she found one, she would shoot Lucas without the slightest hesitation. She knew this as clearly as she knew her own name.

Of course he had none. Cavanaugh had promised to come unarmed, and he could not lie.

"Go. Sit with the others."

Theresa shifted sideways to get to the desk rather than turn her back on him and collapsed almost gratefully to the cool tile. Both her wrists bled from shallow cuts. Cavanaugh sat next to her. Lucas sped past the doors to tuck himself into the L of the teller cages and the exterior wall; he favored his right knee with the slightest limp.

"Well." He retrieved his automatic rifle and switched the handgun to his left hand. "That was exciting. I'll be taking that vest, Chris. I think I'll need it more than you will."

Theresa tried to picture the thoughts crashing about in Cavanaugh's mind. His perfect record had been shot to hell—no pun intended—and he found himself on the wrong side of the phone lines. Would he try to do his job from the inside or give up, let Jason take over? Assuming that his mind hadn't shut down from the shock, how would he play this?

"This has gone from bad to worse, Lucas." She heard him plainly over the ringing in her ears. She had not gone deaf.

"Tell me about it."

"Who are you?" Jessica Ludlow asked of the man who had just dropped down next to her.

"He's the negotiator, Jessie," Lucas told her. "Though he hasn't done such a great job so far. That dog don't hunt, as we say at home."

Cavanaugh asked, "What are you going to do now? Do you have a plan?"

"You know me, Chris. I always have a plan."

"Mind if I ask what it is?"

"I don't mind. Unfortunately, we don't have time to discuss it. Let me have that vest."

Cavanaugh pulled at the Velcro straps and removed the bulletproof vest. The shirt underneath had a circle of blood above the right pocket, and the whole thing dripped with sweat. He slid it across to Lucas but spoke to Theresa. "I'm a little damp."

"You don't smell too good either," she observed.

His dimples appeared, as if he found her attempt at humor reassuring. "We're still alive. We'll make it."

"I know." She didn't know any such thing, but the old defenses reasserted themselves. Act like everything is normal, and it will be. "Where's my daughter? How is she?"

"She's fine. She's across the street, watching this on the monitor."

"You're letting her *watch this*?" Stunned, she let her voice climb to a shout, and Lucas told her to shut up. She barely heard him. "You're letting her see her own mother held at gunpoint? What if—"

She stopped. *What if he kills me?*

"I'm sorry, Theresa," Cavanaugh said to her. "But have you ever tried saying no to your daughter?"

"I do it every day!"

"Well, we haven't had your practice. Besides, every person over there knows that if it were their mother, they'd feel the same way. Her boyfriend's with her, and Patrick keeps checking in. That's all we could do."

She turned her face up to the monitor. *I'm fine, honey. Don't worry. Don't worry.* "How's Paul?"

Again that suspicious pause. "I don't know."

She gave him no shelter from her stare. "Don't know or won't tell me?"

"I truly don't know, Theresa. I know that the hospital spoke to Patrick once, but I didn't even have a chance to ask what they said. I'm sorry." His gaze remained steady, but then this was Chris Cavanaugh, the man who could talk anybody into anything, the man whose entire mission in life was to maneuver and manipulate.

But he couldn't lie either, right? He *would* have been busy, and surely they would have told him if Lucas had murdered a cop. The negotiator would need that information. Paul must be all right. He must be.

"We'll be gone from here soon, and you can find

out for yourself." He lowered his voice to a whisper. "Lucas is getting ready to bolt. I can tell. He's hyper."

They watched Lucas, gun still in hand, armoring himself with the vest. Missy and Brad absorbed his every move, as though waiting to see if he'd put the gun down, or drop it altogether.

Cavanaugh noticed her wrists. "You're hurt."

"So are you."

He felt his chest, grimacing at his own touch. The vest had stopped Bobby's bullet, but he'd be badly bruised for weeks. "Just a flesh wound."

"Ah. A Monty Python fan."

"Isn't everyone?" Then, as if she might not know this, he added, "Eric Moyers is dead."

"I saw it."

"I told him it would be all right."

He didn't appear to be thinking about his perfect record. "Chris, it's not your fault."

For a moment he seemed ready to laugh. "Of course it is! I broke one of the most important rules—never bring family in. You can't predict the results."

"You thought it was the only way to get them to give up."

He leaned back against the marble, his body positioned in a casual slump while his expression stayed anything but casual. "He trusted me. Everyone trusted me."

"Snap out of it." She made her voice deliberately harsh. "Bobby had this planned from the word go. He wanted revenge on his brother, and he used you to get him into the open."

"But he did it so *well*. It's almost like he read my book."

"He probably did, or one like it." She studied Lucas

from her seated position; he seemed flustered by his partner's demise, but not shocked. "These two played us from the very first minute. We assumed they didn't mean for their robbery to devolve into a hostage crisis, but they did. They meant to spend all day here. They meant to kill Eric. Bobby meant to die, and Lucas helped him."

"Why?"

"That's the whole question, isn't it?"

Lucas interrupted her words. Not taking any chances, he had the automatic rifle in his left hand and the handgun in his right. "Okay, Missy and Brad, up and at 'em. I need one little favor, and then you can go."

The young man moaned.

"Come on, Brad, it's your time to shine—make up for being the little whiner you've been all day."

The two bank employees stood up. Brad trembled. Missy seemed to have moved beyond fear to extreme annoyance. "What *now*?"

"Those two duffel bags need to go in my car. They're a little heavy, but you can drag them. It's unlocked— Theresa, you didn't lock the car, did you?"

Sounds still seemed to come from the opposite end of a long tunnel. "I . . . I don't think so. I can't remember."

"If not, come back in and I'll give you the keys." Lucas sounded like a helpful rental-car agent, until he added, "Because if you fail to secure those bags in the backseat of that Mercedes out there, I'll blow out your spine before you make it to the other curb. Got it?"

"Then what?" Missy demanded.

"Then you can go. Walk across the street into the waiting arms of our boys in blue. Or go have lunch at

McDonald's for all I care. I won't need you any-more. The rest of you, move down here. Sit on these steps."

Brad brightened visibly, and he and Missy moved over to the duffel bags. He picked up the straps to one of them and made for the door. He could lift only half the bag off the floor and dragged the remainder of it. Missy did the same.

Lucas followed them, hugging the wall next to Bobby's body. "Put them in the backseat, lengthwise, so that half of each duffel is wedged between the two front seats. Don't leave the car until it's done. At this range I can't miss."

Missy and Brad left without a word, without a back-ward glance for their fellow captives.

The phone rang.

"That," Cavanaugh said to Lucas, "would be Laura. You might want to talk to her."

"I don't think we'll be needing another negotiator. You'll all be going home soon, at least most of you. I can't fit too many people in that car."

Cavanaugh muttered something under his breath.

"What?" Theresa asked.

"He's going to take a hostage with him. I figured he would, but it still sucks."

"There's no way to take him down with one of us in the car?"

"A sniper could get him through the window. They'd have to do it before he gets moving, though. It's risky."

She watched the two freed hostages through the glass door. Brad shoved his duffel into the backseat and then ran, not directly across the street but down the center of it, south toward Superior. Missy strug-gled, maneuvering the two bags into place as Lucas had instructed. Then she walked with defiant calm over to the library building, where three young men in fatigues emerged to welcome her.

"All that money could form a barrier between him and the hostage," Cavanaugh observed.

Lucas surveyed the line. "Eeny, meeny, miney—"

"What happened to letting four people go?"

"That was Bobby's deal, Chris, not mine, and unfortunately it fell through."

"You don't seem real broken up about losing your partner."

Lucas didn't glare at him, not exactly; his face just grew still in a way Theresa had come to recognize as equivalent to a glare. "Bobby was the best friend I ever had, so don't tell me how broken up I am. But I respect his wishes."

"Him dying was part of the plan?"

"I told him to stay where he'd have some cover. He could have hit Eric through the glass or an open door. Bobby worked on his impulse control in therapy, but apparently not enough. He had to *tell* Eric why he was about to die." He took a moment to regroup. Theresa believed him. He hadn't wanted to lose Bobby.

"How did you know I'd produce Eric for you?"

"We didn't, but it was worth a try. The trick was to make you think it was your idea."

Cavanaugh looked as if he'd been slapped.

"Time to go," Lucas told them briskly. "I need somebody the cops would never shoot at. And could there be anything more beautiful, and more vulnerable, than a mother and child?"

Jessica Ludlow gathered Ethan more tightly in her arms, eyes wide.

"Yes, you, my little southern Madonna. And you,

Theresa. You're both coming with me. The guys can stay here. This is how it's going to work—"

"No," Theresa said.

"No," Cavanaugh said. "Leave them here. You can only make things worse for yourself by adding kidnapping to your list of charges."

"Chris, you'll be picking up a pitchfork in hell and still trying to talk St. Peter into opening the gates, I swear. We're not negotiating. We were never negotiating, get it? We needed you to produce Eric and the money, that's all. Now shut up. You, Theresa."

"You don't need me." She emphasized every word. "You have a young woman and a little boy. No one will risk hurting them. I'd just be in the way."

Everyone in the room stared at her as silence flowed in, tamping down the last echo of her voice, pressing on her shoulders like guilt.

"Theresa . . ." Cavanaugh began.

She couldn't look at him. "He won't hurt them. I trust him."

Lucas muttered, "Of all people . . ."

"Leave both of them," Cavanaugh said. "I'll go."

"I just might take you up on that, Chris. I'm sure your heroism would do wonders for the sales of your next book. Even if it's published posthumously." Lucas still wore that cold, closed-down look that frightened her, and it settled on her as if she were the only person in the room. "I think you need to explain this sudden lack of altruism, Theresa," Lucas said, speaking just loudly enough so she could hear him. The security guards almost certainly could not. "It's got everyone quite mystified."

"I want to live, that's all. Leave me and Chris here with the guards. You can't fit us all in that car anyway."

"But I need good hostages. The cops won't shoot at you, their little scientist lady, and they sure as hell ain't going to risk their shining star. He's the only cop who gets on TV without having to be indicted first."

"Let him go," she repeated, desperation spreading through her voice.

"No."

Cavanaugh interrupted. "Why do I get the feeling that you two are having a conversation the rest of us aren't privy to?"

"Can't we just get out of here?" Jessica Ludlow asked. "What are we waiting for?"

Lucas answered without looking at her. "First I need to know what Theresa knows and who she's told."

"I've been stuck in here with you! How could I have told anyone anything?"

Cavanaugh turned toward her, putting a hand to his chest when the movement hurt him. "Told anyone *what*?"

"Go ahead, Theresa," Lucas goaded. "I'm not going to let him go anyway."

Theresa sighed. "This was never about the money. It's about Mark Ludlow's murder."

Jessica stared. "Lucas didn't kill my husband."

"No," Theresa told her. "You did."

CHAPTER 31

3:46 P.M.

Chris Cavanaugh shook his head. "I don't understand."

"Start from the beginning," Lucas instructed her.

She kept her voice steady and strong. "You mean when Mark Ludlow died? Or when you, Bobby, and Jessica met in art therapy at the prison in Atlanta?"

"Talk quieter, unless you want me to have to dispose of those three guards as well. There's no air ducts in this outer wall anyway, so you don't have to be clear for the microphones."

"How do you know about that?" Cavanaugh demanded.

"I studied under an expert. Your book was quite popular at the prison library, by the way—you should let your publicist know."

"Let's *go*," Jessica Ludlow repeated.

"In a minute. Go on, Theresa."

"Jessica's an artist."

Lucas reached one hand toward the young mother, then stopped as he remembered the cameras. But their eyes met, and she smiled, for the first time all day. "She's a fantastic artist. Do you see any of her stuff hanging in her house? No. Ludlow didn't appreciate it, and besides, it was *his* house."

Theresa shifted, drawing her knees toward her chest. "Yeah, he wouldn't even put her name on the deed. So you two met when Jessica worked in art therapy at the Atlanta jail, and you fell in love. But Mark Ludlow got wind of it and asked for a transfer, just as you were about to released?" She made the last sentence into a question, but Lucas nodded. "You followed her here. I'm guessing that's where things went bad."

He said, "All we wanted was a divorce, and custody."

Jessica spoke up, quietly. "I would even have considered *joint* custody. But Mark said no way. He said no court would allow even visitation to someone on felony parole, and I figured he was probably right."

"We had no choice," Lucas said to Theresa. "You're a mother. You must understand."

"So you killed him."

"We argued. Bobby hit him with the gun, just kept hitting. I told you he had poor impulse control."

"Convenient," Theresa said. "But I don't think so. You have a cast-off pattern of bloodstains traveling up your pant leg."

"So I killed him."

"You couldn't be swinging an object and get a neat pattern like that on yourself at the same time. You were standing perpendicular to the swinging weapon, at a slight distance."

"So it was Bobby. Like I said."

"Bobby is wearing khakis, light enough to see any bloodstains present. There aren't any"—her eye fell on his bloodstained corpse—"or weren't. It's possible that for some reason he had time to change his pants and you didn't, but I doubt it. Neither of you has spare clothes in the car. But Jessica had a closet upstairs, and besides, she probably ruined the pants she wore with the bleach she used to clean up the kitchen." She turned to the girl. "You probably didn't plan this, but even though I found the damp mop, I didn't think the floor had been recently cleaned, because Lucas left a coating of sand particles from the floor mats in the car, just as he's done on the marble tile here."

Jessica merely shifted her baby in her arms, her smooth face as innocent as ever.

"You now had a problem," Theresa went on. "You and Bobby dragged the body outside and planned for Jessica to go to work as if nothing had happened, but you knew she'd be the obvious suspect. You had to run off together, but in such a way that Jessica would appear to be innocent. She and Ethan would have been kidnapped by a violent bank robber and presumed dead. No one in Cleveland had any knowledge of your affair, unless Mark confided in a new friend."

"Tell everyone he'd been cuckolded?" Jessica snorted. "He wasn't the talkative type."

"There it is again—you speak of him in the past tense. You said your husband 'didn't' eat with you, not 'doesn't' eat with you, when you weren't supposed to know he was dead."

Jessica glared at her. Lucas frowned.

Theresa kept talking. Any delay would give Frank and the other cops time to figure out what to do. "He wasn't the talkative type, but you are. You told me so yourself. That's the real reason Cherise is dead, isn't it? You told her about Lucas."

She and Lucas exchanged a glance, hers abashed, his merely sad.

"You didn't kill Paul, a cop. You tried to keep your murders to a minimum, but Cherise had to go. The only way this could work is if no one had any idea you two were lovers. Jessica disappeared with a ruthless felon, never to be seen again. A tragedy, but forgotten in a week or two. However, cops—and the public— hate being duped. If they figured it out, you'd be on the evening news from coast to coast."

"But now *you* know," Lucas pointed out, and the fact that he seemed more sad than angry scared her to death. "And Chris here, who didn't have a clue, as I can see from the expression on his face."

"I *asked* you to leave him out of it."

"What I said goes. They'll never strafe that car if he's in it. You, I'm not so sure about—chivalry died a long time ago." He stood up. "Jessie, take the tie-wraps out of the side pocket there and loop their feet together. Just one ankle. Make sure it's tight."

He stood back, holding the automatic pistol. On the monitor it would seem as if Jessica followed his commands out of fear. She slid the sleeping Ethan to the floor, gently propping his head on her purse.

"That's the real reason for the cough medicine, isn't it?" Theresa asked her. "To keep him quiet and still during your getaway. He's really out—I hope you didn't give him too much."

"You think I drugged my own baby?" Jessica kept her voice down, too low for the microphones in the ducts to pick up, and yet she hadn't sounded that angry when accused of her husband's brutal murder.

"I think he hasn't coughed or even sniffled once all afternoon. You stained his nose with the fruit juice to make him look as if he had a cold so that the day-care lady would tell you he couldn't stay there. You came with a convenient supply of snacks for him, since you knew she wouldn't be giving him lunch."

Jessica placed one plastic tie around Theresa's right ankle and one around Cavanaugh's left, then connected the two with a third. She pulled them tight enough to cut off the blood supply. "This whole thing has *been* for him," she declared.

"The same thing on their wrists," Lucas told his girlfriend.

Theresa protested. "No. It hurts."

Jessica slid the strap over Theresa's right hand without hesitation. Theresa held it in place so that it tightened around the bones, to keep it from rubbing the already damaged area. The hand might go numb, but it was the best she could do.

Over at the reception desk, the phone began to ring. Lucas ignored it, as she expected him to. He could not risk crossing that open area where the snipers could sight him through the clear window.

Cavanaugh asked, "What's the purpose of this, Lucas?"

"Here's the plan: Jessie, put Ethan in the rear driver's-side seat. You'll have to drive."

"But I've never even been in that car!"

"Just press the gas and steer. It's an automatic, and we don't have much choice. I'll go out behind you two. The snipers are all on the other side of the street, right, Chris?" When the negotiator didn't answer, Lucas slung the rifle over one shoulder and pulled a handgun from the back of his waistband, pointing it at Cavanaugh's head. Then he repeated the question.

"I don't know! They don't tell me where the snipers are! It's too easy for me to slip and give something away."

Lucas considered this. "That's true, I remember reading that. I'm not worried about the ones on the library anyway. The car will block me," he added to Jessica. "Any on the roof of this building will have to aim straight down, and the awning will block their view up until the last second." He swung the gun's barrel toward Theresa and Cavanaugh. "You two will get into the rear passenger's-side seat. I'll ride shotgun, if you'll excuse the expression."

Theresa formed a picture in her mind, and not a pretty one. She figured that the cops could handle a vertical shot, desperate at this last chance to stop Lucas—and he intended to stay plastered to her back once again. All of a sudden, she wanted to vomit.

"On your feet," he ordered. "Jessie, pick up Ethan. Get ready to run. Move fast, but don't panic—they won't shoot at you. Here's the keys. Get in, start the car, and drive. Don't worry about me—I'll be inside."

Theresa and Cavanaugh got to their feet, gingerly, trying to coordinate their movements. They managed not to fall, but three-legged-race walking required their full attention. She twined a few of her fingers around his. He smiled and gave them a squeeze, but she hadn't done it as a show of moral support. "Try not to yank on my wrist."

"Sure." The smile disappeared.

She felt a twinge of guilt. "I'll try not to bump your chest."

"I don't think that's going to be an option. There can't be a lot of room in that backseat, not with those two duffels in the middle."

"Shut up." Lucas half crouched behind them, holding on to the back of Cavanaugh's shirt with one hand and poking the handgun into Theresa's spine with the other. He kept his head below the level of their shoulders. "Go, Jessie."

Clutching her son, she ran out and around the front of the Mercedes. Lucas pushed, and Theresa and Cavanaugh made for the passenger side in their stumbling gait. He opened the door and slid in. Lucas separated from them, jumped into the passenger seat, and faced them before Theresa could pull in her arms and legs. The barrel of the weapon appeared beside the headrest. He had only to hold down the trigger and she and Cavanaugh became hamburger.

She hoped Rachael was not watching.

"Get in," he said. "Shut the door or I'll shoot you both."

She heard a loud *plunk,* and something struck her calf. Two divots appeared in the pavement outside. She heard more toward the front of the car and retracted her body without thinking. There *had* been snipers on their side of the street, and she hoped that bullets would not penetrate the top of the car. Cavanaugh yanked the door shut, and then they were moving, with her butt on his thighs and the top of her head rubbing the upholstered roof. She remembered to breathe just as they approached the intersection of Rockwell and Sixth.

CHAPTER 32

3:58 P.M.

"Go straight," Lucas instructed, though he did not stop facing Theresa and Cavanaugh in the rear seat. He reached back and locked their door. "Keep up the speed so they can't jump out. Don't stop for anything."

"What now, Lucas?" Chris Cavanaugh asked, and Theresa couldn't believe how calm he sounded. Their bound wrists caused her right arm to bend double and stretch behind her; he slipped his left arm over her head to relieve the strain. The duffel bags created a solid, cloth-covered wall between the two halves of the car. She could only assume that Ethan lay sleeping on the other side. As she ducked her head under Cavanaugh's arm, she noticed a swatch of white at her feet. Her lab coat—she had left it in the car, and Brad had plopped the money-filled duffel bag right on top of it.

"Roll down your window, Jessie." Lucas unzipped the end of the top duffel bag and reached in. He had perhaps six inches of clearance between the top of the bag and the roof of the car, and he pulled out a bundle of money. "Rip the band off this and throw it out."

"How am I supposed to do that and drive at the same time?"

"Just throw it. It doesn't have to be neat, as long as it gets people into the street. They'll slow down the cops."

The negotiator pressed. "Where are you going to go?"

"That's a good question, Chris, but I don't have time to discuss it. Turn right when the road ends, Jessie. Don't slow down any more than you absolutely have to."

"Red light."

"Run it."

"I hate driving!" she snapped at him.

"You'll be fine. Just keep throwing." He rolled his window down a few inches, and even the hot breeze came as a relief. He caught Theresa's eye. "Don't think about jumping out."

She had no intention of it. The idea of the pavement scraping off most of the skin on her face dissuaded her, but more than that, she was not ready to let go of Lucas and Jessica. Paul might be dying because of them, and they were not going to go free. "What about the explosives, Lucas? The ones you cooked up on Jessie's stove last night? By the way, where did you find a health-food store open in the middle of the night?"

"What?" Cavanaugh breathed in her ear.

She prodded the lab coat with her free left foot and felt a thin item under her toes—probably a pen. She never carried much else in her pockets. "You can make plastic explosives with Vaseline and potassium chlorate, otherwise known as salt substitute. It's sold at health-food stores, among other places."

"Didn't use that," Lucas said, tossing loose bills into the wind. "I used Solidox, for welding. There's a twenty-four-hour hardware store in a place called Maple Heights. Turn left on Ninth, Jessie."

Lucas must have removed it from the teller cages across from the security guards, or he would have used it to prevent the cops from pursuing. "So where's the explosive?"

He smiled at her. "Right here, with us."

She thought of a suicide pact but dismissed that immediately. Lucas had planned, very carefully, to get away, and he would not abandon that plan. And whatever else Jessica might be, she clearly was not the kind of mother who'd let any harm come to Ethan.

Harm to Theresa and Chris Cavanaugh, however, was a different story. If they lived to tell, the whole day's efforts would be for naught. Jessica and Lucas would be hunted down, convicted on two counts of murder, and go to jail for the rest of their lives. Ethan would be raised by strangers.

Theresa and Cavanaugh had to die. No other option existed.

Not a pen, she suddenly thought. A scalpel. The sterile, disposable scalpel she'd used to cut the bloody carpeting from the trunk of this car. She had put the protective cap back over the blade and slipped the scalpel into her lab coat.

"The explosives aren't in the car," she pointed out. "We went over it."

"Nope. They're in the backpack."

She and Cavanaugh slid forward suddenly as Jessica hit the brakes.

"Watch it, Jessie."

"A car pulled in front of me. What do you mean, in the backpack? Get them out."

"We *discussed* this."

"The picture's in the backpack!"

"Exactly. The picture that you couldn't resist stealing, even though as soon as they realize it's missing they're going to know that you're not some sweet little innocent secretary!"

Jessica continued to snake a hand into the duffel now and then to throw more money out the window. Theresa could only glimpse the top of the girl's head, not her expression, but she sounded as if her vocal cords were made of solid titanium. "It's a damn *Picasso*!"

"I had the perfect plan! All we had to do was get away, and no one ever would have figured it out, and you had to screw it up because you couldn't keep your hands off some stupid piece of canvas!"

"It's one of the Vollard Suite!"

"It's not worth the rest of our lives!"

Theresa recalled how the dog had barked when Lucas forced Jessica over to the elevators, but not so much, now that she thought about it, when he returned. That was because *Jessica* was carrying the plastic explosives, or at least part of them. Jessica the artist, who knew where the fancy furnishings from the executive's redecorated office had been stored and how a tiny amount of explosive would blow the door's lock, and who returned from that trip with paint flakes on her pants. Jessica, who loved art almost as much as she loved her son, and possibly more than she loved her boyfriend, because she might have ruined their chances for a future together.

This was why Lucas had been so angry when she returned to the lobby with the backpack. Not because she brought less money than he counted on but because he found the painting when he unzipped the bag.

"You had to have the money!" Jessica countered. "Why did we have to hang around for that stupid shipment? We could have lost them in the convention-center traffic if we left earlier!"

"If you hadn't taken that painting, we could have started over again somewhere. You would be an artist, I'd manage the gallery. But if they figure out we worked together, they'll never stop looking for us. We're going to have to stay underground forever now, Jessie, and that's going to take a lot of money."

Theresa continued to watch him but hooked her foot underneath the loose part of the lab coat. Slowly she inched the pocket up as she inched her free left hand down. If Cavanaugh felt her movements, he gave no sign.

Lucas calmed his voice but spoke with teeth gritted against each other in a way that would have been comical if they hadn't been hurtling down a city street in a car carrying $4 million and a bomb. "If it gets destroyed, they'll assume some other bank worker took advantage of the confusion to sneak it out."

"If it just disappears, they'll assume the same thing."

"If he turns around," Cavanaugh breathed into her neck, "we'll strangle him. You may have to grab the gun. Keep the barrel pointed up."

She moved her head in a nod, tiny enough to be taken as swaying with the vehicle. Her fingers dipped into the pocket. She had always appreciated the deep pouches, but now they made it difficult to reach the scalpel. Her thigh protested as she used her foot to pull the pocket a fraction of an inch higher.

It took only the slightest glance down for Lucas to notice her raised knee. "What are you doing? Stop wriggling."

She squirmed more, and the plastic weapon slid into her hand. "There's not a lot of room back here."

But while Lucas watched her, his mind stayed on his girlfriend. "It's your fail-safe, Jessie. If they catch us, you can always say you were coerced. But if they catch us with that painting, they'll know you were in on it with me, and you'll never see Ethan again. Everything I've done has been for you, can't you see that?"

He did it all for love, Theresa thought. *He's been trying to tell me that all day.*

Jessica tapped the brakes, then sped up. "Where are we *going*?"

"Drive into the bleachers. Just like we talked about."

Bleachers? Suddenly Theresa realized why they were heading north on East Ninth, when there was nothing at the end of it but Lake Erie. The Hall of Fame induction concert. Those tall scaffolds covered in rock-and-roll-black cloth on the East Ninth pier, where she and Paul had scouted out the reception facilities on the *Goodtime II*.

"What if I get the wrong spot and hit a pole?"

"Just drive where I point. Brian told me exactly where to go."

"What about them?"

"Keep throwing the money, especially the closer we get." Lucas peered over the headrest. "I'll take care of them."

Theresa's heart sank. Cavanaugh's arm tightened around her waist.

Jessica remained silent, apparently mulling this over. Theresa heard sirens behind them, but not nearly close enough. In Lucas's sideview mirror, she could glimpse pedestrians milling in the street, stopping cars to pick up the scattered bills.

Could she stab him? She'd have to get him in the neck. Disposable scalpels were handy, but also cheap and thin, and they would snap in half at even medium pressure. It would be a one-shot deal. The jugular or nothing. A shallow slash would only make him mad.

She could press it into Cavanaugh's hand. He was stronger, trained in hand-to-hand. Let him do it. He'd have to reach around her, but he could use his right hand, and she would have to use her left. She would be free to grab the gun barrel, to keep Lucas from shooting them in the time it took him to bleed to death.

Because maybe she didn't have what it took to kill a man, and this would be a bad time to find out.

They approached the end of East Ninth, where it dead-ended into the pier. The Rock and Roll Hall of Fame sat to their left, and the World War II submarine, the *Cod,* to their right. The huge stage and seating for the induction ceremony concert rose directly in front of them. The fishy smell of the lake air blew through the car from the open windows.

"How are we going to get to Brian?" Jessica asked.

"We'll stay under the bleachers. Everyone will be looking at the explosion."

The painted guitars outside the rock hall sped by. Jessica couldn't have been driving more than twenty miles an hour, but falling out onto the pavement and possibly a curb at that speed could easily kill them both. Theresa would rather stay in the car, except that the car was going to blow up. Lucas intended to drive the car into the hidden caverns under the seating and set off the explosives. If the bleachers collapsed, it would take even more time before the cops could tally the bodies.

The explosives were in the backpack, and the backpack was in one of the duffels, with the money. The duffels were too heavy to be carried by one person.

"What about the money, Lucas? If you detonate the explosives, won't you lose part of your take?"

"Just one. I can get the other one out."

One of the bags would blow along with the car, for the same reason Jessie now threw bills out the window. Money distracted people, and no one would ever believe that he would have left it behind after all he'd done to get it. If the money wound up in the wreck of twisted metal, then Lucas must be in there as well. It would be months before the DNA got sorted out. He'd salvage enough for Jessie and him to start a wonderful new life together. She'd sell her paintings, and they'd travel the world.

If they got away.

"You'll never make it," Theresa told him. "It's impossible to get out of this car and away from it fast enough. The concert area is a little concrete peninsula, with only one bottlenecked way in or out. Every cop in the city will surround you in thirty seconds, and there's nothing to the north but water."

"And," he reminded her, "boats."

One shot, she thought. As much as she wanted to be the one who took him down, the man who put Paul at death's door, she had to be practical. She had always been practical. Her grandfather had taught her that.

She pressed the scalpel into Cavanaugh's right hand and slipped off the protective cap. He was right-handed, wasn't he? She tried to remember how he dialed the phone. . . . Yes.

She moved her left hand to the back of the front seat, pretending to steady herself as Jessica barreled over a speed bump. "You don't have a boat. You don't even have a car."

"Ah, but, Theresa, what's better than having a boat?"

Cavanaugh squeezed her fingers, but she didn't know if that meant *good luck* or *grab the gun.* "Having a friend with a boat," Theresa said.

"Exactly."

"But you don't have any friends either."

"That's not a very nice thing to say."

Jessica spoke suddenly. "I don't think I can do this."

"Yes you can." While maintaining a firm hold on the gun, Lucas twisted out of his jacket, then produced yet another plastic tie-wrap. "You two, put your hands up here. Just the tied ones."

"What if Ethan gets whiplash?" Jessica fussed.

"He won't. It's just canvas, it won't hurt us. Right there—see the section with the white stripe at the top? Aim for that."

Jessica sped past the end of East Ninth Street, down a narrowed pavement and beyond a sign reading NO UNAUTHORIZED VEHICLES PAST THIS POINT. Spindly trees grew from circles in the pavement, but no other turf presented itself as a soft place to land.

"Give me your hands!" Lucas demanded again, lowering the barrel of the gun to point it at them.

Theresa grasped the headrest with her bound hand and leaned forward, as if she wished to discuss this in private. "Why don't you just shoot us now? You didn't show much enthusiasm for killing Cherise—is that because you don't enjoy it?"

She never heard his answer. Instinctively mirroring, as most humans will, he leaned toward her ever so slightly. She grabbed the gun barrel.

Using the back of the seat as an anchor, Chris Cavanaugh pulled himself forward and struck downward with as much force as he could accumulate in the tight space. The scalpel entered Lucas's neck, and the handle snapped off. Theresa closed her eyes against the spray of blood and felt the burning metal within her palm as Lucas pulled the trigger of his handgun. She let go. The bullets entered the roof.

Jessica screamed.

Lucas put both hands to his neck. For an instant he caught Theresa's eye, his face reflecting pain and disappointment. Blood flowed between his fingers. He brought the gun around again. She moved her hand up to knock it away but couldn't make herself grab the hot metal with her singed palm.

Jessica hit the brakes, instinctively reluctant to hit the black canvas wall.

Then the door came open, and Cavanaugh launched them both into the air. Theresa managed to get with the program just in time to push outward with her legs, trying to clear the doorsill so they wouldn't be dragged alongside the moving vehicle. The car door, trying to blow shut, smacked her in the chest.

Lucas swiveled the gun, following them, but without his earlier lightning-quick ability.

Jessica continued to scream.

Theresa's torso met the concrete, slightly on her right side and with Chris Cavanaugh completely on top of her. The air left her lungs, and she rolled, gasping. Amid the squealing of brakes, the car disappeared behind a black canvas curtain. The shot never came.

Then nothing.

CHAPTER 33

4:01 P.M.

"Theresa?"

She opened her eyes, shut them again. The sunshine hurt too much. Damn, it was hot.

Cavanaugh persisted, patting her cheek. "Theresa. Are you okay?"

She squinted, tried to shake off the liquid dripping into her eyes. It hurt to breathe. "I'd be better if you hadn't landed on top of me."

He made a sound like a laugh and helped her to sit up. One side of his face bled where it had scraped the ground. He held up their bound hands; now both their wrists were bloody. "You don't have another one of those scalpels, do you?"

Her body seemed intact, nothing broken or even bleeding profusely. But it hurt to sit, hurt to breathe, hurt to exist, especially for the right half of her torso—she must have cracked a few ribs. Her lungs worked in short gasps, expanding no more than absolutely necessary.

Sirens wailed around them in a symphony of noise. Most continued past them, skimming the bleachers, but one pulled up in front of them. Mulvaney, Jason, and Frank piled out.

The veteran detective reached her side before the other two got out of the car. "Theresa."

"I'm all right. At least I'm still alive, I mean. Lucas—"

"They're under the bleachers," Cavanaugh cut in.

"We saw it. They won't get far."

"Certainly not Lucas," Theresa said, with only a twinge of hysteria. She let Cavanaugh explain the plan. Mulvaney got on the radio; he instructed the assembling marine units to check all boats in the area for Lucas's accomplice. "Where's the money? I mean, what they didn't distribute to the masses."

"In the car, with the RDX," Theresa said, grimacing as Frank cut apart the tie-wraps with a Swiss Army knife. "How's Paul?"

Frank looked up, into her eyes, and she knew. She knew.

"Mom!"

Rachael bounded from another arriving patrol car before it even stopped moving. Mindless of her ribs, Theresa opened her arms. The impact hurt like hell, and she sobbed for a moment, from relief, and pain, and guilt. "I'm so sorry, honey. This will never happen again, I promise. I promise. I promise."

Abruptly Rachael separated from her, but still grasping her arms with a grip so tight it took her attention off the ribs. "Mom."

"I'm sorry—"

"*Mom.*"

Theresa watched the struggle as her daughter tried to find the right words, to deliver news that no one should ever have to deliver, much less a child to her own mother.

"He's dead."

Confirmation, of something she'd known for hours. She knew it from the pallor of his face when he stumbled past her on the burning street. She knew it from the location of the wound and the amount of blood on the floor of the lobby. She knew it from the refusal of the sergeant and Chris to tell her the truth.

Yet she tried, even as Frank put his arm around her and Rachael laid her raven-colored locks on her neck. "No, honey, the hospital probably—"

"Paul's dead, Mom. I was with him. He died a half hour ago."

Theresa slid her bleeding arms around her daughter and held on.

CHAPTER 34

THURSDAY, JULY 2

In a typical Cleveland change of mood, the temperature dropped thirty-four degrees in three days, and Paul's funeral took place on a cold, wet morning. Theresa found this comforting even as she shivered, more appropriate than a sunny day would have been. Police-department personnel turned out in full force, uniformed and solemn-looking, even the chief and assistant chief and all the department heads. They had plenty of nice things to say about the deceased, and Theresa didn't hear a single word through her own personal fog. Rachael, Frank, and Don kept her cordoned off from most of the mourners, except Paul's family, and all of the media.

They allowed Chris Cavanaugh through, to join her on a bench next to the grave site as she waited for the cemetery traffic to thin and for the strength to walk away.

He gave her a foot or two of space and studied the damp grave. "Glad to see you're not fired."

"Yeah. Leo made some phone calls."

"Jessica is sticking to her kidnapping story. She

must think it's her only chance to get Ethan back, which of course it is."

The break wall had made it easy for the marine patrol to cordon off the boats present, and it hadn't taken long to find Lucas's buddy, the same one who had driven Bobby's car to Atlanta. The former desk clerk at the self-storage place clearly remembered the guy with the missing hand.

Jessica Ludlow had been found with the car, trying to drag a dying Lucas from the passenger seat. He bled out in much less time than Paul had.

"The car never did blow up," Chris went on when she didn't respond. "Lucas never hit the detonator. They even recovered Jessie's damn Picasso, only a little worse for wear."

She nodded. Frank had told her all this, but she let Chris talk anyway.

"What made you suspect her in the first place?"

Speech required an inordinate amount of effort. "The dog. The Browns dog. Those were a limited-edition item, given out by a fast-food place, a long time ago. The Ludlows just moved to the area, so how would they have something like that? She said a neighbor gave it to him, but it seemed in good shape. Odd for someone to keep a collectible like that all those years and then give it to a child you barely know. . . . A tiny thing, but once my mind went in that direction, all the details started to make sense."

"A stuffed dog."

"I think Bobby gave it to him. Lucas wouldn't have had one either, for the same reason, and Ethan kept talking about 'Bo.' Bobby's brother said he was good with kids."

"A stuffed dog. You're something, Theresa." After a moment his voice took on a different tone: "How are you? I suppose that's a stupid thing to ask."

She tried to say that she was still alive, that she'd survive, that she was well, given the circumstances. The words stuck in her throat. "I don't know. What about you?"

"I feel great, actually, ecstatic to be alive. Unfortunately, that's normal. Posttraumatic stress can take weeks to kick in."

"I get that feeling. I think I don't even know what I've lost yet." The idea of PTSD worried her, and as she had done every ten waking minutes for the past few days, she looked around to find Rachael.

Chris followed her line of sight. "How's she handling it?"

"Like a trouper, of course, but that doesn't mean squat. She holds everything in; I taught her that. It's almost a help, how guilty I feel for making her go through this. I'm so determined to put her first now that it takes my mind off—" Her gaze returned to the earthen hole in front of her.

"Guilty?"

"I risked myself. I risked her mother, to save a man we've known for only six months."

"It's your life to risk, Theresa."

You don't have any children, do you? "No, it's really not."

"It was a brave and selfless thing to do. She would respect that."

"I'm sure it would be a great comfort to her during her senior prom, her wedding, the birth of her first child."

The man who made his living ferreting out other people's motivations asked gently, "Why did you do it, then?"

She thought of herself standing in the middle of East Sixth Street, the sun beating her shoulders, Paul collapsed on the lobby floor and bleeding. "I couldn't do anything else."

"If it happened again this afternoon, you'd do the same thing again."

She knew the answer, but it took her a long time to say it. "Yes."

"We all make decisions, Theresa, and we all have responsibilities. Sometimes they line up well and sometimes they don't, but you can only do the best you can. Stop cluttering up your mind with what might have happened, because it's going to take you away from her senior prom, tomorrow's high-profile homicide, or"—he paused—"your next date."

That seemed an odd thing to say. She looked at him. He merely smiled.

"Mom?"

Rachael stood to the side, Leo behind her.

"Yes." Theresa stood up and smoothed her slacks. "I'm ready to go now."

ACKNOWLEDGMENTS AND NOTES

I'd like to thank several people for their assistance in writing this book:

Specialist Lawrence Stringham, my supervisor at the Cape Coral Police Department; Officer Ira Roth, currently of the Cape Coral Police Department and formerly of the New York City Police hostage negotiation team; Freddy Yaniga and Evelyn Drnak, for sharing their knowledge of the Federal Reserve building; my critique partner Sharon Wildwind, for her medical knowledge; librarian Nancy Skabar; my other critique partners among the Sisters in Crime Guppies, for their help with the craft; my editor, Carolyn Marino; and Elaine and Stephanie at the Elaine Koster Literary Agency, who make it all happen.

The Federal Reserve is prohibited by law to render assistance to a private citizen in a commercial venture, so I had access only to the lobby of the building, which is open to the public. There are no teller cages in the lobby anymore; all areas are given over to educational displays. I have no idea what offices are where on the upper floors, and I have no knowledge of any staff members or their personalities, habits, working conditions, or hours. The guards do not wear fatigues but uniforms; I put them in fatigues to make them easily distinguishable from the other two police agencies involved. I have no idea what the FBI's or the Federal Reserve's response to such a situation would be and only a general idea what the city police would do.

The M.E.'s office building as described in these pages has not existed for many years and bears no resemblance to the ultramodern building that now houses the outstanding staff of Cuyahoga County Coroner's Office. Thanks and love to the trace evidence department there—Linda, Sharon, Kay, Dihann, Jim, and Bernie.

I'd also like to thank my husband, Russ, a walking reference source regarding guns and cars; and of course my mother and four siblings, who give me feedback as well as a reason to keep writing.

BIBLIOGRAPHY

Adams, Susan H. "What Do Suspects' Words Really Reveal?" *FBI Law Enforcement Bulletin,* October 1996.

Culley, Lt. John A. "Hostage Negotiations." *FBI Law Enforcement Bulletin,* October 1974.

Meyer, Laurence H. *A Term at the Fed.* New York: HarperBusiness, 2004.

Misino, Dominick J., and Jim DeFelice. *Negotiate and Win: Proven Strategies from the NYPD's Top Hostage Negotiator.* New York: McGraw-Hill, 2004.

Thompson, Leroy. *Hostage Rescue Manual.* London: Greenhill Books, 2001.

Wells, Donald A. *The Federal Reserve System: A History.* Jefferson, NC: McFarland & Co. Inc., 2004.

"I have a building full of dead people," Theresa Mac-Lean told the detective. "I don't have time for one who isn't even dead."

Frank Patrick parked the car against the curb and gestured up at the antique brick architecture in front of them. "Not that we know of. But what woman runs out on a rich husband, a cool apartment, and her five-month-old daughter?"

"A stupid one." Theresa pulled her stocking cap more tightly over the red hair she hadn't bothered to curl, and took in the historic structure from a different perspective. "We're in Lakewood."

"So you did pay attention on the drive over from the morgue. I thought you'd slipped back into your coma."

She ignored the coma comment. "I know this place. You can see it from the rapid transit."

"It used to be the National Carbon Company," he told her. The red brick building in front of her would have looked at home on the Oxford campus; its out-buildings, done in matching brick but with much less style, would not have.

"Why are you involved?" Frank had been a Cleveland homicide detective for eight years, but the well-to-do suburb of Lakewood had its own force, and besides, the woman was only missing.

"Because of her job."

"At the Carbon Company?"

"No, this place has been closed for years. Her husband bought the vacant campus six months ago. I meant *her* job." He opened his door and got out, forcing her to follow suit. The March air hung icy and damp around Theresa's face. She pulled the padded jacket with *Medical Examiner* printed on the back around herself more tightly, knowing it wouldn't do any good. She hadn't felt warm in eight months. But the lettering identified her as one of the M.E.'s staff, a forensic scientist, not a cop, so that witnesses and family members greeted her with a shade more warmth than they did police officers.

She waited for Frank to circle the car. Being the middle of a weekday didn't lessen the traffic on 117th and cars whizzed down the narrow pavement; everyone had somewhere to go and wanted to get there fast. Frank darted out of their way; the homicide detective had a long-legged gait, a mustache to go with his light brown hair, slender and handsome but with no more fashion sense than she had, though she wouldn't dare say so. "And her job is?"

"Escort."

"What?"

"Escort. Was, actually, she quit on her wedding day. One of those pretty girls businessmen hire to take to cocktail parties so they can look like a player. The company—and I use the term loosely—is on West 25th. I remember her boss from his humble origins and have been wanting to bust him for about fifteen years now. So if she's dead, I'm hoping it's got something to do with him."

"It's good to have a goal."

"Hey, I'm not hoping the woman's dead. I'm just hoping to bust her boss if she is. The Lakewood guys are in this with me, but right now they've got their hands full with that family that got wiped out over on Warren, so they don't mind if I look into it. Let's go in, I'm freezing."

"An escort."

"Which means her boss has an opening, if you're looking to make a switch." He grinned. She didn't. He stopped smiling. She felt guilty, because he'd been making her laugh since she was three years old and knew he felt bad that he couldn't do it any more. But she couldn't help it. Her sense of humor had died with her fiancé Paul. "So you dragged me out here for a hooker on a bender?"

Humor fled his face as well. "Just take a look at the place, okay? Pick up some things that we can use for DNA testing if her body turns up and then you can go back to the trace evidence lab and hide behind your glass slides and microscopes."

She scowled, but then followed him up the cracked sidewalk and through the unlocked glass door; Frank had also been pushing her around since she was three and she had gotten used to it. Besides, if she argued with him too long, he'd complain to his mother, who'd complain to her sister—Theresa's mother—who'd give her the concerned *Are you ever going to get your life back together?* looks she'd been giving out for the past eight months. Theresa had gotten used to those, too.

Just keep going, she told herself. It's not like you've got anything else to do.

The lobby smelled coldly musty. "They live in a factory?"

"No, the other buildings are the factory. This building used to be the offices. Apparently he's renovating it as living space for himself and his partner and the programmers. It's high-tech stuff—video games—and those types like to work unconventional hours. Sounds like he plans to be the Bill Gates of Cleveland. I got all this from the Lakewood cop who took the report; he was a whole lot more interested in the architecture than in our errant young mom."

The elevator took an inordinate amount of time to rise one floor, and Frank used the trip to tell her more about the missing Jillian Perry. Twenty-four, native of Cleveland, she lived with her husband of three weeks, Evan Kovacic, and her baby girl. Evan Kovacic owned and operated a video game design firm. He had come home from a downtown meeting on Monday to find the door locked, Jillian gone, and the baby crying in her crib.

"And her husband knew about her former occupation."

"Absolutely. Says Jillian worked as a three-dimensional model."

"Dimensions, right. You keep saying *her* daughter," Theresa said as the claustrophobic elevator shuddered to a halt. "This baby isn't *his* daughter?"

"No. Jillian was pregnant when they met. I guess the father isn't in the picture."

Theresa snorted and nudged the sliding door with her foot to encourage it to open faster. "Great."

"We don't get to pick our victims, Tess."

"Tell me about it." The second floor lobby had fresh carpeting but a gouge in the plaster outside door number 212. Frank gave her a warning look as he knocked, and she straightened her shoulders. *I'm a professional. Focus on the job. What do I need to do right now?*

I care about every victim. Even if she was a drug-addled slut.

Who doesn't give a crap about her own kid.

She thought, These are the things we say about other people in the shuttered rooms of our own minds, the harsh judgments we would never, ever confess to another living soul.

A man about her age—thirty-nine—opened the door. He had black hair cut fashionably close, and wore jeans and a dress shirt without a tie. The untucked shirt had a hard time staying neat over his medium girth. He seemed more like an overgrown boy than a large man. CNN chatted in the background and someone had recently microwaved Italian food.

"Hi, I'm Evan. I'm glad you're on time, I do have to get back to work when we're done. But I let the sitter go home for lunch since I had to be here anyway, so I've got another half hour. Have you found out anything about Jillian? You're Detective Patrick, right?"

Frank introduced Theresa. Never touchy-feely and especially not with distraught family members, she would have been satisfied with a nod, but Evan Kovacic held out his hand so she had to shake it. His fingers felt soft and too fleshy and she couldn't picture him building microchips or whatever it was he did. She let him talk with her cousin while she took in the room.

Walking into the home of a stressed stranger no longer felt odd to her. She had done it at least once a week for the past dozen years. But she no longer found it fascinating, either.

At least it was clean. The polished wood floors gleamed and furniture gathered around the leather sofa held just enough accoutrements of daily living to look comfortable. Lightweight draperies framed the window with a dramatic swoosh. Video game designing must pay well.

"Nice place," she said, interrupting Evan Kovacic's questions. Then she cleared her throat and forced herself to enunciate. Somewhere along the line, talking to people had become an effort. "This is a lovely apartment."

"Jillian did the decorating," Evan told her, biting one nail. "She had—has—a real talent for it."

"I need to see her bedroom and bathroom, please." *Let's grab the DNA samples and get back to my routine.*

"In there." Evan Kovacic waved his hand at the hallway and continued to pepper Frank with questions about how the police go about looking for a woman who disappeared off the face of the earth.

Theresa came to the bathroom first. She had no trouble guessing which toothbrush and razor and hairbrush belonged to the missing woman—Jillian apparently liked pink. Pink hand mirror, pink towels, pink makeup case with pink rhinestones. Theresa donned latex gloves and dropped the items she wanted into three separate manila envelopes. She didn't bother to label them; she could do that back at the lab. As long as the items remained in her custody, they did not have to be immediately sealed. She caught her own face in the mirror for a brief moment, her expression sour and irritated, and left the room.

Stuffing the envelopes into her camera bag, she stepped into the nursery, realized her mistake, and turned to go. But it had been seventeen years since Rachael had been an infant, so she tiptoed up to the gleaming white crib. Mothers never lost their professional curiosity toward other people's children.

Jillian's daughter slept soundly on pink sheets inscribed with the word *Princess*, her little face scrunched, concentrating on some dream or the condition of her diapers or merely the new act of breathing. Light-colored down spread over her skull and both hands made loose fists, the fingernails so impossibly small. Her skin was perfect and her bed smelled of baby powder and warmth.

I should feel something right now. Hope, sorrow, empathy. Anything.

But I don't.

She left the room, backing away from the sleeping child as if the softest footfall might disturb her, though the men's voices only twenty feet away did not.

The Kovacics' bedroom lacked the immaculate quality of the nursery. The bedclothes had been spread out in a quick attempt at neatness; satin sheets—what else?—slipped haphazardly from beneath a chocolate velour cover. The matching nightstands had been segregated—a pink ribbon, a book of crossword puzzles, and a jumble of earrings on hers, a hand-held video game and a ball cap on his. Jillian's dresser held bottles of perfume and several framed photos, which Theresa glanced at. For a professional model—*and I use the term loosely*—there were no posed shots, just candid snaps of a blond woman and various people, Evan, and the baby.

Theresa searched for a hamper. The toothbrush,

hairbrush, and razor should be able to give them all the DNA they would need to compare to the body, if and when a body turned up, but it never hurt to make sure.

She opened the closet. Jillian's half bulged with low-cut blouses and clingy dresses in every color of the rainbow. Evan's half consisted of sweatshirts, T-shirts, and extreme cold wear. Quilted nylon pants with *Faster* emblazoned in yellow down one leg indicated a skier—no, not a skier, she mentally corrected, upon spying a snowboard peeking out of its duffel bag on the floor. Next to it sat a plastic laundry basket. Evan had obviously continued to pitch his T-shirts and briefs at it during the four days Jillian had been missing, making the basket only half of the time, because she had to dig down past four sets of men's under-clothes and a few dress shirts to find more feminine items. Theresa pulled out a skirt, a V-necked sweater and the requisite thong underwear, an article of cloth-ing she could never bring herself to try. It looked like sheer torture. She dropped two of these in a fourth manila envelope; vaginal secretions would provide plenty of skin cells—epithelials—for DNA analysis. They might also reveal sperm that didn't belong to Evan, if there were some boyfriends or clients in the picture, but Theresa couldn't see how that would be relevant. If the underwear was here and Jillian wasn't, then any wayward sperm on it probably didn't co-incide with the crime. If there had been a crime. If Jil-lian hadn't simply found marriage and motherhood too confining, and left them behind with her pink towels.

Theresa stood, listening to her knees creak. She couldn't see what else to do. If Evan had killed his wife he would hardly be letting Theresa poke around unsupervised. She saw no bloodstains or evidence of new paint or carpeting, which might imply a clean-up job. Jillian hadn't left any threatening letters or indiscreet photos lying around, though Theresa hadn't gone through her drawers and didn't intend to. She had come strictly to collect items for future DNA analysis and had no desire to see what professional escorts stored in their bedroom drawers, what people who had a marriage, had a love, had a life kept close at hand. No desire to ponder the contrasts between their situation and hers.

Time to get back to the lab, where the cases were no more fascinating but at least the victims were demonstrably dead. No doubt Jillian would come home after an argument with her mother or new boyfriend or whomever she had gone to.

Inertia kept Theresa from moving long enough to take another look at Jillian's pictures. She had been pretty, certainly, with clear, dewy skin and blond hair falling past her shoulder blades. Even in the hospital delivery room, wet with sweat and exhaustion, she glowed as she held her newborn up for the camera. She beamed in her wedding dress, next to the tuxedoed Evan. She either hadn't gained much weight with the baby or lost it quickly, Theresa thought with a twinge of jealousy. She herself gained and lost the same five pounds every week.

"Is that all you're going to do?" Evan Kovacic asked from the doorway, nodding at her camera bag with its protruding envelopes. "I mean, is there anything else I can give you that would help find her?"

What could she say? *That's it, unless a body turns up?* She glanced at Frank, who stood behind him, but before he could take over, the husband's eye fell on the photos. "She's so beautiful. And not just on the outside. I know she would never have left us, not voluntarily. She loved Cara. She loved me."

Theresa followed his line of sight to the photos. *Thanks a lot, Jillian. Thanks for dragging me across town for five minutes of work, thanks for perpetuating men's fantasy of women as nothing but pretty playthings, thanks for leaving your daughter to be raised by a guy who looks as if he can barely take care of himself. Great job.*

Theresa caught her cousin's eye, trying to signal: Let's get out of here.

Frank ignored her. "Mr. Kovacic, when you returned on Monday, the door was locked? Everything in place?"

"Yes. Jerry and I—Jerry Graham, he's my partner—we'd been at a software association meeting at Tower City all day. We got back about three in the afternoon."

"Who else would have been on the premises?"

"No one, except Jillian and Cara. We're still setting up shop here, Jerry and I. We've got one programmer starting at the beginning of the month and another a week after that and as soon as we get the manufacturing equipment set up we'll take on another designer and about four techs—"

"Was the outside door unlocked? The lobby door downstairs?"

"Yeah, probably. We're in and out all day between this building and Plants Two and Three—where we've begun setting up the equipment—so we don't bother locking it. We haven't had any problems with trespassers, and when we renovated we put in a good deadbolt on the apartment door. Though I doubt Jilly would have had it set during the day. I don't know. I guess anyone could have walked right in—"

Frank headed the man off before his mind could travel too far in that ominous direction. "You've searched the entire property?"

"I sure have. Twice. It's not as hard as it sounds, the buildings are empty for the most part, except for where we're stocking up all the equipment in Number One and setting up the manufacturing process in Number Two. But Jerry and I searched every inch. We can look again now, if you want."

Theresa frowned at Frank. He said, "The officer taking the report did a walk-through with you, right?"

"Yeah."

"I'm sure he would have noticed anything out of place." Like a dead body.

"I can't see why Jillian would have gone wandering around dusty old buildings anyway. It's been so cold, and she thought the dry air was bad for her skin. She was always so careful about her skin." He picked up his wedding picture. "It was all she had, really, her looks."

That didn't sound very nice. Theresa wondered if he always managed to be so tactful, or only when under stress. Yet his eyes filled with tears as he gazed at the photo.

He added, as the level of desperation in his voice climbed steadily, "I know wherever she is, she'll be worried sick about Cara and me. That's why you have to find her. She knows I can't raise a baby all by myself."

This should have been poignant but sounded flat and tinny to Theresa's ears. She did not read anything into that reaction; everything sounded flat to her these days. But then he asked, "Are you two going to do the investigation into Jillian's disappearance?"

"We'll be working on it," Frank assured him. "With the Lakewood police."

Evan Kovacic had smooth skin and short, manicured fingernails; he had tucked in his shirt so that he looked like a frat boy grown up to be pleasant and reasonably responsible. But his eyes—the color of the iris dark and solid, and hard as marble—swept her from the red hair that hadn't seen a grooming product in months to the scuffed Reeboks she wore to cushion her feet during the eight-hours-without-sitting days. He was assessing her competence, Theresa thought, and finding it lacking. Well, screw him.

But then he managed a smile. "Great."

Taught to be polite. Or a lack of confidence in me somehow reassures him. How much does he really want us to find Jillian?

She let her brain wander this path for one brief moment. Jillian and her job had become an embarrassment to the young entrepreneur. Jillian's personality or lifestyle or both had worn him down. He had a good idea where she was—holed up with a boyfriend, on a bender, under the Carnegie bridge with a needle in her arm—and didn't need that publicity. Having had a few days to think about it since making the original report, he now knew that he didn't want her back, but as legal husband and nice guy felt obligated to keep up the pretense.

Or perhaps Theresa saw nothing but pain and deceit in her world these days, and this poor guy had made an effort to keep his self-possession while begging them to bring his wife back. Being left with an infant to raise wouldn't make his busy days easier, and surely Jillian's looks helped him tolerate any other foibles.

"Good-bye, Mr. Kovacic." She left the room and the apartment, taking the steps down.

Outside, the wind cut through her jacket in damp, knife-like slices. They were too close to Lake Erie to avoid the violent air. Trees were bare, the sky an unrelenting gray. Patrons at the station across the street waited in their cars while gassing up. Unexpected sun in the morning had softened the top of the snow, but now it froze to a sheet of new ice once more, the inconsistency harder on living things than a low but steady clime would be. April wasn't the cruelest month in Cleveland, Ohio. March was.

"What do you think?" Frank sauntered up to the unmarked police car, pulling his keys from his pocket and jangling them too loudly.

"About what? Whether this bimbo is coming back or not? How should I know?"

He waited for a truck to pass, then walked quickly into the street to get into the car. Once the doors had closed, he started the car before saying, "You saw the place. Neat, clean. She wasn't some crack whore. The baby's room is—"

"Immaculate," Theresa said. "That could be the nanny, though. She must have been there all day, every day for at least three days, right, if the husband's been at work?"

"He works on the premises, but yeah, the babysitter's been here. I didn't find any trace of drugs," Frank went on. "A little beer in the fridge, that's it."

"How did you get to look around the kitchen?"

"I had a few seconds while he went to see what you

were doing. No prescription drugs in the kitchen cabinets or bathroom. Did you find anything in the bedroom?"

"I didn't really look, just collected some underwear."

He opened his mouth to make a comment, apparently remembered that Theresa was his first cousin, and shut it again. "I ran their financials too. Little bit of credit-card debt—and who doesn't have that, these days?—and a car loan. I didn't have time for more than the basic accounts, but when people run out it's usually because of love or money."

"Same reason they usually murder, too." She didn't know why that popped out, since she doubted Jillian had left due to anything but her own free will.

"Exactly," Frank said.

He spoke as if she had proven some point of his, which irritated her. "Fine. Where is her car?"

"In their garage. The officer who took the original report said it was locked, no sign of damage, no sign of foul play."

"And she's not in the trunk," she said.

"He checked."

"Her purse? Cell phone? Any bank withdrawals?"

"Her purse is still there in the apartment. Phone, money, L'Oreal lipstick in Brilliant Pink, still there. How about it, cuz? When was the last time you left home without your purse?"

"The third grade."

"See why I think it's weird? It's like she went out to get a paper and never came back."

They passed Lakewood Park and she watched the whitecaps kick up the surface of Lake Erie. At one time this case would have interested her, prompted her to a panoply of theories regarding the fate of Jillian Perry. But that was before watching her fiancé bleed to death. Still, for Frank's sake and to forestall that sympathetic look she had come to dread, she made an effort. "What about the nanny?"

"You've got a nasty, suspicious turn of mind," he said, as if the fact delighted him. "Apparently Evan only hired her three days ago; she's fifty-five and a friend of his mother's. They never needed a babysitter before—they live at his company and when Jillian worked, her jobs were mostly at night. I'll look into it, though."

They passed into Cleveland city limits and Theresa grew tired of Jillian Perry and questions with no answers. "Okay. I've got DNA in case her body turns up. That's all I can do for now, so let's get back to the lab. I have to go over the clothes from that woman they found in the park yesterday, make up some more acid phosphatase reagent, run the FTIR samples, order more evidence tape, and maybe eat lunch before Leo comes up with something else to dump on me."

"I'll take you to lunch."

She gave him a skeptical look. Her cousin could be generous to a fault in large ways but had never volunteered to pick up a check in his life. "What do you want?"

"At Pier W. It's on the water."

Especially not at expensive restaurants. "I know where it is. We went there for my senior prom. What do you want?"

"The salty wind in your hair—"

"Lake Erie is fresh water and glaciers give off warmer air at this time of the year. What do you want?"

"Come with me to talk to Georgie, Jillian's boss. The escort service guy."

"I'm not a freakin' cop, Frank. I'm a scientist. I work with microscopes and fibers. I don't interrogate people, and not even lunch at Pier W is worth chatting with a pimp!"

"He's not a pimp," he corrected her, while pointedly missing the I-90 on-ramp. "He's a businessman. Come on, this guy is never around women he can't intimidate or pay off. He won't know what to do with you sitting there."

"Don't you—"

She had almost said, *Don't you have a partner?* Before she remembered that no, he didn't, that his last partner had been shot in a bank robbery, the partner he had more resented than liked, the partner she had been engaged to marry, and since then had managed to circumvent all efforts of the department to assign him another. And she remembered something else, something that had existed in another time, another life—sympathy for someone other than herself.

"Okay," she said. "But I'm ordering lobster. *And* the brie plate."

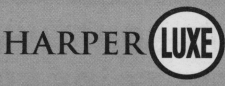

By Lisa Black

TAKEOVER

Coming Soon in Hardcover
EVIDENCE OF MURDER

In the spellbinding tradition of Kathy Reichs and Jeffery Deaver, former forensic scientist **LISA BLACK** *makes an explosive entrance onto the thriller scene with a gutsy and unforgettable new protagonist and a plot that grips and surprises at every turn.*

Being called early to a gruesome murder scene—a front lawn in suburban Cleveland, where a man lies dead, the back of his head crushed in—is not forensic scientist Theresa MacLean's idea of a perfect start to a Thursday. But over the next eight hours her day promises to get much, *much* worse.

When a daring robbery at the Federal Reserve Bank downtown results in a tense hostage situation, Theresa is severely shaken to discover that her police detective fiancé is among the prisoners. Though the charismatic Chris Cavanaugh, the city's best hostage negotiator, has never lost a victim, Theresa fears his arrogance may prove fatal this time around. The best hope, as Theresa sees it, would be if she herself could get inside to gain control of the situation. But what waits beyond the bank's imposing edifice is something far more complex, deadly, and terrifying than an ordinary heist—something that may require an unthinkable sacrifice . . .